VICTORIA PADE

is a *USA TODAY* bestselling author. A native of Colorado, she's lived there her entire life. She studied art before discovering her real passion was for writing. Even after over eighty books, she still loves it. When she isn't writing she's baking and worrying about how to work off the calories. She has better luck with the baking than with the calories. Readers can contact her on her Facebook page.

Books by Victoria Pade

Harlequin Special Edition

The Camdens of Colorado

To Catch a Camden
A Camden Family Wedding
It's a Boy!
A Baby in the Bargain
Corner-Office Courtship
Her Baby and Her Beau

Montana Mavericks: Rust Creek Cowboys

The Maverick's Christmas Baby

Northbridge Nuptials

A Baby for the Bachelor
The Bachelor's Northbridge Bride
Marrying the Northbridge Nanny
The Bachelor, the Baby and the Beauty
The Bachelor's Christmas Bride
Big Sky Bride, Be Mine!
Mommy in the Making
The Camden Cowboy

Montana Mavericks: Striking It Rich

A Family for the Holidays

Visit the Author Profile page
at Harlequin.com for more titles.

Victoria Pade

HOME ON THE RANCH: WYOMING

HARLEQUIN® THE COWBOY COLLECTION

Recycling programs
for this product may
not exist in your area.

ISBN-13: 978-0-373-60135-6

Home on the Ranch: Wyoming

Copyright © 2015 by Harlequin Books S.A.

The publisher acknowledges the copyright holder of the individual works as follows:

Cowboy's Caress
Copyright © 2000 by Victoria Pade

Cowboy's Baby
Copyright © 2001 by Victoria Pade

Printed in U.S.A.

www.Harlequin.com

CONTENTS

COWBOY'S CARESS

Chapter 1

"What's that saying? Life is what happens when you have other plans? I guess that applies to you, Carly."

"No doubt about it," Carly Winters agreed from the back seat of her best friend's car where she sat sideways so her foot could be elevated.

But Deana's comment from behind the wheel was a whole lot more lighthearted than Carly's dejected confirmation. Deana had never been happy about Carly's plans to travel so any interference was welcome to her.

"This hasn't canceled my trip, though. It's just postponed it a little," Carly felt inclined to clarify so her friend didn't think otherwise. "The doctors at the emergency room said I'd be as good as new in a few weeks. And then I'm off like a rocket."

Deana didn't say anything to that. She just turned up the radio and made it seem as if she were paying attention to her driving, as if she had confidence in more of life happening to thwart Carly's plans.

Carly sighed away the feeling of frustration that those thwarted plans left her with—a feeling she was more familiar with than she wanted to be—and laid her head against the seat.

The sun was just rising on the June day she'd been certain would finally be her swan song to Elk Creek, the small Wyoming town where she'd been born, raised and lived almost all of her thirty-two years. Most of which she'd spent thinking—dreaming—about being somewhere else.

But she wasn't headed *away* from Elk Creek. She was headed back to it after spending the night in a Cheyenne hospital emergency room, having her ankle X-rayed.

Luckily she hadn't broken any bones. That could have cost her six weeks in a cast. As it was, her ankle was sprained, the tendons and ligaments were torn, but it was wrapped in an Ace bandage and she'd be able to get around on crutches. And even though it hurt like crazy, she was sure it would heal quicker than a broken ankle would have. Which meant all the sooner that she'd be able to go off on her grand adventure.

Better late than never.

She still couldn't believe it had happened, though. At her going-away party, no less.

The whole thing had been a comedy of errors. There she was, saying goodbye to friends, neighbors and relatives, ready to go home to bed for the last time in Elk Creek, when her sister, Hope, had gone into sudden, hard labor. Their mother had gotten so flustered that in her hurry to reach Hope she'd caught her heel in the hem of her dress. Carly had seen her mother's predicament, dived to catch her and fallen herself, twisting her own ankle to an unhealthy angle while her mother had barely stumbled.

The end result was that Hope had been taken to the medical facility where Tallie Shanahan—the town nurse and midwife—had delivered a healthy baby boy to go with Hope's other three sons, and Deana had taken Carly to the hospital in Cheyenne. Not only had Tallie had her hands full, but she'd been afraid the ankle was broken, requiring the care of a physician—a commodity Elk Creek had been without for some time.

"Maybe this is a sign that you shouldn't go," Deana said from the front seat over the music, letting Carly know her friend was still thinking about her leaving even if Deana tried not to show it.

"It's just a minor setback," Carly countered.

And she meant it, too.

Because nothing—*nothing*—was going to keep her from doing what she'd wanted to do her whole life. Well, since she was seven anyway and her great-aunt Laddy had paid her family a visit and brought photographs of Laddy's travels all over the world.

Carly had studied those pictures until they were burned into her brain, daydreaming over them, wishing she was seeing the sights in person. Somehow, from that day on, Elk Creek had seemed like small potatoes on the banquet table of the world. And she'd made it her goal to get out into that world and feast on it all herself.

Not that that goal had been easy to reach or it wouldn't have taken her so long to get to it.

First, there had been getting her teaching degree in the nearest college where she and Deana could attend economically by staying with Deana's aunt during the process. Once that was accomplished, Carly had returned to Elk Creek to work and save her traveling money. And then, of course, there had been her involvement with Jeremy and the wrench he'd thrown into the works the past few years.

But now all of that was behind her. She'd saved enough money to last a year or maybe more if she was careful. She'd taken a leave of absence from her job. And if she could ever actually manage to get out of Elk Creek, she was going to see everything she'd ever wanted to see and then pick her favorite city to live in. Maybe not forever, but for long enough to give herself a taste of life outside the confines of her small hometown.

She was going to be a cosmopolitan woman.

By hook or by crook.

Even if it killed her.

"It's not as if I'm moving away permanently," she said with a low concentration of conviction, but wanting to console Deana nonetheless. "I just want to see some things. Do some things. Meet some new people. Live outside the fishbowl for a while. Who knows? A little time away and I'll probably get homesick and come back. That's why I only leased my house and why I didn't out-and-out quit my job."

"You won't be back if the grass is as green as you think it is on the other side of the fence."

"Well, even if it is—and it probably isn't—you know it won't make any difference between you and me. We'll still talk all the time, and we can write letters and emails and there's nothing in Elk Creek to stop you from coming to wherever I am."

"It won't be the same as living next door the way we always have."

Carly knew that was true. She also knew she was going to miss Deana and the way things had been since Deana's family had moved into the house right beside her own when they were both four years old. They'd been together through everything from first kisses to burying their fathers within three months of each other.

Carly's leaving would mean no more seeing each other every day, sharing every detail of their lives. No more late-night binges on ice cream when one or the other of them couldn't sleep and they padded across the lawn in pajamas and bare feet. No more consoling each other at the end of a bad date. No more double dates—good or bad. No more filling each other's lonely hours with company. No more shared bowls of pop-corn over tear-jerker movies on videotape to occupy empty Saturday nights. No more impromptu shopping trips or makeover sessions. No more battening down the hatches together in snowstorms. No more working together. No more just being there for each other when either of them needed it for any reason.

But Carly didn't want to think about the downside of leaving town. Instead, she did what she'd been doing to keep herself from dwelling on it since she'd finally decided to do this two months ago: she thought about San Francisco and New York. About seeing Vermont in autumn splendor. About the Alaskan wilderness. About Hawaiian beaches. About London and Paris and Rome and Brussels and Athens and Vienna and Madrid.

About how much she'd always wanted to see it all for herself…

"I still wish you'd come with me," Carly said because that was true, too. She'd tried as long as she'd known Deana to infuse her friend with her own enthusiasm for seeing the world. Short of meeting the man of her dreams on the Orient Express in the middle of her travels, the only other thing that would make the trip perfect would be if Deana had the same wanderlust and they could do it together.

But Carly could see Deana shaking her head even now.

"There isn't anything I want that isn't in Elk Creek."

"Mr. Right," Carly reminded.

"He'll show up one of these days," Deana said with certainty. "And when he does, I don't want to be somewhere else looking at bridges or mountains or leaves or churches or ruins or pyramids."

For as much as they were like two peas in a pod, this was the one area where they differed—Deana was a hometown girl through and through.

And Carly wasn't.

Or at least Carly didn't want to be.

They headed into Elk Creek without fanfare just then. The small enclave's main street—Center Street—was still deserted as Deana drove all the way to where it circled the town square. She turned at the corner taken up by the old Molner Mansion that had been converted into the local medical facility and stopped at the first house behind it. Carly's house. The house her mother had left to her after her father's death, when her mother had decided to move in with Carly's two maiden aunts.

It was a moderate-size yellow clapboard farmhouse with a big front porch, a second level slightly smaller than the lower and a man and a little girl at the oval-glassed front door.

"Looks like you have company," Deana observed as she drove around the station wagon parked at the curb and pulled into the driveway.

"He's not supposed to be here until the middle of the morning," Carly groaned.

"Apparently he arrived ahead of schedule."

"And I'll bet I'm a mess."

Deana reached over and flipped down the visor on the passenger's side so Carly could get a glimpse of herself.

Carly sat up straighter and saw the unruly ends of her straight, shoulder-length auburn hair sticking up every which way at her crown. To get it out of her face she'd twisted it into a knot at the back of her head and jammed a pencil through it.

The blush she'd applied for the party was a thing of the past, although luckily her skin had retained enough color of its own not to leave her looking sickly. Her mauve lipstick was history, too. Her mascara was still in place on longish lashes over topaz-colored eyes, but on the whole she knew she was the worse for wear.

"Not much I can do about it now," she muttered to her reflection as Deana put the idling car in park and got out.

"If you need Carly Winters, I have her right here," Deana called to the people on the porch. "Just give her a minute."

Then Deana opened the rear door and went around to the trunk for Carly's crutches while Carly slid to the end of the seat to wait for them.

"Hi," she said feebly to her guests.

Both the man and the little girl, who looked to be about five or six, had moved from the door to stand at the railing that edged the porch with turned spindles.

The man raised one large hand to acknowledge her greeting.

"Wow," Deana said under her breath as she returned with the crutches, nodding over her shoulder only enough to let Carly know the exclamation was a commentary on the man himself.

As if Carly wouldn't have guessed.

He was tall, no less than six-two, and he looked much more like a muscled, ranch-rugged cowboy than the town's new doctor she assumed him to be.

His hair was a pale, golden brown he wore short all over. His face had the distinctive McDermot lean angles and rawboned beauty Carly knew only too well since his brothers were residents of Elk Creek. His nose was long and thin and perfectly sculpted. His jaw was square and strong. And his lips were thin, kind and slightly sardonic all at once, not to mention way, way more sexy than Carly wanted to notice.

"Need some help?" he asked when he noticed Carly's dilemma, coming off the porch on long, thick legs that were bowed just enough to look as if they'd spent more time straddling a saddle than standing at an examining table.

He wore faded jeans that rode low on narrow hips, and a plain white T-shirt that stretched tight across broad shoulders, powerful pectorals and bulging biceps that made Carly's stomach do a little flip-flop when she got a closer glimpse of them as he joined her and Deana.

"I think I can manage," Carly said, trying to remember what she'd been taught at the hospital about maneuvering the crutches when her brain was really in a haze due to the man's head-to-toe staggeringly masculine glory.

"You must be Baxter McDermot," she said feebly on her way onto the crutches.

"Bax," he amended.

"*Doctor* McDermot," Deana said with a hint of flirting in her tone that, for some reason, rubbed Carly wrong.

In spite of it she said, "I'm Carly Winters and this is Deana Carlson."

"I apologize for showing up so early," he said after a confirming nod of his handsome head. "We were in a motel for the night with World War III going on in the room next to us. We finally gave up tryin' to sleep and figured we might as well finish the trip and catch a few winks when we got here."

"Sure. Of course. There's just been a little setback on this end," Carly said, leaning her weight on the crutches and honing in on gorgeous sea-foam green eyes that stamped him a McDermot without a doubt.

"You aren't leaving town and don't want to hand your house over to us," he guessed with a glance down at her bandaged ankle.

"I'm afraid I had an accident last night and I'm going to have to put off leaving until I'm healed up."

"It's okay. We can stay out at the ranch," he offered congenially.

It might have been better if he'd been nasty about it. If he'd reminded her that they had a contract in the form of the lease that guaranteed she would turn the house over to him today.

Instead, he couldn't have been nicer about it, offering to go to the ranch he and his brothers and sister now owned after having taken it over from their grandfather.

The trouble was, Carly knew that wasn't what he wanted to do or he wouldn't have rented her house in the first place. He'd arranged for the lease because he'd wanted to be closer to the medical facility where he would work—one of the same purposes the house had served for her father when he'd been the town doctor. And there was Bax McDermot's daughter, too. He was determined to be near her so he'd be available to her during the daytime.

Carly knew all this because the real estate agent who had arranged the rental agreement had explained it to her. And now she felt bad that her change of plans had complicated his. She didn't have to be told that if he had to stay out at the McDermot ranch, he'd be pulled in two directions. Not to mention that he wouldn't have this precious time before he actually began seeing patients to get himself and his daughter settled into the house.

He was being such a good sport about it, it just made her feel all the more guilty.

"Listen," she said. "A deal is a deal and according to ours the house is yours as of today. There's a guest cottage just behind it that my dad sometimes used as a makeshift hospital. I could stay there until I'm healed enough to leave and you can have the house. It'll just mean sharing the kitchen, but it will also give me a chance to show you around properly and teach you the workings of the place."

"I don't want to put you out. Maybe I could take the cottage," he offered.

"It's only big enough for one. Besides, I don't mind. It'll actually be easier for me to get around without having to use the stairs in the main house. And it will only be for a little while. As soon as I'm back on two feet I'm leaving. But in the meantime, things won't have to be messed up for you."

He seemed to study her for a sign that she meant what she said.

She aided the cause by adding, "Really, I don't mind."

He finally conceded. "If you're sure…"

"I am."

"Okay, then. Great," he agreed with a slight shrug of broad shoulders and a smile that put dimples in both cheeks and made Carly's head go light.

Not that her reaction had anything to do with him, she told herself in a hurry. She was just overly tired.

"Do you need me?" Deana asked.

Only in that moment did Carly remember her friend, and she was ashamed of herself for having been so focused on Bax McDermot that she'd forgotten her.

"I'm fine," Carly assured too effusively. "Thanks for taking me to Cheyenne and everything else, Dee."

"You'd do the same for me. At least if you were around," her friend said pointedly. "I'll check with you this afternoon. If you need me in the meantime, just holler."

"Thanks," Carly repeated as Deana closed the rear car door then got behind the wheel.

"Nice to meet you," the new doctor said to Deana.

"You, too," Deana answered just before she backed

out of Carly's driveway only to pull into the one next door.

"Short trip," Bax McDermot observed with a laugh as he watched the move.

Annoyance struck Carly for the second time as she caught sight of the big man's gaze following her friend.

She really did need sleep, she decided. Lack of it was making her cranky.

"We might as well go in," she urged, taking her first steps on the crutches.

But heading across the lawn was a tactical error, and by the third uncoordinated three-legged hobble she set one of the crutches in a hole and everything went into a careen.

Bax McDermot lunged for her, catching her just short of falling with both of those big hands on her waist.

"Steady," he advised.

But even though he'd accomplished just that, something about the warm feel of his hands sent things inside her reeling.

"Sorry," she apologized, feeling like an idiot. "I haven't had much practice on these things."

"They work better on solid surfaces."

Before she had any inkling of what he was going to do, he scooped her up into his arms and carried her to the porch on long, sturdy strides, setting her down near one of the posts so she could hang on to it for balance.

The whole trip took only a few seconds and yet that close contact had knocked her for even more of a loop.

So much so that it took her a moment of hard work to regain herself and realize he was introducing his daughter.

"This is Evie Lee."

"Evie Lee Lewis," the little girl corrected.

"Evie Lee McDermot is what's on her birth certificate," Bax explained. "She tacked on the Lewis herself a few months ago. I can't tell you why or where she got it."

"Everybody should have three first names," Evie Lee added. "To tell them apart from everybody else."

"Makes sense to me," Carly agreed, seizing the distraction of the child.

"Why don't you run and get the crutches?" Bax suggested to his daughter.

Evie Lee did just that, dragging them behind her on her return trip.

She was a tiny little thing with blond hair and a face that was the impish image of her father's, complete with beautiful green eyes that Carly knew would break some hearts down the line.

She thanked Evie Lee when she took the crutches from her and was all too aware of Evie Lee's father keeping his hands at the ready to catch her again when she turned and made her way to the front door on them.

"It isn't locked," she informed him when they'd reached it and he seemed to be waiting for her to produce a key. "No reason to lock doors in Elk Creek. It isn't a high-crime area, so nobody bothers for the most part."

"Nice," he commented as he opened the old-fashioned screen and then the heavy oak panel with the leaded glass oval in its center.

Carly hobbled through ahead of him, stopping in the entryway at the foot of the stairs that led to the upper level. "We're all too tired for the tour, so I'll just give you directions, if that's okay."

"Fine."

"The master bedroom is the first one at the top of the steps. I thought Evie Lee might like the one beside it. That was my sister's and it's still all done up for a little girl. I got them both ready for you yesterday, so there's clean sheets on the beds and empty drawers for your things. The bathroom is down the hall a ways, along with the linen closet and the other bedrooms. Down here, you can see the kitchen at the end of this hall. That's the living room—" she nodded over her right shoulder toward the room they could see from where they all stood "—and the dining room is beyond it, connected to the kitchen. There's another bathroom and the den that you get to from under the stairs."

"All we really need for right now are beds."

"Me, too. The cottage is just across the back patio. That's where I'll be if you need me," she said, pivoting on the crutches to face that direction.

"Can I help you get there?" he asked.

"No. I'm fine. Really," she insisted, adding, "Sleep well," just before heading down the hall on her own.

She could feel him watching her the whole way, and she was glad when she finally got far enough into the kitchen to be out of his line of vision.

But somehow that didn't take away the lingering sense of those eyes on her and the inexplicable feeling of heat that they'd caused.

All part of the weird side effects of a sleepless night, she told herself.

But still she hoped she hadn't made a mistake in

keeping her agreement to let Bax McDermot move in before she'd actually moved out.

Because sleep-deprived or not, something inside her was sitting up and taking notice of too many things about the man.

And that didn't have any place at all in her plans.

Chapter 2

For a split second when Bax first woke up he thought he was back in the days of his residency when it wasn't unusual to work a twenty-four-hour shift and catch forty winks in any empty bed he could find, at any time of day he could manage it.

Then he remembered that he was long past that particular portion of his life and he searched his memory until he recalled that he was in Elk Creek, Wyoming, in the bed in one of the rooms in the house he'd rented.

Carly Winters's house.

A wave of satisfaction washed through him.

He was just so damn glad to be out of the city.

He was a small-town boy at heart. Always had been. Except that the small town he'd grown up in had been in Texas rather than in Wyoming.

It had been exciting to leave that small town and go

to medical school, exciting to practice medicine in the hub of that same university since then. But he'd had a change of heart over the past couple of years. A change of heart that had made him want all he'd left behind. For himself. And for Evie Lee. Especially for Evie Lee.

He felt as if his daughter had gotten short shrift in the parent department so far in her young life. His wife had died on the delivery table, leaving Evie Lee semiorphaned right from the get-go. And Bax knew he hadn't been the best of dads since then.

He'd thrown himself into his work to escape a grief that had seemed unbearable any other way, building up one of the largest medical practices in Denver. That had meant sixty- and seventy-hour workweeks, being on call most nights and weekends, and generally putting fatherhood second.

It had meant leaving Evie Lee in the care of a string of live-in nannies. Not all of whom had treated her well.

He wasn't proud of any of that.

But he was going to rectify it.

Here and now, he thought as he opened his eyes to glance at the clock on the bedside table.

Three o'clock on a Sunday afternoon and a new life had begun for both him and Evie Lee. He'd make sure of it.

Bax yawned, stretched, then clasped his hands behind his head and had a look around the room that had been predesignated his.

The bed was a fair-size four-poster. At the foot of it was a television on a stand against the facing wall. A tall, five-drawer dresser was to the right of the bed. And a door that no doubt led to a closet was to the left.

The whole room was painted a serene shade of

beige, with the woodworking all stained oak. Crisp
tieback white curtains bordered the two large windows
on either side of the television, with scalloped shades
pulled down to the sills of both.

The room was comfortable. Functional. Charmingly
old-fashioned.

He liked it.

And he wondered if this had been Carly Winters's
own room.

Probably not, he decided. It didn't smell the way
she did.

Not that it smelled anything but clean. But he sort of
wished it had that faintly lingering scent of honey and
almonds that he'd caught a whiff of when he'd carried
her to the porch. It was a nice smell.

A nice smell to go with a nice-looking lady, he
thought.

Sure, she'd shown the wear and tear of a long night
in an emergency room. But despite that, she was still
a head-turner.

Besides smelling great, her hair was so smooth and
silky and shiny, it had made him want to yank that
pencil out of it and watch the tresses drift like layers
of silk down around her face.

A face that glowed with flawless, satiny skin.

She had a rosebud of a mouth that was pink and
perfect and much too appealing even without lipstick.
She also had a cute, perky nose that was dotted with
only a few pale freckles he wouldn't have noticed if he
hadn't been so close.

Artfully arched eyebrows and long, thick lashes ac-
centuated stunning, unusual eyes, too. Brown eyes, but

shot through with golden streaks that made them the color of topaz. Sparkling topaz.

Her body hadn't been anything to ignore, either. She was on the small side, weighing next to nothing when he'd lifted her. But petite stature or not, when she'd put her arm around his shoulder to help bear some of the burden, he'd felt a more than adequate breast press enticingly into his shoulder.

Oh yeah, it was all nice. Very nice...

And strange that he should remember everything about her so vividly.

Particularly when the other woman he'd met that morning was just a vague blur in his mind. He wasn't even sure he'd recognize the other woman again if he met her on the street, and for the life of him he couldn't recall her name.

Yet every detail of Carly Winters was right there in his mind's eye.

Making him stare up at the ceiling with a smile on his face...

Cut it out, he told himself.

But that was easier said than done.

In fact, it was damn difficult to get her out of his thoughts, he discovered when he tried.

Maybe it was just that he was in her house, in a room that might have been hers. In a bed she might have slept in...

The idea of that stirred even more uninvited responses inside him, and he wondered where the hell it was all coming from.

But wherever this reaction was coming from, he put a concerted effort into chasing it away, reminding himself that he hadn't moved to Elk Creek to think...

or feel…things like he was thinking and feeling at that moment. It just wasn't in his game plan.

He'd come to the small town to concentrate on practicing medicine and to raise his daughter hands-on, full-time, which was why it had been so important to live a stone's throw from where he worked. And he wasn't interested in trying to add a woman to the picture. He'd already made that mistake once, and he wasn't going to make it again.

But not even the reminder of his second marriage, which was the worst thing he'd ever done in his life and in Evie Lee's, not even his determination to conquer those thoughts of Carly helped to get the image of her out of his head. Or stopped those stirred-up feelings that went with them.

"Must be the house," he muttered, convincing himself that the place was somehow infused with the essence of her, and that was why he couldn't stop thinking about her, remembering how she'd looked, smelled, felt in his arms.

But as soon as she was gone and he and Evie Lee had settled in and taken over the place, all that would be different. The house would be theirs and Carly Winters would only be a faint memory.

He was sure of it.

He just wondered how long it would take for her to be well enough to leave.

And that was when he realized he hadn't even asked what was wrong with her or what kind of an accident she'd had.

"Some good doctor you are," he chastised himself.

But he *was* a good doctor. Ordinarily. In fact, he'd been named Doctor of the Year for the past four years running. Yet meeting Carly Winters had thrown him off-kilter.

Oh yeah, something very strange was going on, all right.

But strange or not, topaz eyes or not, honey-scented hair or not, it didn't matter. Before long Carly Winters would be gone and he was going to be the best damn doctor Elk Creek had ever had. And, more importantly, the best damn dad Evie Lee could possibly have.

And that was that.

Except that even as he sat up and swung his legs over the edge of the mattress his first thought was whether Carly was up and about yet.

And if their paths might cross again anytime soon…

Carly might have slept longer if not for the quiet humming that was coming from beside her bed.

There was no real tune to it and it was terribly off-key, so she knew from the start that it wasn't coming from the clock radio on the nightstand. And since no one had any reason to be in the cottage at all, let alone while she slept, the sound brought her abruptly awake.

Her eyes opened to the sight of the youngest of her new tenants sitting patiently on the dated, barrel-backed chair that was against the wall to the left of the bed, facing it.

Evie Lee was dressed just as she'd been when Carly had first seen her on the porch—short pink overalls and a white T-shirt dotted with rosebuds. But her wavy blond hair was matted and standing up on one side as if that were the side she'd slept on and hadn't bothered to brush or comb since getting up.

If Carly had to bet on it, she'd wager that Evie Lee

had woken up and come exploring without her father's knowledge. He was probably still asleep. Or at least thought his daughter was.

"Hi," the little girl said when she saw Carly's eyes open.

"Hi."

"I got tired of sleepin' and I came to visit you. Is that okay?"

"You can visit me any time at all," Carly answered.

Evie Lee glanced around. "I like this place. It's like a big playhouse."

That was true enough. The cottage was one large room—with the exception of a separate bathroom. Only the furniture divided the open space into sections. A double bed, the antique oak nightstand and the visitor's chair Evie Lee was occupying made up the bedroom. A round, pedestaled café table with two cane-backed chairs and a wet bar were the dining area. A pale-blue plaid love seat, matching overstuffed chair and a television comprised the living room, although the TV was positioned so that it could be seen from anywhere in the room.

The cottage had a history as a guest house and also as a sometimes hospital room where her father had put up patients he'd wanted to keep a close eye on.

It was pleasant and airy, though, with off-white walls of painted paneling and ruffled curtains on the windows to give it a homey atmosphere.

"I don't remember your name," the little girl said bluntly.

"Carly."

"Is that what I can call you, or do I have to call you Miss or something like at school?"

"You can call me Carly."

"You can call me Evie Lee Lewis."

"Thank you," Carly said with a smile, sitting up in bed and bracing her back against the headboard. "Have you been to school yet?" she asked the little girl.

"I went to kindergarten before the summer and when the summer is over and it's schooltime again I'll be in the first grade. You go all day long in that grade. I hope I like it. I hope it's not too much stressful. Alisha had a lot of stressfuls and then she'd go to bed and I wouldn't want to have to go to first grade and then have to go to bed."

"Alisha?" Carly repeated, her interest sparked at the mention of a woman's name.

"Alisha was my sort-of mom for a while but she didn't like me. She liked my daddy. But she didn't like me. She said I was a bad kid and that I was a stressful and a pest and a pain-in-the—"

"Where did she go?"

"Away. My daddy sent her away because she locked me in the closet because I was naughty one day and I put on her shoes and messed up some of her lipsticks."

The thought of putting this little girl or any other child in a closet raised Carly's hackles. "Sounds like your daddy did the right thing by sending her away."

"He was really mad."

"Good for him. He should have been."

"How did you hurt yourself?"

"I fell and sprained my ankle."

"I got a bad scratch on my elbow. See?" Evie Lee displayed the underside of her elbow. "I got it on Mikey Stravoni's slide and then I got a scab but I picked at it till it comed off and then it bleeded all over the place and my daddy said 'I told you not to pick off that scab' because he's a doctor."

Carly laughed at the lowered-voice imitation, enjoying the child who looked so much like her father that staring at her conjured flashes of the man himself in Carly's mind's eye. Flashes that left her with more eagerness to see him again than she wanted to acknowledge.

"Does your ankle hurt?" Evie Lee asked.

"A little."

"Sometimes if you pinch yourself really hard somewhere else you'll forget about it."

"I'll remember that."

"Could I play with your crutches when you don't need 'em?"

"Sure, but they'll be awfully big for you."

"You have pretty eyes."

"So do you."

"I have pretty hair, too," Evie Lee said matter-of-factly. "Will you show me how to put a pencil in it?"

"I will if you want me to. But we could probably put something prettier than a pencil in it."

"Okay," Evie Lee said with enthusiasm, her pale eyebrows taking flight with the anticipation. "My daddy is no good at hair combing. He says he could do surgery better. Do you have any l'il kids?"

"I'm afraid not. I'm not married."

"Me, neither. My daddy isn't neither, too. Are there any l'il kids around here to play with?"

Carly eased herself to the edge of the bed, letting both feet dangle over the side to test how her ankle felt when it wasn't propped up. It hurt more, but it wasn't unbearable.

"There's a little girl up the street," she answered.

"How old is she?"

"I think she's six."

"That's good. That's how old I am—six. I just turned it and I got Angel Barbie for my birthday because she's the prettiest one."

"You'll have to show her to me."

"I could go get her now."

"I think we'll have to do that later. My sister is at the medical building where your daddy will be working. She just had a baby last night and I want to go over and see how she is."

"What kind of baby?"

"A boy."

"Can I come with you?"

Carly laughed again, not minding the little girl's chattiness or persistence. "It's okay with me if it's okay with your dad. But we can't go without checking with him first."

Evie Lee hopped out of the chair. "I'll go ask him right now."

"I want to clean up and then I'll come across to the house to check with him."

"I'll clean up, too," Evie Lee said as if she liked the idea.

The child ran for the door, opened it and turned back to Carly. "See ya."

"See ya," Carly answered.

And out went Evie Lee.

Since Carly wasn't too sure whether or not the little girl might return within minutes—alone or with her father—she wasted no time getting to her crutches and heading for the bathroom.

But on the way she realized she was wearing only her slip, that the dress she'd had on the night before was tossed over the back of the love seat, and that she hadn't brought any of her things with her from the house.

That meant she couldn't take the fast shower she had in mind or so much as run a comb through her hair or brush her teeth or fix her face or change her clothes.

It also meant that if Bax McDermot was up and about, she was going to have to meet him looking even worse than she had the first time.

Not a proposition she relished.

But what was she going to do? She was in the cottage and everything she needed was in the house. She didn't have any choice.

Her only hope was that he was still asleep and she could slip in and out before he woke up.

With that in mind, she put her dress back on over her slip and made her way out of the cottage.

The cottage was separated from the main house by only an eight-foot, brick-paved breezeway. The breezeway was covered on top but open on either side so it could be used as a patio in good weather. There was a cedar wood bench seat along one side, but Carly had left the rest of the patio furniture—chairs and small tables—in the garage so far this season. Minus the clutter of it, she maneuvered herself and the crutches across the breezeway without impediment.

When she reached the back door, she peeked in the window that filled the top half of it and spotted Evie Lee alone in the kitchen, standing on a ladder-backed chair to get herself a glass of water.

Carly knocked on the door to draw the child's attention and then opened it enough to poke her head in. "Is your dad around?"

"He's in the shower so I didn't ask him yet about going with you. But he'll be out in a little bit."

Carly didn't want to think about Bax being in her shower. *Naked* in her shower…

"I need to get up to my room. All my things are still in it."

Evie Lee jumped down from the chair as if it were a tall cliff. "Okay. Come on."

Carly pushed the door open wide with the end of one crutch and got herself through it. But as she did, it occurred to her that if she didn't let the new doctor know she was coming inside, she was liable to bump into him accidentally. As he left the bathroom after his shower. Maybe not dressed…

And while that possibility erupted some wild goose bumps on the surface of her skin, she knew she couldn't let it happen.

"I think it might be a good idea for you to go up and warn him I'm here."

"It's all right. He's always in the shower for a looong time. Come on," Evie Lee encouraged with a flapping wave of her hand, shooting off ahead of Carly.

Carly didn't seem to have a choice but to follow, wishing the whole way that she could just send Evie Lee to get what she needed.

But most everything was packed and Carly had closed the suitcases to make sure she could. Evie Lee was too small to deal with what it would involve to get into them.

The stairs to the upper level presented a problem

and after several attempts with the crutches, Carly conceded that she needed help.

Since Evie Lee was already on the landing at the top, Carly said, "I'm going to need you to carry the crutches up for me. But why don't you let your dad know I'm coming first."

Evie Lee shrugged and did her little-girl-happy-dance until she was out of sight.

Carly heard her holler through the door to her father that Carly was there, but no answer came in response.

"He can't hear me," Evie Lee said a moment later, at the top of the steps again. "It'll be all right. I told you, he'll be in there for a really, really long time."

The prospect of standing there waiting for that really, really long time was not appealing. Especially when the alternative was that Carly could get in and out of her room without seeing him at all.

"Okay. Come and get the crutches for me, then."

The child obliged and while Evie Lee dragged them up in front of Carly, Carly used the banister to aid in hopping one step at a time on her good foot.

It was noisy and awkward and Carly kept up a silent chant of *Please don't let him come out of the bathroom, Please don't let him come out of the bathroom,* the whole way.

When both she and Evie Lee had finally made it to the top and Carly was on the crutches again, she realized that sometime during the trip the shower water had stopped running. Not a good sign.

Before she moved from that spot at the top of the stairs, she said, "It sounds like your dad is out of the shower. Knock on the bathroom door and yell in again to let him know I'm out here."

"Okay," the child agreed as if she just didn't understand what the big deal was.

But Evie Lee barely made it to the door when it opened before she had the chance to do or say anything. And out stepped Bax.

It was obvious he was fresh from the shower. His short hair was still damp and all he had on was a pair of faded blue jeans that rode low on his hips. His feet were bare and so was his entire upper body—broad shoulders, big biceps, muscled pectorals, flat belly and all.

And an even worse case of goose bumps sprang to the surface of Carly's skin than the mere thought of the same scenario had caused.

"Whoops," Evie Lee said at the look of surprise on her father's face. "I was just comin' to tell you Carly was out here."

"I'm sorry," Carly was quick to say. Once she could drag her eyes off his chest. "I didn't bring any of my stuff with me to the cottage, and I was trying to get to my room for it now. Evie Lee knocked before and called in to you, but you must not have been able to hear her."

And didn't Carly just want to crawl into a hole rather than face him looking the way she did!

Bax recovered himself and granted her a smile that made her suddenly feel wobbly on the crutches. "No problem. Do you want to use the bathroom up here?"

Hot, steamy air was wafting out into the hallway, smelling like a far more manly soap than she'd ever used. The idea of stepping into that was too arousing to entertain.

"No, I'd rather just take my things down to the cottage."

"How did you plan to do that?" he asked reasonably.

Only then did it occur to her that he was right. How was she going to manage suitcases and crutches, too?

"I guess I hadn't thought it through," she admitted.

"I don't mind if you want to use the bathroom up here, but if you'd rather not I can carry your things down to the cottage for you."

She didn't know how he could be so calm and collected when she felt like a blithering idiot.

But then, he wasn't looking at the magnificent specimen she was looking at. He was looking at her, dressed in the same rumpled sundress she'd gone to her going-away party in, her face unwashed in more hours than she wanted to think about and her hair straggling around her ears, weeping for a comb.

"It would be great if you could bring my suitcases down to the cottage," she said when she found her voice. "There's a full bathroom down there. In fact, it's better equipped for someone incapacitated because my dad sometimes had patients stay there. Well, not in the bathroom—I mean, he'd have patients stay in the cottage. But the bathroom has grab bars and a seat in the shower and—"

She stopped herself before she babbled anymore.

"Anyway," she said, "I'd really appreciate it if you could bring my suitcases down. That would be great."

"Why don't you show me which room is yours and I'll get them," he said.

Carly pointed with a nod of her chin to the end of the hall. "It's that one."

"Can I go with Carly to visit her sister in the hospital?" Evie Lee said then.

Carly explained what the child was talking about as she followed Bax into her room.

"So I have two patients already," he said as he put Carly's carry-on bag under one arm, picked up the smaller of the other two to tote in one hand and then hoisted the largest in the opposite hand.

"I don't think there were any complications or anything," she answered, trying not to watch the flex and swell of his muscles in the process. "Tallie Shanahan—she's our nurse and midwife—delivered the baby, and when I called from Cheyenne, she said everything was fine. So I don't know if you'd call Hope and the baby your patients."

"I should still look in on them. How about if we all go together? You can show us the way."

"Sure. That would be fine," Carly said, feeling anything but fine.

She hated that just being near this man could reduce her to some kind of bumbling schoolgirl.

She took a deep breath to try to get control over herself. "I'd like to shower first, though," she added.

"Need help?"

"No!" she said in too much of a hurry before being sure if he was teasing her, flirting with her, or if he was offering medical aid.

But the glint in his green eyes and the hint-of-the-devil smile that brought out his dimples made her inclined to think he was teasing. And flirting.

"Like I said," she continued, "the shower is equipped for people who aren't at their best. Besides, they told me at the hospital that I could unwrap my ankle to bathe and then just wrap it again, so I shouldn't be too handicapped."

"Did they show you how to wrap it again afterward?"

"No, but I'm sure it won't be too hard."

"You might be surprised. If you wrap it too loose, it won't do any good and too tight will do damage. Why don't you leave it unwrapped and I'll do that for you before we go over to the hospital? At least I can teach you how to do it right so you can take care of it yourself from here on out."

There was no mistaking his more professional tone.

"Well, okay," Carly agreed without enthusiasm. Somehow just the thought of his touching her—even only her ankle—made flutters of something she didn't understand go off in the pit of her stomach.

"Let's get you back downstairs then," he suggested.

Carly did an ungraceful about-face on the crutches and headed for the stairs again.

At the top of them she hesitated, unsure how best to make the descent.

"You probably ought to go down on your rear end," came the advice from behind her in a deep, baritone voice edged with amusement once more.

There was no way she was going to sit and slide down those stairs while he watched!

Carly ignored his recommendation, handed Evie Lee the crutches again and bounced on her good foot from step to step much the way she'd gone up.

Granted, it wasn't an improvement in the grace or aplomb department, but at least it was quick and didn't involve her rear end.

Once she was at the bottom she held her head high, accepted the crutches from her tiny assistant, and led the way through the house, back to the cottage with Bax and Evie Lee both following behind.

Only when she was in the middle of the cottage again did she turn to find that Bax McDermot was trying to hide a laugh. At her.

"Are you always this headstrong?" he asked.

"I got here, didn't I?"

He just chuckled and raised her bags. "Where shall I put these?"

"Set the big one on the table, the carry-on on one of the chairs beside it and the smaller bag in the corner," she instructed. "If you wouldn't mind," she added to soften the command.

The cottage had never felt as small to Carly as it did then. Bax was a big man and he seemed to fill the space with a heady masculinity that seeped through Carly's pores and made her almost dizzy.

She couldn't keep from watching as he did as she'd told him. Her gaze was glued to his bare back where it widened from his narrow waist to the expanse of his shoulders in smooth-skinned glory. No doctor should have a body like that, she decided. It put too many other men to shame.

And she had to fight the itch in her palms to reach out and run them over the hills and valleys of honed muscle.

Then he turned to face her once more and tearing her eyes off his chest again became a battle she almost lost until she reminded herself that the last thing in the world she wanted was to be attracted to a man right now. Any man.

But it still took a force of will to yank her gaze up to his face.

Too bad that didn't allow her any relief. Because the chiseled planes of his ruggedly perfect features only made her feel dizzy all over again.

"Need me for anything else?" he asked.

Needs were just what were churning inside her, but none he could meet in front of his daughter.

Or anywhere else, for that matter, without disrupting Carly's plans more than they'd already been disrupted.

And she wasn't going to let that happen.

"No, thanks. But thanks for helping me get my stuff down here."

"How long shall I give you before I come back to wrap your ankle?"

"Half an hour?"

"Perfect."

Yes, he was. Damn him, anyway.

"Come on, Evie, let's do something with your hair," he said to his daughter then.

The little girl skipped out ahead of him, clearly oblivious to her father's effect on Carly. As was Bax, Carly hoped.

But only after they'd both left and closed the door behind them did Carly breathe freely again.

The trouble was, this time she couldn't blame her response to Bax McDermot on lack of sleep. She had to admit that it was purely a reaction to something about the man himself.

But she had too much at stake to let it get beyond goose bumps and weak knees and itchy palms and dizziness and flutters in her stomach. She likened her reaction to sneezing when she got anywhere near ragweed—inevitable, inescapable, and over as soon as she got away from the ragweed or took her antihistamine.

She just needed to get away from Bax McDermot.

Which was exactly what she would be doing in just a few days.

In the meantime, she'd simply have to grit it out and keep reminding herself that she didn't want anything to foul up her plans any more than they already had been.

Because unfortunately she didn't think her antihistamine would be of any help with this particular reaction.

Chapter 3

Carly took the fastest shower of her life. Not an easy task when she had to do it standing on one foot like a flamingo lawn ornament. But there was absolutely, positively no way she was going to come face-to-face with Bax McDermot for the third time without being presentable.

With that in mind—actually with Bax in mind—she gelled her hair to give it body and let it air dry while she slipped into a pair of flowing rayon overalls in a red-and cream-colored batik print over a tight-fitting short-sleeve T-shirt.

She applied just enough blush to give her high cheekbones a healthy glow, mascara enough to accentuate every single eyelash and a pale gloss that guaranteed kissable lips.

Of course that kissable part didn't matter, she assured herself, ignoring a second eruption of those stomach flutters at the thought.

By then her hair was dry, so she brushed it and pulled it to the top of her head in an elastic scrunchee and let the slight bit of natural wave on the ends have its way.

A scant splash of perfume was the final touch. Even though she knew there was no call for it, she couldn't resist. She just rejected any thought that her desire to smell sweet and sexy and alluring had anything to do with the new town doctor.

She was in the midst of stashing the perfume bottle back in her carry-on bag when the knock on the cottage door came.

She took one quick look at herself in the full-length mirror on the bathroom door, approved of the improvement, and called "Come in," in a voice she hardly recognized because it sounded so giddy and unlike her.

Bax only poked his handsome head through the door. "Are you ready for us?"

"Sure," she answered after clearing her throat, this time sounding as calm as if she hadn't just hopped around the place like a rabbit in fast-forward mode.

"You *look* ready," he said, stepping inside and giving her the once-over as he did. Then he dimpled up with an appreciative smile that made her crazed hop worth it.

At least it would have if she'd been admitting to herself that she cared.

Behind him came Evie Lee, closing the door and turning to Carly, too. "Daddy wouldn't put a pencil in my hair," the little girl complained rather than saying hello.

Carly didn't mind the omission. She was grateful for the distraction from Bax's dimples and lowered her gaze to the child.

Evie Lee's hair no longer stood up or was matted on one side. It was combed smooth all over, but merely left to fall loosely around her thin shoulders.

"Could you put the pencil in it now and maybe another time we could use a barrette?" Evie Lee persisted.

Carly looked to Bax for permission. "Do you mind?"

He rolled his eyes, shook his head and answered so slowly it was clear he'd been exasperated with the subject before ever getting to the cottage. "If she wants a pencil in her hair and you're willing to put a pencil in her hair, then be my guest and put a pencil in her hair."

"I'm willing," Carly said with a laugh at his controlled loss of patience.

Since she was near the table and chairs where her suitcases were, she pulled the free chair out from under the table and sat on it.

Both the pencil Carly had used in her own hair earlier and her brush were close at hand so she motioned Evie Lee to stand in front of her.

Evie Lee came on a twirl of delight, stopping with her back to Carly.

It took only a few swipes of the brush to pull the silky tendrils off the child's neck. Then Carly twisted Evie Lee's hair into a loose knot at the crown and stuck the writing implement through it.

"There you go," Carly said when she'd finished.

Evie Lee ran for the same mirror Carly had used moments before to check her own appearance and preened before it.

"Oh, that's so cute!" the little girl said.

Carly laughed again, enjoying Evie Lee's enthusiasm.

"What do you say?" Bax prompted his daughter.

"Thank you, thank you, thank you!" the child gushed.

Bax sighed out another breath as if he were glad to have that over with and said, "Okay, now for more important things than pencils as hair doohickeys."

That drew Carly's attention back to him.

Until that moment she hadn't noticed he'd brought with him a black medical bag much like the one her father had carried. He set it on the floor by her feet, then hunkered down on his heels in front of her. Opening the bag, he took a fresh bandage from it as Carly hiked up her pant leg just to midcalf, exposing an ankle swollen to triple normal size and turned a variegated shade of midnight-and-blueberry blue.

"You did a number on this, didn't you?" Bax observed, studying the results of her fall. "So, what was your diagnosis?"

"Sprained ankle with torn ligaments and strained tendons. But no broken bones," Carly recited.

"How did it happen?" he asked, still surveying it with only his eyes.

Carly explained the chain of events that had landed her sprawled on the floor at her going-away party.

"Well, at least you can say it happened in an attempt to do a good deed," Bax said when she'd finished the story, barely suppressing a laugh at her recounting. "Let's get it wrapped again for you. It'll feel better."

And with that he cupped her heel in the palm of his hand and raised it to rest on the thick, hard ledge of his thigh.

There wasn't anything the slightest bit unprofessional or improper or out of the ordinary about what he did. Yet that was all it took for the whole array of sensations to kick in again, adding streaks of lightning to the list as they shot from her ankle all the way up her leg when he began to wrap the bandage expertly around her foot.

No doubt about it, having him touch her was not a good idea.

She didn't know how hands that big could be so warm and gentle when they looked as if they belonged on the reins of a horse instead. But gentle they were. Exquisitely, enticingly gentle.

And worse than all the sensations going through her again was the intense desire to feel the touch of those hands on other places. Much more intimate places...

He was explaining to her how to wrap the bandage, but she only realized it belatedly. When she did, she yanked her thoughts out of the instant reverie his touch had elicited and tried to concentrate so she could perform this task for herself.

"We can soak this a couple of times a day and keep it elevated as much as possible," he was saying. "But mainly with an injury like this you just have to wait it out."

"Too bad. I'd do just about anything to speed up the healing process," she heard herself say all the while she was thinking, *Anything to speed up the healing process and get me out of town and away from everything being near you does to me.*

He didn't seem aware of the internal turmoil he was causing with his ministrations, though, which was one thing to be grateful for, Carly thought. Still, it would have been nice to be able to turn off the turmoil altogether.

When he'd finished with the bandage, her ankle was wrapped perfectly. He lowered her heel to the floor much the way he'd raised it to his thigh before and Carly suffered pangs of disappointment that the whole thing was over even as she silently screamed at herself to stop the insanity that seemed to overcome her every time she was around this guy.

Bax closed the bag and took it with him as he stood. "Done," he announced.

Carly only wished her response to him was done, too.

But even though it wasn't, she pretended it was, got to her good foot and hopped to where her crutches waited against the wall not far away.

"Thanks," she said, not sounding genuinely grateful and regretting the flippancy in her tone. After all, it wasn't *his* fault she'd turned into a sack of mush over him. He didn't even know what was going on with her. So, feeling guilty, she added, "I really appreciate this."

"Glad to do it," he assured. But as he watched her wiggle around for the right position on the crutches, wobble, then right herself, his expression turned dubious. "Maybe we should drive to the medical center rather than walk," he suggested.

The idea of being in an enclosed car with him was too dangerous at that point. Carly would have crawled to the medical building rather than that.

"It's only across the way. I'd have to walk farther to get out to the car than to get where we're going. There's a path from the backyard over to the Molner Mansion."

"The Molner Mansion?" he repeated as Carly led the

way to the door. He still managed to get there enough ahead of her to open it for her.

She explained that the three-story redbrick building had belonged to one of the founding families of Elk Creek and had been donated to the town as the medical building. She also told Bax and Evie Lee that it contained what would be Bax's office, examining rooms, the emergency center, the dental office, outpatient surgery facilities and two rooms that acted as hospital rooms when the necessity arose.

By then they'd reached the mansion and again Bax held the door open for her and Evie Lee to enter before him.

"Do you want a tour of the place?" she offered.

"How about tomorrow? Afternoon naps always leave Evie hungry, so I thought maybe we'd just visit our patients and then go home and I'd whip up some supper for the three of us. Which reminds me, thanks for stocking the refrigerator. That was really thoughtful."

Carly could feel her face flush. Doing a good deed was one thing, but it embarrassed her to have it mentioned.

"It was nothing," she said as she pushed the button for the single elevator that had been installed in the building to accommodate moving patients from one floor to the other.

Carly had ridden the elevator more times than she could begin to count, but never had it seemed so small.

Or smelled so good.

She breathed in the same scent that had come out of the bathroom with Bax when she'd met him in the hall of the main house, enjoying the second helping of it more than she wanted to. She was glad the trip to the second floor was quick.

But she was also slightly disappointed again when it was over and she had to leave the confines that allowed her the heady indulgence.

Maybe the fall that had sprained her ankle had knocked something loose in her brain, she thought, and left her a little nuts.

It didn't take much to tell which room her sister was in because that was where the voices and laughter were coming from when they got off the elevator, so Carly led Bax and Evie Lee there, too.

One step inside the room changed the tone of things for Carly. The room was full of people visiting Hope and the baby, people who gathered around Carly to ask about her ankle, people who were interested in meeting the new town doctor and his daughter, people—Hope's in-laws—who wanted to show off the most recent addition to Hope's family.

The good thing about the whole situation, Carly thought, was that it gave her a break from Bax and diffused his effect on her. And at that point she was glad for any small favors.

They spent until nearly eight o'clock visiting with everyone before Bax finally cleared the room to examine Hope and the baby. When he had, he, Evie Lee and Carly headed for home again, leaving Hope with her company.

By then Carly had had a long while to lecture herself about how silly she was being over Bax McDermot, and she was convinced she could stop her vulnerability to him if she just put her mind to it.

But putting her mind to it was a whole lot easier

when he was at a distance and they were both surrounded by other people than it was when she was sitting at the table in the kitchen of her family home, watching him make mile-high sandwiches for their dinner.

"Nice people," he was saying about the townsfolk he'd just encountered. "I'll bet this whole place is filled with more like them."

"It is," she confirmed, trying not to stare at the best rear end she'd ever seen as he stood at the counter.

"Your sister and the baby are doing well. I told her she could go home tomorrow."

Carly laughed. "She'd probably rather not. There are three more boys waiting for her there, so her rest will be over."

"True enough," Bax agreed, laughing with her in a deep, rich chuckle that sluiced over the surface of her skin like warm honey.

He brought three plates to the table, complete with sandwiches, chips, pickles and olives, then hollered for Evie Lee to join them as he poured milk for his daughter and iced tea for himself and Carly.

Evie Lee must have been on her way to the kitchen even before the bellow because she popped through the swinging door right then.

"Know what?" she asked her father, her tone full of excitement. "There's a bedroom way up high with pictures all over the walls of castles and mountains and all kinds of stuff. Could it be my room instead of that other one?"

Bax looked to Carly, questioning her with his expression.

"It was my room up until a year or so ago," she explained. "It's in the attic. There's travel posters on the walls."

"Ah," Bax said, nodding. "Is it off-limits?"

"No. Evie Lee can use it if she wants. And if you don't mind having her that far away from you."

"It's not far away," Evie Lee countered. "If I leave the door open, you could still hear me if I called you."

"If it's all right with Carly, it's all right with me."

"Oh goody! Can I eat my dinner up there now? It'll be like a picnic."

"Okay, but you'll have to be careful with your milk. Come on, you carry your plate and I'll take the glass," he instructed before excusing himself from Carly for a moment.

She spent the time he was gone working on her self-control yet again, looking around the warm, familiar country kitchen awash in blue and white, trying to get her bearings. To ground herself.

But then Bax came back and sat across from her at the round mahogany table.

And that was all it took for her to notice the color of his eyes as if for the first time, turning her to mush once more.

"That room is nearly wallpapered in posters," he said, referring to her old bedroom as he settled in to eat. "Are any of those places where you're headed?"

Carly swallowed a bite of sandwich she'd taken to camouflage her latest response to him. "All of them, with any luck."

"Looks like you've been planning it for a long time."

"It seems like forever. Since I wasn't much older than Evie Lee."

"And just when you were about to leave, this happens." He nodded in the direction of her ankle.

"It's only a minor setback."

They both ate some sandwich before Carly picked up the conversational ball and got it rolling again. "Have you traveled at all?"

His eyebrows arched and he nodded as he finished his bite. Then he said, "Some. My brothers and I did a summer-long trip through Europe after I graduated college. I saw most of what you have posters of upstairs and then some. Then I came back here, went to medical school and did a stint in the Peace Corps afterward. Saw Africa that way."

"Wow. And now you want to be in Elk Creek?"

He laughed again. "Don't sound so shocked. I've seen enough to know a small town like this one is still the best place to put down roots, to raise a family. But it's good to go out into the world and have a look at it all before you make that decision if you've a mind to. Helps you to know what's right for you and what's not."

Okay, it was ridiculous, but there was a part of Carly that wasn't happy that he was so in favor of her leaving. She couldn't help feeling as if he were trying to get rid of her.

Or maybe she just would have preferred him trying to convince her to stay.

One way or the other, this whole day since she'd met him had been the strangest of her life.

And she was more than ready to put an end to it.

She'd finished her sandwich, so she pushed the plate away. "I should get going," she announced, even though it seemed as if they'd just started to actually talk to each other and she was cutting that short.

But Bax merely nodded, putting no effort into stopping her from leaving the house, either.

"Are you sure you'll be all right out in the cottage?" he asked.

"I'll be fine," she answered. "Better that than those stairs."

"So, we'll just leave the back door open and you can come and go as you need to use the kitchen—is that how we're doing this?"

"That'll work fine. I shouldn't need anything else—especially upstairs—so you won't have to worry about my being in the hallway when you come out of the shower the way I was today."

He grinned at her, dimpling up again. "That wasn't any big deal. With a daughter in the house I have to be careful about how I walk around anyway."

"Still…" she said, remembering all too vividly the sight of his naked chest and feeling all over again what she'd felt then.

Carly pushed herself to her good foot and put a crutch under each arm.

"So, tomorrow you'll show me my office?" he asked, confirming what they'd mentioned at the medical building when he'd declined the tour of the place.

"Sure."

Bax stood then, too, and went ahead of her to the back door to open it for her. "I sleep with the window open, so if you need me during the night, just call," he said as she started to pass through the door.

Needs she was certain were nothing like what he was referring to sprang to the forefront of her mind once more. But all Carly said was, "I think I'll be fine."

And then she did something catastrophic.

She glanced up at him as she passed in front of him to get through the door. Close in front of him. And an intense image of him kissing her good-night flooded through her.

This really had been the most bizarre day she'd ever spent.

"See you tomorrow," she said in a hurry, forcing herself to look down at the ground instead of up at him and moving the rest of the way out of the house.

But as she hobbled across the breezeway, feeling his eyes following her, she couldn't stop herself from wondering what kind of a kisser he would have been if he actually had kissed her good-night.

And then she could have kicked herself for the thought.

Because something told her that he would be as good at that as he was at handling sprained ankles.

And she had to fight hard against the desire to find out for real.

Chapter 4

As Bax searched the cupboards for a can of coffee the next morning he kept an eye on the guest cottage out back.

The curtains were all pulled and there didn't seem to be any signs that Carly was up and about.

But then it was barely six and there wasn't any reason she should be up that early.

There wasn't any reason *he* should be up that early. Except that he'd dreamed about her and the dream had snapped him awake and left him with such an adrenaline rush he hadn't been able to go back to sleep.

Much as he'd wanted to. To revisit the dream.

Because what a dream it had been!

Carly, stepping out of the bathroom the way he had the day before. A towel wrapping her naked body. Steam all around. Her hair twisted and held in place with that pencil, just as it had been when he'd first seen her. One long slender arm reaching up to pull the pencil out. Her hair cascading to her still-damp shoulders. A secret smile on that rosebud mouth. Shining topaz eyes giving him a come-hither wink. And then the towel falling away...

Somewhere in recalling the dream Bax had stopped looking for coffee. Instead, he was holding on to the edge of one of the counters like a runner catching his breath.

And he actually did need to catch his breath. Along with calming down the rest of him before anybody walked into the kitchen and saw him in the state the memory had left him.

He straightened, arched his back, and told himself he was being a damn fool.

Then he let out a deep sigh and restarted the search for coffee.

Maybe a hot, dark cup of the stuff would help get him on track again.

Not that anything else had.

"Bingo!" he muttered to himself when he spotted a can of coffee grounds in the same cupboard where the cups were stored.

He took the can down, fiddled with the coffeemaker until he figured it out and then measured the grounds, adding one more scoop than he ordinarily would have in the hope that an extra-strong brew would have some effect on these unwelcome thoughts he'd been having about Carly Winters.

Caffeine as the cure-all.

Once the coffee was on its way he replaced the can and settled in to wait for the liquid to brew.

And as he did, his gaze wandered out the window over the sink to the cottage again.

Was she sleeping? Probably. In pajamas? Or maybe a frilly little nightgown? Or nothing at all…?

"Hurry up, coffee," he said to the machine, desperate for something—anything—to stop the thoughts of Carly.

It had been like this since he'd first set eyes on her the day before. He didn't understand it. And he couldn't curb it. No matter how hard he tried. And he had been trying. But it was as if she were stuck like glue to his brain and he couldn't pry her loose.

Not that it was torturous having her on his mind. Or at least it wouldn't have been if things were different. If he was in the market for a relationship. After all, there was something really appealing about her. She was beautiful and cute at the same time. Thoughtful and independent. Sweet and sexy…

And flustered. She'd been very flustered for some reason.

Maybe she'd sensed the things he'd been thinking about her. The attraction he felt for her.

He'd done his damnedest to hide it. To seem as if he were hardly noticing her at all. But maybe he hadn't done that any better than he'd actually fought his attraction to her. And maybe if she'd sensed it, she'd figured him for some kind of maniac.

Hell, he felt like some kind of maniac.

What rational man would be so bowled over by a little wisp of a woman he'd just met? What rational man wouldn't be able to stop thinking about her? Wondering how her hair would feel slipping through his fingers. Wondering if he could make her writhe with pleasure if he touched her in just the right spots. Wondering what it would be like to kiss her...

There he was, doing it again. Daydreaming. Night-dreaming. Fantasizing...

What the hell had gotten into him?

He checked the coffeemaker and found the tar-black liquid waiting for him. He filled a mug with steaming coffee, sipping it gingerly rather than allowing it to cool at all.

But that didn't help, either.

Carly was still right there in his mind's eye. Skin like fresh cream. The thickest eyelashes he'd ever seen. Those perky little breasts...

"Geez," he groaned at himself and his own inability to escape his mental wanderings.

It was as if he'd suddenly developed some kind of obsession with her. Like a starving man craving a steak and not being able to think about anything else until he got one. No doubt about it, he felt like a starving man. And she was definitely the lean, succulent steak he was craving.

He drank more coffee, flinching at the scalding his esophagus took as punishment.

It was just a damn good thing Carly was leaving town, he decided, or he was liable to be the worst doctor Elk Creek had ever seen. Preoccupied. Distracted. All het up...

That was why he'd encouraged those travel plans of hers that had been postponed because of her ankle. With the way things had been so far, her leaving Elk Creek had started to seem like his only chance for salvation. Too bad he couldn't put her on the first train out of there.

But fast on that thought came a gnawing in his gut that let him know that wasn't really what he wanted at all.

Okay, so maybe a part of him wanted her to stick around. Wanted to get to know her. Wanted to delve deeper into what he'd so far only seen on the surface. Wanted to explore what made her tick. To know if she was as wholesome and homespun as she seemed, as fresh and funny, as bright and beguilingly sexy.

Sexy again…

He seemed to have *that* on the brain, too.

But no matter what he wanted, he reminded himself sternly, the last thing he *needed* was a woman in his life right now. Let alone a woman he couldn't stop thinking about. A woman he couldn't even escape in his sleep. A woman he was itching to see when he wasn't with her. Itching to touch when he was.

A woman with an agenda of her own that didn't mesh with his.

"Been there, done that."

And he wasn't going to do it again.

No, what he *was* going to do was keep on fighting the attraction he had for Carly because there was just no place for it. Not in his life and not in hers.

And while he was waging the battle, he'd hold on to the hope that the attraction wasn't bigger than he was.

Although at that moment, standing there staring across the breezeway at the cottage once more and imagining himself slipping in to watch her sleep, waking her with a soft kiss, he wasn't convinced that what was happening with him wasn't already a little out of hand.

* * *

Plain blue jeans. A simple white, short-sleeve, V-neck T-shirt. Her hair in a French braid. Just a little light mascara, blush and lip gloss.

Carly was absolutely certain she had herself under control as she made her way across the breezeway to let Bax know she was ready to go with him to the medical building and show him his office.

No more fluttering insides. No more weak knees. No more goose bumps. No more of anything that had plagued her the day and evening before. She was her old self. She'd avoided the temptation to wear something special and made sure to dress the way she would have for any other sunny Monday morning. And she was convinced that the whole attraction thing was just some kind of fluke she had finally overcome with a good night's sleep.

Then Bax opened the main house's back door in answer to her knock.

And there he was, dressed not much differently than she was in snug-fitting denim jeans that hugged his hips and stretched taut with the hard bulge of well-developed thighs, a work-worn chambray shirt with the sleeves rolled to his biceps and a pair of cowboy boots more suited to ranching than to doctoring. He smelled of that clean, spicy soap again, and as she breathed it in he smiled at her with those dimples and those great green eyes. And the whole package hit her like a ton of bricks.

So much for being in control and back to her old self.

She even swayed on her crutches as she stood there, to such an extent that he reached for her with both hands on her shoulders to steady her. Hands that seemed to sear right through her shirt and brand her.

Lord, but she wished this reaction to him would stop!

"Ready to go?" she asked cheerily, drawing herself up stiffly enough to slip from his grip.

"Sure. Are you okay this morning?"

Even a slight frown beetling his brow only added to the man's handsomeness. Damn him anyway.

"I'm fine," she answered too brightly, overcompensating.

"You look good," he said, his gaze going from head to toe to head again, broadening his smile and leaving her wondering if he was flirting.

But before she had a chance to decide, he glanced over his shoulder and yelled, "Evie Lee! Let's go. Carly's here." And his young daughter came barreling through the kitchen's swinging door.

"Carly's here?" she repeated as if Carly were a gift-laden Santa Claus come to pay her a midyear visit.

"Good morning, sweetie," Carly said, appreciating the delighted welcome and the diversion from Bax.

"Oh, let me see your hair today!" the little girl demanded effusively, charging around her father, out the door and around to Carly's back. "That's so pretty and fancy, too! Can you do that to me?"

"Sure. It's just a braid."

"Daddy can't do things like that."

"How about playing beauty shop later?" Bax said to his daughter. "Carly came to take us to my new office right now."

"Can we do my hair later?" Evie Lee asked Carly.

"As soon as we get back," Carly promised.

"Then let's go so we can hurry up and come home."

The two adults followed the child's lead, heading down the same path they'd taken the night before.

Along the way Bax asked how Carly's ankle was today and she told him it was better, even though, in actuality, it was more swollen and black and blue than it had been. She was afraid if she told him the truth, he might want to examine it. And if he examined it, that meant he might touch it. And she knew too well how powerful his touch could be.

Nice. Gentle. Warm. Arousing.

Definitely much, much too powerful to leave her with a clear head. And she was determined to keep her head clear, if it was the last thing she did.

But in the process of thinking about keeping a clear head, Carly made the mistake of bringing Bax into the medical building through the front door rather than the rear. Unlike the previous night when the only other people in the place had been in Hope's room on the upper floor, today there were folks milling around everywhere.

Tallie Shanahan—who had been handling all minor medical treatments since arriving in town only a few weeks earlier—was just calling a patient to one of the examining rooms when Carly, Bax and Evie Lee entered the building. Tallie would soon be Bax's sister-in-law since she was engaged to his brother Ry, but Carly knew that Tallie had only met Bax over the telephone during his interview. So when Tallie glanced up at the threesome as if they were more patients, Carly had to introduce Bax. Once she did that—with the whole waiting room within hearing range—Tallie had no choice but to do a general introduction to the half-dozen people eavesdropping. And despite the fact that the introduction included the information that he wasn't there to work yet and was taking a few days to get his bearings, people were eager to shake his hand and tell him their ailments.

Carly was a doctor's daughter so she knew this came with the territory. And since it was her fault that she'd brought him in the way she had and made him fair game, she also knew she had to be the one to ease him through the waiting room as best she could.

It was no simple task, but as Tallie went on to see patients, Carly finally managed to get Bax, Evie Lee and herself through the door behind the reception desk and into the hallway that led to the office and the examining rooms.

"The office is at the end of the hall," she said, leading the way.

It had been her father's office for forty-four years, until his death six months ago. Carly had been in it since then, but only when she, her mother and sister had cleared her dad's things out of the old scarred walnut desk not long after the sudden heart attack that took his life.

Crossing the threshold into the office now was more emotionally difficult than she'd expected as memories of her father flooded her.

She put some effort into shaking them off by facing Bax from the center of the room and apologizing for not bringing him in the back way. But the whole time he was assuring her it was all right, she could feel the urge to escape this place that had been the very essence of her dad.

"Let me point out a few things," she said, hating

that she sounded so fragile. "And then I'll get out of here so you can do whatever it is you want to do here."

She cleared her throat when what she was actually trying to do was strengthen her voice. Then she continued. "The key to the desk drawers is in the top one. That same key locks and unlocks the credenza. I guess they've always been a set. We cleared my dad's stuff out of them both so they're all yours—"

Her voice cracked at the mention of her father and it seemed to alert Bax to how tough this was for her. He took over.

"I saw the shelves of patient files behind the reception desk, so I'm figurin' that's where they're kept, and Stella—if I'm rememberin' her name right—the receptionist, will likely be the one to ask for any of those I might need. Right?"

Carly nodded.

He pointed his chin in the direction of the old leather sofa that was against the wall facing the desk. "My guess is that that couch has seen its fair share of catnaps. Those bare nails on that wall over there are where your father's diplomas were hung and where mine will go. But I noticed there's no screen on the window. Is that because he climbed out of it once or twice to give himself a breather without having to explain it?"

That made Carly smile, which she was reasonably sure had been the point of the unrealistic assumption. But she was just grateful that his joke helped diffuse some of her tension. "I think the screen is just being fixed, but sneaking out the window is probably not a bad idea."

Bax walked to the wall that faced the desk. The worn leather sofa against it had seen better days, but what drew his attention was the wall itself. Floor to ceiling, end to end, it was a collage of photographs.

"Explain this for me, though, would you?"

Carly hobbled to stand beside him as Evie Lee climbed onto the couch to get a better look, too.

"Wow, look at all those pi'tures."

"It started with the first baby my dad delivered," Carly informed them both. "He took a snapshot of the family and pinned it up here so he could see it whenever he wanted. He was so proud of that very first new Elk Creek citizen he'd helped bring into the world. The pictures just snowballed from there. It got to be a tradition. Not only for him to take photographs of new babies, but of new patients, and kids—or even grownups—in fresh casts or when the casts came off broken arms or legs. Of people he helped one way or another. Sometimes, even if folks moved out of town, they'd send him pictures with notes on how they were doing and he'd put those up, too. It got to be sort of a goal for everyone to have their picture on Dad's wall. I suppose you could say this is the gallery of his practice. Of most of his life. We didn't have the heart to take it down."

Tears suddenly sprang to Carly's eyes. She blinked them back and in spite of the fact that Bax had been studying the photographs and not looking at her, he seemed to sense the wellspring of emotion that had been tapped.

Without so much as glancing at her or taking his eyes off the wall, he reached a hand to her back and rubbed it softly.

The gesture was no more than an offer of comfort and that was how she took it. But it was an offer of comfort that melted something inside her. Something more than the sensual awakening it brought with it, more than the sparks it lit in her at his touch.

It melted some of the internal starch she'd been using to resist him and she wanted badly to turn to him, to lay her cheek against his vast chest and feel him engulf her in those oh-so-able arms.

And that was when she knew she was in real trouble with this man. Because not only was he drop-dead gorgeous and so sexy it seemed to infuse the air around him, he was also a nice person. A compassionate person. A person, like her father, who would be a good doctor for Elk Creek.

"Of course you're free to take the pictures down now that the office is yours," she said softly when she had some control of herself again.

Bax slid his hand up to her neck, gave a slight squeeze and let go.

"I like it," he said, still studying the wall. "It'll be a great icebreaker when I ask patients to pick themselves out for me. Besides, it's a sort of legacy, isn't it? And legacies shouldn't be tampered with."

There wasn't anything more right he could have said and Carly finally hazarded a glance at him. "Thanks," she murmured.

"Nothin' to thank me for," he claimed, meeting her eyes with his.

For a moment Carly lost herself in those green depths. The urge to turn into his embrace only got stronger and in that same moment something seemed to connect them. To isolate them from everything else and leave them in the center of their own universe.

Carly had the oddest sensation that there was something predestined about this whole thing. Predestined and out of her hands...

"Can we go home now?"

Evie Lee was part of what Carly had forgotten about, but the sound of the child's voice reminded her that Bax's daughter was still very much with them. It seemed as if Bax had also lost track of Evie Lee because the little girl's question snapped him out of that moment of silent reverie, too.

Bax looked away first, but not in any hurry and clearly reluctantly.

"I told you we were going to need to spend some time here, Evie," he said to his daughter.

"But I want Carly to do my hair."

Before either Carly or Bax could comment about that, Tallie knocked on the door they'd left open and said, "I'm sorry, Bax. I know you didn't come in to see patients today, but I have a few out here who are insisting they have emergencies that can only be taken care of by a doctor now that they know there's one on the premises."

Bax chuckled good-naturedly. "It's okay. I'll see them."

"Thanks," Tallie said as if he'd answered her prayers, then disappeared as quietly as she'd come.

"That's my fault," Carly acknowledged. "If I'd brought you in the other way, no one would know you were here and you wouldn't have to go to work before you're ready to. So how about this. I'm going upstairs to see Hope and the baby before they leave and Evie Lee could come with me. Then we'll go back to the house and braid her hair and I'll keep her busy while you take care of things here."

"I don't expect you to be my baby-sitter."

"But finding one is probably one of the things you were going to do before you thought you'd have to start dealing with patients, isn't it?"

"Yeah," he admitted. "But still—"

"I don't mind. Besides, Evie Lee can be a big help to me while I'm on these things." Carly raised one crutch to demonstrate what she was referring to.

"I can get stuff for her and help her with stuff, too," Evie Lee chimed in, clearly liking the idea.

Bax lovingly roughed up his daughter's hair. "You promise you'll behave yourself and do everything Carly tells you?"

Evie Lee nodded vigorously.

"And you're sure you don't mind?" he asked Carly.

"I'm positive."

"Okay, then. I appreciate it."

"Oh goody, goody, goody," Evie Lee cheered, leaping off the sofa. "Let's go."

"I guess I'll see you ladies at home in a little while," Bax said.

"There's no rush," Carly assured him as she made her way to the door.

But before she left the office something caused her to turn and look back at Bax where he stood in the center of the room.

Even though she still had pangs of loss, she felt as if she'd handed over what her father had loved dearly to someone her dad would have approved of. And liked.

Almost as much as she did.

Chapter 5

Word traveled like wildfire in Elk Creek, so it was no surprise to Carly that by midafternoon there were patients lined up around the block to see Bax. The town had been a long time without a doctor and even though Tallie had done a good job since moving back, even though there had been an occasional week of a visiting doctor's care, there was a fair share of the population who felt their medical needs had gone unattended.

Carly was racked with guilt for having been the cause of the avalanche of patients to befall Bax, so when he called at five to say he still had a waiting room jam-packed with people and didn't know when he'd get home, she assured him there was no hurry, that she was enjoying Evie Lee's company, and that they would have dinner waiting for him when he got there.

But when he got there, *they* weren't waiting for him.

Only Carly was because it was nearly ten o'clock and Evie Lee had fallen asleep on the couch in the living room.

Carly was sitting at the other end of the sofa watching the child sleep when she heard the back door open. She told herself that the speed with which she got to her good foot, onto her crutches and headed for the kitchen was merely because she didn't want Bax to come into the living room and wake his daughter.

But deep down she was fighting a rise of pure eagerness to see him again.

Bax was standing at the sink when she slipped through the swinging door. He was facing away from her, washing his hands. With the water running, he didn't hear her come in.

She should have announced herself, but for a moment she just stood there, her already intense attraction to him strengthening with every second.

It wasn't the width of his shoulders in the chambray shirt. It wasn't the narrowing of his waist. It wasn't even that derriere that was so remarkable. It was something about the back of his legs. Long, thick, hard legs, spread slightly apart, sexy and so strong they looked as if they could brace the weight of the world.

And Carly had an image of them bare of the tight jeans, straddling her...

"Hi," she said softly, yanking her gaze upward and hoping that if she let him know she was there it would help push away the image, the thoughts, the desire.

Bax glanced over his shoulder at her as he turned off the water and reached for a paper towel from the holder underneath the cupboard to dry his hands.

"Hi," he answered as he turned and leaned against the counter's edge.

His chiseled jaw was whiskered with the full day's growth of beard, and it only added to his appeal in her eyes. He looked rough and rugged and more masculine than she could bear.

She knew she should tell him what he needed to know, say good-night and get out of there, but she'd been so hungry to see him again since they'd parted that morning that she just couldn't make herself do it. And despite telling herself she owed him a little company while he ate, it was nothing more than a feeble excuse when the truth was that she just couldn't resist having her own hunger satisfied.

"I made a casserole. It's still in the oven," she said, trying not to feast on him with her eyes. But that wasn't easy. Five-o'clock shadow or no five-o'clock shadow, he didn't look any the worse for wear. There were hardly any signs that he'd just put in a twelve-hour day. Instead, his green eyes were as bright as ever and if anything, he seemed even more at ease.

"Great. I'm starved," he said in answer to her announcement.

But Carly was so lost in the sight of him that it took her a moment to recall what he was responding to.

When she did, she crossed to the stove, propped both crutches under one arm and used a hot pad to take the dish out of the oven.

Setting it on the stove top was as far as she got before Bax came to lend a hand. "Let me do this. And while I eat, let's soak that ankle of yours. I brought a footbath and some Epsom salts from the office."

Oh good, a valid reason for staying.

"Go sit at the table and let me set it up," he instructed.

She did as she was told, unwrapping the bandage while Bax filled the footbath and brought it to her.

He made sure the water level was high enough and the temperature just right, then he returned to the stove for the casserole.

"There's salad in the fridge and beer or iced tea to drink," she informed him as he put the dish on the table near the plate, napkin and silverware she'd arranged for him when she and Evie Lee had eaten.

He made a second trip for the salad, a jar of Caesar dressing she'd made and the tea.

"Can I get you something?" he asked.

"No, thanks. I'm fine."

Carly watched him serve himself, and while she did she said, "Evie Lee is sleeping on the couch. She tried to wait up for you, but she didn't make it."

"I figured she was down for the count. She never stays awake past nine, no matter how determined she is. But I hate it when I miss her."

"That's my fault. I really am sorry about today. I know better than to bring the doctor in the front door," she apologized for her faux pas again.

"It's okay. There were a few folks who really did need to be seen. And much as I wish it wasn't true, Evie is pretty used to my working late. Besides, I'm not worried that this will be the norm, so don't beat yourself up over it."

Carly appreciated how he was taking the whole thing.

She also appreciated the sight of him eating, that sleek jaw working as he chewed....

"Good stuff," he complimented when his mouth wasn't full.

The hamburger, green beans and gravy casserole with mashed potatoes on top was hardly gourmet fare. "You're probably just starved," she said with a laugh.

"That, too," he agreed, dimpling up for her. "How did you spend the day?" he asked then.

"Hope and the baby were on their way out when we got upstairs, so we went along home with them. Evie Lee got to meet my nephews—they're two, three and four—and being the advanced age of six herself, she mothered them all."

"Ordered them around is more like it."

"That, too," Carly agreed with him, laughing again. "We had lunch over there and then came home when it was everybody's nap time. Evie Lee swore she doesn't take naps anymore, so I didn't make her—I hope that was okay."

"She was right, she doesn't take them. She barely took them when she was a baby. So what did you do when you got here?"

"We did her hair and I read to her and we colored and that took up the afternoon. Then we fixed supper and put a puzzle together and she fell asleep in the middle of my reading to her again tonight."

"Sounds like a full day."

"Not as full as yours, but full enough."

"I hope she didn't wear you out or keep you on that foot too much."

"No on both counts. She didn't wear me out, I had a great time with her, and she didn't keep me on my feet too much because she waited on me every chance she got. Of course, I had to call her Nurse Evie Lee Lewis, but that was just part of the game."

It was Bax's turn to laugh. "Sounds like she played nurse while you played teacher."

"I wasn't playing. I am a teacher."

"Ah, that explains it. Of little kids?"

"Junior high. Geography."

He nodded knowingly. "I should have guessed that one. Goes along with that wanderlust of yours."

"Mmm," she agreed, wishing *wander*lust was the only kind she was feeling these days.

Bax had finished eating by then and cleared the table, leaving the dishes in the sink so he could rejoin her. He sat in the same chair he'd used before, but this time he lounged in it, draping one arm over the back of it and stretching the other out on the tabletop.

Carly suddenly found herself interested in the coarse hair that speckled thick forearms and wrists, another element of his masculinity that thrummed something sensual inside her.

"Would you mind telling me about your dad?" he asked then. "It's looking like I have some pretty big shoes to fill."

That made Carly smile and helped her rein in her thoughts.

She forced her glance up to his face once more. "You do have big shoes to fill," she told him kindly, but in no uncertain terms.

"Your father's patients surely do miss him."

"He was a good man. An old-fashioned country doctor who knew his patients inside and out. He loved them and they loved him."

"I got that message today. Even my genuinely ill patients spent as much time tellin' me how great he was as they did tellin' me how sick they were. Was your dad a hometown boy?"

"Born and raised. So's my mom. They always said that being an Elk Creek native made it hard for Dad to be taken seriously when he first started his practice here. Some folks wouldn't even go to him right off the bat. They said they knew him when he was an ornery, mischief-making kid, so how could they turn around and trust him with their health care? He almost didn't stay because of it. He and Mom were thinking about leaving Elk Creek—or so the story goes."

"What changed their minds?"

"Mom got pregnant with Hope, for one. They didn't want to raise a family anywhere else. And a few emergencies came up that proved Dad's salt. Little by little, folks came around. Like they will with you, if you're worrying about it because they gave you a rough time today."

Bax's grin let her know she'd hit the nail on the head. "And your dad ended up being loved by all," Bax finished for her.

"He was always loved by all. It just took some time to be loved and trusted as a doctor."

"But when it kicked in, it kicked in but good, from what I heard today."

Carly conceded that. "My dad had two things going for him—he really, truly cared about these people, and he was the kind of man who made sure nobody in town went without a turkey for Thanksgiving or toys for their kids on Christmas. He saw being a doctor as more than just pill pushing. He *talked* to his patients. He made them all friends. He found out what was going on in their lives, in their heads, in their hearts, so he had the whole picture. He was like a father to everybody, I guess."

"And how was he as a father to you?"

"Oh, he was good at that, too. I can't remember more than a handful of nights in my whole growing-up years when he wasn't home to tuck me in. Even if it just meant running over for five minutes from sitting at someone's bedside, he'd make sure he was home to tell me to have sweet dreams."

"Are you sure he didn't climb out that office window to do it?" Bax asked with a laugh, clearly thinking of the day he'd just put in and the impossibility of getting away himself.

"Maybe he did and that's why the screen is in such bad shape," she agreed, playing along. "I'm just saying that my dad was really conscious not to forget about his family. If he'd been away a lot or one of us kids felt as if we hadn't seen enough of him, he'd let us spend a day at the office with him, being his assistant—even if we had to ditch school to do it."

"Sounds like he was quite a guy."

"He was."

"Kind of like his daughter is quite a woman."

That came out of the blue and brought a blush to Carly's cheeks. "I don't know about that," she said, deflecting the compliment and wishing she could as easily deflect the steady stare of his eyes as she realized that he hadn't taken them off her the whole while they'd been talking.

As the heat from his gaze seeped all through her, it made her aware of just how cold the water in the footbath had become and that gave her another diversion.

"I think my ankle has soaked long enough. The water's getting pretty cool."

Even that didn't cause an instant reaction. For a moment Bax just went on studying her, smiling a small, secret smile, as if he liked what he saw.

But then he bent over and dipped a finger in the water to test it.

"Yep, cold, all right. Better get you out of there."

"There are towels on the shelf above the dryer in the laundry room," she informed him.

The laundry room was just off the kitchen to the right and Bax was back with towel in hand before she'd done more than raise her foot out of the now chilly bath.

He hunkered down in front of her the way he had the night before and scooped her foot into the towel, a medical version of Prince Charming trying on Cinderella's glass slipper.

"I can do that," Carly said as he began to blot her skin dry, careful not to press too hard and hurt her.

But Bax went right on doing it, studying the increased swelling and bruising while he was at it.

"I know it looks worse," she said, trying to keep her own perspective and not lose herself too much in the pleasure of his ministrations. No matter how tempting it was to just sit back and indulge in the tenderness of his touch.

"Par for the course," he answered. "It may look even worse tomorrow, but then it should start to improve. You did one hell of a job on it."

"You can leave it unwrapped. I have a clean bandage at the cottage and I can wrap it myself over there," she said then, almost afraid of what any more contact with him would inspire in her.

"Okay," he agreed, slipping the bath out of the way so she could gingerly set her foot on the towel he laid out on the floor.

As he took the bath to empty in the laundry tub, Carly gathered up the used bandage, put it in her pocket and got up onto her crutches again.

"You don't have to go," Bax said, returning from the laundry room for the second time. "It can stay unwrapped for a little while." He seemed disappointed at the obvious sign that she was ending the evening.

"It feels better if it's wrapped. Besides, you've had a long day. I'm sure you want to relax."

He grinned at her with a hint of the devil in the corners of his supple mouth. "Who said I wasn't relaxed?"

"You know what I mean."

Carly headed for the back door and Bax crossed with her on just a few strides of those long legs she'd had unholy visions of earlier.

As they reached the door and went out into the breezeway, he said, "I understand there are some folks I should see on a couple of the outlying spreads around here. I called the ranch to let my family know I was in town but wouldn't be able to get there today the way I'd planned, but we arranged for me to take Evie out there to stay tomorrow while I do some travelin' to the other places. Gives me a chance to get an idea of what all I'm lookin' at and see whatever folks I need to. Then I'll go on back to the ranch for dinner."

Carly didn't know why he was outlining his next day's plans for her, but she did know the thought of him being busy and away and her not getting to see him deflated her spirits much more than it should have.

"Sounds good," she said without any enthusiasm.

"I also heard from more than one source today that you're pretty popular with folks around here, particularly with some of the older ones. I was told that you used to do house calls with your dad when you could and that havin' you along would be a feather in my cap when I go to introduce myself to some of the less sociable souls out in the countryside. Not to mention that I could use a guide to give directions to find these people. Think I could persuade you to come along?" he concluded, finally getting to the point.

The air was pumped back into Carly just that quick. Even though she knew it shouldn't have been.

He'd made the request sound innocent enough. Harmless enough. But Carly knew better. She knew that any time spent with him was dangerous because she liked him too much. Because for some reason she didn't understand, she was particularly susceptible to him.

So, just say no, she told herself.

But saying no meant just what she'd thought before—it meant he would go off tomorrow and do his business and she wouldn't see him at all.

And she hated that eventuality so much, she couldn't inflict it on herself even if it *was* what she *should* do.

"What do you say?" he persisted, making her realize she'd let too much of a pause linger while she argued with herself.

"Sure. I don't have anything else to do tomorrow," she heard herself say before she was completely sure she was going to agree.

"Great. I'd really appreciate it. We don't have to go too early, though. Maybe around eleven?"

"Fine."

Great. Fine. No problem. Except for the racing of her heart at just the idea of the next day and being with him again.

Carly crossed the breezeway, wishing it were about a mile longer so maybe the night air could have more chance of cooling her off.

Although if Bax went along—the way he was going along now—no amount of distance would have helped.

When they reached the cottage, he opened the door for her, but he stood half blocking it so she couldn't go in. Instead, she was left facing him, looking up into eyes that seemed to delve into her.

"Thanks for taking care of Evie Lee today and tonight. And for the supper."

"No thanks necessary. I enjoyed it." And him. Everything about him…

He went right on staring down at her, studying her face as if he were learning it.

Then, when she least expected it, he raised a hand to brush the backs of his fingers against her cheek in a feathery stroke.

"I hope I didn't upset you by asking you to talk about your dad."

She shook her head. Upset was definitely *not* how she was feeling. "Being in his office was a little hard, but talking about him only brings back good memories."

Bax nodded. Slowly. Never taking his eyes off her.

"I really do appreciate everything you did today," he repeated, this time in a voice that had gone deeper, softer, more intimate.

"No big deal," she responded, her own voice joining the intimacy.

He went on looking at her in a way that seemed to draw her to him. That seemed to block out everything else, leaving them alone in that space and time.

And then he leaned in closer and kissed her.

It was just a brief peck of a kiss, although it wasn't timid or abrupt or the way a young boy might snatch a smooch from a young girl.

It was confident. Smooth. Intriguing.

It was just short.

But not so short that it wasn't enough to give her a taste of lips that felt even better than they looked. Enough to set a whole lot of things in her atwitter.

Then he smiled down at her again, looking pleased with himself. Or maybe with her. Or with the kiss. Or maybe with everything all rolled together.

"Night, Carly," he said.

"Good night," she answered, hating that her voice sounded so small, so starstruck.

He stepped out of her way then and said, "See you in the morning," and left her on the threshold of the cottage.

But somehow she felt as if she were on the threshold of more than just the guest house.

And as she stepped inside she couldn't help wondering what a full-fledged kiss from him would do to her if just a peck could leave her feeling as if a whole new door had just opened in her life.

Chapter 6

Carly had never been a late sleeper so when Deana knocked on the cottage door at ten the next morning and called, "It's me," Carly was already up, showered and dressed in a sunny yellow, cap-sleeve A-line dress that went all the way to her ankles. She was in the process of fastening her hair only inches from the ends with an elastic ruffle to hang in a low, loose ponytail, so she merely yelled back, "The door's open."

"I come bearing fresh bagels and cream cheese," Deana said as she let herself in.

One look at Carly standing in front of the mirror on the bathroom door and Deana added, "Wow! How come you're all dressed up?"

"I'm not 'all dressed up.' This is just a sundress."

"That you usually reserve for summer parties."

"I have to go with Bax to introduce him to the people on the farms and ranches outside of town and then have dinner at his family's place. I don't want to do all that in jeans."

Deana's well-shaped eyebrows reached for her hairline. "One day I don't see you and you're calling him Bax as if the two of you are old friends and he's taking you to eat with his whole family?"

"It isn't the way you're making it sound," Carly said as she sat at the table and pointed to the other chair for Deana.

Carly had pushed her open suitcase to the wall so half the table was usable, and she'd set her carry-on bag on the floor to free both chairs, mainly thinking of Evie Lee but now accommodating Deana, too.

Deana set the sack she was carrying on the table, produced two cups of coffee from it, two cranberry bagels and a small tub of cream cheese. Then she sat down herself.

"How's your ankle? I wanted to get over here yesterday, but my sister had a crisis—Clive broke up with her. I had to rush over there at the crack of dawn and didn't get home until after midnight last night."

"That's okay. There isn't anything you can do here anyway. It's just a matter of time and hobbling around on the crutches."

"Does it hurt much?"

"Sometimes, if I try to put any weight on it or when the bandage is off, but it's not a big deal. How's your sister? I know she was thinking she and Clive were on the verge of getting engaged. She must be heartbroken."

"She is. But we both know she's better off without him and I think she'll see that when the worst of the shock is over." Deana took a sip of coffee and changed the subject. "Now, what's going on with you and the good doctor?" she demanded with the same inflection she'd use if Carly was about to tell her the principal of the school where they both worked was moonlighting as a drug smuggler.

"There's nothing *going on* with me and the good doctor. I just seem to have inherited the job of showing him around and introducing him to everyone."

"Which means spending a lot of time with him," Deana concluded as they divvied up the cream cheese and started to eat.

"It's kind of hard not to spend time with him under the circumstances. He's living in my house and we're sharing the kitchen. He's taken over my dad's practice. And he's also looking after my ankle."

"You lucky dog you."

Deana's envious sigh made Carly recall that her friend had seemed to have quite an appreciation for Bax when they'd all initially met on the front lawn the other morning.

It also restirred the twinge of jealousy Carly had felt, but she didn't want to think about that.

"Did you kind of have your eye on Bax?" Carly asked tentatively, unsure exactly what to say, but thinking she should somehow address the subject.

Deana waved a hand at her as if she were shooing away a fly. "I thought he was drop-dead gorgeous and the best hunk to hit town in a while. But if he's managed to snare your interest, that's even better. You can have him and maybe he'll have a friend for me. It could all work out great!"

"He hasn't managed to snare my interest," Carly

protested too much. "But if he had, why would that be even better and make things work out great?"

"Because if you fall head over heels for our new town doctor, you'll stay in Elk Creek. And I'm all in favor of anything that makes that happen, even if it means you get the guy and I don't."

"Deana—"

"I know. You're going to say you let a man tie you to this town once and you won't do it again. But I can hope, can't I? Besides, Bax McDermot is a whole lot more man than Jeremy ever was. He'd be worth being pinned to Elk Creek for eternity."

There was no disputing that Bax was more man than Carly's former fiancé had been. There wasn't any comparison at all.

But she didn't want to think about Bax's good qualities any more than she wanted to think about that dumb jealous twinge.

As she and Deana sat eating their bagels, though, Carly knew it would have been the perfect time to encourage her friend to go after Bax. Maybe even to offer to set them up on a blind date.

Yet Carly just couldn't make herself do that.

No matter how hard she tried.

"You do like him, though, don't you?" Deana said then as if she were reading Carly's mind.

"There's nothing *not* to like. He's nice, understanding, kind, compassionate, caring, considerate. He has a good sense of humor, great hands. He's a good father—"

"Hold it. What was that *great hands* part?"

That had slipped out. Carly had been hoping Deana wouldn't catch it.

"Surgeon's hands. It just meant that he'll be able to do operations well when he needs to."

Deana laughed out loud. "That is *not* what you meant. Has he gotten his hands on you already?"

"On my ankle. Only in a medical capacity."

"And you liked it, didn't you? And not in just a medical capacity."

"So he's gentle. So what?"

Deana smiled like a kid who'd just found precisely what she asked for under the Christmas tree. "This is better than I thought."

Carly rolled her eyes. "Deana, as soon as my ankle heals, I'm leaving Elk Creek just the way I planned. And no man—not even Bax McDermot—is going to change that. I let that happen before, and I will not let it happen again," she said forcefully.

"We'll see."

"I mean it."

"Okay. You mean it," Deana conceded without conceding anything at all because she was still smiling like the cat that ate the canary.

So prove you mean what you say and fix her up with Bax, a little voice in the back of Carly's mind challenged her.

But in that instant when Carly imagined the new doctor's hands on her friend—in any way, medical or not—in that instant when Carly imagined Bax giving Deana even the kind of almost-nothing kiss he'd given her the night before, Carly's hackles rose so high she still couldn't make herself do it.

And worse than that, she almost felt a hint of an inclination to actually stay in Elk Creek to keep it from happening.

"This is crazy," she said, not realizing the words were going to come out until they had.

But Deana took them as a comment on their conversation, unaware that Carly was talking to herself about her own thoughts.

"Crazy or not, I'll take what I can get when it comes to any chance of you not leaving," Deana said. "And crazier things than this have happened. With Bax McDermot in town, Elk Creek may have a whole new appeal for you."

"Please don't get your hopes up, Deana," Carly beseeched.

But she could see that her friend's hopes were already up.

And as much as Carly didn't want to admit it, she knew something was up with her, too.

She just didn't know quite what it was.

"So what, besides the lollipops you haven't offered me yet, is in the bag?" Bax asked with a nod at the paper grocery sack near Carly's feet as she sat in the passenger seat of his car.

They'd stopped at the McDermot ranch to say a brief hello to his family, then left Evie Lee to the afternoon her uncles had planned for her, an afternoon of playing with the animals and riding the horses.

Carly had dipped into the bag to send a rainbow-colored sucker with the little girl for later, and now that Carly and Bax were on their way to the outlying farms and ranches, Bax's curiosity about the grocery sack she had packed before they left seemed to have gotten the better of him.

Carly glanced at him, trying not to notice how good

he looked in his khaki-colored jeans and crisp white shirt with the sleeves rolled to his elbows.

"I'm sorry. I didn't think you'd want a sucker."

"Think again," he advised with an ornery smile tossed her way as he drove down the deserted country road.

Carly reached into the sack and produced the same kind of lollipop she'd given his daughter. She unwrapped it and held it out to him.

Rather than taking it with his hand, he leaned over and took it with his mouth, grinning up at her before straightening in the seat and focusing once again on the road.

It was a playfully intimate gesture that warmed Carly more than she wanted to admit. Especially since they were alone in the middle of nowhere, in the close confines of his station wagon.

She forced her own eyes straight ahead, too, trying not to be so aware of the way he moved the candy around in his mouth.

When he'd settled it in the bulge of one cheek, he said, "So, what are we in for this afternoon?"

Talking about that seemed like safe territory. And Carly was grateful for anything that might keep her mind off the heady scent of his aftershave filling the sun-warmed interior of the car and infusing her with too strong a sense of his masculinity.

She jumped right into the subject.

"Be prepared for plenty of stories about sprains, broken bones and months on crutches. Having me along will inspire everyone who's ever had a similar injury to tell you about it."

"Great. It'll give us a good opening. Who's up first?"

"The Marris family. Their farm is about four more miles out. They have eleven kids and another on the way—that's who the lollipops are mainly for. Three of the kids are prone to strep throat and four to ear infections, and even though they're great, well-behaved kids, it helps to have a reward waiting after you examine them."

"I'll remember that. Twelve kids, huh?"

"They wanted a big family."

"I'd say a dozen kids qualifies. What's the age range?"

"Eighteen months to seventeen, with two sets of twins in the mix. But you'll always find the kids and the house spotlessly clean, and they come into town every Sunday for church."

"So they're good people is what you're telling me."

"Good enough that we all try to make things easier for them if we can. Sometimes Kansas—she owns the general store—opens up just for them after the Sunday service if they haven't been able to get in to do their shopping any other time. And my dad met them at the office after church, too, on occasion, if one of them was under the weather. They're nice enough folks to do a little extra to help them out. And if you do, it'll be worth your while. Helen Marris makes the best zucchini bread in the county and she'll reward you with a loaf for your trouble."

"Okay. I like zucchini bread as much as the next guy."

"Good. I'm glad to know you'll do what you can to help out, too. I think that's what being a small-town doctor is all about—being flexible, taking an extra step now and then."

Bax pretended to strain for a glimpse into the sack. "So, that accounts for the suckers. But I can tell there's more than that in there."

"There's a couple of fishing magazines for Murray Abrams—the old issues nobody's reading in the waiting room anymore. Some people call him Murray the Grouch because he's so cantankerous. Don't be surprised if he greets us with a shotgun and even shoots a load over our heads before he realizes who we are. But don't let it phase you. It's a test of your mettle. He really isn't such an ogre when you get to know him."

"He's the diabetic Tallie told me about."

"Right. But the other thing is that you can't *ever* let him see a needle. Dad was able to treat his diabetes with oral meds so far and it's a good thing because I don't know what would happen if he had to use injections. If you have to give him a shot for any reason, make sure he's lying flat on his back on the bed because he passes out cold."

"Okay. Good to know."

Carly continued with her roll call of the patients Bax would be meeting today. "There are quite a few elderly people. It's not unusual for these big spreads to be passed down to the kids and grandkids—"

"The way ours was."

"Right. And a lot of the older folks have stayed on to live. There's one couple—the Krupcheks—who are both in their nineties and in a constant state of World War III. They'll tell you they're getting a divorce and one or the other of them will try to talk us into taking them into town to live with some of their other relatives. But if you cajole them a little, it'll pass. They've been threatening divorce for as long as I've been alive and nothing ever comes of it."

"And how long is it now that you've been alive?"

He'd eased into that pretty smoothly.

But Carly didn't resent the question. She was secretly flattered by his interest.

"Thirty-two years. You?" Two could play the same game.

"Thirty-six. Thirty-seven next month."

"Oh, you're old," she teased him, purposely omitting the fact that she, too, would be another year older in only four days.

"What do we *old* people get out of your magic bag?"

"Jam, raspberry chutney or pickled green tomatoes."

"Homemade?"

"I have summers off work, remember? These jars are the end of last year's gardening and canning."

He nodded and gave her a look out of the corner of his eye. "Can't do much gardening or canning when you're out traveling around."

"I think the world will survive without it."

"You never know."

What Carly did know was that he was just giving her a hard time. She opted for ignoring him and went on with what she'd been saying.

"There's also some romance novels in the sack. Minnie Oliver is eighty-six, but she just loves them. She says that no matter how old the heroine is, when she reads those books she's that same age. She says they keep her young. She also says she likes them steamy. The hotter the better."

"Maybe I'll have to keep my eye on her," he said as if the elderly woman might try to seduce him.

"You don't have to worry about Minnie, but I should warn you about Candy Woodbine. She will likely want to tap dance for you and her tap dances look more like tame stripteases—not that she gets down to her Skivvies, but expect some shedding of scarves or sweaters or whatever she can spare."

"Yeah?" Bax asked with mock interest in his tone. "How old is she?"

"Seventy-three, but she's still kickin'—that's what she'll tell you—and a little charm tossed back at her will tickle her to death."

"At seventy-three maybe I shouldn't be tickling her to death," Bax joked.

"You know what I mean—it'll thrill her."

"So, I'm not only the doctor, I'm also the marriage counselor and Cary Grant?"

"Something like that," Carly said with a little laugh. "There's also Frank Montoya. He's eighty and he'll bend your ear about the flood of 1929 when his family was stranded on the farmhouse roof, watching their pig float by. Don't cut him off even though the story will go on for a long time or you'll hurt his feelings."

Bax glanced at her. "That's important to you, isn't it? With all these people. That I don't hurt their feelings."

Carly shrugged. "They're nice people."

"So are you."

That made her cheeks heat and she didn't know what to say. So instead she went back to what she'd been talking about. "Frank loved that pig. Don't be alarmed if he tears up."

Bax gave her another pointed glance, chuckling kindly at her.

"Oh, and if Benny Mathis wants you to take a look at a problem with one of his animals, humor him. Every symptom he tells you his cow or horse or goat or dog has is really what's going on with him. He just doesn't like to complain for himself."

"Is that it?"

"There's more people we'll see, but those are just some of the quirks you'll come across."

"Good thing you warned me. I could see myself getting into some real trouble without you."

"I think you'd probably have done all right on your own." She thought he could probably do all right on his own with anything or anyone.

But then maybe she was biased.

The dirt road that led to the Marris farm came into view then. Carly directed Bax to it, and from that moment on she consciously tried to take a back seat to him. At each house they entered from then on she introduced him and did her best to blend into the woodwork.

She wasn't terribly successful because everywhere they went she was well-known and well liked while Bax was the newcomer people were a little shy of.

He didn't seem to mind and included her himself at every opportunity.

Along the way Carly got to see Bax in action, and it only confirmed her earlier opinion that her father would have approved of this man who had taken over the care of the people who had meant so much to him.

If there was such a thing as a born country doctor, Bax was it.

There was no pretension, no arrogance, no talking over anyone's head. He blended just the right amount of socializing with the practice of medicine, and not even Cary Grant could have charmed everyone more adeptly.

Carly didn't think there was a single home he left without having won over the folks inside. To the point where she felt confident that the next time he made the rounds to the outlying farms and ranches he'd be welcome not only for the gifts and tokens he made note to return with, but also just for being himself.

And Carly realized as they wrapped up the final visit of the day that she felt a little jealous again.

Jealous of the fact that Bax was only beginning these visits while they were likely the last she'd ever make.

Not that it mattered enough to stay in Elk Creek, of course.

But still, she fought a twinge of regret she hadn't anticipated.

Regret that she wouldn't be along on his future visits.

Especially when they seemed to make such a good team.

Chapter 7

It was after six by the time Carly and Bax made it back to the McDermot ranch.

Since Carly had lived all her life in Elk Creek, she'd known the place when it had been the Martindale ranch—Bax's grandfather Buzz Martindale's spread.

That was long before Buzz's daughter—Bax's mother—had eloped with a man Buzz hadn't approved of. Years of estrangement had finally ended, and when it had Buzz had turned over his house and land to the grown grandchildren he hadn't known before that—Shane, Ry and Bax McDermot and the other brother and sister that Carly had yet to meet.

The original house had been a small farmhouse, but since Shane and Ry had developed a new breed of cow and reaped the success that had come with it, they'd added onto the original home.

So much so that Buzz's old place wasn't much more than the entry to the new, sprawling ranch-style house.

Carly never passed the property without marveling at the addition and that held true as Bax parked in front and helped her from the car.

It was a beautiful place with twin wings gracefully spreading out on either side of the main entrance where separate bedroom suites opened onto a wraparound porch.

Bax didn't bother to knock on the front door when they reached it. But then, this was his house, too. He was merely renting hers for the sake of convenience.

He held the door open for her to go in ahead of him, waiting patiently as she maneuvered on the crutches she wished she could throw into Make-out Lake.

"Anybody home?" Bax called once they were inside, standing in the wide-open entryway from which both wings could be accessed on either side. Straight ahead was the living room, then the formal dining room, and then the kitchen out back.

It was from the kitchen that someone answered.

"We're on the patio."

Bax swept an arm out to let Carly know he wanted her to go first, and they made their way through the tastefully decorated living and dining rooms to find Bax's brother, Shane, filling tall glasses with ice and tea.

"'Bout time you got back," Shane greeted them in a tone that took the complaint out of his words. "We're eatin' outside tonight. Barbecuing. That's where everybody is already. Want tea or soda pop or a beer?"

Bax looked to Carly.

"Tea would be good," she added.

"Tea for me, too," Bax added.

Shane handed two of the glasses he'd filled to Bax, took two more and led the way through the French doors onto the bricked patio where thickly cushioned lawn furniture was occupied by Shane's twin brother, Ry, Shane's wife, Maya, Ry's soon-to-be wife, Tallie, and Buzz.

"Daddy!" Evie Lee shouted when she spotted Bax before anyone else had even noticed that Shane hadn't returned alone.

"Evie!" Bax answered, echoing his daughter's enthusiasm as everyone said hello.

The little girl left a cardboard crate full of kittens to charge her father. "I been swimmin' and everything today!" she announced, going on to give a recounting of an active afternoon.

"...and when the kittens get a little bit older I can have one. Or two or the whole box!" she finished, clearly repeating what someone had said in answer to whether or not she could have a kitten.

"I don't know about that," Bax hedged. "We might just have to visit them here. Our lease may not let us have pets," he said with a wink at Carly.

"Uncle Ry and Uncle Shane got you a present. A whole horse!" Evie Lee added as Bax led Carly to a chair at the big round table where everyone was sitting.

When Carly had shucked the crutches to sit down, Bax took the seat beside her.

"Is that so? A whole horse, huh?" he responded to his daughter's statement, but cast a quizzical look at his two brothers.

They were both giving that same devilish grin Carly had seen on Bax's face, stamping them all brothers.

"He's a buckin' bronco," Evie Lee said. "See him? Over in that place next to the barn? He's soooo pretty and he looks nice but Uncle Ry says he's not as nice as he looks. But they brought him in from bein' wild just for you."

"Gee, thanks," Bax answered facetiously.

"There was a time when this daddy of yours was the best of us all at ridin' a horse like that. Isn't that so, Ry?" Shane said.

"True enough," Ry confirmed.

"Bet it isn't true anymore, though," Shane added, obviously goading Bax. "Not now that he's a big-time *doctor* and all citified. Probably doesn't even remember how to ride a horse at all, let alone one that's tryin' to buck 'im off."

"Bet you're right," Ry agreed again.

"Could you still do it, Daddy?" Evie Lee asked, picking up the gauntlet her uncles had thrown down.

Bax grinned the grin of a confident man. "Probably could."

"*Probably* could? Or *could?*" Shane prodded.

"Never know," Bax answered.

"Not unless we get your rear end up on his back to see."

Carly looked at the sleek black stallion across the yard. Evie Lee was right, it was a beautiful animal. But Carly had been around these parts long enough to know that no matter how docile a wild horse might appear to be, trying to ride it would bring out the worst in it.

"It's been a busy day," she interjected as if that nullified the idea, because the thought of Bax anywhere near the stallion made her uneasy. Even though she knew it was none of her business and she had no right to be nervous. Or to say anything at all.

But it was that pointed comment from her that Bax seemed to hone in on more than any of his brothers' baiting.

"You don't think I can do it, do you?" he asked in a quiet voice for her ears alone.

"I can't imagine why you'd want to."

"It's a pretty good rush," he said by way of explanation. But the lazy smile that stretched his lips as he looked at her made her think that he knew how his riding the horse would unnerve her and was just ornery enough to do it to get a rise out of her.

But Carly was just ornery enough not to let it get a rise out of her.

Or at least not to show it.

Instead, she merely arched an eyebrow at him.

Unfortunately he seemed to interpret that as a challenge.

He set his glass on the table and stood. "Get me a pair of gloves and some chaps so I don't ruin my pants," he ordered as if they were instruments he needed to perform a surgical procedure.

"Eee-haw!" Buzz hooted, getting into the spirit of things.

"Stay on 'im the regulation eight seconds and we'll do the saddle breakin' for you," Ry said as if setting the terms of a bet.

"But let 'im throw you before that and you come out here to do it yourself," Shane added.

"Deal," Bax answered.

Then he threw Carly another wink. "Good thing we have crutches handy, just in case."

"You can't do much good as the town doctor if you're laid up," she told him.

"Careful or I'm gonna take that as an invitation," he said, purposely misinterpreting her words.

"Come on, if you're gonna do this thing, do this thing," Shane urged and the three brothers headed for the barn.

"I want to see this!" Evie Lee announced, following behind.

"Sometimes I think there's just too big a streak of boy in every man," Tallie said.

"Mmm," Maya agreed while Buzz merely chuckled and got up into the walker he'd needed to get around since breaking his knee several weeks before.

"Guess we all better go out there," Tallie said as the older man made slow progress across the yard. "We may have to pick up the pieces. Can you make it all right, Carly?"

Carly assured her she could, and the women headed for the paddock where the unsuspecting horse waited.

It wasn't long before Ry, Shane and Evie Lee joined them and Buzz at the paddock rails while Bax came out through the barn's side door directly into the enclosed area with the horse.

Carly had wondered why Ry was carrying Bax's white shirt, but when she spotted Bax she understood.

His khaki jeans were covered with the leather chaps he'd requested, his hands were protected by fingerless gloves strapped tight around his thick wrists, and he'd traded his own shirt for a ragged chambray one.

He looked every inch the cowboy with leather reins slung over one shoulder as he approached the stallion, talking softly to it, soothingly.

The animal raised its head from where it had been peacefully munching grass to watch Bax, but it didn't shy away. It stood its ground almost as if it were curious as to what the human had in mind, but showing no fear.

"We used to say that Bax thought like a horse," Shane said to the spectators in general.

But that didn't put rest to any of Carly's tension. She just hoped Bax knew what he was doing.

Although she had to admit he seemed to.

He had sugar cubes in his left hand and when he got close enough to the horse he held one out for him. The animal nibbled it out of his palm, keeping a wary eye on him the whole while.

The treat bought Bax permission to go a few steps nearer until he could feed the stallion the cubes with the animal's nose nearly up against his chest. He kept on murmuring something Carly couldn't hear, but she imagined his deep voice saying endearments and she thought if she were the horse, that in itself might be enough to tame her.

But rather than endearments, she realized he was probably making friends with the animal the way she'd watched him make friends with his patients all afternoon. Charming him. Gaining his trust.

And when he had, he hooked the reins through the driving bit of the bridle and eased them over the stallion's ears.

Carly knew it was probably a feeble hope, but she couldn't help thinking that maybe the horse would just let Bax ride him as Bax stepped around to his side.

Bax smoothed the animal's hind quarter and kept on talking to him as he wrapped the reins around one hand. Then he grabbed hold of the mane with the other and swung a leg up over the horse's back in one smooth, lithe motion.

For a split second the horse just stood there.

But then the fact that he had a rider registered and he took off like a shot, racing several yards, stopping cold, rearing to kick his front legs in midair, lowering them so he could buck with his hind legs, then taking off again to repeat the process. Again and again.

Never had Carly seen an animal as determined as that one to rid itself of a rider.

But Bax didn't merely hang on for dear life, he rode the horse, staying with it, absorbing the shock of each buck, each rearing up that made the animal seem like a giant to Carly.

Beside her, Ry went from observing the event to checking his wristwatch, but for Carly it was an endless eight seconds.

Her heart pounded in her chest and it was as if every jolt of the animal jarred her, too.

Yet even as afraid as she was for Bax's safety, she had to admire what she saw. The way he handled the animal was an impressive sight. His power and strength met that of the beast and he came out the victor when Ry finally yelled, "Time!"

And then, with all the adeptness of a stuntman, Bax actually managed to leap from the bucking bronco's back and land on his feet in a run that took him away from the still-rearing animal.

Buzz and the other McDermot men hooted and hollered and cheered for him, and he faced it with a grin that said he'd enjoyed every second of the ride.

He folded one arm across his waist and took a bow.

Then he came to the rail to climb the first rung and swing himself over the top to again land on his feet amid backslaps from his family.

Evie Lee was jumping up and down, clapping her hands and parroting her uncles' and great-grandfather's cheers, but Bax's gaze sought out Carly.

His eyes locked on hers for a moment, beaming with pride and pleasure, and for that brief time it seemed as if they were the only two people there.

And, Lord, how she wished it were true...

Then he pulled off the gloves and handed them to Shane, unfastened the chaps to slip them off and before Carly knew it, he'd also shed the work shirt and was reaching for his white one from his brother.

It took her so unawares that she didn't have time to brace herself before she was confronted with his naked torso the way she had been on Sunday when she'd caught him coming out of the shower.

Only this time she was having even more difficulty tearing her gaze away from shoulders and biceps that were all tight flesh over hard muscles—not what any doctor acquired in the course of his duties.

The span of his chest was daunting and delectable at once, and Carly's mouth went suddenly dry as her eyes stuck on the slight smattering of hair there, at the vision of brown male nibs, at the six-pack of taut abdominal muscles down his middle to the sexiest navel she'd ever seen peeking from above a pair of jeans.

The whole picture took her breath away and made her head reel as much as if she'd been on that wild horse herself. Her hands ached to be pressed to him, to learn for herself if his skin was as smooth as it looked. As warm. As wonderful...

Then on went the white shirt, blocking her view and, somewhat belatedly, Carly realized that someone had suggested the steaks be put on the grill. Ry had left to take the reins off the stallion and the group was moving back toward the house, leaving Carly and Bax alone.

The silence around them as Bax buttoned his shirt and jammed the tails into his waistband seemed to Carly to shout of her attraction to the man, so she swallowed hard and fought to find her voice.

"I guess you are good at wild horse riding," she said.

He smiled a quirky kind of smile that raised only one corner of his mouth. "Just showin' off," he admitted. "I've had a lot of experience from my misspent youth. I was always the one crazy enough to do the bronc bustin'. I guess once you get the feel for it, you never lose it."

Carly understood having the feel for something.

Or maybe it was having the desire to feel something that she really understood....

"Well, don't do it again," she heard herself blurt out.

Bax laughed. "Yes, ma'am," he said as if accepting a command. Then his tone turned satisfied. "Had you all riled up, did I?"

Riled up. Aroused. Hard to tell the difference if there was one.

"It isn't that you scared me or anything," she denied to save face. "It's just that Elk Creek needs its doctor in one piece."

"I suppose that's true enough. But think of it this way—I only had to spend eight seconds up there. Now my brothers have to do the actual saddle breaking. So I came out ahead and so did Elk Creek."

"Still…"

He leaned over to whisper in her ear much the way he'd whispered to the horse. "Careful or I'm gonna start thinkin' you care."

"I do care. For the town's sake. For Evie Lee's sake."

"And for your sake?"

"I just don't want to share my crutches," she claimed with her nose in the air.

"There's a lot of things I'd like to share with you, but crutches aren't one of them," he said with a bad-boy grin and an unmistakably lascivious glint in his eyes.

Ry came out of the barn just then, having retrieved the reins and put them away.

"Well come on, you two, looks like we're finally eatin'."

Bax did a courtly sweep of his arm. "After you," he said to Carly in a bedroom voice that turned her blood to molten lava.

But she merely shook her head as if she'd just suffered a silly joke and headed for the house again.

Matters weren't helped, though, when Bax fell into step beside her and put a hand at the small of her back.

As always his touch spread a heat all its own, lighting a fire to the already molten lava.

Carly and Bax didn't have another moment to themselves the rest of the evening. At least not until they left the ranch.

Evie Lee had fallen asleep before dessert was served and had been put to bed with an assurance that one of her uncles would take her home in the morning. That left Carly and Bax alone in the car on the way home.

The temperature hadn't cooled much with the setting sun so all the windows were rolled down to let the air flow through. Carly was grateful for that. It helped diffuse some of the intimacy of being in the dark car with him.

"Tomorrow's the meet-and-greet reception," he said, disrupting the quiet hum of the motor as he drove.

"That's right. I'd forgotten about it. I didn't expect to be here."

"But since you are, would you charge me extra for comin' to it with me? I already owe you for introducing me to everyone and giving me the briefing about them beforehand."

Carly had laid her head against the seat back and she kept it there even as she turned to look at him. "I didn't know I was charging you for today."

"You could. For being my consultant. Except that the service you provided was priceless."

There was an edge of teasing to his tone, and his dimple was showing in the cheek that she could see.

For a moment Carly lost herself in the sight of his profile. It was as well-chiseled as the front view, and she got lost in the sharp jawline for a moment before she recalled that they were having a conversation.

"The reception is in the evening, isn't it?" she asked to pull her thoughts back into order.

"At six. In the church basement so folks aren't coming to the office and expecting me to work. I'd really appreciate it if you'd come with me."

Not just be there, go *with* him.

"I think I can do that," she said, despite the warning alarm in her head that told her she should refuse. That he didn't really *need* her there. That they were spending too much time together. That she was liking him much too much…

But the agreement was already given and she couldn't take it back.

"Great!" Bax said in response to her acceptance. "Now I'll be lookin' forward to it."

"Weren't you before?"

"You know how those things are—you have to be center stage the whole time. Makes me uncomfortable."

"A lot of people would like being center stage. It would be a big ego boost for them."

"I'm more of a hands-on guy myself," he said with a sideways glance at her to go with the innuendo.

"Mmm," was all Carly answered, thinking that his hands on her had definite appeal.

Not that she'd ever say it.

They'd reached Elk Creek by then. It was after ten o'clock, all was quiet and it suddenly seemed to Carly that she'd gotten her earlier wish—it truly felt as if they were the only two people in the world.

And she was liking *that* too much, too.

Bax pulled into the driveway in front of her house, stopped the engine and wasted no time getting out. He came around to her side to open the door and held her crutches for her as she got out.

"Want to trade houses for the night?" he asked then.

"Trade houses?"

"It just occurred to me that without Evie Lee at home I could sleep in the guest cottage and you could have a night in your own bed if you wanted," he explained as they went onto the porch and in the front door.

"That's okay. I'm all set up in the cottage and you're settled into the house. Besides, I don't mind. I've always liked the bed out there."

For the first time in her life the mention of *bed* felt wicked. Titillatingly wicked.

Maybe because the moment she'd said the word she'd realized that within a short time that was where they'd both be—in their respective beds. But what had popped into her mind was the image of Bax in her bed in the cottage rather than in the one he was using upstairs.

In her bed in the cottage with the sheets dropped low enough to bare the naked chest she'd seen earlier.

In her bed in the cottage with the sheets dropped low enough to bare the naked chest she'd seen earlier and her in bed beside him...

Carly tried to push the instant fantasy into oblivion, but it was stubborn and she ended up deciding the best thing to do was to end this evening and get a safe distance from the man who was provoking the unwelcome thoughts.

So she didn't pause inside but instead headed straight for the back door.

Unfortunately Bax went with her to hold open that door. Then he went out into the breezeway and across to the cottage with her, as well.

And there she was at the cottage door, with Bax in the soft glow of the motion detector light that had turned on as they'd come outside.

She had to take a good, hard look at his white shirt to force herself to remember that he was, in fact, fully clothed or she didn't think she could keep herself from falling into his arms. On purpose.

"Thanks for everything you did today," he was saying when she yanked herself back into reality.

"Don't think anything about it. I enjoyed myself.

It was good to see all those people before I left." And she *was* going to leave, she reminded herself firmly. Soon. And nothing was going to get in her way this time. Not even a man who stared down at her with sea-foam eyes that delved into her soul and turned her insides to mush.

Not even a man whose lips she suddenly recalled the feel of much too vividly...

"Before you leave," he repeated, more to himself than to her, as if he were reminding himself the way she'd just reminded herself.

But if he'd intended that reminder the way she'd intended hers—as a caution that whatever was happening between them had no future—it didn't appear to help.

Because he remained standing there, studying her face, smiling at whatever it was he saw there.

"We should probably call it a night," Carly said then, trying to hang on to her resistance but hearing the words come out in a voice that was nearly breathless and far more sensual sounding than she'd intended.

"Probably should," he agreed in a raspy tone of his own.

But he didn't move from that spot where he stood close in front of her. So close she could see every long eyelash that shaded his eyes.

So close she could feel the heat of his big body.

So close she could have arched her back and her breasts would have touched his chest...

"And I probably shouldn't, but I'm gonna kiss you good-night again," he added then.

His low, deep voice and the sight of those handsome features put together in such rugged perfection mesmerized her. The only thing Carly could think to say was, "Probably shouldn't," in a way that sounded more inviting than anything else.

"Probably shouldn't," he agreed just before he lowered his mouth to hers.

But tonight the kiss he gave her was not merely a brief peck. Tonight it was a full-blown, genuine kiss with lips that knew just the right amount of pressure, just the right amount of persuasion to entice her lips to part slightly to match his, to give as good as she got.

Tonight it was a kiss that drew her in. That rocked her.

That left her knowing somewhere deep inside that things would somehow never be the same again.

And then it was over.

Bax straightened away from her. He captured her eyes with his once more and she could tell she wasn't the only one of them to have felt the earth shake.

"Probably shouldn't have," he whispered, as if talking to himself.

But the fact remained that he had.

They had.

And as Carly said good-night and went into the cottage, all she could think was that she wanted more.

No matter what it put into jeopardy.

Chapter 8

"Boy-oh-boy, do they get up early over at that place," Evie Lee announced the following morning at the breakfast table.

Bax was still slightly bleary-eyed. Shane had called at five-thirty to tell him Evie Lee was ready to come home, and here it was 6:07 and she was eating a bowl of cereal and chattering with vigor when he could usually count on her staying in bed until seven.

And since Bax had had some trouble falling asleep the night before, it wasn't easy keeping up with her.

"They gots a rooster," Evie Lee continued, "that makes lots of noise and it waked me up. Not like the cock-a-doodle-doo noise in the cartoons. It makes a worser noise than that."

Bax smiled at his daughter's inexperience with country life. But then for the six years she'd been alive he'd been practicing medicine in Denver and there wasn't a rooster crowing at dawn in a high-rise apartment building. This was just the kind of thing he'd come to Elk Creek for—so Evie Lee would have a taste of what he considered real life. The kind of life he'd known growing up.

Just then Evie Lee hopped off the chair and headed for the back door. "I wanna go tell Carly what the kitties did this morning."

"Whoa, hold on there," Bax said in a hurry, stopping her just short of charging out. "It's too early to go bargin' in on Carly."

"But she said it was okay for me to visit her anytime."

"Not at six in the morning. She's probably not even up yet."

"Then I'll wake her up," the little girl said reasonably. "I'll make the rooster sound for her."

"Uh-uh." Bax gave his daughter a firm stare and wiggled a hooked index finger, motioning her to come back to the table.

"But I *like* Carly," Evie Lee moaned.

"I like Carly, too, but that doesn't mean we can disturb her." Even though she was disturbing the holy hell out of him and his sleep patterns. He couldn't stop thinking about her long enough to get any rest.

But that was his own fault.

Evie Lee dragged her feet back to the kitchen table and climbed onto her chair to take another bite of cereal. And just that fast her pique changed to a new interest.

"You like Carly, too?" she asked.

"She seems nice," Bax said, downplaying the truth.

Because the truth was that he liked her a lot. Enough to have been up until the wee hours of the morning thinking about her. Picturing what she might be doing out in the cottage. Calculating how much distance separated them. Wondering what would happen if he crossed that distance and appeared on her doorstep. Imagining himself finding her in some slinky, low-cut little nightgown, her hair hanging loose and free and silky around her shoulders, her face all pink and pretty from a fresh scrubbing, her topaz eyes wide with surprise but her rosebud mouth smiling a welcome. That same rosebud mouth he'd kissed twice now. And was dying to kiss again. And again. And again. Before they moved on to so much more...

"Do you like her for a girlfriend?" Evie Lee asked, interrupting his wandering thoughts.

"She's just a nice person," he hedged, uncomfortable with his daughter's probing into something he wished wasn't happening at all.

"I heard the big grandad say you mittened her."

Bax had to think a minute to figure out what that statement meant. He knew the *big grandad* was Buzz. That was Evie Lee's version of great-grandfather. But it took him a moment to figure out why Buzz would say anything about Bax, Carly and mittens.

Then it occurred to him.

"You mean *smitten?*"

"Okay. But you don't have any smittens, do you? I never saw you put any on Carly."

Bax laughed lightly. "*Smitten* isn't the same as *mittens.* It means *like,* too."

"Oh. Then the big grandad thinks you like Carly. A whole bunch."

Bax just took a drink of his coffee rather than commenting on that.

"Do you like her like you liked Alisha?"

There was a note of caution in Evie Lee's voice even now when she said the other woman's name.

Not that Bax didn't understand it. Alisha had been both their nightmares.

What he couldn't tell was if Evie Lee was asking that question because she was concerned he might repeat with Carly the mistake he'd made in his second marriage.

And it wrenched his heart to think his daughter might have those concerns. That part of his past was something he'd regret and feel guilty for having put Evie Lee through for as long as he lived, but he hoped she could put it behind her.

"You don't have to worry about my bringing home any more stepmothers, Evie," he assured her quietly.

"I wasn't worryin' about *that*," she said. "I was just wondering if you like Carly. I like her and I think she likes me."

"I think she likes you, too."

"Alisha pretended she liked me at first but she didn't."

Another wrench of his heart—to know that this little girl carried with her the knowledge that her former stepmother hadn't liked her.

"There wasn't anything wrong with you, you know? Alisha was just not a nice person and she fooled us both. She was who deserved not to be liked. Not you."

"But Carly *is* a nice person."

That was a statement without any trace of uncertainty in Evie Lee's voice. It was something Bax was grateful for. If he and Evie Lee were going to be in such close proximity to Carly even for just a short while, he was glad Carly was so patient and friendly toward his daughter.

"Yes, I think Carly is a nice person, that's why I said it."

"And I think she really likes me, not just pretends, because she laughs at my jokes and she has a good time playin' the Candy Land game with me and she even gived me a hug the other day when I said something she thought was cute. Alisha never did that."

"I think Carly really does like you, too."

"Then I think it's okay if she was your girlfriend."

Bax chuckled again. "Thank you for your permission," he joked.

"You're welcome," Evie Lee answered seriously. "If I can't go see Carly, then I'm gonna watch cartoons till I can."

"All right."

Evie Lee hopped down from the chair for the second time and Bax watched her do a sedate skip through the swinging door, aching with love for her. Aching for the pain he'd caused her by bringing Alisha into her life.

Never again, he vowed for the hundredth time since his second marriage had ended.

Never again would he let a woman like Alisha anywhere near his daughter.

And once more he thanked his lucky stars that Carly seemed genuinely fond of Evie Lee. That she didn't appear to mind having Evie Lee around since Evie Lee enjoyed Carly's company so much.

"Like father, like daughter," Bax muttered to himself, sliding low in his seat so his head could rest on the back of the chair and he could catch forty winks.

But napping came no easier than full-blown sleeping had the night before.

Instead he was thinking about just how much *he* enjoyed Carly's company. More than he'd enjoyed any woman's company in a long, long time.

They seemed to be such a great fit.

He liked talking to her. Listening to her. She was so down to earth. So uncomplicated. So sweet-natured. So accepting. So kind. So funny. So thoughtful.

She had a touch of naiveté about her that was a breath of fresh air to him after Alisha. Being a small-town doctor's daughter gave Carly a certain amount of built-in status, yet she didn't seem to know that. She didn't seem to realize how well thought of she was. Or if she did, she took it all in stride because he hadn't seen any signs of it inflating her ego.

He couldn't think of anyone better to tell him about the townsfolk. She had a way of giving him insight into his patients, into their strengths and weaknesses, all the while making them sound so amusing, so interesting, so human and likable, that he ended up seeing them as whole, three-dimensional people before he even met them.

And as for what she was doing with Evie Lee, he couldn't put a price on the gift she was giving his daughter. Carly was letting Evie Lee feel that she was a likable little girl again, rebuilding the self-esteem Alisha had damaged.

He was crazy about the way Carly looked, too. Not only was she beautiful, but it was as if her warmth, her intelligence, her humor were all reflected in her face to give it a deeper kind of beauty than Alisha had had. And he sure as hell couldn't get the picture of her out of his mind, he liked it so much. Head to toe, she was perfect. Shiny hair. Adorable face. A body he was itching to know more of...

Okay, so he was hot for her along with everything else. No sense denying it.

Hotter for her than he'd been for anyone since his first wife. Definitely hotter than he'd been for Alisha even though she'd been incredibly gorgeous. Hotter than he had thought he'd ever be for anyone again.

Carly had an under-the-surface, beguiling sort of sexiness that left him consumed with wanting to know if her skin was as satiny as it looked. With wanting to trace every inch of her body with his fingertips. With wanting to feel her pressed so close to him, he didn't know where he ended and she began. With wanting to fill his hands with those small breasts. With wanting to bury his face in her hair, in the soft side of her neck. With wanting to bury himself inside her.

He just plain wanted her. So bad, it was something that seemed to emanate from the marrow of his bones.

And he didn't know how to shake it.

If only he could find just one fault, he thought. One thing that would turn him off.

But he couldn't. No matter how hard he tried.

And he did try.

Then just one fault occurred to him. Not a flaw in Carly herself, but a fault in what came with her—she was leaving town.

And *that* was a negative. A great big fat negative.

Or was it? a voice in the back of his head asked.

Bax opened his eyes and gave up trying to nap. Instead he stared at the ceiling, looking at things from a different perspective suddenly.

Maybe the fact that Carly was hell-bent on leaving town was a positive thing.

He wasn't ready to jump into another serious relationship. In fact, he'd come to Elk Creek with every intention of avoiding it. But what about a not-serious, short-term relationship? With a genuinely good person? Wasn't that something else entirely?

It was.

It was also something that might work out pretty well, now that he thought about it.

What was wrong with a brief encounter with a woman who made him feel terrific again? Who made his daughter feel terrific again?

Both he and Evie Lee knew Carly was leaving before long. And didn't that knowledge give them a sort of armor that would keep them from getting dangerously close to her? Didn't the fact that she wouldn't be around for long make getting too close impossible? Wouldn't it keep either of them from becoming attached to Carly?

And knowing that, why couldn't they have fun with her while she was around? What harm would there be as long as he kept in mind that this was only a temporary situation? As long as he reminded Evie Lee of it?

He took a minute to analyze everything, but even after he had he couldn't come up with any harm that would be caused or any reason why he and Evie Lee couldn't have this time with Carly. She was starting him off on the right foot with his future patients. She was making this transition in both his life and that of his daughter pleasant and easy. Why shouldn't those benefits be embraced and appreciated and reveled in? Why should he be fighting it?

Okay, so maybe the attraction he had for her threw a curve into things. But if he made sure to foster no illusions about her being around forever, about any chance of a long-term, serious relationship, why couldn't he and Evie Lee enjoy her company? So long as he knew the score he couldn't get hurt, could he?

He didn't think so.

And he didn't think Evie Lee would get hurt, either, because she knew as well as he did that Carly was leaving, that this whole arrangement had a limit to it.

So maybe he could relax a little and just enjoy what was going on between him and Carly.

He just had to keep the reins of his emotions in hand so that if they started to run too wild he could pull them back into control.

But unless that happened he couldn't see any reason not to let the reins go slack, not to ride this out until it came to its natural conclusion. He couldn't see any reason to go on fretting over it.

So he wasn't going to.

What he *was* going to do was let himself indulge a little. Let himself relax. Let himself relish what time he did have with her.

And then, when the day came for her to leave, he'd kiss her goodbye and watch her set off on that trip of hers. No different than sending a friend off on a vacation.

Except that what he was feeling for Carly was a lot more than simple friendship.

And suddenly the thought of kissing her goodbye and watching her set off on her own brought an odd twinge to his gut that told him that even though he'd just talked himself into all the reasons her not sticking around indefinitely was a positive thing, he was having some trouble keeping it in mind.

But still, that was the reality of their situation. She was here now and she'd be gone before long.

So while she was here, he'd enjoy it. Enjoy her.

And when it was over?

She would have left him with a good footing in the community and a daughter who felt better about herself.

"And maybe with a heart that's a little broken," he muttered to himself as if someone else were injecting another viewpoint.

But even if that ended up being the case, he'd just deal with it. After all, he'd lived through losing his wife and the mother of his child to an early, unexpected death.

He'd lived through an ugly divorce.

He could live through putting Carly on a train and watching her leave after only a few days of knowing her.

Couldn't he?

Sure he could.

He just had to make sure he didn't lose sight of the fact that she was going.

But then, it wasn't something he thought he was likely to forget.

Carly had spent the day with her sister, helping out where she could with the new baby and Hope's other three kids.

She'd left home early, making her way on the

crutches from the cottage, down the path that led to the medical building and around the corner to Hope's house. Because she'd gone out that back way, without going into the kitchen in the main house first, she hadn't seen either Bax or Evie Lee all day.

As she took a second shower and shampooed her hair late that afternoon, she tried not to think about how much she'd missed them both.

How could that be? she asked herself.

She barely knew either of them and yet a few hours apart had left her dying to be with them again, wondering what they'd done today, feeling that no matter what they'd done, she was sorry not to have done it with them.

Lately she was beginning to think she'd lost her mind.

What possible difference could it make to her *what* they'd done without her? Or if they'd missed her, too—which was the other thing on her mind.

And yet there it was—it did make a difference to her.

It was all probably due to the fact that Bax was new in town, she reasoned. He was someone she didn't know the way she knew everyone else in Elk Creek. And the unknown was always more interesting, more intriguing than the known.

That was all there was to it.

That was probably even why she'd caught her mind wandering to Bax all day long. Why she'd had such trouble concentrating on anything anyone said to her while visions of his sharply planed features danced through her head. While images of those broad shoulders, that well-muscled chest, that hard, flat belly swam before her eyes. While memories of his lips on hers made her turn to jelly...

She scrubbed her scalp extra hard, then rinsed her hair, trying to wash away those very same thoughts right then.

"It's just the novelty," she said, as if saying it aloud would make it more convincing.

Because she wanted to be convinced.

She *didn't* want to be racked with thoughts of the man, with this sense of loss for having not spent a few hours with him. It was only a matter of days until she left Elk Creek, and if she felt this way now, what was going to happen to her then?

It was just dumb, she told herself sternly as she turned off the water and reached outside the shower door for her towel.

The whole thing was dumb.

Lying in her bed last night reliving that good-night kiss again and again. Closing her eyes and pretending he was there with her, kissing her once more. More than kissing her. Dreaming about him when she did finally fall asleep. Waking with him in her thoughts first thing in the morning. Fantasizing about him all the while she should have been listening to her sister and her nephews and the other people who'd come to visit.

It was all dumb. Dumber than dumb.

"So stop it," she commanded herself. "He's just another guy."

Except that didn't ring true even out loud.

Bax wasn't just another guy.

He was a guy whose eyes could melt her insides with a glance. He was a guy who had a way about him that made her forget everything else when she was with him. He was a guy whose smile lit a fire in her blood.

Why couldn't she have met him before? Before his Peace Corps days. Before he'd married. Before he'd developed ties that bound him. When they could have seen the world together.

Better late than never... a little voice in her head said.

But she didn't necessarily agree with that.

What was good about meeting him now?

On the other hand, it suddenly occurred to her that maybe a little time with him now, before she left, was better than no time with him at all.

That gave her pause. Or maybe the appeal of that idea was what gave her pause.

But either way, it left her thinking about what she'd been telling herself the whole day—basically to put as much distance as she could between them, to refuse to do things like this meet-and-greet with him, to avoid him.

But what if instead of that—which she obviously wasn't pulling off anyway since she was getting ready for the meet-and-greet, after all—she just gave in to the urge to spend time with him now, while she could?

Because really, what was the worst that could happen? she asked herself as she left the bathroom and limped to where she had a brand-new pale-blue summer dress waiting for her on the bed.

The worst that could happen was that when she left in a few days she'd miss him and Evie Lee the way she had today. And that wasn't too horrible.

Okay, so the hours had seemed to drag. So she hadn't enjoyed herself much, or enjoyed any of the other people she'd been with. So she'd watched the clock and counted every minute that passed until she could be with Bax again.

But when she was finally off on her trip, when she was in the middle of someplace new, meeting more new people, wouldn't she be so completely engulfed in the experience that she wouldn't even think about Bax?

It seemed so to her.

And if she felt a little of what she'd felt today?

She'd call it homesickness and wait for it to pass.

Because surely it would.

Wouldn't it?

It would just have to, that was all there was to it.

And in the meantime, she could have the memory of these days spent with him to carry with her. To relive in her mind on long plane rides, at lonely moments, lying in bed in some strange place.

She could consider meeting Bax now as just the beginning of her adventure. Someone new to get to know the way she'd meet new people in her travels and want to get to know them.

That didn't seem so unreasonable.

"Or maybe it's just an excuse," she muttered to herself.

But excuse or no excuse, she knew spending time with him was what she was going to end up doing one way or another, so she might as well put the best spin on it that she could. And the best spin she could think of was that Bax coming to town now was just an opportunity to practice dealing with someone she hadn't known her whole life. To work on a skill she'd need when she finally left Elk Creek.

Certainly that spin made her more comfortable than

admitting she was giving in to spending time with Bax because she was mind-numbingly attracted to the guy.

She just hoped she wasn't fooling herself.

At least not too much…

Chapter 9

The meet-and-greet should have been called the meet-and-greet-and-bring-the-new-doctor-a-casserole because so many women came bearing foil pans for Bax and his daughter.

It happened frequently enough that when Bax spotted someone approaching with their offering, he began to whisper his guess as to what kind of casserole it might be.

Of course his guesses got more and more farcical as the evening wore on—cream of outdated encyclopedia pages from Nan Carpenter, who looked like an old-fashioned librarian with her hair in a bun; duck à la dill weed from Maude Benchley, who had a mallard embroidered on her blouse; long drink of watercress custard from Prissy Palicomo, who stood a full six feet tall.

It was all silly but not unkind and his comical conjectures teased Carly at the same time for the descriptions and commentaries she made as sidebars to her own introductions.

Nearly the whole town streamed in and out of the church basement, and what was scheduled to be a two-hour reception stretched until nearly ten o'clock at night. But for Carly the time flew by.

She and Bax stayed together in what was actually a two-person receiving line, which meant it was a concentrated evening of being with him. And even though Carly did what she'd done the day before as they'd visited the outlying farms and ranches—performing the introductions, then trying to fade into the background as Bax got to know the townsfolk—there was still no question that she was with him. That they were sharing the evening. That she was enjoying herself.

When the church basement finally saw the last of the people who'd come to meet Bax, there was a tableful of the casseroles along with cakes, pies and various loaves of banana, zucchini, cranberry and poppy seed breads for him to take home.

Luckily he'd driven his station wagon so that Carly wouldn't have to walk. It gave him a way to get everything home.

By then Carly's ankle was throbbing and since she couldn't help load the goodies into the back of the station wagon anyway, she sat on one of the folding chairs that lined the walls and put her feet up on another.

Evie Lee, who had had a full evening of meeting and playing with just about every child in town, joined Carly to lie down on the chairs beside her, laying her head in Carly's lap.

"Tired?" Carly asked.

"No, not me," Evie Lee claimed as she closed her eyes and fell instantly asleep beneath Carly's hand smoothing her hair.

Carly smiled down at the cherub and then rested her own head against the wall and closed her eyes, too, as Bax and several of the husbands of the Ladies' League members who had given the party and were doing cleanup detail began to make trip after trip to the car.

She lost track of time, but it didn't seem long before Bax's voice interrupted her reverie.

"Looks like my girls have had it," he said when the gifts of food were all loaded and he'd come back for her and Evie Lee.

Carly opened her eyes and smiled at the "my girls" part, feeling a warm flush of pleasure to be included.

"Mmm," was all she answered, continuing to smooth Evie Lee's hair, but looking all the way up the long length of Bax.

He was wearing cowboy boots, a pair of gray corduroy slacks and a dove-gray shirt with a charcoal tie as he stood smiling that secret smile of his.

"Guess I better get you both home," he said then.

He bent over and scooped his daughter into his arms, and the sight of the small child held against her father's broad, capable chest warmed Carly, too.

"Want me to come back and carry you out?" he offered, only half teasing. "I'm betting you've been on that ankle of yours too long tonight."

"It's putting up a little fuss, but I'm fine," she said as she retrieved her crutches from the floor in front of the chairs and got up onto them again.

But the flinch that escaped then wasn't from the pain in her ankle, it was from the rawness under her arms left by too many hours on the crutches.

Bax seemed to know that. "Even pads don't help those arm pieces after a while, do they?"

"Sounds like you know from experience."

"A little. Broke my leg when I was a teenager and did my time on them. They're murder."

"You can say that again."

He didn't, though. Instead, they both called a quick good-night to the cleanup crew and made their way out of the church basement.

The cooler, fresh air outside felt like heaven to Carly and she took several deep breaths of it as Bax laid Evie Lee on the back seat and maneuvered a seat belt around her. Then he helped Carly into the passenger side and they went the short distance home.

Once they got there Bax backed into the driveway and turned off the engine. But before he made a move to get out from behind the wheel he turned to Carly. "I want to take a look at your ankle. How about if I put Evie Lee in bed, set up the footbath and you can soak in it while I get all this stuff out of the car?"

"Okay," Carly agreed. She didn't need a lot of persuading because not only did the foot soaking sound good, so did the thought of prolonging the evening with Bax and honing those getting-to-know-you skills she'd talked herself into as she'd dressed for this evening.

In the time it took Carly to get into the house and unwrap her ankle, Bax had his daughter in bed and was ready with the footbath in the living room so Carly could sit comfortably on the couch to use it.

She felt a little guilty for not being able to help him

carry in the food, but that didn't keep her from watching him as he did. In fact, she was a rapt audience, memorizing every detail.

There was a slight, unconscious swagger to the way he walked. It came more from being a little bowlegged than from ego, but it was so sexy it made her mouth water.

He kept his back straight, not hunching even as he carried casseroles stacked from waist to chin, and she couldn't help remembering just how impressive that same back was when it was bare, wishing suddenly that he would chuck the gray shirt and finish the chore that way.

Even from a distance, there was no denying that the man was lethally handsome. So lethally handsome that she wanted that face, that body, his every movement, every nuance, etched into her brain like a mental videotape she could replay again and again when she was far away from there. From him.

But no matter how hard she tried to ingrain his image into her mind, she wasn't sure if her memory would ever do him justice.

It took him nearly half an hour to unload the car and store everything, but then he came back to Carly with a towel flung over one shoulder, carrying a plate filled with slices of various sweet breads and two glasses of iced tea. He set the goodies and drinks on the coffee table and then sat beside her on the sofa, pulling the towel from his shoulder.

"How are we doing?" he asked.

"Better," Carly answered, knowing he meant her ankle. But her answer included more than that because her ankle wasn't the only thing to improve with his arrival.

"Let's have a look," he ordered, bending over to make a sling out of the towel and catching her foot in it as she raised it from the water.

Then he took hold of her leg and swung her so she was sitting crossways on the couch with her foot in his lap so he could pat it dry and study her injury.

Carly reached down to remove the strappy sandal she wore on her other foot so she didn't soil the sofa and was grateful for the fact that her dress was long and the skirt full enough to stay draped around her legs to maintain her modesty.

"Doesn't look like we did too much damage tonight," he said as he examined the foot and ankle. "Swelling's down some. Bruising is right on track. Want me to wrap it again or shall we let it breathe a little?"

"Let it breathe. I'll wrap it again before I go to sleep."

"Okay." He tossed the towel to the floor and sat back, keeping hold of her foot to do a gentle massage of her toes. "Does this hurt?"

"No. It feels good." Great, in fact. Wonderful. Warm. Tender. Arousing…

It occurred to her that she should have said it hurt so he'd stop, that she was safer if he didn't touch her.

The trouble was, then he might have actually stopped.

"Did you find a place in the refrigerator for all those casseroles?" she asked instead.

"In the refrigerator, in the freezer on top of the refrigerator and in the big freezer in the laundry room, too. Looks like I won't have to cook for a year."

"At least," Carly agreed.

"It was amazin' to have so many people think of me, though. There aren't too many places where you get treated that well."

Carly hadn't thought of it that way. It was all just part of Elk Creek's customary welcome, a welcome she'd have been a part of had she planned on being here. But seeing it through Bax's eyes, she guessed it was something special.

"Folks here are thoughtful," she said.

"More than I've found in other places. Looks like I made a good choice in this town."

"I think so."

He grinned at her. "Then how come you're leavin' it?"

"Just to see what else is out there. Not because there's anything wrong with the town itself." And she was surprised at how defensive she sounded.

Bax must have picked up on it because he left that subject and went back to the previous one. "Think there's any Engelhart casserole in the bunch?"

"Engelhart casserole?"

"It's something my wife—my first wife—used to make. That's what she called it. I don't know if it's a real thing or not. It was a concoction with ground beef and noodles and cheeses and I don't know what all. I just know I liked it and haven't had it since she died. But with that many casseroles I was hoping there might be one Engelhart among them."

"I don't know. I can't say I've ever heard of it or of anybody around here making anything called that,"

Carly said, wondering if his mentioning his first wife allowed her an opening to pry. Just a little. To soothe her curiosity.

But opening or not, she decided to pry anyway.

"Your first wife was Evie Lee's mom, right?"

"Mm-hmm," he confirmed, seeming more interested in her foot than in anything else.

"What happened to her—if you don't mind my asking?"

"She died about an hour after Evie Lee was born. She had a brain aneurysm on the delivery table."

"Without warning?"

"Not a clue. The pregnancy was normal, healthy. Labor had seemed fine. No signs of toxemia. And then—boom—she blew a vessel. They had to take Evie Lee cesarean, rush Lee Ann into brain surgery. But they couldn't save her."

"You must have been devastated."

"To put it mildly."

"And there you were, left with a newborn."

"Left with a newborn and a double-duty job practicing medicine and teaching."

"Did you have help?"

"My sister came to stay. It was a good thing because I knew how to deliver babies, but taking care of them once they were here was not my area of expertise. I had to be walked through it as if I were a baby myself. I guess I learned, but to tell you the truth, I couldn't swear I could do it again. Most of that first year is a blur. I just got through it somehow. Barely."

"And after the first year?"

"My sister had to go back to her own life and I was on my own. It wasn't easy, but we managed. Well, I managed. Evie Lee got shuffled more than she should have. I felt bad about that. Real bad. That's part of why I ended up marryin' again."

"To give Evie Lee a sort-of mom—she told me she'd had a *sort-of mom* named Alisha." Carly thought it was better not to say what else Evie Lee had said about Alisha.

"*Sort-of mom* is a better title than Alisha deserved," he said, his tone much different than it had been when he'd talked about his first wife. Much harsher, much harder.

"Evie Lee didn't seem too fond of her," Carly confessed as a means of prying a bit more.

"Evie Lee didn't like Alisha at all. With good cause."

That seemed to stall things.

Carly took a different tack to keep it going. "How long were you married?"

"Less than a year. She was a nurse—that's how I met her. I didn't have time to be out doing a lot of socializin'. But I worked with Alisha and that made it easier than maybe it should have been to get close to her. We dated some. She was pretty—on the outside, anyway—and I thought we had the same values, the same goals, the same agenda…."

He drifted off for a split second, then came back to finish what he'd been saying.

"She pretended that she loved kids—Evie Lee in particular. One thing led to another."

"You married her."

His hands were still gentle and careful, but there was more pressure in them all of a sudden. A sign, Carly thought, of strong feelings about whatever had happened with his second wife.

"I married her," he said as if it left a sour taste in his mouth. "She quit her job. Said she wanted to be a full-time mom, stay at home with Evie Lee."

"It didn't work out that way?"

"Oh, Alisha wanted to stay home, all right. But not to be with Evie. She wanted to shop and go to fancy lunches and play some kind of social-climbing game. Guess she figured a doctor for a husband—even a former good ol' Texas boy of a doctor—was the first step."

"What about Evie Lee?"

"Evie Lee tied her down. She interfered with Alisha's agenda." That word again, hit hard and disparagingly. "Evie was four when I married Alisha. Alisha thought it was time for preschool so she sent her there two afternoons a week. That was okay. No harm in it. But that was just the beginning. She looked for any way to get rid of Evie—play groups, baby-sitters, day care, shoving her off on neighbors—anything so she could be free to hobnob."

"And Evie Lee wasn't happy about it."

"Evie Lee wasn't happy, period. She was quiet. Sullen. Fearful. But she didn't say anything against Alisha. I talked to one of the psychiatrists at the hospital. He recommended a child psychiatrist at Children's Hospital in Denver and I went to see him, even brought Evie to see him. He did a workup on her. Said she was having normal adjustment problems to the introduction of a stepmother. Nothing to worry about."

"So you didn't worry."

"I still worried. Kept taking her to the shrink. But I still didn't know what was really going on when I wasn't home."

"How did you find out?"

"I came home one day when Alisha wasn't plannin' on it. She was having a tea party for some women she thought were hot stuff. Apparently Evie was exiled to her room to keep her out of the way. But a tea party was right up Evie's alley. She'd gone into our room, gotten into Alisha's things. Shoes mostly, and lipstick to pretty herself up—"

"And decided to invite herself to the party." Carly would have smiled at the thought of the little girl dressing herself up and joining in if the tone of this wasn't so ominous.

"Alisha got furious—something she apparently did a lot when she was alone with Evie—and locked her in a closet. That's where I found Evie. Crying in a closet. Terrified of the dark. Her arm bruised from where Alisha had grabbed her to throw her in it."

Bax accidentally bent her ankle too much and Carly involuntarily pulled away from his grip.

"Did I hurt you?" he said, alarmed.

"Just a little. My ankle isn't very flexible."

"I'm sorry," he said effusively, instantly returning to a much softer massage. "I guess just thinking about this riles me up."

"What did you do about it?"

"Alisha was out within the hour."

"And you divorced her."

"Got a lawyer the next day. And took some serious stock of myself and the life I was leadin'."

"Which is what led you here to Elk Creek."

He nodded somberly.

"Evie Lee doesn't seem too much the worse for wear," Carly said because it was true and because she wanted to ease some of the guilt she could see he was carrying around.

"There are residual effects. But I'm working on it. Her being around you has seemed to help."

"Me? I haven't done anything."

"You like her. You treat her well, that means a lot."

And his massage was suddenly deeper, more penetrating. Just the way his green eyes were when they met hers then.

Carly couldn't have pinpointed when exactly a change had taken place. But it had. A change in the air around them.

It was filled with intimacy. And Carly had a new awareness of Bax, a more heightened awareness. Of every tiny detail. Of the way his brow creased to let her know he'd been struck by the same sense of closeness between them. Of the way all his features came together to form a rugged, masculine sort of beauty. Of the way his mouth turned up at the corners even when he wasn't smiling. Of how sharp his jawline was. How thick his neck where it dipped into the collar of his shirt.

She realized only then that somewhere since leaving the church he'd taken off his tie and opened the collar button of his shirt. She could see only a hint of the hair smattering his chest, but it was enough to remind her of the magnificence of that chest. The magnificence that carried through in broad shoulders and incredible biceps and thick forearms and wrists, and those hands that were no longer massaging her foot but now caressing it…

"Evie and I are both a little bit nuts about you," he said in a soft voice that lightened the tone of things.

"Maybe you're just a little bit nuts, period," she teased him, sounding much more seductive than she'd intended.

"Maybe I am," he agreed with a half grin that dimpled only one cheek. "But Evie Lee is a pretty good judge of people."

Bax held her eyes with his, and even if Carly had wanted to break away she didn't think she could have. Something about the depth of his gaze kept her hypnotized, enthralled, enchanted.

Why did he have to be so great-looking? she wondered. So great-smelling? So great all around...

He reached one hand around to the back of her neck then to guide her forward, nearer to him, as he leaned to the side enough to meet her.

There was no question that he was going to kiss her, and Carly's pulse went into overdrive, beating hard and fast with anticipation. With excitement. With wanting.

And then he tilted his head so he could press his lips to hers and Carly knew only in that first touch of his mouth how hungry she'd been for it. Starved, in fact.

This kiss was different than the two that had come before, though. Deeper. Richer. Like heavy cream compared to skim milk.

His lips were warm and wonderfully adept as they parted over hers, urged hers to part, too.

His other hand came to the side of her face, drawing her closer still, as his mouth opened farther, enticing hers to do the same as his tongue began to explore the sensitive inside of her lips, the tips of her teeth, her tongue...

This was a kiss that teased and courted and meant business at the same time, as mouths opened wide and tongues danced and parried so freely Carly wondered why they hadn't been doing this all along since they were so good at it.

And they *were* good at it. As good as if they'd been doing it forever.

He knew just when to be aggressive, just when to be subtle. When to be bold and in command. When to let her take the lead.

He knew how to light a fire in her blood so that flames ignited every secret spot in her body and made her ache to be touched, to feel his arms around her, his hands other places...

But before that happened, he stopped, ending the kiss with a determination that seemed reluctant, leaving Carly hungry for more.

He half sat, half fell back against the couch cushion the way he'd been before, looking at her again with eyes that seemed to regret the abrupt conclusion to what they'd been sharing so intently. So pleasantly...

"You're a dangerous woman, Carly Winters," he said in a raspy voice that partly teased and partly didn't.

"I've been told that," she said, seizing the teasing part to answer with a joke of her own.

She looked up into his eyes and knew what he was thinking as clearly as if the thoughts were in her own head. He was remembering two wives, one a mistake, and a daughter he was determined to protect from hurt.

And Carly understood why he hadn't wanted the kiss to go on, to go further.

Even though it left her yearning and burning inside.

But for her own sake, too, she knew it was best. It was one thing to practice getting to know someone new and another thing altogether to lose herself in the man the way she just had.

"I think it's time for me to call it a day," she said, swinging her legs to the floor. She slipped on her sandal, gathered up her discarded bandage and her crutches.

"You don't have to walk me to the cottage," she said in a hurry when Bax started to his feet to do just that. "Truly. It'll be better to clear my head if you don't."

Because she knew what would happen at the cottage door. He'd kiss her again. And once he did she wasn't sure either of them would stop it.

"Just stay where you are," she added more strongly than she felt.

And then she made her exit, wishing it could be more graceful.

Wishing more that she wasn't making it at all. That she was right back on that couch with him, his mouth locked onto hers, his hands in unspeakable places sharing the delight with the rest of her body.

And somehow Carly also knew as she went out into the breezeway alone that sleep wasn't going to come easily tonight. That her bed was going to seem awfully empty and lonely.

Because what she had no choice but to admit to herself was that she had a weak spot for Bax.

A very, very sweet weak spot...

Chapter 10

Ordinarily Carly appreciated a little irony. But the irony of making up her mind to spend time with Bax and then not seeing him was hard to appreciate.

And by three o'clock Friday afternoon as she and her mother finished their visit to the town boardinghouse, Carly had not laid eyes on Bax since leaving him sitting in the living room on Wednesday night after the hot kiss that had knocked her socks off.

The boardinghouse was actually Elk Creek's version of an old folks' home. It had been the original schoolhouse, and when the new one had been built, the Partridge sisters had bought the old building with the intention of turning it into a hotel. But there wasn't a lot of call for a hotel in the small town, and economics had required that Lurlene and Effie change course. So it had become the boardinghouse, and from there the boarders had proved to be mainly elderly people unable to live alone any longer.

Currently there were eight women and three men renting rooms from Lurlene and Effie, all of them considerably older than the fifty-nine-year-old twins and in various stages of needing assistance.

The beauty of the place was that everyone helped everyone else—the more capable picking up the slack for the less capable. And since no one was too infirm, it all worked out very well and left Lurlene and Effie free for other pursuits along with overseeing the house and providing meals.

Carly had been ending her Friday afternoons there for as long as she could remember. Sometimes she played cards with some of the residents, sometimes she read to them, sometimes she danced with old Mr. Elton who swore no one could cut a rug the way Carly could.

And always she brought what she was asked to bring—the newest movie released on video, library books, a bottle of brandy for Mrs. Gordon who insisted she was a teetotaler and couldn't possibly go into the liquor store to buy the brandy she needed purely for medicinal purposes.

Carly had said her goodbyes on the Friday before—certain it was her last—but since she was still in town this week, she didn't want to pass up the opportunity to see everyone one last time. Only today she'd asked her mother to come along, too, to drive her and help her carry in the shopping bag full of things one phone call had told her they all wanted.

Carly and her mother were just leaving the two-story Georgian redbrick when she heard, "Hey, stranger!"

She glanced up from watching the front stoop stairs

as she descended them to find Bax and Evie Lee coming up the walk.

"Well, hello, Dr. McDermot," Carly's mother said before Carly could.

"Call me Bax, please, Mrs. Winters," he answered.

"And I'm Madge," Carly's mother responded.

Carly had already heard her mother's stamp of approval for the new doctor, and it was there again in the tone of her voice.

"Hi," Carly said somewhat belatedly.

It was funny, but just that initial sight of him was at once a balm and a tonic to her spirit. Not that she'd been aware of feeling in need of either, but one glance at him—even in cowboy boots, a pair of faded blue jeans and an old chambray shirt that made him look as if he'd just come from working the range—and it was as if everything inside her was set right again.

"Hi, Carly!" Evie Lee chimed in, helping Carly to broaden her spectrum.

"Hi, sweetie."

"We came to talk to a baby-sitter," Evie Lee announced.

"Carly knows, Evie. She recommended Miss Effie," Bax said to his daughter. Then to Carly he said, "Where've you been? I haven't seen hide nor hair of you. And I've been lookin'," he added slightly under his breath and with a note of intimacy that erupted little tingles of delight in her bloodstream.

It also didn't hurt to know he'd missed her.

"I helped Deana with some paperwork for summer school yesterday and we went to the movies last night. This morning I was at my sister's house, and this afternoon—"

"She always visits here on Friday afternoons," Madge interjected, sounding proud but also a bit like Carly's sales representative.

Carly just wasn't sure what her mother was selling, though.

"Where have you been?" Carly countered, figuring if he could ask her point-blank, she could do the same with him.

"Spent yesterday mostly at the office, going over files and settlin' in—I sneaked in the back way so nobody'd know I was there. We had Ry's bachelor party last night so Evie Lee and I both slept over and today I helped get things ready for the wedding. Until a little while ago when Evie and I came in to keep our appointment with Miss Effie and get dressed for tonight."

That accounted for why their paths hadn't crossed although Carly wasn't too thrilled with the news that Bax had spent the previous evening at a bachelor party.

Not that it was any of her business.

"Are you ladies comin' to the wedding?" Bax asked then, including Madge with the question even though his interest seemed more on Carly.

"I'm afraid I can't make it," Madge answered first again. "I have to stay with Hope and the children. I've already sent my regrets."

"Sorry to hear that. How 'bout you, Carly?"

"I'll be there." Eagerly since it meant seeing him, but she didn't add that.

"Goin' with anybody special?"

"Deana and her sister."

"How 'bout goin' with me…and Evie Lee instead?"

"Oh, that would be nice," Madge answered before

Carly could. "Deana wouldn't mind. She has her sister to go with anyway."

Carly shot a curious glance at her mother, wondering what she was up to.

But whatever it was, Carly wasn't about to turn Bax down, if that was what her mother thought.

"What do you say?" Bax asked.

"Won't you be busy? I know you're one of the groomsmen and Evie Lee is the flower girl," Carly hedged just so she wouldn't appear to be too much of a pushover.

"That's only during the ceremony. We'll be free agents after that."

He said that with a smile that made it seem as if he and Carly were sharing a secret, and Carly couldn't have refused him even if she'd wanted to.

But once more her mother beat her to the punch. "Won't that be nice—to be together for the reception. Carly would be happy to go with you."

Carly gave her mother a sideways look, then glanced back at Bax to find him amused.

"What do you say?" he asked in a tone that focused on her alone.

"Okay. I suppose that would be all right."

"Great."

"And tomorrow night," Madge added then, "we're having a little dinner and ice cream and cake for Carly's birthday. Would you and Evie Lee like to come?"

Carly looked at her mother again, more directly this time, knowing for sure that Madge had something up her sleeve. Something that rang of matchmaking.

"Tomorrow's your birthday?" Bax asked Carly.

"Guess I can't deny it now."

"I'll go! I'll go!" Evie Lee answered eagerly.

"We like birthday parties," Bax said, including himself in his daughter's enthusiasm.

Madge took it as an acceptance of her invitation. "Oh, good. We're having it at Hope's house. You can just come with Carly."

"We'll be lookin' forward to it."

"So will we," Madge said, poking Carly with an elbow.

Bax looked at his watch. "We'd better get inside or Miss Effie will think we have bad manners."

Carly was only too happy to have this encounter end despite how good it was to see him. Her mother's antics were beginning to border on embarrassing.

"What time do you need to be out at the ranch tonight?" Carly asked then.

"We can leave about six-thirty."

His eyes were on hers again, giving off a warmth that seeped in through her pores and heated her all over.

"Six-thirty," she repeated. "I'll be ready."

"She'll be ready," her mother repeated as if Madge would personally make sure of it.

They all said goodbye then, and Bax and Evie Lee went inside as Carly and her mother made their way to Madge's car.

"What was that all about?" Carly demanded as they both got into the sedan.

"What was what about?" Madge said innocently.

"You know what. Accepting his offer for me to go to the wedding with him, inviting him for tomorrow night."

"I was just being friendly."

"You were being more than friendly. You were trying to set us up."

"Why would I do something like that when you're about to leave town?"

"Good question. You tell me."

"I wouldn't think of such a silly thing," Madge said. But then she added slyly, "Even though it's as plain as the nose on your face that he likes you and you like him."

Madge wasn't as straightforward as Deana, but Carly knew her mother was no happier about her plans to leave town than her friend was. And that, in her own way, Madge had the same hope that Bax could alter Carly's plans.

"I do like Bax," Carly admitted, realizing as she did just how true it was. "But that doesn't change anything. I'm still going to travel."

Madge didn't respond. She just poked her chin in the air and pretended to concentrate on her driving.

But even without any more comment from her mother, Carly had an inordinate urge to repeat herself, to impress upon her mother that she meant what she said, to put more force behind it.

She controlled the impulse, though, knowing too much protest would only prove her mother's point.

Carly hadn't cursed the crutches quite as much as she did that evening when she dressed for the wedding.

After a shower, a shampoo, air drying her hair to a silky sheen and carefully applying just enough makeup to accentuate her features, she slipped into a slinky black dress she'd bought with the idea of looking as sophisticated as she imagined everyone else would in cities like New York or London or Paris.

The dress was silk crepe with spaghetti straps, a hem at midthigh and a cut so perfect it skimmed her body just close enough to hint at what was beneath it without actually giving anything away.

She also had a pair of barely there three-inch heels and sheer black hose to go with it. But the whole effect was less than perfect with a bandage wrapped around her foot and ankle, and the wooden crutches as accessories.

And less than perfect was not what she was aiming for. She wanted to look absolutely perfect.

Not because she'd be seeing so many friends and family at the wedding. But because she'd be there with Bax.

She wished that wasn't the case, but what was the sense in kidding herself? She hadn't dug out the dress she considered her Paris dress to wow people who had known her since she was in diapers. It was Bax she wanted to wow.

It was Bax she was doing everything for lately.

Bax she really did like…

Admitting as much to her mother that afternoon in front of the boardinghouse kept niggling at her.

The moment she'd said it, she'd known that *liking* him was an understatement. A serious understatement.

But if she didn't just *like* him, then what did she feel about him?

"Don't think about it," she advised herself.

Because if she thought about it, she might have more to deal with than just being attracted to the man. And the attraction was enough to deal with all by itself. Add feelings to it that were more than mere *liking* him, and then where would she be?

Maybe not in Paris or London or Rome or New York.

"So just don't think about it!" she said more vehemently.

And for once she took her own advice.

Because it was one thing to come to terms with wanting to spend time with him while she was still in Elk Creek, but even thinking about feeling anything more serious about Bax was not something she could do. Not without risking things she wasn't willing to risk.

So instead, she told herself there wasn't anything to think about and she put on a mauve-colored lipstick, jammed the crutches under her arms and headed for the main house.

Before being alone led to anymore delving into things she didn't want to delve into.

Attraction. Infatuation. That was all that was going on with her when it came to Bax, she swore to herself as she crossed the breezeway.

Simple attraction and infatuation that came out of enjoying his company, out of having fun with him, out of not being blind to his charms, his handsomeness, his sexiness.

But it was nothing as serious as what had gone on between her and Jeremy.

Nothing as life-altering as that.

So she was still safe.

"You're here!" Evie Lee said when Carly knocked on the back door a few minutes later. "Could you do my hair so it looks nice? Daddy says he's just gonna put a brush in it and leave it and that won't be pretty enough for a flower girl."

"How about a braid like we did that first time?" Carly suggested, grateful for the distraction of the little girl in the frilly midnight-blue dress with the silver sash.

After all, who could think about silly things like feelings when Evie Lee had a hair crisis?

"Evie Lee? Where are you? I need to brush your hair now or we'll be late."

Bax's voice came from upstairs and just that was enough to make everything inside Carly stand up and take notice.

"Carly's here and she's gonna do my hair," Evie Lee hollered back.

"Thank heaven for small favors," he called in return.

Evie Lee went running out of the kitchen then, returning moments later with a hairbrush and a rubber band.

Carly had pulled a chair away from the table and sat in it so Evie Lee could stand in front of her. Which Evie Lee did, with a twirling flourish to make her skirt billow out around her.

"Did you get to meet Miss Effie?" Carly asked as she French-braided the little girl's hair.

"Uh-huh."

"Did you like her?"

"She's nice. Like a gramma. She's gonna baby-sit me when my daddy goes to work and she said we could bake cookies and go to the park and stuff."

"That sounds good." And more appealing than Carly wanted to admit. Appealing enough to cause Carly a twinge of jealousy to add to the list of feelings she didn't want to explore.

"But she doesn't know 'bout makin' French braids and puttin' pencils in my hair. That's one bad thing," Evie Lee was saying. "I won't be pretty if you go away."

The little girl's words didn't come out plaintively, but the statement made Carly's heart ache anyway as she recalled what Bax had said about all his daughter had been through with her stepmother and the blow her self-esteem had taken.

"You're pretty no matter what anyone does with your hair," she told the child.

"But I'm prett*ier* when you do it nice."

"How about if I talk to Deana about doing your hair for you sometimes, on special occasions? She's just next door and I'll bet she'd be happy to," Carly suggested, wondering as she did why the thought of Deana taking her place didn't sit any better than the idea of Evie Lee baking cookies and going to the park with Effie Partridge rather than with her. Especially when it wasn't really *her* place at all to do any of those things with Bax's daughter.

"Okay," Evie Lee agreed reluctantly. "But it won't be the same as when you do it."

"It won't be the same for me, either," Carly heard herself say in a quiet voice that surprised her.

"What won't be the same?" Bax asked as he came into the kitchen.

Carly didn't glance up from what she was doing, but just the sound of his voice closer by, the feel of his presence in the room, erupted a whole new set of feelings too powerful to ignore.

"It won't be the same if the lady next door combs

my hair into a braid the way Carly does when Carly goes away."

"Are you leavin' sooner than I thought?" Bax asked with what could have been a note of alarm in his tone, although Carly wasn't sure.

"Not until my ankle heals," she answered.

"So you're just making provisions for the future."

Provisions that rubbed her wrong.

"We were just talking," she said, finishing Evie Lee's braid to look up at Bax for the first time since he'd joined them.

There weren't a lot of men in Elk Creek who could wear a tuxedo and seem as right in it as they did in blue jeans. But Bax was one of them. And a single glance at him was enough to take Carly's breath away.

Tall, lean, muscular, and very dashing—he still bore a hint of rugged masculinity.

He didn't have the entire tux on, though. The jacket was in place—hanging from broad shoulders as if it had been cut especially to accommodate them—and he wore the flawlessly tailored pants, the crisp white shirt and the bow tie. But he was carrying the cummerbund in one hand.

He held it up and said, "Would you consider doing me next?"

Again Carly couldn't be sure if his voice was flecked with something more than his words conveyed. But the half smile and the quirk to his eyebrow lent credence to what she took as innuendo.

And there were a number of things she could think of to do with him, none of them as innocent as helping him on with his cummerbund.

"I wanna see me!" Evie Lee announced then, dashing out of the kitchen to leave Carly alone with Bax in a stew of sexually charged air.

"I can't hook this thing to save my life," he said then, referring once more to the waistband. "Would you mind?"

"No," she answered simply, succinctly, unable to say more because her head was still swimming with other thoughts about him and the effect that the sight of him was having on her, making her pulse race and little sparks dance in the pit of her stomach.

Bax slipped off the suit coat and draped it over one of the chairs. Then he came to stand where Evie Lee had been moments before, turning his back to Carly.

It didn't help matters that she was eye level with his rear end. Or that the trousers smoothed across it just so, leaving no doubt that it was a great male derriere.

"I don't even know which way is up and which is down with this thing," he was saying, but to Carly the words seemed to come from a long way away as she fought an inordinate urge to see that terrifically sexy posterior bare of everything.

Then she caught herself and realized she needed to say something in response.

"Here, let me see it," she finally managed to reply.

She assumed from the shape of the cummerbund that the straight edge was the bottom and the arched edge the top. But having decided that, she was left in need of reaching around Bax to set it at his waist.

Not a good idea.

Because once her arms were around his middle, that was just where they wanted to stay. Her arms around him, her cheek pressed to his hard back...

But of course she couldn't do that and she told herself in no uncertain terms to stop these unwelcome thoughts and behave herself.

Although it was difficult to heed her own warnings when his hands brushed hers as he tried to hold the front of the cummerbund in place to free her to fasten the back. That simple contact sent shards of glittering delight straight into her bloodstream. Not only did she want to keep her arms around him, to press her cheek to his back, but she wanted to feel more of his touch against her hands, sliding up her arms, pressing her to him...

The yearning for all that got so strong, Carly could hear the blood rushing through her veins and she knew if she didn't pull herself together in a hurry she'd be sunk. So she reclaimed her hands, made quick work of hooking the waistband, and said, "There!" much too cheerily.

"Thanks," he said, his own voice an octave lower than usual for no reason Carly could fathom.

Then he stepped away, retrieved his jacket from the chair back and put it on.

"Yep, feels like a monkey suit, all right," he said as he tugged at his cuffs and set everything right.

"You look wonderful," Carly heard herself say softly and much too breathlessly before she even knew she was going to voice what was going through her mind.

Bax only acknowledged the compliment with a rakish smile before motioning to her with one hand as if he were trying to levitate her. "Come on, let me get a gander at you."

Ogling him was one thing. Carly was less comfortable being the ogle-ee.

But she could hardly stay sitting there, so she used

the table for support and stood without the crutches to mar the effect.

His sea-foam-green eyes went from her head to her toes and back up again—the return trip accompanied by a long, slow whistle of approval.

"Now there's a good example of a little bit of a dress leavin' just enough to the imagination to whet a man's appetite," he said appreciatively, clearly enjoying the sight for a moment longer before tossing another glance downward. "But what about that high heel?"

"What about it?" Carly asked with a look down at her only shod foot.

"High heels and crutches don't mix."

"I did just fine coming over here."

"You're riskin' broken bones," he warned.

"I'll be okay."

"Either that or you'll end up with worse than a sprained ankle. But then, on second thought, that'd keep you around longer, so I guess I should just shut my mouth."

Evie Lee rejoined them then, saying as she did, "Isn't it time to go?"

Bax seemed reluctant to take his eyes off Carly, but with his daughter insinuating herself between them he didn't have much choice.

"Daddy? Did you hear me? Isn't it time to go?" the little girl repeated when she didn't get an instant response.

"I suppose it is," he said, still without taking his eyes off Carly, all the while smiling that secret smile that somehow seemed to wrap the two of them in their own private cocoon.

"Then let's go," Evie Lee persisted.

Bax took a deep breath and sighed it out as if he would have preferred staying there indefinitely, giving Carly the once-over.

But then he reached for her crutches, keeping them away from her. "You're sure about this?" he asked.

"I'm an expert on those things by now," she assured him.

He gave her a dubious, sideways glance, but handed them over and Carly got up onto them with aplomb. Then she headed across the kitchen to prove her ability.

"What did I tell you?" she said as she made it to the swinging door.

But when she glanced over her shoulder to see if he was admiring her competency, she instead discovered him admiring something else—her derriere—before he realized he'd been caught at it. He simply raised his gaze and smiled a wicked smile.

"Oh yeah, you're good," he said, this time with too much innuendo to mistake.

He stepped up to push the swinging door open for her and once she and Evie Lee had gone through it and were headed for the front door, Bax made his way to Carly's side to keep a hand at the small of her back just in case she stumbled.

And as far as Carly was concerned, that was only a benefit of the high heels and crutches combination.

A benefit that was worth whatever risk she was taking.

Chapter 11

The wedding was held outside on the patio at the Mc-Dermot ranch. White lanterns were strung all around, their strings wrapped in vines and white roses. The aisle down which Tallie Shanahan walked was bordered with candles on white pillars that were also wrapped in vines and roses, and she came to a stop in front of the minister where she and Ry met beneath an archway trimmed to match.

It was a beautiful ceremony, with Ry's brothers standing as groomsmen, his sister, Kate, and Tallie's friends, Maya and Kansas, serving as the bridesmaids.

Since this was the first Elk Creek had seen of the fourth McDermot brother, Matt, and the sole sister, Kate, they drew almost as much attention and curious stares as the bride and groom. But from where Carly sat with Deana and Deana's sister in the rows of white chairs set out for the guests, she only had eyes for Bax.

All the brothers were strikingly handsome men. But to Carly, only Bax stood out from the crowd and she could hardly wait for the I dos to be said and the kiss to be over so she could have him by her side again.

But before that could happen, Tallie and Ry were presented as man and wife. While all the guests filed through a receiving line to congratulate the happy couple, tables were set up and the rows of chairs were dispersed around them.

Out came a fully stocked bar and by the time everyone was ready to sit down, an elaborate dinner of poached salmon, crown rib roast, new potatoes, grilled vegetables, Caesar salad, French bread and wine was served.

Evie Lee had met up with other kids and was more interested in playing than in eating, and since Deana and Deana's sister shared a table with Bax and Carly, conversation was general but lively.

Only after the meal, when the band began to play dance music, were Carly and Bax left alone as Deana and her sister were led onto the floor by some of the single men.

"Don't let me keep you if you're dying to trip the light fantastic," Carly felt obliged to say.

"I think I can live one night without dancing," Bax said wryly.

It was a relief to Carly. She would have been crushed if he'd gone off to dance with some of the other single women who kept throwing him come-hither smiles.

"What about you?" he asked. "I met a man at the boardinghouse today who told me to get that ankle of yours fixed up on the double so you could get to dancin' with him again."

"Mr. Elton," Carly said. "I think he keeps forgetting that I'm leaving town and won't be there to dance with him one way or another."

"He also said if he was a little younger, he'd be waltzing you down the aisle."

Carly laughed. "He's a character."

"*Has* anybody ever waltzed you down the aisle?"

"You mean, have I ever been married? Somewhere in my deep, dark, mysterious past?"

"Something like that."

"Nope. Never."

"Are the men around here crazy or blind or what?"

"I think they must be," she deadpanned. "It isn't as if I haven't had the chance, though. I was engaged, as a matter of fact, until about five months ago."

"You were?"

"To a man named Jeremy Smythe. He worked for the newspaper that serves all four counties. But he lived in Elk Creek. At least, he did before we broke up. Then he moved to Pinewood."

"I drove through Pinewood on my way here. It's a lot like Elk Creek."

"Small town in the center of farms and ranches—it's a *lot* like Elk Creek. It would have to be to get Jeremy to move there." She hadn't meant that to sound as disparaging as it had.

"Who broke up with whom?"

"I guess I did it. But not without provocation."

"He was a cheater? A con artist? A manipulative creep?" Bax guessed with levity and a splash of hopefulness in his tone.

"He misled me."

"Ah, a liar."

Carly flinched. "Jeremy isn't a bad guy. It's just... well, like I said, he misled me."

"How?"

Carly glanced out at the wedding celebration they were in the midst of, realizing as she did that Bax had a way of focusing so intently on her that it was almost as if they were alone. It helped her confide in him even though she hesitated.

"I've always wanted to travel. I told you that."

"About getting the bug from your aunt when you were a kid," he said, proving he really did listen to what she told him.

"Right. I've been to Cheyenne and Denver, to Las Vegas on a junket some teachers took, but that's it. I've never seen an ocean. I've never been to Disneyland. I want to go to the Smithsonian. I want to see the White House and the Eiffel Tower. I want to see the leaves change color in Vermont in the autumn. I want to spend Christmas in London, New Year's Eve in New York. I want to see Paris. I want to see Spain and Greece and Ireland and Scotland and all of Europe. I want to see China and Japan. I want to ride the Orient Express and—"

She cut herself off, knowing she'd gotten carried away on her favorite topic.

"Anyhow," she said with a laugh as she got back to the point. "From the time we met two years ago, all through our year-long engagement, Jeremy made me think he wanted to do it all, too. With me. That we were going to travel the world together."

"But it never happened."

"No, it never happened. I'd talk and talk, and he'd say he wanted to go, too. But not only didn't he ever take any steps to make it happen, when *I* would, he'd throw a wrench into the works. He'd all of a sudden have some kind of health problem. He'd have back spasms, he'd think he might be on the verge of gall-bladder surgery—which he never had. Once he thought maybe he had kidney stones—something else he never had. Or he'd swear his folks needed him home. And every time, he'd tell me I was just selfish to be thinking about traveling when there were other things more important. Then, of course, I'd cancel the trip."

"Until…" Bax prompted.

"Until he told me he couldn't get away from work and I found out otherwise."

"How did you do that?"

"I found out it wasn't that he *couldn't* get away. The truth was that he *wouldn't* get away. I had his editor's daughter in a class and during a conference the man started to tell me how thrilled the paper would be if we ever got our act together and started that traveling we were always talking about. Apparently the newspaper had offered to continue Jeremy's salary if he kept writing articles and columns about our travel experiences and faxed them in. Jeremy had told me two days before that he couldn't leave because the paper had refused to let him do just that."

"So he was a liar."

That still sounded so harsh. But it was true. Carly just didn't confirm it outright.

"I confronted him, and along with telling me more about how selfish I was, how I only thought of myself, he finally admitted that he didn't want the same things I did. He'd only acted like he did to hook me. But when it came right down to it, he didn't want to travel—he didn't *like* to travel—and he was actually intimidated by the thought of going outside the confines of small-town living. In fact, he'd figured if he could just get me to the altar, I'd forget all about the rest of the world, settle down and quit dreaming my silly dreams—that was how he put it. He said if we just got married and had a few babies, I'd get to like the life I'd been born to—again, those were his words."

"Sounds like it was a good thing you found out what was on his mind before you married him."

"That's what I thought." Although it had still been difficult. And painful. She'd cared about Jeremy. She'd thought they were going to see the world together. She'd looked forward to it.

"So you broke it off with him," Bax said, coming full circle.

"So I broke it off with him." And in the process felt disillusioned and disappointed and angry with herself for letting him manipulate her as long as he had. Angry with herself for letting her feelings for Jeremy blind her to what was really going on, to the fact that he was doing his best to pen her in. Angry with herself for wondering if her dreams really were silly...

"And then you packed your bags," Bax said, interrupting her thoughts.

"First, I agreed to finish out the school year, applied for a sabbatical from my teaching job and put my house up for rent."

"And *then* you packed your bags."

"And sprained my ankle." And met you...

"And now, as soon as you're back on two feet, you're going to see all those places by yourself."

He'd said that in an upbeat way. So why had it sounded so lonely to her?

She ignored the feeling. "Just as soon as I can."

Bax leaned in close and said, "For what it's worth, I don't think your dreams are silly. The world is an amazing place, and there's nothing wrong with wanting to see it."

The man truly had a knack for saying the right thing.

"Thank you for that," she said quietly. "And you've seen some of it, so you're talking from experience, right?"

"Right. I haven't done the Orient or been everywhere you mentioned in the States, but I've been enough places to know there are things out there worth seein'. And as for the guy thinking you'd just forget about what you want if he could tie you down—big mistake. Nobody wants to be *tied down*."

"That's what your ex-wife said, isn't it? About Evie Lee."

He confirmed that with raised eyebrows. "It's good that you know what you want and are going after it straightforwardly, without hurting anybody else in the process. There's nothing wrong with wanting to get out a little, see some things. For me, doing that and living in some big cities along the way helped me know better when I was ready to make the commitment to a family. It made me appreciate places like Elk Creek all the more. That other guy was dead wrong thinking to steal that from you and expectin' that you'd be content without it."

Again, all the right things to say.

But somehow Carly thought Bax looked and sounded a little sad saying them.

Then he sat up tall in his chair, as if someone had infused him with energy and put a devilish smile on his face. "For now, though, I have you where I want you and I think we could use some champagne. What do you say I snitch us a bottle? If I'm not mistaken, it's French, so we can consider it warming you up for your trip to Paris."

"Sounds good."

"I'll be right back."

He left then, in search of the champagne, and Carly watched him work his way through the guests—some he knew and some who introduced themselves along the way. And as she kept her eye on him, she couldn't help wondering what was really going through his mind, if her talking about being penned in had brought up too many memories of his ex-wife, or if he was sorry to hear the same sentiment from her.

But by the time he got back he seemed in such high spirits that she forgot to think any more about it.

Instead, she let herself be carried away by his charm, his wit, all the attention he lavished on her, and those good looks that were enough to wipe out every other thought she'd ever had.

She let herself just revel in being with him.

Because if she couldn't be in New York or London or Paris, there wasn't another place on the planet she'd rather have been than with Bax.

Carly and Bax didn't leave the wedding reception until nearly eleven and the party was still going strong. For everyone but Evie Lee. She was exhausted to the point of being slaphappy so they said their good-nights and went home.

Because it was so late and Bax had to help his daughter out of her flower girl dress, Carly left him to it and made her own way to the cottage, wishing the night wasn't over, but resigning herself to the fact that it was.

The problem, though, was that after hours in the summer night air, the cottage felt hot and stuffy. And since she wasn't actually tired, she opted for a quick change of clothes—cutoff shorts and a simple tank top—opened all the windows to let in some of the cooler air, and went outside to sit on the swing that had hung between the two huge elm trees in the backyard for as long as she could remember.

She sat on the single plank seat, dropped her crutches to the ground and hooked her elbows around the ropes that connected it to the tree branches, but she didn't put the swing into motion. She just rested there, letting her head fall to one of the ropes as her gaze wandered up to the main house.

The house where Bax was at that very moment.

The kitchen light was on downstairs, but so was the hall light upstairs and his bedroom light, too. The curtain wasn't drawn on his bedroom window and even though she saw him pass by the window several times—wearing less of the tux with each passing—it wasn't as if he were standing right there and she could watch him undress.

But she was imagining it just the same. Remembering what he had looked like that first day when she'd caught him coming out of the shower wearing only jeans. And what he'd looked like that evening at the ranch when he'd shed his shirt after riding that wild stallion.

She was remembering, too, what had gone through her when she'd fastened his cummerbund earlier. Remembering watching him during the wedding ceremony. And all through the evening.

And she thought that it was the hardest thing she'd ever done not to get off that swing and go into the house, up the stairs to that bedroom, to do more than just watch.

He came to the window then. To open it more than it was.

Carly was sitting perfectly still, so she didn't know what caught his attention, but something did because she saw him take a second look to see what—or who—was out there.

When he recognized her, he waved. Smiled. Then disappeared.

The light went out in the bedroom and Carly assumed he'd gone to bed, leaving her to fight images of that on top of everything else.

But then she saw a shadow move in front of the kitchen window and there he was again, this time coming out the back door to be with her after all.

He'd put on a plain white T-shirt and a pair of disreputable jeans with a rip at the knee. He was barefoot—just as she was—and he looked so incredible that her mouth nearly watered at the sight. Certainly her pulse picked up speed.

"What are you doin' out here?" he asked as he crossed the yard to her.

"I guess I didn't get enough fresh air tonight." Or enough of him, either, but she didn't add that.

"Want a push?" he offered, nodding at the swing.

"No, that's okay. It makes more noise than you'd think."

He went around behind her then, to the park bench that nestled between the two tree trunks under the canopy of the elms' entwined branches where her mother had spent summer afternoons reading in the shade. He sat with one foot on the seat so his knee could brace an elbow and made himself comfortable.

Carly spun around to face him, letting the ropes cross over her head. "Aren't you tired?" she asked.

"Nope, can't say I am," he said with a glance that seemed to take her in all at once and let her know she was the cause of his insomnia. Just as he was the cause of hers.

"What's up for tomorrow?" she asked, just to make conversation.

"I'm part of the cleanup crew out at the ranch. That'll probably take most of the day. Then we have your birthday party tomorrow night, as I recall. Happy birthday—almost—by the way."

"Thanks. But you don't have to go to the party if you don't want to. I know my mother sort of put you on the spot."

"I wouldn't miss it," he said emphatically.

"I have to warn you that my two aunts are slightly eccentric. They'll both get crushes on you the minute you walk in the door. They do it with any man who pays them a visit—that's how they'll see you being there, paying *them* a visit."

"Are you telling me that it doesn't have anything to do with me personally?"

"Don't take offense," Carly confirmed with a laugh. "I'm just letting you know that my aunt Gloria will fol-

low you like a puppy while Aunt Tasha will flirt out-
rageously the whole night—even if both of them have
trouble recalling your name."

"I see. Well, I think I can handle it. I know all too
well what it's like to have a crush," he said pointedly,
his eyes shooting a message all their own that seemed
to warm the cool night air around them.

Then he poked his chin her way. "Why don't you
come over here and let me rub your foot?"

There were things she wanted him to rub, but tonight her foot wasn't one of them.

"It's late and we'd have to unwrap it and I'd have to
wrap it all over again. It's okay."

"Then why don't you just come over here and sit
with me?"

Said the spider to the fly…

But it was an invitation Carly couldn't resist. An
invitation she didn't want to resist.

So she didn't.

When he reached out a hand to her, she took it and
let him pull her gently to sit beside him on the bench.

Then he stretched his arm along the seat back behind her but not touching her. Much as she wished he
would because she craved the feel of his arm around
her.

"So, is this crush you mentioned recent?" she heard
herself ask, flirting more than she knew she should.

"Mmm. As we speak," he answered with a hint of
that secret smile toying with his lips.

"Anybody I know?" she persisted, aware that she
was playing with fire. And not caring.

"I think you've met once or twice. She's a little bit
of a woman with brown hair that shines red in the sun,

eyes the color of topaz, and skin like cream. I think she used to teach junior high geography."

"Doesn't sound like anybody I know," Carly joked even as she flushed beneath his compliment and the scrutiny that went with it.

"The trouble is," he continued, pretending he was greatly wounded, "she doesn't know I'm alive."

"I can't believe that," Carly countered as if they weren't talking about her. "I'll bet she notices more about you than you think."

That seemed to please him. "I wonder," he said hopefully.

He was looking into her eyes, giving her more of the secret smile as he seemed to search for something.

She didn't know what. But she did know that sitting there the way they were, surrounded by the darkness of night, shadowed even from the moon by the tree branches, she felt removed from everything but Bax.

Every sense was tuned in to him. Every nerve ending cried out for his touch. And nothing else seemed to matter but that moment. The two of them. The charge of pure sexual energy in the air around them...

Bax cupped her chin in the circle of his thumb and forefinger then and tilted her face up a little more so his mouth could find hers, slowly, softly, warmly.

Carly's eyes drifted closed as she gave herself over to his kiss, a kiss she'd been craving since the last one they'd shared the night before.

His arm came around her from the back of the bench, his other slipped under her knees and he lifted her to his lap so he could hold her closer and deepen the kiss even as his lips parted farther and his tongue came to play.

Maybe it was all the champagne she'd had at the wedding reception. Maybe it was the intoxication of the night air. Or the intoxication of just being in his arms, but Carly felt no doubts, no reticence, no hesitation.

She was where she wanted to be. With this man who seemed to have gotten into her bloodstream, into her every waking thought and a fair share of her dreams, into her heart…

He kissed her with a new intensity. A new hunger, as if what they'd shared before had only whetted his appetite.

And Carly answered every bit of it with an intensity, a hunger of her own. She wrapped her arms around him, let her palms ride the hard muscles of his back, let them even slide beneath his shirt to indulge in the pure delight of the hard, bare expanse all the way to his broad shoulders.

His skin was smooth and warm and seemed to feed her soul, it felt so wonderful. Their kiss turned urgent and she could feel how much he wanted her as the sure sign of it rose against her hip. And she wanted him just as much. So much that it was an ache deep inside her. So much she couldn't help arching her back to let him know she needed more of his touch.

He was a quick study, slipping big, capable hands under her tank top to her bare back and then around just to her rib cage.

She didn't know if he was teasing her again or just taking his time, but she thought that if he didn't do more than that—and fast—she was going to shatter like blown glass under too great a pressure.

And then one hand started a languorous path upward until he found her breast, encasing it, kneading it, learning every curve.

Her breast had never been as sensitive as it was at that moment. Alive with wanting him and he made it come alive even more.

He found the hardened crest, circling it, pinching gently, rolling it and tugging at it and driving her wild.

She didn't know what there was between herself and Bax, what drew her so inescapably to him, but she knew there was magic to it. Magic to his touch. Magic to him and how much he could make her want him even without trying, let alone now, when her every sense was singing beneath his attentions.

She wanted him so much it hurt. Wanted him to go on kissing her forever. Touching her forever. She wanted to stay right there in his arms forever.

But for some reason that thought suddenly set off an alarm in her head.

Or maybe it was that thought along with having talked about Jeremy earlier so that, too, was fresh in her mind.

But whatever had set off the alarm, she couldn't stop thinking that it was feelings like she was having at that moment—feelings that had been less powerful for Jeremy than they already were for Bax—that had kept her from doing what she'd wanted. Feelings that had tied her to Elk Creek…

"No…no…we…"

It was difficult to get the words out. To give voice to the battle that was raging inside her between wanting Bax, wanting all he was doing to her, wanting what could come, and being terrified of what it might mean later on.

But he got the message.

His glorious hand retraced the path to her back and then he removed it from under her tank top.

His kiss softened, slowed. Stopped.

He laid his forehead against the top of her head and took several deep breaths.

"No?" he repeated.

"I just…Maybe this isn't a good idea," she finally managed to murmur.

He didn't say anything for a moment. He just let silence linger as he seemed to fight for some control of his own.

Then he said, "Okay. You're probably right."

He didn't sound totally convinced.

But then neither was she.

How could anything that felt as incomplete as this did be where they should stop?

But she knew it wouldn't be wise to start it up again, either, so she just let it alone and pushed herself off his lap to sit more primly beside him before her own willpower could get any weaker than it already was.

"I should…go in," she said, still stammering over words she didn't want to say because they distanced her further from what she really wanted. What her body was crying out for yet.

Bax nodded his agreement, but he didn't move. He looked almost as if he couldn't. As if he were incapable of it.

"I'm just gonna sit here a minute. Get myself…in order."

Ah. She hadn't thought about the advantage of a woman's body carrying all that desire on the inside rather than the outside the way a man's did.

"I'll see you tomorrow," he said then, as if he preferred being left alone.

"Okay."

Carly got up onto her crutches again and headed for the cottage without looking back because she was too afraid if she did she wouldn't be able to make herself go.

But his passion-husky voice stopped her halfway.

"Carly?"

"Yes?"

Silence again.

Carly waited.

But in the end all he said was, "Good night."

"Good night," she answered, knowing that wasn't all he'd intended to say without knowing what he had.

But there was so much on her own mind that she didn't try to explore his.

Instead, she went the rest of the way to the cottage, wondering how she was ever going to get any sleep when what she was taking to bed with her were raging, unsatisfied desires that no amount of reason could chase away.

And it occurred to her that she'd never in her life been so torn.

Because she wanted to leave Elk Creek to see the world as much as she always had.

Which was just about as much as she wanted Bax...

Chapter 12

The postwedding cleanup the next day took until the middle of the afternoon. By the time the job was finished Evie Lee had campaigned to spend the night at the ranch so Bax returned to Elk Creek alone.

He didn't go directly home, though. With Carly's birthday in mind he drove farther into town, down Center Street where the shops and businesses lined either side of the wide avenue in a long, facing row of quaint old buildings.

The particular shop he was looking for was about three quarters of the way to the train station that ended Center Street on the south. When he reached that particular shop, he parked nose-first in front of it.

The building was a single-story square box painted white and trimmed with bright-blue awnings over the door and windows to break up the starkness. Inside was the local travel agency and a small luggage store combined.

Who could be easier to find a gift for than someone about to embark on a long trip? he thought. Travel alarm. Travel umbrella. Travel tote. There were any number of things he could get Carly for her birthday.

Except that as he sat in his car, staring at the place, Bax couldn't make himself get out and go in.

The problem with all those travel gift ideas was that they shouted encouragement for her to travel.

And how could he encourage what he found himself wishing like crazy wasn't in the offing?

That wasn't a good sign, he realized.

But there it was, washing through him like a tidal wave. He wanted her to leave about as much as he wanted to have open-heart surgery.

And for some reason, the force of just how much he didn't want her to leave surprised him.

What was all that stuff he'd thought before? About it being okay to have a brief encounter with someone he knew was leaving because knowing she was leaving would act like armor that would keep him from getting too close to her? From getting attached to her?

Well, so much for that.

That armor had apparently been as flimsy as tissue paper.

Because there he was, feeling both close to her and attached.

And hating the thought of her leaving so much that if it had been a wall, he'd have put his fist through it.

How had this happened? he asked himself as he stayed sitting in his car, staring at the travel agency as if it were evil incarnate.

But there was no clear answer because even though it hadn't taken much time, it still seemed to have sneaked up on him.

Maybe if he hadn't watched the way she was with the folks of Elk Creek—laughing and joking and listening delightedly to every story anyone wanted to tell her—maybe then he might not have developed a soft spot for her.

Maybe if he hadn't watched her with Evie Lee, giving his daughter the attention and bolstering that had made the little girl beam, maybe then he might not have come to appreciate Carly and every nuance about her.

Maybe if he hadn't heard what the elderly residents of the boardinghouse had had to say about her—how much she did for them, going out of her way to provide some of that same sort of attention she'd given Evie Lee and adding a little spice to their lives—maybe then he might not have started to just plain like her more than anyone he'd met in a long, long time.

Maybe if he hadn't studied the way her eyes glittered gold. Maybe if he hadn't noticed how shiny her hair was. How flawless her skin. How great her body. Maybe then he might not have found himself itching to touch her, to hold her, to make love to her.

Maybe if he hadn't done all those things, he wouldn't feel as if he had a lump of lead in his gut every time he thought of her leaving.

But he had done all those things.

And when they were added to that initial attraction that had nearly knocked him for a loop the first time he'd set eyes on her, it made for some damn overwhelming feelings rolling around inside him.

Feelings he hadn't bargained for when he'd decided to indulge in this time with her before she left.

Feelings that wouldn't let him get out of his car to buy her a gift that would say, *So long, have a nice trip....*

So he started the car engine again and backed away from the curb, parking a second time at the very end of Center Street in front of a store of an entirely different sort.

This tiny shop took up one storefront of a building that looked as if it had originally been a two-story Victorian house. Now it was split into three sections on the ground floor—the jewelry store, the barber shop and an accountant's office—with the local real estate office occupying the top floor.

But it wasn't a haircut, a tax return or a real estate investment he was interested in.

When he finally got out of the car, it was the jewelry store he headed for.

As he did, a small voice in the back of his head asked if jewelry might be too personal a gift.

But how could it be any more personal than the way he felt about Carly? was the answer he gave himself. Because like it or not, what he was feeling about her was definitely personal.

The jeweler greeted him when he crossed the store's threshold. He was an older, bald-headed man who came out from behind a table where a bright work lamp lit pieces of a watch he was working on.

"What can we do for you today?" the shopkeeper asked.

Bax looked around, having no idea what he might actually buy.

His gaze settled on the first of three cases, but displayed there were engagement and wedding rings. And even though his glance hesitated there longer than it should have, he bypassed it. The second case held watches and cocktail rings, which seemed too *im*personal to him, but the third contained necklaces, bracelets and brooches and those seemed to strike a chord.

"I need a birthday gift," he informed the jeweler then, leaning over the case to have a look at what was inside.

Bax didn't have any trouble choosing. The first thing that caught his eye was a white-gold lariat necklace that he could just picture around the porcelain column of Carly's neck, dropping slightly below the hollow of her throat, the dangling ends pointing downward to those small breasts that tempted him beyond rational thought.

Those small breasts that had felt so incredible in his hand the night before....

He cleared his throat. "Let's have a look at that necklace," he said, pointing to the lariat.

The older man slipped it out of the case and onto a piece of black velvet to show it off to best effect.

"How much?"

The jeweler told him, but Bax barely heard the answer because he was still too lost in the mental image of how it would look on Carly. Instead, he merely said he'd take it, and waited while the shopkeeper wrapped it up for him.

It only struck him then that there might be more to the lariat's appeal than his simply liking it. What was he trying to do? Lasso her with it? that voice in his head asked again.

The idea didn't sit well with him. It wasn't something he wanted to do to her. And even if that was what he subconsciously had up his sleeve, he knew it was a futile attempt.

She's leaving one way or another, he told himself sternly. And again the truth of it was like sandpaper along an open wound.

Why was this bothering him so much all of a sudden? he wondered.

But he still couldn't figure it out.

"Is this for your wife?" the jeweler asked from where he was tying a red ribbon around the package.

"No. I'm not married," Bax answered.

"Must be for someone special, though," the man insisted. "Someone you care about."

"Mmm," was all Bax answered.

But he couldn't stop thinking about the man's comment even as he paid for the necklace and took the small gift out to his car.

Someone he cared about...

Was that why the thought of Carly leaving was eating at him so persistently now? Because he *cared* about her?

Bax shied away from that notion as he backed out of the parking space and retraced his path up Center Street.

But even as he tried to think of other things, the idea that he'd come to care for Carly kept niggling at him.

Cared about...

What exactly did that mean? Besides that he didn't want her to leave town.

It was a troubling thought.

Because what occurred to him as he worried about it was that somehow, when he wasn't looking, when he'd least expected it, he'd gone right ahead and gotten in over his head with her.

In over his head with someone who was going to take off like a shot the minute she was able to and leave everything and everybody behind.

Was that something she realized? he wondered. That when she left this place she'd be leaving behind all the perks of this small town she seemed to fit so perfectly into? That she'd be leaving behind family and friends who loved her? Family and friends she seemed to revel in herself?

Surely she must have considered that.

But what if she hadn't? What if, in her determination to hightail it out of there, she'd overlooked much of what was great about Elk Creek and everybody in it?

Maybe someone could point it all out to her...

Okay, so it wasn't likely to make any difference, he admitted before his hopes could get too high.

But then again, pointing out to her what she'd be leaving behind couldn't do any harm, either.

Could it?

He didn't see how.

And if he didn't see how it could do any harm, then maybe he could put a little effort into it himself.

Because the more he thought about the fact that he cared about her, the more certain he was about one other thing.

There was a better than even chance that when she left, she'd take his heart along with her.

And that wasn't going to be any easier to lose than she was.

Because maybe...just maybe...he more than cared about her....

* * *

Carly's party that evening was at Hope's house around the block. Bax drove, but the ride was so short Carly didn't have time to do more than ask where Evie Lee was and hear the explanation before they were pulling up at the curb in front of her sister's place.

The house was much like Carly's—a two-story clapboard farmhouse—only it was painted Salem blue, trimmed in white and wore a Happy Birthday, Carly! banner strung from the porch eaves.

"Don't forget I warned you," Carly said to Bax as he turned off the engine.

He just smiled, got out of the car and rounded it to open her door.

He looked as handsome as ever, dressed in dark-blue jeans and a crisp white Western shirt with a collar and pointed yoke of midnight-blue, and as Carly eased out of the passenger side and onto her crutches she feasted on the sight out of the corner of her eye and wished she was spending the next few hours alone with him.

That wish wasn't granted for longer than it took them to reach the front porch before Carly's nephews burst from the house shouting jubilant happy birthdays to her.

And so the party began.

Bax was more the center of attention than Carly was, but she didn't mind. It gave her the chance to watch him from a distance. To study him. To enjoy the sight of the big man roughhousing with the little boys, exchanging sports anecdotes with her brother-in-law, goodnaturedly humoring her mother and both of her aunts.

The trouble was, what she witnessed didn't help dilute any of her attraction for him. Any of her rapidly growing feelings for him. Any of her desire for him.

So, as much as she loved and appreciated her family, Carly couldn't help counting the minutes until she and Bax could say good-night.

Of course, once they did she started to wonder how she was going to keep their time together from ending prematurely, but he took care of that when he pulled into the driveway at ten o'clock and said, "I haven't given you my present yet. How 'bout I bring that and a bottle of wine out to the cottage for a change so I'm the one who has to go home afterward?"

Carly laughed. "Oh, good. It's been such a long trek for me to get home those other times."

He just smiled, got out of the car and again came around for her.

Carly went ahead of him through the main house and out to the cottage, wanting to make sure her tiny, temporary lodgings were in order before he followed.

Luckily she didn't have much tidying up to do because he didn't give her ten minutes before he was knocking on the cottage door.

"Come on in," she called as she let a sense of decadence have its way with her and lit the room with only the three vanilla candles that decorated the center of the coffee table in front of the love seat that made up the biggest part of the living room section of the guest house.

Bax did as he was told, bringing with him a small, gaily wrapped package, a bottle of wine, two glasses... and bare feet—something Carly noticed right off the bat.

"New boots. They were killing me," he said when

he caught the direction of her eyes. "Hope you don't mind."

Since she'd already shed her own single shoe she could hardly complain.

Not that she would have, anyway. She liked the relaxed, comfortable intimacy of his bare feet.

She liked it a lot.

But then there wasn't anything about Bax McDermot that she didn't like.

"I don't mind," she answered a little belatedly, going to the couch to sit and letting her crutches fall to the floor.

Bax joined her there, sitting at an angle that had him almost facing her.

"If you take this—" he held the gift out to her "—I can pour the wine."

Carly was only too happy to oblige, curious as to what he'd gotten her.

"Can I open it?" she asked as he did as he'd promised and filled both glasses with ruby-red liquid.

"Sure."

She was half expecting a pen-and-pencil set from the size and shape of the box and was pleasantly surprised to find a necklace inside.

"Oh, this is beautiful," she said, taking the silver lariat from its bed of velvet.

"I hope you like it."

"I love it," she said honestly.

She had on a denim sundress that was cut like a jumper though demurely enough not to need a shirt of any kind underneath it. Instead, the neckline split at the cleavage to expose a hint of white lace that gave the illusion that she had on a second layer when in fact she didn't. It left her throat and the upper portion of her chest bare—the perfect accommodation for the necklace.

She fastened it around her neck and then used her wineglass as a makeshift mirror.

"It really is beautiful," she reiterated.

"I'm glad you like it," Bax said, his eyes so intent on the necklace and the portion of her body where it rested that Carly could almost feel his gaze like a lover's caress.

He pulled his gaze upward with what appeared to be some difficulty then and Carly could have sworn her skin grew cooler with the loss.

"Happy birthday," he added.

"Thank you." She tried to turn down the wattage of her smile, but it wasn't easy when she was as thrilled as she was with her gift. "And thanks, too, for being so nice to all my family tonight at the party."

"I wasn't just being nice. I was havin' a great time. How often can a man have three gorgeous women catering to his every whim?"

"My mother stuffing you with enough food for three people, my aunt Gloria making you sing show tunes with her at the piano, and my aunt Tasha trying to drag you off to dance with her every two minutes? Anybody who'll go through all that as patiently as you did tonight can't be all bad."

Bax gave her the devilish grin. "Maybe not *all* bad. But a little. When it counts."

The innuendo in his voice went along with the grin and only increased the sensuality that had already begun to simmer in the air around them.

"You don't fool me, though," he said then.

"Was I trying to?"

"You make it sound as if you didn't get a big kick out of everything tonight and I know better."

Carly had the grace to laugh. "I like my aunts," she confessed.

"You like your aunts and your family and the folks at the boardinghouse and everybody we visited out on the farms and ranches the other afternoon, and the whole rest of this little town and what makes it tick. I'm startin' to think you're just one big fraud, pretendin' that you can't wait to get away from everything and everybody."

"I beg your pardon," she said in mock offense. "I don't speak badly of Elk Creek or anybody in it. I love Elk Creek. I just want to go out and see the rest of the world, too."

"Elk Creek is gonna miss you."

"Me? I don't know about that."

"I do. I think you're one of the town's sweethearts." That made her blush.

"And I think you're gonna miss Elk Creek more than you think, too."

"Is that so?"

"It is," he said with confidence. "You may go out and find the Eiffel Tower and big-city lights and fancy restaurants and museums and galleries, but you won't find such clean air and so many folks thoughtful enough to bring food to the new town doc, or so many folks who look out for each other the way they do over at the boardinghouse—the way you do for them over at the boardinghouse. You won't find so many people wantin' to tell you those stories you love listenin' to or so many folks who care about you the way they do around here. And I'll tell you somethin' else, I'm gonna hate the thought of you bein' out in that big bad world by yourself with not nearly enough people recognizin' just what a gold mine of a woman you are."

"A gold mine of a woman?" she repeated with a laugh, not taking any of what he said too seriously because there was a note of levity to his tone the whole time he talked.

"An old-fashioned girl who has the biggest heart in town. Who's trusting and giving and sweet and—"

"Stop!" she said with another blush and another laugh, this one embarrassed.

Bax looked deeply into her eyes, holding them with his sea-foam-green ones. "'Round here you're appreciated the way you should be. But out there…"

He made that sound as ominous as a melodramatic comic book and Carly laughed.

"Out there," she repeated in the same vein, "lurks ogres and monsters and evildoers of every ilk. Is that it?"

He grinned. "I was pouring it on a little thick, is that what you're tellin' me?"

"Just a little. But it's a refreshing change of pace. My mother and Deana usually opt for other tactics to convince me I shouldn't go."

"Maybe because they don't want to lose you," he said then in a quiet voice that no longer joked or teased. "And maybe I don't want to, either."

His eyes were still delving into hers and that, coupled with words that had an impact of their own, made Carly weak-kneed and lightheaded suddenly.

She set the glass on the coffee table and used the motion as an excuse to tear her eyes away from Bax, a little afraid of that impact and the weak-kneed, light-headedness that went with it.

But when he put his wineglass on the table near hers and turned back to her again, the spell was still weaving itself around them and Carly lost herself in that sight she was always starving for—the sharp planes of that handsome face that drifted through her dreams like an enticement.

"I have such a crush on you," he nearly whispered, making her smile once more. "A crush and then some," he said more to himself than to her as he leaned toward her and caught her lips with his in a soft kiss that began and might have ended there except that Carly met him halfway, kissed him back and went on kissing him, indulging in that bliss she never got enough of.

She'd been doing a lot of thinking about Bax since the evening before. A lot of thinking. A lot of yearning. A lot of wanting. A lot of wishing he was with her. Alone with her. Holding her…

And right then she wasn't thinking about leaving Elk Creek. She was only thinking about this man who made her blood boil in her veins. Who had carved out his own special spot in her every waking thought. In her heart. This man who made every nerve ending in her body sing and scream at once for more of him. More of his kisses. More of his Midas touch.

She was only thinking that when she was with him everything felt right. She felt complete in a way she'd never experienced before, with anyone else.

There were times, she decided, when it was good—no, necessary—to surrender to all those feelings, all those cravings and yearnings and desires. Just to surrender to the moment. To that one man…

And tonight felt as if that time had come.

So Carly went on kissing him, letting him kiss her with those supple, talented lips that began the magic. That slowly drew her to him, to their own private province where nothing mattered but the two of them, the feelings she had for him and the sensations that he was awakening within her with lips that were parted over hers and a tongue that had come to court, to play, to seduce.

His arms came around her, pulling her more closely to him, cradling her head in one hand as he deepened their kiss, pressing her backward.

She slid her arms around him, too, molding her palms to the honed, muscular mountains of his back, of his broad shoulders.

His mouth abandoned hers to kiss her eyes, her cheeks, her chin, her throat, and when he returned to her lips it was with a new intent, a more serious intent that sparked stronger passion, stronger desire in her.

So much passion, so much desire, that she ached for the touch of more than his lips. Ached to feel his hands not just bracing her. Ached to know more of the wonders of his touch than she had already.

Her back arched all on its own, relaying the needs of her flesh.

Bax got the message. He eased her farther back until she was resting flat against the sofa, with him beside her, his hands free to glide along the bare surface of her arms, her shoulders, her collarbone, worshiping the feel of her skin as if it were something he'd never experienced before, arousing every inch he touched and awakening an even greater need in her before answering that need with a course that reached its goal at her breast.

The dress had prohibited her wearing a bra and now she was glad for that, glad that there was only one layer shielding her from him. Because even that one layer seemed like too much.

Another arch of her back to meet his kneading hand let Bax know what she wanted. What she needed. And he finally slid that hand inside the denim.

Carly couldn't suppress the groan that escaped her throat at that first meeting of warm, masculine hand and soft, engorged flesh.

But it was a groan answered by Bax with one of his own as his mouth worked over hers in an open urgency and he explored the lush curve, the hardened nipple, the straining globe of her breast.

He found the zipper that closed her dress in back and slid it only far enough to slip the straps off her shoulders and lower the bodice. For a split second, cool air brushed across her bare skin and then he reclaimed her in a gentle, demanding, teasing, tormenting touch that drove her wild.

His mouth left hers once more, this time kissing and nibbling a path down the column of her neck to the hollow of her throat, and farther, finding just the beginning swell of her breast even as his fingers rolled the kerneled crest between tender, expert fingers.

And then he took that oh-so-aroused nipple into the hot moist velvet of his mouth, suckling, nipping, circling it with his tongue until Carly could barely breathe the pleasure was so great.

But she was still greedy for more. More of the feel of him. More of his body. More of him.

She tugged his shirt out of his jeans and made quick work of the snaps that held it closed, sliding it off him as soon as she was able.

His skin was hot and taut, satin over steel where muscles bulged and tensed with the power they contained.

But even that wasn't enough and so she let her fingers dive into the waistband at his spine, smoothing their way to his sides and even a little toward the front, giving as good as she got in teasing him, taunting him, even as she writhed beneath the glory of his mouth at her breast and cursed what remained of her clothes and his.

And then he stopped.

Slowly. Reluctantly. Kissing a path upward until he wasn't kissing her at all and instead looked down into her eyes, searching them.

"You didn't think this was a good idea last night," he said in a ragged, raspy voice. "Has that changed?"

"I can't think of any better idea now," she barely managed to say as every cell in her body cried out for him.

"You're sure?"

"Oh, yes…oh, yes…" she breathed both in answer to his question and to the hand that had found its way under her skirt to brush feathery strokes on her thigh just above her knee.

"Then let's do it right."

Bax rolled away from her and got to his feet. He leaned over and blew out the candles, leaving the room dusted only in moonlight as he bent to pick up Carly, whisking her across the small room to her double bed.

But he didn't lie her on the mattress there. Instead,

he set her carefully on her feet, kissing her again as he slid the zipper of her dress the rest of the way down and then pushed it and her panties to fall around her ankles.

Carly was only too glad to be rid of the barriers and hardly hesitated before reaching for the buttons of his jeans, unfastening them and giving that last article of clothing a shove that sent them to the floor, too, where Bax kicked them completely off.

It left him as naked as she was. Magnificently naked and so incredible to behold that that first sight of him, of his burgeoning desire for her, made her heart pound and her hands itch to touch him.

And touch him she did. That long, hard part of him that proved he wanted her as much as she wanted him.

Again he swept her up into his arms, this time swinging her around to the bed, lying her there and joining her, his spectacular body following the length of hers, one thick thigh across her legs, holding her a willing prisoner as he recaptured her mouth with his.

He reached an arm over her to catch her hand, threading his fingers through hers, palm pressing palm as he raised her arm above her head.

Then he rose just enough to kiss the soft inside of her wrist, trailing those same downy kisses to the inner curve of her elbow, to the juncture where arm met body, to her shoulder, to the spot where her shoulder turned into her neck.

He rained kisses all the way down to her breast once more, to her nipple, all tight and yearning. To the delicate underside of her other breast. To her flat belly where his tongue traced her navel.

And then lower still...

Her eyes flew open in part surprise, part pleasure, as

that warm, seeking mouth reached her. Her back came up off the bed and the "Ooh," that came through her lips came on a long, low, breathy sigh that was unlike anything she'd ever heard herself utter.

Then, when she could hardly breathe with wanting to feel their bodies united, he rose above her again in a glory of moonlit male beauty, finding his place between her legs, finding his home inside her.

Not all at once, but slowly, patiently, carefully, slipping into her until he'd achieved a perfect fit.

He moved only slightly at first. So slightly that it was just a pulse.

And then a second pulse.

And a third…

Carly flexed her hips into his, absorbing each movement no matter how slight, easing her own muscles in glorious answer to every withdrawal, waiting with growing anticipation for that next glorious plunge.

All the while she let her hands ride along on his back, filling themselves with massive shoulders, sliding down the expanse to his waist, reveling in the feel of that sexy derriere.

He quickened the pace then.

Faster.

Faster.

Diving into her farther and farther. Striving. Straining. Racing.

Passion grew apace with his speed and lit sparks at the very core of her.

Sparks that ignited into embers. Embers that flamed to life to blaze through her in white-hot flames that curled her spine completely off the mattress, that threatened to sear her with ecstasy so unbelievable, so incredible, so miraculous Carly wasn't sure she could endure it even as she cried out for more and tried to hang on to every exquisite moment. The same moment she felt Bax tense above her, within her. The same moment when she heard him call her name in a voice that sounded tortured and triumphant at once.

And then, too soon, the flames' blaze cooled to embers, to sparks. Until finally just pinpoints of light glittered all through her as both she and Bax calmed, quieted and relaxed so that every part of them melded together, entwined, as one.

There were no words to say in the midst of a union beyond measure. As hearts seemed to reach out to each other and join as completely as their bodies had.

Bax only pressed the gentlest of kisses to Carly's brow, held her tight and rolled them both to their sides where neither of them could resist the exhausted tug of sleep.

But even as Carly drifted off, wrapped in the cocoon of his body and feeling more wonderful than she'd ever felt in her life, she was a little afraid.

Afraid that the change to the grand scheme of things that she'd been so sure wouldn't happen might have just happened anyway…

Chapter 13

Of all the times in his career that Bax had been roused out of a deep sleep in the middle of the night, never had he wanted to ignore his pager more than that night.

But the only people who had the number wouldn't use it unless it was an absolute necessity, so he had no choice but to slip his arms from around Carly where she slept so peacefully beside him, find his pager in his discarded pants pocket and then answer the 911 code.

Elk Creek's baby boom had struck. Three of the four babies due to increase the town's population decided to make their appearance all at once. And Bax could hardly complain about leaving Carly's bed when Tallie Shanahan—Tallie McDermot now—had had only the second night of her marriage and what should have been her honeymoon ended abruptly, too.

When Bax got to the hospital portion of the medical facility just fifteen minutes after the call for help that Tallie had sent, he found his new sister-in-law with her hands more full than one midwife and a singular nurse's aide could handle. Ally and Jackson Heller, Ivey and Cully Culhane and Della and Yance Culhane were all about to welcome their new arrivals.

Luckily there were no complications, but both Bax and Tallie could have used roller skates to get around as the hours of labor and then the deliveries passed. And yet, even as busy as Bax was, Carly kept sneaking into his thoughts.

Carly, so warm and soft in that bed he'd left.

Carly in his arms. Carly beneath him, their bodies keeping perfect rhythm, fitting together as if they were two halves of a whole.

Carly calling his name at the height of passion.

Carly laughing, snuggling in beside him, every curve and hollow of her body molding to every hill and valley of his.

But it wasn't only their lovemaking and the afterglow that kept wafting through his mind.

There were also thoughts of Carly listening with such delight to the stories of the elderly Elk Creek residents.

Thoughts of Carly dancing with old Mr. Elton.

Of Carly bringing Mrs. Gordon brandy.

Of Carly with Evie Lee.

Of Carly with her family, humoring her quirky aunts, playing with her nephews, cradling her sister's new baby.

And then, too, there were thoughts of Carly pregnant and having a baby of Bax and Carly's own making....

The bottom line was that no matter how hard he

tried throughout the rest of that night and into the early dawn, he couldn't stop thinking about her.

And even though he kept pushing the thoughts aside to deliver the laboring mothers—boys for Ally and Jackson, and for Ivey and Cully, and a girl for Della and Yance—the thoughts stayed with him. Got stronger. More insistent.

Until, on the way out of the medical building when everything was under control and mothers and babies were all resting comfortably, he finally gave in and explored those thoughts that had refused to stop.

Something had happened in the past twelve hours, he realized.

Something had happened during making love to Carly that had gelled his feelings for her, that had started him wanting more of her. More from her.

Because what he was thinking had gone beyond merely being unhappy with the idea of her leaving town. Beyond being loath to lose her.

It had gone to a strong, sharp image of the future. His future. With her in it.

Somehow, out of the blue, his thoughts had gone to a strong, sharp image of making Carly a part of his life.

A big part of it.

But that was exactly what he'd sworn not to do with any other woman for a long, long time to come. And certainly not with a woman who likely didn't want that kind of commitment. Not when it meant it would tie her down.

Tie her down...

That didn't sit well with him as he got into his car and headed for the McDermot ranch to pick up his daughter in the early morning sunshine. In fact, he hated the sound of it.

He didn't want to tie Carly down.

He just wanted her. In his future. In every day of it. In every night of it...

But how could he have one without causing the other? How could he have her in his future and not tie her down?

"Good luck coming up with a plan for that," he muttered to himself as he drove through the open countryside toward the ranch.

She'd seen right through his plan to point out the good things about the small town. She'd seen right through him, laughed as if he'd only been joking, and that had been that.

And now he wanted more than just for her to stick around.

Would she laugh at any hint of that, too? Would she even consider it?

And if she considered it, if she actually agreed to do it, then what? Would she feel *tied down* the way Alisha had? Would the same things happen?

"Then what would you have?" he asked himself.

But he knew the answer. He might have the kind of mess he'd had before. The kind of mess he was determined to spare Evie Lee.

His daughter was playing out in front of the ranch house when he pulled up the road that led to it and she stopped bouncing the ball she'd been dribbling to wave to him, her delight at seeing him written all over her cherubic face.

He couldn't do anything else that would hurt her,

that was all there was to it. And he shouldn't even be thinking about it.

So again he pushed the thoughts out of his mind as he parked the car and got out, telling Evie Lee he was going inside to say hello to everybody before he took her home.

Yet once he'd done that, along with letting his family know the outcome of his and Tallie's night's work, once he and Evie Lee were in the car headed away from the ranch, those same persistent thoughts of Carly came right back.

And worse than before, they came back with a new edge to them. An edge that wouldn't allow him to so much as imagine a future without her when he tried.

"Is Carly home? Does she know about the babies?" Evie Lee asked then, interrupting his mental musings.

"She knew the babies were trying to be born, but not that they have been. And it's so early she might still be in bed."

In the bed he'd left her in. The bed where he'd made love to her and sealed the fate that made it seem impossible for him to say goodbye to her.

The bed he wished he was sharing with her now. And forever...

"You like Carly a lot, don't you?" he heard himself ask his daughter before he was even sure he was going to broach the subject at all.

"Yep. A whole lot. We're friends."

"Mmm."

He hesitated to pursue what was on his mind, but in the end that, too, had a will of its own that he couldn't fight and he said, "Would you ever want to be more than friends with her?"

"You mean like *best* friends?"

"Or even more."

"What's more than best friends?"

"Like Alisha was," he said tentatively.

"Carly's not like Alisha," Evie Lee insisted defensively, wrinkling her perky little nose at the very idea. "Carly's nice. Even when you're not around. She's better than Alisha."

"Does that mean you wouldn't mind having Carly be, say, your stepmother? Or would you rather just keep her as your friend?"

He was walking on eggshells, unsure if he should even be saying any of this to his daughter but concerned about so much as entertaining any of the thoughts that had been riddling him since leaving the guest cottage without first knowing how, exactly, Evie Lee felt about Carly.

Evie Lee gave his question serious consideration. Serious enough to let Bax know she wasn't taking the suggestion lightly.

"Not that that's going to happen," he felt inclined to interject. "I'm just wondering what you thought about something like that."

"Isn't Carly goin' on her trip no more?"

"*Any*more," he corrected. "And yes, as far as I know, she is. I was just—"

"Pretend talkin'?" Evie Lee finished for him.

"Yeah. Pretend talking. What-iffing."

"Well, I didn't think I would ever want you to get married to no one else ever again."

"*Any*one else."

"*Any*one else. Ever again."

"I can understand that," he said.

"But I like Carly. And if she was my mom, she could comb my hair all the time and play with me and read to me and I guess that would be okay. 'Less she turned into like Alisha was. But I don't think that could happen because Carly's not the same as Alisha."

Except that she might feel as *tied down* as Alisha had felt.

Back to that.

But it wasn't something he could ignore and he knew it.

What if he somehow managed to convince Carly not to leave town, to become a part of his life, of Evie Lee's life, and she felt as tied down as Alisha had?

As Bax pulled into the driveway at home, he realized that even if Carly ever felt as tied down as Alisha had, she wouldn't do what Alisha had done. Because Evie Lee was right, Carly was not like Alisha.

Carly was a natural nurturer. A natural mother. She mothered everyone. She'd been mothering Evie Lee already.

There was also none of Alisha's selfishness or self-centeredness in Carly, no matter what her former fiancé had tried to pin on her. Carly was generous and giving to a fault. She put other people ahead of herself, of her own needs and desires. Carly was definitely *not* Alisha.

But still, regardless of the fact that she wouldn't punish anyone else, the last thing Bax wanted was for her to *feel* tied down. Or not to do what she'd wanted to do since she was a child herself.

Maybe *he* was being the selfish one, he thought as he and Evie Lee got out of the car.

Maybe just thinking about trying to change Carly's mind about leaving was pure selfishness.

And that didn't sit any better with him than the thought that what he had in mind, what he wanted of her, might tie her down.

So what are you gonna do? he asked himself as he ushered his daughter into the house, feeling torn and tormented and at the same time elated to be even just that much nearer to where Carly was.

He could keep his mouth shut, he thought, answering his own question.

Although that meant watching her leave town—and maybe his life—forever.

But maybe that was the high road—not letting her know how he felt about her. About her going. Making sure he didn't influence her or alter her plans or even make her think twice about leaving.

But high road or not, he didn't think he could actually do that when it meant most certainly losing her.

He couldn't let her just walk away without talking to her about it all. Because if he did, he knew he would spend the rest of his life wondering what might have happened if he had just been open and honest with her. If he'd just let her know he didn't want her to go.

Of course talking to her meant that he had to spill his guts. He had to lay everything out on the table.

Including his heart.

It meant that he'd be taking the risk that she didn't feel the same way he did. That she didn't feel the same way about him that he felt about her.

It meant he could still lose her.

But he didn't see any other way to deal with this.

So he had to take the risk.

He had to hang on to the hope that he wasn't making a mistake.

And he had to see if he could find a way that neither of them would come out on the losing end.

Brilliant sunshine flooded the guest cottage and woke Carly up early.

She opened her eyes to the empty side of the bed where Bax had been until the middle of the night when he'd been called away. She couldn't help smiling at the indentation in the pillow beside hers, smiling at the memory of soft kisses waking her to tell her he had to go deliver babies.

She longed for him to still be there. To be looking into his face at that moment. To be molding her naked body to his. To feel his arms come around her, pulling her close. To kiss his bewhiskered face. To make love again...

But since he wasn't there to do any of that, she had to content herself with just the pillow indentation.

She reached over and swept her fingertips along the curve, imagining it was warm from the heat of his body, resting her hand in the very center of it as if it connected her to him, willing him to come back to her bed.

But she could only stay there wishing for so long before she finally decided she had to get up, get dressed, get on with the day.

She made it as far as getting up, showering and dressing in her pink-and-white-striped sundress before a knock on the cottage door raised her hopes anew.

Cursing the crutches that kept her from running to answer the knock the way she wanted to, she called, "Come in," and then held her breath until the door opened and she could see who her visitor was.

She couldn't be sure if the sun really did seem brighter from behind Bax or if she just perceived it that way because she was so thrilled that it was him opening the door and coming in.

And again she had the urge to run, this time to run to him, to throw her arms around his neck and kiss him and pick up where they'd left off the night before.

But instead she just said a cheery, "Hi," not wanting to seem as eager as she actually was.

"Mornin'," he answered in a sexy voice and with a lift to his eyebrow as he took in the sight of her from head to toe and seemed to like what he saw in her fresh-scrubbed appearance, her hair hanging loose around her shoulders.

It was only fair that he approved of the way she looked, Carly thought, since she was feasting on her first morning view of him, too.

He'd showered—she could tell because his hair was damp and the scent of soap and aftershave had come in with him. He wore a pair of faded jeans and a black Henley T-shirt that hugged every bulging muscle of his well-developed torso.

And all Carly could think was that there they both were, clean and put together, and maybe they could muss each other up all over again.

But Bax didn't seem inclined to do that as he remained standing just inside the door he'd closed behind him.

"Are there new babies?" Carly asked then.

"Three," he said, filling her in on the details.

When he'd finished outlining how busy he'd been while she'd gone on sleeping, she said, "Are you tuckered out?" almost hoping he was because she had vi-

sions of his napping for an hour or so in her bed and
then crawling in with him.

"No, I'm not tired. I want to talk to you. Somethin'
about all those babies got me to thinkin'."

"Births and deaths—I guess they'll do that to you,"
she said. But for some reason the tone of his voice, the
look of solemnity on his handsome face, alarmed her
slightly.

"It got me to thinkin'," he continued, "about you
and me and the future and this traveling thing you're
hell-bent on doing."

This traveling thing?

Carly didn't want to hear that the way she had. But
to her it sounded so much like her former fiancé's ref-
erences to her "silly little dreams" that she couldn't
help being rubbed wrong by Bax's phrase.

"My plans, you mean," she corrected defensively.

"Your plans. They've been botherin' me all along.
Since meetin' you and likin' you and…well, since
comin' to feel about you the way I do."

He took a deep breath and sighed it out, switching his weight to one hip. "I just don't want you to go,
Carly," he said matter-of-factly. "I want you here, in
my life. I want you to be a part of my life. I want us to
have a life together. I'm in love with you."

"Oh."

It was probably not the best thing to say. But he'd
shocked her so thoroughly that it was the only thing
that would come out of her mouth.

If he expected more, he didn't show it. He just went
on. "I know it's quick, but there it is. I'm crazy, madly,
wildly in love with you and I want you to stay here and
marry me. I want you to be Evie Lee's stepmom. I want

to have kids of our own and live here in Elk Creek until we're two shriveled-up old prunes who die holdin' hands on our porch swing sixty years from now."

"We don't have a porch swing." Okay, that was worse than *oh*. But she was still so stunned by all he was saying that that, too, had just come out on its own.

But once more Bax continued with what he was saying as if what she'd said wasn't important yet. "Here's what I've been thinkin'."

He took a few steps toward her, but for some reason Carly didn't move to meet him halfway. She stayed glued to the spot, and she even discovered herself stiffening up a bit, although she wasn't sure why she did that, either.

Bax must have seen it because he stopped in his tracks, still a fair distance away when it seemed as if he'd intended to come closer.

But it didn't keep him from continuing with what he'd been about to say.

"I've been rackin' my brain with how things could work for us," he said then. "What if I promise you at least one trip every year? Come hell or high water. Would that persuade you to stay?" But he didn't stop long enough for her to answer. Instead, he forged ahead. "I could get a doctor in here to sub for me and we'll go wherever you want to go. We'll see every single place you want to see. Together. I know it won't be exactly what you planned. It won't be all at once. You won't be living anywhere but here. But you'll see it all. And you'll have something to look forward to every year. Elk Creek really is a great little town and this way you wouldn't be leaving it behind, either. You'd still have your life here with the people you love, the people who love you…."

He was saying more in that vein, but Carly was feeling herself splitting into two parts even as he was laying it all out for her.

She knew where he was going with it and there was the part of her that was tempted by what he was proposing. Marrying him. Being a mother to Evie Lee. Seeing the world with Bax by her side. It was very enticing.

But there was the other part of her that kept thinking that she'd heard the promise he was making before. From Jeremy. A promise that had never been kept.

And if that promise hadn't been kept by Jeremy, how could it be kept by Bax of all people? Bax who was the new doctor.

She was a country doctor's daughter, after all. She knew better then anyone what that entailed. Emergencies and births and outbreaks and any number of obligations that had left her parents rarely leaving town for anything.

Carly felt her head shake before she even knew what she was going to say, stopping Bax's avalanche of words with the movement.

Then she heard, "It won't work," come out of her mouth.

"What won't work?"

"All of it. Any of it. Maybe you mean what you're saying—"

"*Maybe?* There's no maybe about it. What do you think? That I'm like that other guy? Just blowin' smoke to keep you around until you give up the idea of ever leaving at all?"

"I don't think you're being realistic. I think you're making a promise you can't keep even if you mean to."

"*Even if I mean to?* I'm giving you my word, Carly, that you'll see all the places you want to see. That I'll make sure of it. That I won't let anything stop us. That I'll make absolutely certain that contingencies are made for everything that might come up."

He sounded so sure of himself.

And it was tempting.

Oh, was it tempting.

To marry Bax. To have him all to herself forever and ever. To sleep every night in his arms the way she had the night before. To make love with him. To make a family with him. To see the world with him.

Carly couldn't have fantasized anything more appealing.

But she'd been blinded by a man once before. Blinded to the reality of things.

And even if Bax wasn't intentionally misleading her the way Jeremy had, even if he meant every word he said, she knew what was more likely to happen.

She knew that the promise would get broken. She knew that the first thing to go by the wayside would be her trips.

And worse, she knew that she'd feel penned in just the way she had with Jeremy.

That she'd start to resent Bax, just the way she'd resented Jeremy.

That she'd start to feel as if her dreams really were silly.

That she'd feel diminished and petty and selfish—just the way she'd felt with Jeremy every time he'd come up with a reason, important or otherwise, why a trip had to be canceled or postponed.

And she just couldn't let any of that happen. Not again.

Her head shook of its own volition. "No. It just won't work," she said softly, hearing the pain in her own voice before she even felt it.

"It *will* work because I'll make it work," he insisted.

"I just don't think you can," she said firmly. "There will be medical problems you need to take care of and family matters that come up and kids to raise and problems and emergencies and—"

"And nothing that can't be handled. I'm telling you, I'll handle it, Carly. I won't let you take second place to anything."

"And then you'll be torn and harried and resentful and I'll feel guilty and selfish if I make you go through with the trips or penned in or tied down and resentful if I don't…." She put some effort into calming her voice because it had become as agitated as she envisioned them both feeling. "That's not good. It's no way to have a marriage. It'll chip away at us. At our relationship. And then where will we be? We'll be right where I ended up with Jeremy.

"It just won't work between us, Bax," she made herself say. "You've come here to be the town doctor. To put down roots. To raise Evie Lee where you can be a constant, handy part of her everyday life. And I'm packed and ready to leave the way I've planned since I was Evie Lee's age. That's how things are. You're ready to settle in. I'm ready to leave. And that's how things have to be. You won't be happy abandoning Elk Creek when it needs you—and it will *always* need you. You won't be happy leaving behind Evie Lee—or more kids—so we can traipse around the world. And if I stay, if I give up what I've always wanted, what I've always dreamed of and planned for, then I'll feel trapped...the way I felt before."

"Trapped," he repeated as if she'd hit him with the word.

"I'm sorry."

"And you're wrong. We both have family here to look after kids, and kids do fine being away from their parents for short spans. Or we'll take them with us. There's Tallie here to pick up the slack medically and other doctors who can come in temporarily. One of the great things about this place is that folks do for other folks. They help out. They care. So there are ways, Carly. Ways to make it all work. That other guy found ways to keep it *from* working. But I'm not that other guy any more than you're like my ex-wife. And I won't resent anything. I sure as hell won't make you feel penned in or tied down or trapped."

She knew his intentions were good. But there was too much at stake. Too much that could tear them apart or make her feel bad about herself or make him feel things about her that she never wanted him to feel.

"I'm sorry," she said again. And then, with finality, "It's just...it just won't work."

"Only because you don't want it to work," he accused.

But there was no sense trying to deny that even though it wasn't true. No sense trying to make him understand what she believed would happen because she'd seen it all happen before.

So she just turned her back to Bax to let him know there was nothing more to say.

"Think about this, Carly. Think about what you're cutting off here."

But she shook her head again. Stubbornly. Without looking at him. Because she was certain that she could see into the future where, if she agreed to what he wanted—to what a part of her wanted—they'd both have a life fraught with the kind of pitfalls she'd already encountered with Jeremy.

"Damn it, what do I have to do to prove to you that I can make this work? That I can give you what you want?"

"You can't," she barely whispered, so, so sorry that she believed it.

"You're wrong," he said once more.

But there didn't seem to be anything else for either of them to say, and so Carly just stayed where she was, her back to Bax, until she heard him leave.

And that was when the pain struck her like a body blow.

Chapter 14

The rest of Sunday and all of Monday and Tuesday were the longest days of Carly's life. Maybe because she hadn't slept either Sunday or Monday night, so there didn't seem to be any break from one to the other, she thought as she sat soaking her foot in Deana's living room late Tuesday afternoon.

She'd moved out of the guest cottage within hours of her confrontation with Bax, telling Deana that the small house was making her claustrophobic when she'd asked to stay with her friend and neighbor.

But that was all she'd told Deana.

Carly wasn't sure why she hadn't confided in her friend. Certainly it was the first time in her life that she hadn't.

But she almost felt as if Deana wouldn't understand. Who *could* understand, after all? Carly wasn't altogether sure she understood herself. Not late at night, lying in the lonely twin-size bed in Deana's guest room, thinking about Bax and Evie Lee. Missing them both because she hadn't seen hide nor hair of either of them since Sunday morning. Wondering if they missed her. Wondering what Bax was doing. Wishing she were back where she'd been on Saturday night...

She'd spent a good part of those three days with her sprained ankle in a pan of water, trying to hurry the healing process so she could finally leave Elk Creek and put this whole thing behind her. That thought was the only thing that sustained her, that kept her from crying buckets of tears and being a complete mess.

But the truth was, even thoughts of traveling weren't helping a whole lot.

And that was an oddity she couldn't fathom.

No matter what bad or unpleasant or upsetting things had ever happened to her, daydreaming about seeing the world had always been her outlet. It had always had the power to comfort her, to soothe her. It had always allowed her an escape.

Until now.

Now not even that eased the heaviness in her heart. The constant knot in her stomach. The sleeplessness. The lack of energy or enthusiasm. The doldrums.

The thinking about Bax...

But still she kept telling herself that if she could just get out of town she'd be all right. Then she'd be able to put aside thoughts of him. Longings for him. Wanting him more than she wanted food or water.

Wouldn't she?

Of course she would.

Deana's doorbell rang just then, but it didn't have

any effect on Carly. Not the way it had when she'd first moved in. She'd stopped perking up at the sound and waiting with baited breath as images of Bax being outside on the porch danced through her mind.

Now she knew better, knew that if he hadn't come around yet, he never would. So not so much as a glimmer of hope sprang to life at the sound.

Not that she *wanted* him to come around. Because she didn't. What good would it do anyway? Nothing had changed. Nothing could be changed by his coming around. In fact, she knew she'd only feel worse than she already did if she had to look even one more time at those chiseled features that turned her to mush, or at that body that singed her from the inside out with cravings. So it was good that Bax had never been on the ringing side of the door. When Deana came from the kitchen to answer the bell this time, Carly barely looked up from staring at the carpet.

Until Deana said, "Well, Evie Lee Lewis! Hello, there."

"Hi," Carly heard the little girl's response. "Is Carly here?"

"Why, yes, I believe she is. Would you like to come in and see for yourself?"

"I would," Evie Lee confirmed just before Deana pushed open the screen door and in came the little girl who was almost as much a feast for Carly's eyes as Bax would have been.

"There you are!" Evie Lee said as she bopped into Deana's living room in her bright-red overall shorts and white T-shirt, spotting Carly on the couch.

"Hi," Carly answered, fighting the unexpected wash

of tears in her eyes and wondering what had gotten into her.

"I'm not s'pose to be here botherin' you but I was thinkin' and thinkin' 'bout you and so I came to see you. But don't tell my dad 'cuz he said he know'd you were over here 'cuz he saw'd you but that I wasn't s'pose to bother you."

"You're not a bother. You're never a bother," Carly was quick to assure, knowing she sounded starved for the child's company but unable to hide what she was feeling.

"Maybe I could get us some lemonade—how would that be?" Deana offered.

"I like lemonade," Evie Lee agreed. "And cookies, too. I like cookies, too."

Deana laughed. "I'll see if I can round up some of those, too."

Evie Lee crossed to the sofa and sat beside Carly. "Is your foot still hurt?"

"I'm afraid so. It's getting better, though."

Deana must have let her dog Sam in the back door then because the schnauzer came running into the living room barking his head off at Evie Lee as he did.

"He won't hurt you," Carly said, trying to quiet the dog.

"I know. I play with him through the fence in back sometimes when he's outside when I'm outside."

The dog finally stopped barking when Evie Lee petted him.

"He's a nice dog," Evie Lee decreed. "Kinda like the kittens at the ranch only louder."

"He does tricks," Carly said. "Do you want to see them?"

"Yeah!"

Carly put Sam through his paces, making him sit up and shake hands and roll over and play dead. Then she said, "Say 'please,' Sam. Say 'please.'"

Sam complied with a staccato yap.

"Oh, that's so cute! Now make him say 'Evie Lee Lewis!'"

Carly laughed and teared up again for no reason she could fathom, aching to wrap her arms around the adorable little girl and hang on tight.

"'Please' is all Sam can say," Deana informed as she rejoined them with a tray holding three glasses of lemonade and a plate of cookies.

Sam lost interest in anything but the cookies when Deana set the tray on the coffee table and Evie Lee knelt down on the floor nearby to have a closer look herself.

When she'd chosen a vanilla wafer and taken a sip of her lemonade, the little girl said, "This is just like a tea party." Then, to Carly she said, "Did you ask Deana 'bout French-braiding my hair yet?"

Carly was more in control of herself again and laughed once more at the child she took such delight in. "Not yet," she answered before explaining to Deana. "I told Evie Lee that when I'm gone you might braid her hair for her for special occasions."

"Sure, I'd be happy to," Deana said. "Want me to do it now?"

"Yeah! That would be good 'cuz I'm goin' out to stay at the ranch tonight and then I'll look pretty."

"I'll get a brush and a rubber band," Deana said, heading for the bathroom.

"You're going to spend the night at the ranch?" Carly

asked Evie Lee, then hating herself for being so curious about why Bax would be sending her to the ranch. But she couldn't keep herself from remembering much too vividly what they'd done together the last time Evie Lee had been away on a sleep-over, and that curiosity about what he had planned without her was unbearable.

"I'm goin' to spend a whole while with them. And we're gonna have a barbecue and I can swim in the pool and play with the kittens and everything."

"Your dad must be real busy," Carly fished.

"He's pretty busy, all right."

"Seeing patients and getting into the routine of work, I imagine…." Carly said, subtly inviting Evie Lee to expand on the subject.

"And doin' a lot of stuff at home, too. On the telephone and stuff."

Deana came back with the hairbrush, a rubber band and a hand mirror then. She sat on the chair facing Carly and motioned for Evie Lee to kneel in front of her where the little girl would be in the right position to have her hair combed.

"I was at Miss Effie's some of the time yesterday and today," Evie Lee offered. "We had fun. We went to take walks and she bought me ice cream, but she doesn't know how to do French braids."

"Miss Effie's nice, though," Deana said.

Carly watched as her friend brushed and braided Evie Lee's hair, the two of them chattering away, and her heart hurt at the sight. She'd never felt so left out. So jealous. So much like someone on the outside looking in.

Maybe she really was selfish, the way Jeremy had accused, she thought. Because shouldn't she have been happy for Evie Lee? Deana could braid her hair the way she liked, and Miss Effie could take her for walks and buy her ice cream, and Evie Lee could have sleepovers with the rest of her family at the ranch, and go on having an all-round wonderful time without having any need for Carly.

"There you go," Deana said when she'd finished, holding up the hand mirror for the little girl to see herself.

"Oh, that's pretty! Isn't it pretty, Carly?"

"Beautiful," Carly answered, hating that her voice cracked and that once again those strange tears filled her eyes. "You look beautiful, sweetie."

Evie Lee handed the mirror back to Deana. "I better go now before my dad knows I was here. But can I come back sometime?"

"Anytime," Deana answered. "But I think your dad will know you've been somewhere when you show up at home with a new hairdo."

"Oh."

The quandary on Evie Lee's face was precious, but even so Carly couldn't let her fret for long. "I think it'll be okay if you tell your dad you were here. I was glad to see you."

"And I didn't say nothin' bad, did I?"

"You didn't say anything bad at all. We just had a nice visit."

"Okay." Evie Lee went to the door by way of Sam, where he lay on the floor near the coffee table, petting him and telling him goodbye. Then to Carly and Deana she said, "See ya," and out she went while the two women watched her go.

Only when Evie Lee was outside and the door was

closed behind her did Deana settle back in her seat to stare at Carly.

"All right. I've had it. What's going on with you?" she demanded.

"I don't know what you're talking about."

"Bull! I've been keeping my mouth shut, waiting for you to tell me, but I guess you're never going to unless I pry it out of you. But here you are, nearly crying at the sight of that little girl, and so now I'm prying. I know you didn't just feel cooped up in the cottage. I can see that something happened between you and our new doctor over there and I want to know what it was."

Carly considered holding the line that nothing had happened. But something about seeing Evie Lee had raised too many things to the surface to go on not confiding in her best friend.

So Carly let it all flood out. The whole story. Start to finish. Omitting nothing. And finally letting Deana see just how much of a wreck she was.

When she'd finished, Deana merely shrugged and said, "You love him," as if that summed up everything and there was no doubt whatsoever that it was true.

"I loved Jeremy, too," Carly countered.

"Not the same," Deana insisted. "You may have loved Jeremy, but you weren't *in* love with him. Not the way you are with this guy. I think Jeremy was just the dress rehearsal. But this is the real thing. And you aren't going to be happy leaving the real thing behind, no matter where you go or what you're doing or seeing."

For once there was nothing in Deana's tone that hinted at ulterior motives of her own. Carly knew her friend wasn't saying any of this because she didn't want Carly to leave town. Deana was merely stating the facts as she saw them.

"Jeremy played on your dreams of traveling to get you interested in him," Deana continued. "He made himself sound like the perfect partner, and I think that was the whole basis of your feelings for him—he was more travel companion than life partner. So when you finally figured out that he wasn't going to travel at all, there wasn't much left between you *except* feeling penned in. But from what you've said about Bax, from what I've seen when you're with him and what I saw today with Evie Lee, I'd say there's a lot more going on there. And you'd better think about it, Carly. Before you go running off. Unless I'm mistaken, I'd also say that even Elk Creek looks different to you with him around and you'll be making the biggest mistake of your life if you leave him and us behind now."

Okay, so that last might have been somewhat on Deana's own behalf, but it didn't lessen the merit in what she'd said.

Before Carly could respond to any of it, though, the telephone rang and Deana went to the kitchen to answer it, leaving Carly alone to meditate on her friend's wisdom.

Uppermost in her mind was Deana's view that Carly hadn't been *in* love with Jeremy, that Carly had seen him more as a travel companion than as a life partner.

She'd never thought of it like that before, but as she considered it now, she realized her friend could be right.

Not that it had been intentional or conscious or even something Jeremy hadn't instigated and participated in himself. But yes, she and Jeremy had seemed to click when he'd begun talking about wanting to travel as much as she did. And yes, she'd counted on the two of them traveling together. And yes, only when she'd accepted that that wasn't ever going to happen had she started to resent him and feel penned in.

And no, she hadn't seen Bax in that light because she'd known from the get-go that he wasn't likely to do much traveling.

On the other hand, Bax as a life partner?

Carly could definitely see that.

And it was more appealing than anything she'd ever imagined with Jeremy.

But more than the difference between travel companion and life partner, was Deana right about the difference in how she felt about Bax? Carly asked herself. Had Jeremy only been the dress rehearsal for falling *in* love with Bax?

Carly thought about it. She examined her feelings then and now.

And she had to admit that her friend was right on that score, too. She'd loved Jeremy, but she hadn't been *in* love with him.

And she was *in* love with Bax.

Head over heels, deeply in love with him.

So in love with him that she wanted to be with him in a way she hadn't wanted to be with Jeremy—every minute of every day. Every minute of every night. Forever and ever. For the rest of her life.

So in love with him that she wasn't feeling the same interest, the same preoccupation, the same obsession she'd always felt with traveling, with seeing the world. Because suddenly none of that seemed worth anything if she didn't have Bax.

That realization rocked her to the core.

Never in her life had she felt that way about anyone. Never in her life had there been anyone or anything that had had the power to alter her dreams, her fantasies, of traveling.

Until now.

And now all she could think was that maybe she'd rather stretch out her travel plans to one trip a year with Bax than go anywhere for any amount of time without him.

Than risk losing him.

But what if those once-a-year trips didn't come to be? a little voice in the back of her mind asked. What if she stayed in Elk Creek, married Bax and never stepped foot out of the small town again?

That gave her pause.

And truthfully, she was afraid it would cause some anger, some resentment. Some of the feelings she'd ended up having with Jeremy.

But Bax isn't Jeremy, another voice in her head reminded her.

Jeremy had misled her.

Okay, he'd out-and-out lied to her. He'd *tried* to trap her.

But that wasn't Bax and she knew it. It wasn't something Bax would do. He didn't think her dreams were silly. He'd even agreed that the world was an amazing place and that there was nothing wrong with wanting to see it.

He'd also vowed that they'd have a trip a year, that he'd do whatever it took to accomplish it. And she believed him. She believed that he would work it out because that was the kind of man he was. Because he wasn't selfish the way Jeremy had been when it came right down to it. She'd seen Bax put his daughter first, seen him put his patients first—even before they were technically his patients—and she knew he'd meant it when he'd said he would never let her come second to anything.

Bax wasn't deceitful or manipulative the way Jeremy was, either. And he wasn't stuck in the kind of rut Jeremy had carved out for himself.

No, Bax would do everything he could to keep his promise and she knew it.

And if marrying him meant life here in Elk Creek?

Suddenly that seemed okay, too. Because yes, Deana was right again, and Bax being a part of the town did give it a new dimension for Carly. An added dimension that helped give everything more depth for her.

Not to mention that in his own way, he'd opened her eyes to things about Elk Creek that she'd always taken for granted, that she'd come to overlook— the goodness, the kindness, the thoughtfulness of the people; the closeness and caring they all shared; the strength of community. Things that she knew she'd never find in impersonal big cities.

And where else but Elk Creek could she and Bax spend every day never too far apart? Where else would they have so few distractions from each other? Where else could they raise their kids without ever having them far from sight?

Only in Elk Creek where Carly would be the person who braided Evie Lee's hair and taught her to bake cookies and took her to the park and watched her grow.

Only in Elk Creek where Bax could walk across the

yard to have lunch—and maybe some other afternoon delights—with her.

Those were all things that had never seemed important until Bax and Evie Lee had come into her life. But they were things that held more appeal now than she could resist.

And when images of those things flitted through her mind, they left Carly certain that Deana had been right about one more thing. If she left Bax behind, if she left Evie Lee behind, if she left Elk Creek behind, it *would* be the biggest mistake of her life.

Carly pulled her foot out of the water it was soaking in then, deciding she'd wasted enough time, that she was going to dry off, bandage her ankle, get onto those crutches, hobble-march next door and tell Bax she loved him. That she loved Evie Lee. That she wanted to marry him. To live her life with him in Elk Creek. To see the world one trip at a time with him.

But she only got as far as bandaging her foot before the sound of several voices came from outside just as the doorbell rang again.

"I'll get it," she called to wherever Deana was since her friend hadn't returned from answering the phone.

Carly got up onto her crutches and went to the door, curious about the sounds coming from outside still and wondering if Evie Lee had collected a whole group of friends to bring back with her.

But when Carly opened the front door it wasn't to a bunch of children. It was to a contingent of adults. Her mother, her sister, her brother-in-law, her aunts, Miss Effie and Miss Lurlene and Mrs. Gordon and Mr. Elton, some of the Hellers and the Culhanes and a slew of other family and friends.

"Is this a lynch mob?" Carly joked, uncertain what was going on.

Then Deana came from somewhere else in the house, carrying Carly's packed bags just as Carly's brother-in-law and one of her cousins swept her up into a chair made of their clasped hands and deposited her in a wheelbarrow.

"The train's waiting and you're finally getting out of here!" Hope announced.

"Oh, no, I can't—"

"People more handicapped than you travel. You're doing fine enough on your crutches to get around and we're making sure no more of your trips get canceled," her mother added.

"No, you don't understand," Carly tried again.

But to no avail.

The men took her suitcases from Deana and Deana picked up the crutches that had fallen when Carly had been relocated to the wheelbarrow. All of a sudden everyone was in motion—including her—as the lot of them headed for Center Street, everyone talking at once about sending postcards and Paris and missing her and not worrying about anything and on and on as Carly kept trying to tell them to stop.

The thought of all her friends and family getting together to whisk her away to the train station so she could finally have her dream was so sweet and funny and kind and thoughtful that it only made her want to stay in Elk Creek all the more. But no one was listening to her protests. Not even Deana who'd been instrumental in convincing her to choose Bax over leaving.

Instead they wheeled her down Center Street, gaining more and more people who cheered her on and only made the noise more impossible to be heard over, forming an impromptu parade past Kansas Heller's general store, past Margie Wilson's café, past all the other shops and businesses, past Linc Heller's Buckin' Bronco honky-tonk, all the way to the train station....

Where Bax McDermot was leaning against one of the posts that held up the roof over the platform beside the old-fashioned yellow-and-white station house.

His arms were crossed over his chest. His weight was all on one hip. And he was smiling a Cheshire cat smile as Carly was pulled from the wheelbarrow to be carried up the platform steps to him.

"Bax?" she said almost as if she didn't recognize him.

"I told you I'd do what I had to do to get you on your trips. And I'm provin' it," he shouted over the din.

"But—"

"But nothin'."

"You don't understand," she said over the cheers as he pushed off the pole and picked her up into his arms.

"You'll have all the time you need later on to say whatever it is you want to say," he told her, carrying her to the three-car train waiting on the tracks behind them. "Now wave to everybody and tell them goodbye," he instructed.

"No! I don't want to go without you!" she said instead, panicking at the thought.

Bax just laughed. "Good thing...because you aren't. Now wave and say goodbye," he repeated.

Still unsure of what was happening, Carly did as she was told, waving over his shoulder as he climbed the stairs to a passenger car.

And then they were in a private compartment, away from some of the commotion still going on outside.

Bax set her on the double bed pulled down from a side wall of the compartment and stepped back, hands on his hips, staring down at her.

"Say you'll marry me," he commanded. "That we can have the honeymoon first and the wedding as soon as we get back."

Carly laughed, hardly believing what she was hearing. "It's a little unconventional, but yes, I'll marry you after we have our honeymoon. I was going to tell you that anyway—"

He cut off her words with a hand raised palm-outward, stepped from the compartment to the entrance steps again and called, "It's okay, she said yes. The wedding's on for when we get home."

Another cheer went up from the crowd, making Carly laugh once more even as tears of joy filled her eyes.

But she'd blinked them away by the time Bax returned to close and lock the compartment door behind him and fall against it as if blocking any escape.

"Now, what was it you were tryin' to say?" he asked as the first turns of the train's wheels set them into motion.

"I was trying to say that I love you and I'd made up my mind to marry you and stay in Elk Creek— except for those once-a-year trips you promised me. You didn't have to prove you were good to your word. I believed you."

"Not before you didn't."

"Let's just say it took a little thinking out to get me there."

Bax pushed off the door and came to stand in front of her. He pulled her to her feet while still bearing most of her weight so she could balance on her good foot, holding her braced with his arms around her waist.

"Are you tellin' me I did all this for nothin'?"

She laughed once more. "Basically. But it was pretty impressive."

"Damn right it was."

"Where did this train come from, anyway? This isn't the time of day it hits town and this isn't the same train."

"I have connections with the railroad from years of my family moving cattle this way."

"And where are we going?"

"Denver first. Then Paris. We have ten days."

"Ten days that Evie Lee is spending at the ranch," Carly guessed, remembering what the little girl had told her earlier.

"And ten days that a friend of mine is comin' to town to take care of the medical side of things while Tallie and Ry go off on their honeymoon, too. I told you arrangements could always be made." His expression turned more serious then as he looked down into her eyes with those glorious sea-green ones of his. "I love you, Carly. I'll never let you feel penned in or tied down or trapped. And if you ever have even an inkling of any of that, all you have to do is let me know and we'll be on the next train out of town, headed for wherever you want to go."

But standing there in the circle of his arms, Carly couldn't imagine ever feeling anything but as wonderful as she felt at that moment.

"I love you, too," she said. "And even before you had

me kidnapped I'd made up my mind that I wanted to be with you and Evie Lee in Elk Creek. That I didn't want to be anywhere that you weren't with me."

His supple mouth stretched into a slow grin just before he kissed her, a kiss that was soft and warm at first but rapidly turned deeper, branding her as his.

He picked her up into his arms once more, laying her on the bed and coming to lie beside her, kissing her again, this time with a flash flood of passion that Carly was only too eager to answer.

He undressed her and she undressed him, all in a flurry of anxious fingers. Then hands began to explore, to find and stake claim with a new abandon born of the knowledge that they truly did belong to each other.

And as if their first lovemaking had only been the hors d'oeuvre, they feasted this time. Savoring every kiss, every touch, every caress, every inch of naked, aroused flesh until neither of them could wait any longer and Bax slipped inside her to take her to the limits of ecstasy where they clung together as they peaked at once, reaching the pinnacle that stamped and sealed their love, their commitment, and the life they would share.

And then they lay, still entwined, sated and blissful in the blush of lovemaking that Carly knew was really only the beginning of everything for them.

"I love you, Carly," Bax repeated.

"I love you, too."

"Will you marry me and be my wife and be Evie Lee's stepmom and mom to however many other kidlets we have and see the world with me, too?"

Carly smiled against his chest and yet again felt her

eyes grow damp with happy tears. "That has to be the longest proposal in history."

"I wanted to make sure I covered everything. What's your answer—for the record?"

"Yes. My answer is yes, I will marry you and be your wife and Evie Lee's stepmom and mom to however many other kidlets we have and see the world with you."

"Then I can die a happy man."

"But not for sixty years—you promised me sixty years."

"At least," he whispered.

Carly felt him relax and slowly fall asleep as she settled in, comfortably molded to his side, the train bouncing along beneath them.

And somehow she knew in her heart that she would never feel any regrets for this, for changing her plans, for altering her dreams.

Because in Bax's arms was all the world she needed. All the world she would ever need.

And anything else would just be a bonus.

* * * * *

COWBOY'S BABY

Chapter 1

Most of the McDermot family was gathered in the living room when the roar of an airplane flying so low over the house made it impossible for normal voices to be heard. Conversation halted and all eyes turned upward as an excited Matt McDermot said, "That's gotta be Brady. Four o'clock on the dot, just like he said."

Matt's expression showed his pleasure. But the arrival of her brother's old college roommate and best friend had just the opposite effect on Kate McDermot. She felt a wave of pure panic.

"Where are you going?" her brother demanded when she stood suddenly to leave the room.

"I thought I might take a little nap before dinner," she lied.

"Now? Just when Brady's gettin' here? Don't do that. I told him to land in the north field and I'm going out to pick him up right this minute. I'll have him back here before you know it and you'll want to see him, won't you?"

Not really, she was inclined to say. In fact, not at all. Brady Brown happened to be the last person on the face of the earth she wanted to see.

But she couldn't say that, so instead she said, "Sure. But maybe I'll just freshen up first."

Then she made a subtle dash to her suite of rooms, closed the door tightly behind her and leaned against it for added measure.

As if that would help.

But unfortunately it was only a stopgap measure, and she knew it. Eventually she was going to have to face Brady Brown whether she liked it or not.

Her family didn't know how she felt. They didn't know any of what had happened between her and Brady Brown. They didn't know anything about what was going on now.

But plenty *had* happened.

And there was plenty going on now.

To Kate's dismay.

She'd moved to the small Wyoming town of Elk Creek at Christmastime to live on the ranch she and her four brothers had owned since their grandfather had turned it over to them. She'd needed a change of scenery. A change of lifestyle. A change all the way around.

If only she'd made the move and let it go at that.

But after a Christmas during which her brother Matt had become engaged to a woman named Jenn Johnson, who he'd found in a snowstorm on the side of the road, Matt had talked his brothers and sister into a trip to

Las Vegas. He was to meet up with Brady to celebrate their mutual thirtieth birthdays on New Year's Eve.

Kate had been reluctant to go.

Taking off on the spur of the moment, without making plans, to a place like Las Vegas, wasn't something the ultraconservative accountant usually did. But she'd been in a pretty bad funk, and in an effort to lift her spirits all of her brothers had put pressure on her to go.

So, more to humor them than anything else, she'd let herself be persuaded.

Of course, only after she'd arrived in Las Vegas had she realized that Matt had an ulterior motive. He was fixing her up with Brady Brown. And since all four of her brothers were paired off with their wives or soon-to-be wives, it was impossible for Kate and the also solo Brady not to be thrown together as a couple.

Luckily—or maybe not so luckily—Brady had made things easy on her. She was reasonably sure the cowboy crop duster hadn't had any advance warning that he was going to have Matt's sister on his hands, but he'd been great about it. Fun, funny, charming, courtly. Kate had found herself having a surprisingly good time in spite of the impromptu arrangements and being with a man she'd heard of but never met before.

But the truth of it was that she'd had *too* good a time.

New Year's Eve. Two birthdays. A lot of champagne. Being left alone with Brady after everyone else had gone off to celebrate privately in their own rooms. Las Vegas lunacy. And something that had run deeper in Kate. Much, much deeper…

At a time in her life when old feelings of being undesirable, unappealing and unattractive had resurfaced with a vengeance, Brady Brown had made her feel very desirable, very appealing, very attractive.

And the impact of even a false sense of being desirable, appealing and attractive to a jaw-droppingly handsome man who made heads turn when he walked into even the most crowded room was nothing to sneeze at. Especially in addition to way, way too much champagne. It had all gone to her head.

So when passion had erupted between them and Kate had confided her deepest secret to Brady—that she was still a virgin at twenty-nine and was fed up with saving herself for a marriage that never materialized—inebriated reasoning had somehow made it seem like a good idea for him to whisk her off to a wedding chapel at the stroke of midnight where an Elvis impersonator had performed the ceremony that gave permission to relinquish her virginity in a night of abandon that she barely remembered the next morning.

The next morning…

Kate couldn't think about that next morning without cringing.

Married. She'd actually gotten married, she shrieked silently, pushing away from the door and beginning to pace, because thoughts of what she'd gotten herself into left her too agitated to stand still any longer.

The whole thing seemed unreal.

But then, how could a person take a ceremony seriously when it was performed by an Elvis impersonator? Plus, she'd had so much to drink beforehand that everything had had a fuzzy glow to it.

But fuzzy glow or no fuzzy glow, the wedding had been real and the marriage certificate on the hotel room's bureau had proved it.

She hadn't been gracious about it. Which was part of why the memory of that next morning made her cringe. And part of why she didn't want to face Brady again.

She'd behaved pretty abominably. She'd let him know in no uncertain terms that if their marriage was real and legally binding it needed to be unbound. In a hurry.

Brady had agreed. He'd even been nice about it. He'd tried to calm her down. To make her see it in a lighter vein. To infuse a little humor into the situation.

But Kate had been having none of *that*.

It was a horrible, horrible thing they'd done, she'd told him. An incomprehensible, unconscionable thing. A completely irresponsible, foolish, foolhardy, immature, stupid thing. And it needed to be rectified immediately.

Brady had given up his attempts to reason with her or put things into a different perspective. He'd finally just assured her he would take care of it. He'd even conceded to her insistence that they not let Matt or any of her other brothers know what they'd done.

"Just relax. It'll be okay," he'd said. "I'll have the marriage dissolved one way or another."

Those were the last words he'd spoken to her before Kate had slipped out of his hotel room, sneaked back into her own room across the hall and pretended to have the flu for the remaining day of the trip so she didn't have to see Brady again.

And that had been the end of it. At least the end of any time she'd had to spend with him. Or so she'd thought. Until now.

A week ago she'd received a plain, type-written envelope containing a note from him informing her he would have divorce papers for her to sign when he got to the ranch for the visit she hadn't known he was about to make.

And since then she'd learned that seeing him again wasn't her only problem.

The thought of just how complicated things were suddenly deflated Kate. She sat on the edge of her bed and sighed a sigh that was really more of a groan.

For what seemed like the millionth time she asked herself how she could have gotten into this predicament. After all, she was the most careful person she knew. In every way. Careful, cautious, conservative. She never took a wrong step because she never took a step without thinking about it ahead of time. Without analyzing it. Without judging it from all angles first.

She drove a plain, practical sedan. She saved her money. She had a retirement plan. She wore muted colors and high necks and flat-heeled shoes and heavy coats in winter and sunblock in summer. She didn't speak out of turn. She ate in moderation. She exercised. Her whole life had been in order.

Well, it had been until Thanksgiving, anyway, when her longtime fiancé, Dwight, had pulled the rug out from under her by eloping with someone else. But even then she'd still tried to keep her life as neat and tidy as possible. She'd worked hard to keep her devastated emotions under control and undercover. And she'd given long thought to moving to Elk Creek before she'd made her decision to actually do it.

But then in one single night she'd completely blown it. All that order. All that control. All that conservatism and caution. Out the window.

"Shouldn't I have been allowed just one indiscretion

without paying for it like this?" she asked the unseen forces that seemed at work in her life now.

And even if she had to pay for that one night of indiscretion, why did the payment have to be so steep? It just wasn't fair.

"Brady's here!"

Kate heard someone make that announcement in the distance right then, and tension renewed itself and turned into needles prickling along the surface of her skin. So much so that sitting still suddenly became impossible for her.

She lunged to her feet and started pacing the room once more.

Brady's here. Brady's here. Brady's here...

It was a chant in her head, and it made her want to run away. It made her want to just get in her practical sedan and drive off into the March sunset without a word to anyone. Never to return and have to reveal what was really going on with her. To anyone. Certainly not to her family. And certainly not to Brady Brown.

But she couldn't do that and she knew it. She couldn't even stay in her bedroom hiding out from everyone. From him. She was going to have to go out there and look him in the eye again. And pretend she wasn't more confused, more scared, more worried, more muddled than she'd ever been in her life.

Good luck....

"Kate? Are you comin' out? You didn't fall asleep in there, did you?" Matt called through her door.

"I'll be right there," she answered, hoping her brother didn't hear the uncertainty in her voice.

She straightened her posture in hopes that a stiff

spine might lend her courage, and took a look at herself in the mirror on the dresser.

The clothes she had on were okay—jeans and a heavy-gauge mock-turtleneck sweater with a single diamond knit into the front. But her face was so pale.

She pinched the high crests of her cheekbones until they turned color but that didn't help the wide, deer-caught-in-headlights look in her light green eyes.

"Buck up," she ordered her reflection as she ran a brush through her chin-length, riotously curly brown hair pulled back with a headband.

Then she applied a light shade of lipstick and massaged some lotion into her hands and up her arms to her elbows in hopes that that would help alleviate some of the skin-prickling tension that was still attacking her.

"You have to go out there," she told her image in the mirror as she did. "You don't have a choice."

But maybe it wouldn't be so bad, she tried to convince herself, picturing in her mind how the next several hours were likely to play out.

She would slip into the living room and say a simple hello from the sidelines—which was also where she would stay.

Brady would be involved with Matt, catching up, trading stories. He would probably hardly know she was anywhere around. He definitely wouldn't whip out the divorce papers in the middle of her whole family and demand that she sign them on the spot.

They would all have dinner and she'd keep herself as busy in the kitchen as she could so she wouldn't have to spend too much time in the same room with Brady. Then the evening would end and he'd go off to his rooms and she'd go off to hers and that would be that. He probably wouldn't even have a thought about their rash wedding or what had followed it.

And he also wouldn't have the slightest inkling of what she'd found out only four days earlier.

That the consequence of their single night of abandon was that at this very moment she was pregnant with his baby.

Chapter 2

Everyone in the living room was laughing when Kate finally ventured back there. She was only guessing, but she assumed they were laughing at something Brady had said. He could tell a joke as well as any professional comedian, which had made him the life of the party the whole time they'd all been in Las Vegas two months before.

Her family was so caught up in him, in fact, that no one noticed her standing in the arched entry from the foyer, and it gave her a chance to take a look at him.

How could he be more handsome than she remembered?

But he was.

He was as tall as her brothers—at least six foot three. A tower of long legs, narrow hips, flat stomach, wide chest, broad shoulders and big biceps.

There wasn't an ounce of fat on him, but there were muscles galore. Muscles his clothes couldn't hide. Especially since he was wearing jeans tight enough to show off his great thighs, and a long-sleeved knit shirt that hugged his perfectly veed torso like shrink-wrap.

And as if the body wasn't enough to give her heart palpitations, he had a face to die for, too.

He had swarthy good looks. His hair was the color of French roast coffee beans—not quite coal-black but close. He wore it just a touch long and combed it with a hint of a part on the right side, sweeping all of it casually away from his face.

His skin had a natural tan to it, a golden glow that would brown up in the summer but merely gave him the look of robust health and vitality now.

And there were his features to top it all off.

Oh, he was gorgeous!

But not pretty-boy cute. He had a masculine, rugged, almost craggy kind of beauty that said he was born that way and didn't do anything to accentuate it.

His chin was strong and well defined, his lips turned up at the corners as if he were in perpetual good humor. His nose was straight and perfect, his eyebrows slightly full, and his eyes were a pale blue-gray beneath long lashes.

And when he smiled the way he did right then, there were creases that animated his face. Creases that hammocked his chin from dimples in his cheeks, creases that crinkled the corners of those eyes that glimmered with vibrancy, creases that bracketed that lissome mouth full of blindingly white teeth.

It all made for a powerful package. Powerful enough not to help the muddle Kate was already in and making something flutter inside her that had nothing to do with the baby she was carrying and everything to do with that baby's daddy and the pure animal magnetism he exuded.

A magnetism that made her step farther into the room even as another part of her wanted to run in the opposite direction just so she could get things under control.

"There she is!" Matt said from the center of the group when he spotted her. "We thought you'd gotten lost."

She had. For a moment. In the sight of Brady Brown.

But now she struggled to find her way back to some semblance of normalcy so she could play the charade she needed to play to keep her secrets.

"Say hello to Brady," her brother urged.

"Hello, Brady," she parroted, trying to make a joke out of the obvious return of Matt's overt matchmaking attempts.

But there was no joke in that first moment Brady's eyes rested on her.

Her heart started to beat double time, she felt her face flush, and although her skin still felt prickly, it didn't seem to originate in tension anymore but in something entirely different.

"Hi, Kate," Brady said in the lush baritone voice she'd forgotten about. His tone was edged with formality, though. A formality she thought might indicate he was leery of her.

But then why wouldn't he be leery of her after the way she'd treated him New Year's morning?

"Brady was just telling us about being stranded in

a one-runway airport in the middle of nowhere for the past twenty-four hours," Matt said to update Kate.

"Which is why I need a shower before keepin' company with civilized people," Brady added, directing the comment at Kate. "How 'bout you show me where you folks want me to bunk? Let me clean up some?"

Kate's pulse redoubled at the prospect, even as she wondered why he didn't have Matt show him to his rooms.

But she couldn't be rude and deny a guest his request, so she forced a small smile she hoped looked better than it felt and said, "Sure."

Brady poked his chin in the direction of the front door. "My bags are there. Just let me grab 'em, and you can lead the way."

Kate saw Matt nudge her other brother Ry with an elbow and knew Matt was feeling pleased with himself, thinking that he was in the midst of a second chance at getting Kate and Brady together.

If only you knew how much trouble you've caused, Kate thought. But she turned and retraced her steps out of the living room rather than saying anything.

Brady followed behind as Matt called after them. "We thought we'd put 'im in the rooms next to yours, Kate. Junebug got 'em all ready."

Terrific. This just gets better and better.

The house had two wings on either side of the central portion where the living room, dining room and kitchen were lined up. Both wings contained bedroom suites that allowed for privacy no matter how many of the McDermots were in residence.

The suites all had their own bedroom, bathroom and sitting room, complete with fireplaces, wet bars and French doors that allowed entrance from or exit onto the porch that wrapped around the front and sides of the place.

There was also a den and a recreation room, but Kate didn't want to prolong her time with Brady enough to give him the whole tour, so she merely took him down the hall to the right of the entrance. She went past her own door to the one beside it without saying a word, until they'd reached the entrance to the guest room Brady would be using.

"There you go," she said simply, opening the door for him but not stepping inside.

Brady craned his neck just enough to peer through the opening before he tossed in his duffel bag and slid his suitcase after it. Then he turned toward Kate, but his gaze didn't drop to her face until after he'd glanced over her head, as if to be certain they were alone in the hallway.

"I wanted to have a minute with you right away to let you know I'll be discreet about everything," he said then. "In case you were worried that I might blurt out something."

"I wasn't worried. About that," she added under her breath.

A small frown tugged at his dark brows. "Are you okay?"

"Of course. Why wouldn't I be okay? Don't I look okay?" She was too quick to answer and she regretted it.

"You look great," he said as if he meant it. "But you don't look happy to see me."

Which wasn't very hospitable. And he was being

more than polite. There was thoughtfulness in his effort to reassure her he'd be keeping their secret.

Kate took a deep breath and called upon her own manners. "I'm sorry. I didn't mean to be a shrew. This whole thing is just—"

"Weird. Uncomfortable. Embarrassing. I know. It is for me, too."

It was odd, but knowing that, knowing he not only understood how she felt but was feeling the same things—well some of the same things, anyway— helped. It was comforting. Like having a comrade in arms.

"What do you say we start over?" he suggested then. "Wipe the slate clean of Las Vegas and of everything up to this minute and pretend we've just met?"

Oh, if only it were that easy.

But nothing was made any easier by her being contrary or nasty so what was the point? Especially when there was so much more they were going to have to deal with than he knew yet.

She held out her hand to him. "Hi. I'm Kate McDermot. Matt's sister. Happy to meet you."

Brady chuckled a little and accepted her hand to shake.

Not the best idea in the world.

Because only when that big callused mitt closed around hers did she recall what truly wonderful hands he had. Strong, adept, powerful, commanding. And with a touch that felt like kid leather. A touch she suddenly remembered feeling on other parts of her body and liking much too much.

"Friends?" he said then, still holding her hand and apparently having no idea what it was doing to her.

"Friends," she confirmed through a constricted throat.

Then he let go, and Kate told herself to breathe again, to act normal, to ignore the fact that that one touch had made her blood run faster in her veins.

"You wanted to shower," she reminded, since he was still just standing there, still giving her the once-over.

"Right."

"There should be towels in the cupboard in your bathroom and fresh soap in the dish. The wet bar is probably stocked—feel free to help yourself. If you need anything else just holler."

"Thanks. I'm sure I'll be fine."

"Then I guess I'll just see you at dinner. With everyone else," she said, wondering if her cheeriness sounded as false to him as it did to her.

She finally managed to take a few steps backward, and as she did he said, "It's good to see you again, Kate."

"You, too," she answered mechanically.

Then she gave him a little wave and hightailed it back to her own rooms where she again closed herself in and leaned against the door.

Only this time she needed to wait for everything Brady Brown had put into motion inside her to settle down—her pulse, the blood racing through her veins, the prickles on her skin, the warmth where his hand had held hers....

This wouldn't do, she told herself firmly. It just wouldn't do to be susceptible to the man. She had to keep a level head and view this situation from a practical standpoint. She'd veered off the straight and narrow with Brady once, and look at how much trouble she'd gotten into. She wasn't going to let it happen again. Regardless of how great looking he was or how charming or how nice or how sexy.

No sir. Not her. Never again.

Not if it was the last thing she ever did.

But as she pushed away from the door with the strength of her determination not to let Brady have any effect on her, she realized that even if it wasn't the last thing she ever did, it just might be the most difficult.

Brady unpacked a few things, shucked the clothes he'd been wearing too long now and headed for the shower.

Matt had a nice place here, he thought as he went from the bedroom that was as big as a studio apartment into a bathroom luxurious enough to have been in a four-star hotel.

Yep, a nice place all right. A nice place filled with nice people.

So far it seemed as though his friend's idea that he check out Elk Creek for some property to invest in was a good one. Which was part of why he was there—to see the spreads Matt had called him about.

And none too soon.

Matt had told him that three different ranches were either up for sale or had owners who were making noises about selling, just when Brady had been looking for an excuse to get up here. Just when he'd been looking for something that he could use as a cover for his other reason for coming.

He needed to have Kate McDermot sign the divorce papers that would dissolve their marriage.

Their *marriage*. It shouldn't be called that. It

wasn't a marriage, after all. At least not in any way that counted.

What it was was the most insane thing he'd ever done in his life.

He still couldn't believe he'd actually *married* her.

But then, he'd been in a crazy state of mind, he recalled as he stepped into the steamy spray of the shower.

Of course, he hadn't realized he'd been in a crazy state of mind at the time. In fact, he'd thought he was over the craziness that had struck after his breakup with Claudia. After all, they hadn't been married. They'd only been living together. And not for long. Sure, he'd known his pride was still bruised from her walking out on him, but he'd really thought he'd gotten past everything else.

And even the bruised pride had felt on the mend the longer he'd been with Kate in Vegas.

That had come as a surprise to him. But then, having a good time with her had come as a surprise to him, too.

Brady had known within fifteen minutes of meeting up with Matt and his family that his old college roommate had a fix-up up his sleeve. To tell the truth, Brady had been initially PO'd about it. A fix-up with his best friend's sister? That was just asking for trouble as far as Brady was concerned. It was a no-win situation.

Then he'd met Kate.

He'd liked everything about her on sight. She was more beautiful than she seemed to realize, with that buttermilk skin and those huge eyes the color of kiwi fruit.

Her mouth was lush, and she had high cheekbones

any supermodel would envy, plus curly hair that danced around a face as perfect as a Greek goddess.

And then there was that compact body with those great breasts that were just the right size....

Oh, yeah, one look at her and he'd gone from PO'd to thinking it might not be so bad to spend some time with her. As long as he kept everything light and friendly and aboveboard. What harm could it do to escort her here and there? he'd asked himself. And the answer he'd come up with was: no harm at all. A few days of enjoying her company and making Matt happy, then they'd go their separate ways.

For a while he'd thought he was pulling that off, too. He'd just been having fun, looking forward to meeting Kate at breakfast every morning and filling the rest of the day and evening with gambling or sight-seeing or shopping or taking in a show together.

Then little things had begun to strike him.

Like how sweet she could be. How nice. Like how much more fun he had when he was with her than when he wasn't. Like the fact that she had the most terrific laugh that came out sounding like wind chimes and turned her from terrific looking to stunning and made a sparkle come into her eyes that could light up a whole room.

And then it was New Year's Eve.

His and Matt's birthdays.

And there he'd been, with his best friend and his best friend's family, with Kate, having one of the best times he'd ever had. Which had included a record number of toasts with plenty of champagne—not his drink of choice but it had been poured like water that night.

And the result of everything put together was that he'd gotten carried away.

Okay, so taking Matt's sister to a wedding chapel and marrying her on the spur of the moment probably qualified as more than just getting carried away.

But that's where the insanity part had kicked in again.

By then he'd been aware that he was attracted to Kate. But maybe not how much. And if she'd been another woman he would have just tried coaxing her into spending the night with him.

But she hadn't been another woman. She was Kate. Sweet Kate. Matt's little sister. And a virgin.

Brady still didn't know how she'd arrived at twenty-nine years old with her virginity intact. Or why. But when she'd confided in him that she was a virgin, he'd known he couldn't just make love to her because they'd both been so inclined. There had to be more to it than that. It had to be special. It had to be ceremonious.

And what had his liquor-soaked brain come up with?

Marriage. They should get married....

Brady stood under the pelting spray of the showerhead and let it beat down on his face as if it might wash away the stupidity in that reasoning from two months ago.

But it didn't help. What else but *stupid* could you call marrying your best friend's virgin sister and then taking her to bed?

Monumentally stupid.

Especially when that sister woke up the next morning feeling about it the way Kate had.

What a rude awakening that had been!

Before he'd so much as thought about what they'd

done, she'd been out of bed, frantic and ordering him to rectify it.

Sure he agreed what they'd done had been dumb. But did she have to be so appalled? So outraged? So downright repulsed?

His pride hadn't just taken another strike, it had taken a full body blow—and then a knee to the groin when she'd gone on to let him know she was so horrified by having married him and slept with him, that he had to promise never to tell her brothers.

Of course, telling her brothers was not high on his top-ten list of things to do, either. But again, it wasn't an ego booster to know the extent to which Kate was disgusted by the whole situation.

That was about when he'd decided he wanted to kick himself for having fooled around with her in the first place. For having put his friendship with Matt in jeopardy. For not having seen ahead of time that Kate wasn't anywhere near as attracted to him as he'd been to her.

And rebruised pride or no rebruised pride, Brady hadn't been left with a doubt in his mind that the best thing for everyone was to do exactly what Kate had ordered him to do just before she'd run out of the room as if she couldn't stand to spend another minute with him—dissolve the marriage.

Which was what he had contacted a lawyer for the very next day.

So now, as soon as she signed the papers and they filed them, it would finally be over and they could put it behind them. Once and for all.

Finished with his shower, Brady got out of the stall

and wrapped a towel around his waist. Then he used another towel to clear the mirror to shave.

As he did, he couldn't help wondering if, when he could put this fiasco behind him, he would also be able to get Kate McDermot off his mind.

Because that's where she had been for the past two months. Stubbornly, continuously, vividly on his mind. No matter what he tried to do to dislodge her.

But would some simple paperwork accomplish that? Especially when seeing her again had done what it had done to him?

Even surrounded by her family and at a distance, he'd still felt her presence the very instant she'd walked into the living room. It had been as if the temperature had suddenly risen. As if everything were brighter. As if all the colors around him were more vivid.

And that was before he'd so much as glanced at her.

Then he'd looked up and seen her for the first time since New Year's morning, and he'd been struck all over again by how beautiful she was in that quietly understated way of hers. With those sparkling green eyes and that wildly curly honey-brown hair shot through with streaks of gold, and those tender lips he remembered kissing until they'd grown puffy....

Damn if he hadn't wanted to walk away from the rest of her family and go to her, take her in his arms, kiss her again the way he had that night....

Brady nicked himself with his razor, drawing blood.

"That's what you get for thinking those kinds of things," he told himself as he tore a corner from a tissue and pressed it to the wound.

And why the hell was he thinking about this now? He'd already made one huge mistake with that woman and she'd let him know what she thought of him for it.

So what good did it do to be wallowing in this damn attraction to her?

No good, that's what.

"So shake it off," he ordered.

And that's exactly what he was going to do.

Even though a part of him was itching to do something entirely different. To do a little courting. A little charming. A little wooing…

But that was the stupid, crazy part of him.

Because if there was one thing he'd learned in the past year—and learned the hard way—it was that no amount of tenacity or persistence, no amount of wooing or wining and dining or gift giving, could change a woman's feelings once she'd decided she didn't want him.

And Kate McDermot had made it more than clear the morning after their wedding that she didn't want him. Or anything to do with him.

So he was here to visit Matt, to look at some property, to get the divorce papers signed, and that was it.

And if Kate McDermot could still rock his world just by walking into a room? Too bad.

He wasn't giving in to the attraction. He wasn't letting it put him in any position where he could be dealt another emotional body blow the way Claudia had done.

And if he and Kate had had one incredible night together? Obviously it hadn't been as incredible for her as it had been for him.

So that one night was all they were ever going to

have together. Because he just didn't need any more grief.

And that's all there was to it.

Chapter 3

"Go on in with your company," Junebug Brimley told Kate, making a shooing motion with her hands in the direction of the door that led from the kitchen to the dining room.

Junebug was the McDermots' housekeeper. All six feet, three hundred pounds of her.

"I want to help," Kate informed her, trying to do what she'd decided to do to get through dinner that evening—make herself as scarce as possible by staying in the kitchen.

"Don't need your help," the booming-voiced woman told her bluntly. "Raised a passel of sons who ate like bears comin' out of hibernation at every meal. I think I can put on this dinner without too much strain."

"But we're all here tonight," Kate reminded her.

All being those family members who lived in the big

house built to accommodate them—her twin brothers Ry and Shane, their wives, Tallie and Maya, and Ry's nearly three-year-old son, Andrew, Matt, Jenn and Kate, along with Bax—Elk Creek's doctor who lived in town—and his wife Carly and his going-on-seven-year-old daughter, Evie Lee, plus Brady.

"All or not, I can do it myself," Junebug said, holding firm. "You're missin' time with Matt's friend in there."

"That's just it—he's Matt's friend. Not mine. I don't have anything to say to him."

"I heard the two of you liked each other fine in Las Vegas," Junebug said slyly.

"He's a nice enough man. But that was then, and this is now, and he's here to visit Matt, not me."

Junebug eyed Kate as if she could see right through her. "He's a handsome cuss. And single, same as you. Maybe you ought to try thinkin' of somethin' to say to 'im."

"I'd rather not."

"Could be you could get a little romance goin'."

"I'm not in the market for a romance. If I was, I might go after one of those six handsome cuss, single sons of yours," Kate countered, teasing the gruff older woman.

"Which one would you like? I'm tryin' my best to get 'em married off but they're too mule-headed for their own good."

Kate laughed in spite of having her bluff called. "I don't want one of your sons, either, Junebug. I'm not interested in fooling with any man right now."

"Should be."

"Well I'm not. And Matt's as bad as you are about

Brady—he's trying to throw me together with him by hook or by crook. So do me a favor and put me to work in here."

Junebug looked her up and down, as if debating about granting Kate's wish.

Then she went to the swinging door that connected the dining room and said, "Would somebody get Kate outta my kitchen so's I can do some dishin' out of this food without her underfoot?"

"Thanks," Kate said under her breath.

Junebug grinned. "Two by two—that's how we're meant to walk this earth."

Kate just rolled her eyes at the woman as demands for her to go into the dining room were voiced in answer to Junebug's request.

So, with no other choice, that was what Kate had to do.

Rather than serving appetizers buffet-style Junebug had had everyone take their seats at the dining table. But the only place setting that wasn't already occupied when Kate joined her family was the one directly across from Brady.

She would have preferred being situated farther away from him and without much of a view of the houseguest, but as it was she had to take the sole remaining spot.

The McDermot family was once more laughing at something Brady had said as they passed hors d'oeuvres of bruschetta, cherry peppers stuffed with proscuitto and cream cheese, and blue-cheese torta served on crackers. Kate didn't attempt to join in the fun but merely slipped into her seat, wondering as she did if she'd been manipulated once more by Matt, or if all her brothers, sisters-in-law and Matt's fiancée were conspiring against her.

"Brady's been in Alaska since we saw him in Vegas," Matt updated Kate then.

"Ah," she said, unsure what else she was suppose to contribute to that.

But Shane saved her the trouble by asking if Brady had done any hunting or fishing while he was there.

As Brady talked about his adventures, Kate couldn't help checking him out.

He'd obviously taken that shower he'd been headed for. He looked refreshed, and she could smell the spicy scent of cologne or soap or whatever it was he'd used. She only wished she didn't like it so much.

He had changed into a less-worn pair of jeans and a crisp white dress shirt with the sleeves rolled to midforearms and the top button unfastened. It wasn't unusual attire by any means, but what those slight exposures let her see made her all too aware of more details about him than she wanted to be aware of. His thick, straight neck, for instance, and the wholly masculine hollow of his throat. Powerful-looking forearms and wrists that were unaccountably sexy. Not to mention big, blunt-fingered, capable hands.

He'd washed his hair, too, and recombed it, along with shaving away the shadow of a day's growth of beard so that his raffishly handsome face was free of anything that could hide its glory. And even the way his razor-sharp jaw flexed when he chewed somehow tweaked a sensual nerve inside her.

Why hadn't Junebug let her stay in the kitchen? Kate lamented to herself as she fought not to look at Brady, not to be so impressed by him.

But there she was, with nowhere to run and a mysterious disability that left her unable not to study his every movement, unable not to hang on his every word as he told stories about Alaskan winter days when light only dawned for a few brief minutes.

Alaskan winter days that left Kate thinking about endless hours of darkness that someone else might have shared with him....

She was grateful when Junebug finally served dinner and allowed her a distraction from that thought. And the odd bit of something that felt like jealousy that came with it.

The older woman had made Caesar salad, a crown rib roast, braised potatoes and carrots and home-baked rolls. Ordinarily Junebug either prepared dinner in advance and left it to be reheated when the McDermots were ready to eat, or left the cooking for someone else to do so she could go home to her own family. But on special occasions she catered and served the whole meal.

Tonight was one of those nights. So not until all the food was on the table did she inform them that dessert was ready and waiting in the kitchen whenever they wanted it and that she was leaving them to their own devices.

As everyone bade her a nice evening and dug into her delicious fare, Matt said, "I have it set up for you to take a look at those three spreads tomorrow, Brady. Ted Barton's ranch next door is probably the best of the lot but he hasn't made a firm decision to sell yet. The other two have been on the market for a couple of months. The houses on them aren't in as good shape as the Barton place. 'Course I know you care more about the land and the barn than where you'll be livin', but still."

Kate stopped cold and paid closer attention to what was being said as her other brothers chimed in with information on land that was for sale around Elk Creek.

Was she understanding this correctly? Was Brady buying property? *Here?* Was he *moving* here?

It was news to Kate. And not good news. She'd thought that after getting through this visit he would go back to Oklahoma. It had never occurred to her that he might be in Elk Creek permanently.

Suddenly she could feel the blood drain from her face and a cold clamminess settle over her.

"You want to buy a ranch *here?*" she heard herself blurt out with no small amount of alarm.

For the first time since she'd sat at the table, Brady leveled blue-gray eyes on her. "Thinkin' about it," he answered simply enough.

Her brothers continued filling him in on the pros and cons of each property and what might or might not be factors in the sale prices as they all ate. But Kate couldn't seem to swallow so much as a morsel of food from that moment on. She just kept thinking, He could be here to stay. He could be here to stay....

Most of the rest of the evening was pretty much a blur to her after that. She pushed the food around her plate and pretended to be interested in what was being said at the table. She even managed a remark or two when she'd been silent for longer than she should have been.

But the truth was, she heard almost nothing as the idea of Brady ending up as her next-door neighbor tormented her.

And when she could finally excuse herself without raising eyebrows, she stood to do just that.

Only, before she actually got to say her good-nights, Matt said, "By the way, Kate, we're all tied up tomorrow, so I thought maybe you could show Brady those properties he needs to see."

"Me?" Kate said, the alarm again in her tone.

"You know your way around well enough now. None of the places are hard to find. It'll give you somethin' to do."

"Who says I need something to do?" Kate said lamely and much too quickly, sounding like a put-upon younger sister who didn't appreciate her big brother taking liberties with her time.

"What do you have to do?" Matt challenged.

For the life of her, Kate couldn't think of anything except that she wanted to strangle her brother.

Then Brady piped up. "It's all right. Just draw me a map. I'm sure I can find the places myself."

It was clear that Brady had noticed she didn't want to play tour guide, and Kate not only knew she was being rude again, but she could feel the tension in the room because of it.

Yet Matt still wouldn't let her off the hook. "Kate doesn't have anything planned she can't rearrange. Do you?"

All eyes were on her, and she knew her next words would set the tone for the rest of Brady's visit. If she refused, everyone would be aware of just how much she didn't want to be around him. They would all want to know why—especially since she and Brady had seemed to hit it off so well in Las Vegas. And her entire family would be embarrassed by her behavior and feel awkward whenever everyone was together.

But if she didn't refuse she was going to end up spending the whole next day with Brady. Alone with Brady. And all the unsettling things merely being around him did to her.

Maybe strangling Matt wasn't harsh enough punishment.

Kate took a breath and opted for keeping the peace and maintaining appearances. "Sure I can rearrange things. No problem. I'd be happy to show you around," she said without enthusiasm.

"Great," Brady answered much the same way.

With nothing more to be said, Kate finally told everyone good-night and went to her rooms, thinking of ways to get even with her brother as she did.

That was still what she was thinking about an hour later when a soft tap sounded on her door.

"If this is you, Matt, you're dead meat," she muttered to herself.

She'd undressed by then, and before answering the knock she pulled on a navy-blue velvet robe over the supersize T-shirt she was wearing to bed. But she didn't fasten it, because she assumed her late-night visitor was her brother and he'd seen her in her sleepwear innumerable times before. He'd probably come to gloat about his victory or chastise her for not being more warm and friendly to Brady, she thought, letting the robe hang open to her ankles and padding in bare feet to fling open her door.

But it wasn't Matt standing in the hall outside. Or any of her other brothers, either. It was Brady.

"Oh!" she exclaimed, fumbling instantly with the open sides of her bathrobe to pull them around her.

But not before Brady's gaze dropped enough to take in the Wyoming Women are Wild, Wicked and Willing printed across the front of her shirt—a gag Christmas gift from Matt that caused just the corners of Brady's mouth to tilt upward.

Kate yanked the tie belt around her waist and tied it to make sure she was wrapped up good and tight.

"I'm sorry to bother you," Brady said in a hushed voice, obviously to keep his impromptu visit clandestine. He raised his chin, pointing in the direction of the room behind her. "Can I come in?"

She wanted to say no and avoid more of what it was doing to her to merely think about having him in her rooms, alone, this late at night, wearing nothing but a T-shirt and a bathrobe.

But he had a manila envelope in one hand and enough of an air of formality about him to let her know he was only there on business.

Business she needed to attend to.

So Kate stepped back and motioned him into the sitting room.

He didn't hesitate to come in, but he did take a quick glance up and down the hall a split second before. And he made sure to close the door behind him as soon as he could. Very quietly.

That spicy scent that had caught her attention at dinner wafted in after him, and Kate had the urge to close her eyes and take a few deep breaths. But she resisted. She also tried not to notice how Brady seemed to fill the room just by his presence in it, tried not to

feel the warm rush of something that seemed dangerously like excitement.

But trying and succeeding were two different things.

Brady held up the manila envelope. "Divorce papers. As promised," he said, as if he'd brought a trea-
sure map they'd both been searching for.

It didn't feel good to her, though, and Kate didn't
know why.

"I wanted to go over them with you," he continued. "To make sure you know what's in them. Not that
they're complicated, but just to make sure we're clear
on everything."

"Okay," she said, hearing the clipped tone of her
voice and resolving to amend it. The divorce had been
at her insistence, she reminded herself. It was what she
wanted. It was the logical thing to do.

And the baby? a little voice in the back of her mind
asked.

But she didn't know yet how she was going to handle
letting Brady know about the baby, and she certainly
wasn't inclined to blurt out the news to him right then.

"Why don't you sit down?" she invited primly, nodding toward the sofa, two overstuffed chairs and the
coffee table that were positioned to face the fireplace
and the French doors on the outside wall.

"Thanks."

He crossed the room in long strides of massive legs
she had no doubt could control a stallion with nothing
but their pressure.

But the fact that he went ahead of her to the couch
left Kate with a view of his backside, too. A view she
couldn't resist taking in. A view of broad shoulders

and a straight back that narrowed to his waist and to a rear end that made her mouth go dry.

She might have been a virgin until two months ago but that didn't mean she hadn't done her fair share of looking at men's physiques—especially their derrieres. And Brady's was the best she'd ever seen.

Only when he sat down and deprived her of the sight did she realize she'd been ogling him and cut it short to follow him to the sitting area of the room.

He was at one end of the sofa, so she sat in the chair that was at a forty-five-degree angle to it, grateful that she wouldn't have to sit beside him to see the papers he was setting out on the coffee table. But even from there she caught a whiff of the clean, spicy scent of him, and it went right to her head.

Maybe it was the pregnancy, she told herself. She'd noticed that her sense of smell was heightened, so maybe it wasn't so much that he *really* smelled wonderful, but that she merely had some kind of illusion that he did.

Except that it didn't seem like an illusion. It seemed as if he just plain smelled terrific.

"This is pretty straightforward," he said then, flipping through the pages as he spoke. "A simple dissolution of marriage. Basically what's on all these pages amounts to declarations that we have no joint property or assets to split up, no mutual residence for one of us to keep and the other to move out of, no children so no custody or visitation issues."

Kate's mouth went dry, and she didn't hear the rest of what he was saying.

No children so no custody or visitation issues…

Somehow it hadn't occurred to her that the baby she

was carrying should be included in the divorce papers. Custody and visitation? Those were things she hadn't even thought about.

Of course, she hadn't really thought about much of anything in terms of Brady and the baby. She hadn't had time to think about it. In the four days since she'd had her pregnancy confirmed, she hadn't thought about much of anything except the fact that she actually was pregnant.

It had come as such a shock. The first period she'd missed hadn't even made her curious. Her cycles had always been irregular and it wasn't unusual for her to skip a period, so she hadn't thought a thing about it. It was only when she realized she'd missed a second one that she'd put two and two together.

And in those four days since she'd taken the home pregnancy test and then gone in to see a doctor in Cheyenne to have it verified, she'd mainly been walking around in a daze. About the only thing she'd actually thought through was that she wanted the baby. But beyond that, well, she was still just trying to come to grips with everything.

"Don't sign anything," Brady was saying, the first words to penetrate her thoughts since child custody and visitation. But "Don't sign anything" seemed to come as a reprieve, so maybe that's why it got through to her.

"Read it all when you have a chance," he advised, "that way you'll know what's there. Then it has to be signed in front of a notary. When we've done that, I'll send it back to the lawyer and he'll file it with the courts."

"A notary," Kate repeated to prove she was listening and to cover up that she hadn't been before.

"It's all just a formality, but we have to do it right for it to be legal."

"But Elk Creek is a small town. If we get a notary here word is bound to leak, and this won't be only between you and me anymore."

"We'll work something out. Maybe we'll trump up an excuse to fly into the nearest town and do it there in a day or so."

That seemed like a reasonable solution. And with Matt in matchmaker mode, her brother would likely not question any time she and Brady shared.

"And that's about it," Brady concluded, tapping the edges of the pages on the coffee table to make sure they were all even before he laid them on top of the envelope. "I'm sorry it took so long for me to get here with this. But my buddy in Alaska had an accident that put him in the hospital, and if I hadn't gone up there and flown for him until he was back on his feet, he would have lost his charter company."

"It's okay," Kate assured. "I thought it would take some time."

The mention of Alaska brought a return of that strange twinge of jealousy she'd felt earlier. And that strange twinge of jealousy compelled her to say, "So Alaska, huh? You talked at dinner about all you did there, but I imagine you met a lot of interesting people, too."

"Sure. I met a lot of interesting people. It's an interesting place."

"Anyone…special?"

She didn't have the courage to look straight at him when she asked that, so she pretended to restraighten the divorce document before slipping it back into the manila envelope. But out of the corner of her eye she saw Brady smile for the first time since he'd come into the room. A small smile, but a smile she remembered well from Las Vegas. A smile that made a warm rush of something she couldn't pinpoint run through her.

Unless of course the smile was due to a happy thought about another woman....

"Did I meet anyone special?" he repeated.

"You know, like did you run into Eskimos or fur trappers or bear hunters?" she persisted.

"I met a few of all those."

"But not many women, I imagine. I read not long ago that there's still a low ratio of women to men. Is that true?"

"Are you askin' if we should add adultery as grounds for the divorce?" he joked.

"No," she said as if the very thought were outlandish.

"Well, you can relax. I was too busy for romance, and what you read is right, I didn't run into many women. Especially not many available ones. The irreconcilable differences as grounds for the divorce will have to stand."

"That doesn't matter to me. I was really only curious about Alaska's population," she fibbed. Badly.

"Either way."

Despite the fact that he seemed to have seen through her, the news that he hadn't hooked up with another woman in the past two months brightened Kate's spirits considerably. Although she didn't want to think about why it should.

Then he changed the subject. "Seems like you've

managed to keep the whole marriage thing under wraps."

"Nobody knows anything," she confirmed. *And you don't know all you think you do.*

"That's good. Then we'll be able to take care of it without anyone being the wiser."

Oh, if only that were true for the long run....

"And what about you? Are you still mad at me?" he ventured carefully, as if he were afraid he might set off the same reaction he had on New Year's morning.

Kate was embarrassed at the memory of her behavior and decided this was the opportunity she needed to apologize for it. "I know I went a little wacko the next morning. It's just that doing what we did... Well, it was so out of character for me. I'm such a straight arrow...." She wished this were coming out more smoothly, but the awkwardness of the situation was making for a bumpy road. "Anyway, I want you to know that in spite of what I said then, I accept that I'm just as responsible as you are for this whole thing."

"So I'm not the devil incarnate anymore?" Brady asked with a note of wry levity to his voice.

"No. I was out of line that next morning. My memory of New Year's Eve isn't clear but it's clear enough to know that no one twisted my arm. I was all for getting married. And the rest," she added under her breath.

Brady's smile stretched into a grin. "Why am I gettin' the impression that you're blamin' yourself now?"

Maybe because she was. Or at least she had been for the past four days, ever since finding out she was pregnant.

Which also happened to be about the same time she'd begun hearing her mother's voice in her head.

Her mother's voice from her growing-up years when her mother had done a lot of preaching about the girl in any girl-boy relationship being the guardian of the gate.

It wasn't something Kate had thought about in years. But suddenly there it had all been again.

The guardian of the gate.

The guardian of the gate, who wouldn't be in this pickle if only she'd maintained some control, some moderation in the amount of champagne she'd consumed on New Year's Eve. If she hadn't given in to her own baser needs, no matter how strong they'd been. If she'd resisted the temptation of sweet, seductive words, the temptation of the handsome cowboy. If she hadn't allowed herself to be swept away by the desires he'd raised in her....

Maybe Brady read the answer to his question in her expression, because when she didn't say anything he said, "Things are pretty foggy in my memory, too, but as I recall, getting married was my idea. You just thought it was a good one and went along with it. I think that makes the blame pretty much equal."

Kate shrugged, still feeling at fault no matter what he said. But what was the use in arguing about it? "I just wanted you to know I don't bear you the kind of ill will I did that next morning."

Brady chuckled—a deep, rich sound that rolled from his throat. "That was definitely ill will all right. I was grateful there were no knives in the room or you might have gelded me. You made it clear you thought I was a big bad beast."

Kate flinched at the reminder. And the truth in it. "I'm sorry. I was out of line. It isn't what I think of you now." What she thought of him now was that he was too good-looking and charming and charismatic and sexy for her own good.

"But you still weren't too happy to see me today," he said, sounding as if he doubted her claim.

"Were you happy to see me?" she challenged in return.

He didn't answer right away. Instead he stared at her with eyes so intense she could almost feel his gaze. So intense she finally had to look directly at him, too, to see if she could read what he was thinking.

But before she could he let out another of those wry chuckles and said, "I didn't expect to be happy to see you, no."

Did that mean he had been? Because that's what it sounded like. And the possibility that he'd been happy to see her made something inside her dance.

Then he looked away, as if he didn't want her to see what was in his expression. And he changed the subject once more. "Don't feel like you have to go through with showing me around tomorrow. I know Matt railroaded you. He seems to have his matchmaking hat on again. Or is it *still?*"

"You don't want me to show you around?"

"No, it isn't that," he said quickly. "I had a good time checking out Vegas with you. It'd be nice to learn about Elk Creek the same way. It's just that if you'd rather not—"

"No, it's okay," she heard herself say for no reason she understood. Here he was, giving her a break, and rather than take it, she was getting herself in deeper by making it seem as if she *wanted* to be his tour guide.

Maybe it was because memories of what a good time she'd had with him in Nevada had sprung to mind and made the prospect of repeating it appealing to her. So appealing that she'd forgotten for a moment that she was supposed to be steering clear of him.

"You're sure?" he asked.

Too late now even if she wasn't.

So, trying to cover her tracks, she said, "Matt will never let up if he doesn't think he's getting his way."

"Matt," he muttered, as if he'd thought her reasons had been her own. And for a split second he looked disappointed.

But then he seemed to rebound. "You think we should play along with his matchmaking, just to keep him off our backs?"

"It might be our only chance." *Oh, you fraud, you,* a little voice in the back of her mind chastised, when a part of her knew full well that she wasn't merely agreeing to spend time with Brady to appease her brother.

"We'd only be pretending, of course," she said. "And there wouldn't be anything to it but things like letting ourselves be thrown together once or twice. We talked about being friends, and that would really be all we were doing. It's just that Matt wouldn't know it."

"Only pretending," Brady repeated.

But there seemed to be some reservation in his tone, and Kate wasn't sure why.

"Unless you don't want to," she said, reversing course in case he was having second thoughts. "I mean, if you want to just hang out with Matt, we can sit him down and tell him point-blank that what he wants to happen is not going to happen, no matter what he does."

"You think that would help?"

Kate hated that he sounded so hopeful.

"It might."

"Or it might not," Brady pointed out. "But if we go along with a few of his maneuverings—"

"And then tell him we're just going to be friends after that, we'll have something to back it up. We can say we tried but we just didn't click."

"Sounds like a plan," Brady agreed. "And it'll be the perfect cover for getting to a notary with these papers, too."

"True."

"So, tomorrow. Matt wants to give me the tour of this place in the morning. Why don't we shoot for leaving around one in the afternoon? After lunch?"

"Fine."

Had they really just talked themselves into spending part of Brady's visit to Matt with each other instead?

They had. And Kate couldn't believe she'd let it happen. Hadn't she spent nearly every minute since she'd found out Brady was coming thinking of ways to stay away from him?

What had gotten into her?

But Brady stood just then, and she stood with him, hoping that if he left, she could get a handle on what she'd just done.

He didn't leave, though. Instead he was studying her again, as if he wanted to relearn her face.

"You really do look good," he said after a moment.

"You, too." She'd meant that to be a simple volley, but it had come out much more seriously, much more heartfelt, and she had the sense that she'd just exposed something she shouldn't have.

"Tomorrow then," she reminded, hoping he'd take the hint before she gave away anything else.

He didn't respond, though. He just continued star-

ing at her, looking into her eyes now in the same way
he had just before he'd kissed her for the first time in
Las Vegas.

Was he going to kiss her?

Alarms went off in her mind that told her to move
away. To shove him toward the door, if she had to, to
get him out of there.

But that wasn't what she did.

Instead she stayed rooted to the spot, gazing up into
those eyes that were the color of a summer sky before
a storm, her chin tilted, thinking about the way his
lips had felt against hers New Year's Eve—sweet and
gentle and oh, so adept....

But a kiss didn't come.

All of a sudden he broke the hold he'd seemed to
have over her and repeated, "Tomorrow. Afternoon.
To keep Matt happy." Then he headed for the door.

Kate didn't follow. She couldn't have, even if she'd
wanted to, because thinking about him kissing her and
then not being kissed had somehow left her drained. As
if dashed anticipation had sapped her strength.

Brady opened the door, peered out to make sure the
coast was clear and then said, "'Night."

"Good night," she answered, watching him step out
into the hall.

Only after the door closed softly behind him did
Kate feel as if she were breathing freely once more.
But as she found the strength to go into her bedroom,
it occurred to her all over again that she'd just agreed
to precisely what she shouldn't have agreed to—spending time with Brady.

What was there about the man that always had her
doing the wrong thing? Even when she knew just how

wrong it was? How much of a mistake it was? What was it about him that attracted her to him even when she didn't want to be? That had her thinking about kissing him even when she wanted him to leave her alone?

She didn't understand it. Not any of it. But then, there were a lot of things she didn't understand about herself and her actions since meeting Brady. In fact, she'd been more confused than she'd ever been in her life.

Maybe she'd had some kind of breakdown over Dwight and just hadn't known it, she thought, as she got into bed and pulled the covers up to her chin. And then she'd met Brady right after that, and maybe meeting someone in the middle of a breakdown caused a person to do bizarre, out-of-character things. And to go on doing bizarre, out-of-character things.

But she didn't actually think a person could have a breakdown and not know it.

Which left her back where she'd started—with no explanation for why she'd done the things she'd done with Brady on New Year's Eve or why she was doing the things she was doing now.

Right now.

Because even as she hashed through it all in her mind, at that moment there was still a part of her that was actually disappointed he hadn't kissed her.

And if that wasn't confusing, nothing was.

Chapter 4

One of the good things about knowing she was pregnant—if you could call it a good thing—was that Kate finally knew why she'd been waking up nauseous every morning. Without revealing her condition, she'd done some subtle, conversational questioning of Shane's wife, Maya—who had found out she was pregnant at Christmastime—and garnered some help for it. Maya had said she'd had morning sickness early on, and to counteract it she'd kept soda crackers on her nightstand to eat before she'd even raised her head from the pillow each morning.

So that was what Kate had started doing—sneaking soda crackers into her room at night to nibble the minute she woke up.

The next morning, as she lay in bed doing that her thoughts trailed back to the previous evening. To

Brady. And to what to do about him in conjunction with this baby that was making her feel so bad at that moment.

Should she tell Brady she was pregnant now, before the divorce went through? she asked herself. Or later? Or at all?

She really hadn't had time yet to think about whether or not to tell him, but Brady's offhand mention of custody and visitation had made her realize she had to at least consider what she was going to do.

It was tempting not to tell him at all. Ever. To just keep the baby to herself. To have it be her baby and her baby alone.

But in spite of the temptation, she knew that wouldn't be the right thing to do. The baby wasn't hers alone, and she knew Brady had a right to know about it.

But when? Sooner rather than later seemed to be the answer to that. At least it was the answer since he might be moving to Elk Creek. If he ended up living nearby, eventually he would notice. And count back. And know. And she didn't want him finding out that way. That was the coward's way.

But that still didn't mean she had to tell him immediately. Immediately being before the divorce was final.

And waiting until it was final appealed to her. With good reason.

It hadn't been easy for Kate to grow up with four brothers. And not just in terms of bumps and bruises, practical jokes and teasing and horseplay that overlooked the fact that she was a girl at all. Growing up surrounded by men had also given her an insider's view into some other aspects of that gender. Good-looking men had plenty of wild oats to sow and just as many women willing to have a part in sowing them.

She learned how men talked—and thought—about some women and some situations with women. Also, regardless of the fact that they might enjoy the favors of a woman who got drunk and spent the night with them, men didn't think highly of her the morning after.

And if that woman got pregnant? Then they considered the man trapped.

Trapped...

That wasn't only a concept she'd garnered from her brothers, though. She had proof. Kelly McGill—her best friend since kindergarten.

Kelly had gotten together with a friend of Matt's when they were all in high school—Buster Malloy. Kelly and Buster had been madly in love. Inseparable. They'd even been voted the couple most likely to grow old together, and they'd assured everyone that was true.

Then Kelly had gotten pregnant and everything had come apart, even though a quickie marriage followed Kelly's graduation and the end of Buster's first and only year of college.

Maybe the baby wasn't even his, Kate had heard him say to Matt one afternoon when they hadn't known she was in the next room. Matt had discouraged that idea, reminding Buster that Kelly hadn't so much as looked at anyone else.

"Then I'm trapped, is that what you're saying?" Buster had demanded, sounding furious.

Trapped—the same thing Kate's brothers had said about other guys in Buster's predicament. The same thing she'd heard them talking about after Matt's conversation with Buster, agreeing that, yes, Buster was trapped. Stuck. That he had no way out....

The cracker Kate was slowly munching wasn't helping as much as usual because suddenly she felt her bile rise in spite of it.

Or maybe it was what was going through her mind that was churning her stomach. Because she had no doubt that Brady felt the same as her brothers did about things like an inebriated woman he hardly knew spending the night with him.

And getting pregnant.

He would feel trapped. Stuck. And nothing good could come of that. Nothing good had come of it for Kelly, that was for sure.

Kate knew all her friend had gone through since her shotgun wedding to Buster, because Kate had been right there to hold Kelly's hand through the worst of it. Like right after Buster's frequent rants at Kelly for ruining his life. Like when Buster had shirked his responsibilities to Kelly and the twins she'd delivered six months after their wedding and Kate had needed to pay Kelly's rent so she and the twins wouldn't be evicted because Buster had disappeared with their rent money. Like when Buster had announced that he wanted out— that was how he'd put it, as if he were demanding his release from the cage of his marriage to Kelly.

Kate had been there to hold her friend's hand then, too, when Kelly and Buster's relationship had become one battle after another over everything. Poor Kelly had been left not only with two boys to raise and support on her own, but with a broken heart and a whole lot of questions about how Buster could have stopped loving her so suddenly, so completely. How he could have turned into someone Kelly didn't even recognize. How he could have come to hate her.

But the answer had always been the same—Buster had come to all of that because he'd felt forced to marry Kelly since he'd gotten her pregnant. He'd felt trapped and stuck.

And if it wasn't enough for Kate to have seen with her own eyes how bad a situation the unplanned pregnancy had put her friend in, she'd had Kelly on the phone the night before her doctor's appointment reminding her how bad things still were, even ten years later.

Kate fought another overwhelming spell of nausea, wishing even as she did that Kelly hadn't been leaving for a vacation in Mexico the same day Kate had gone to the doctor in Cheyenne. Kate had told her friend she was afraid she might be pregnant but now that she knew for sure, now that she was facing Brady, she craved Kelly's support.

Not that she couldn't guess what her friend would tell her if she could talk to her, Kate thought.

Kelly would say to let the divorce go through before Kate told Brady anything. Kelly would say that just learning about the baby would likely make Brady feel some sort of obligation, but at least if he was already off the hook in the marriage department Kate could make it clear that she didn't need anything from him. That besides being part owner of the ranch she was also opening an accounting and bookkeeping service in town and would make an adequate living at that, so she could afford to support both herself and the child. And, while raising a child alone was a daunting proposition, millions of women did it and she could, too. Kelly was, after all.

"But if I tell him before the divorce is final, he won't believe I mean it," Kate said out loud, as if she were actually talking to Kelly. He would believe she didn't want the divorce at all. That she wanted him to stay married to her.

And he'd most definitely feel trapped.

But Kate was bound and determined that Brady Brown was not going to feel—or be—trapped by her.

No man was going to be married to her because he *had* to be. No man was going to accuse her of the things Buster had accused Kelly of. No man was going to blame her for ruining his life.

The cracker hadn't worked at all and Kate flung the covers aside and made a mad dash to the bathroom where she spent the next twenty minutes being miserable.

When the bout was finally over, she went to the sink, splashed cool water on her face and brushed her teeth.

Being alone in all this was definitely not something she would have chosen for herself. In fact, recalling what Maya had told her about Shane made Kate feel a little jealous. Apparently her brother had waited outside the bathroom door for his wife every time she'd gotten sick, ushered her back to bed and served her fresh crackers when she'd thought she could tolerate them again.

That would be nice. Much nicer than the way things were for Kate—having to suffer through the illness alone, all the while hoping no one realized she was ill at all and why.

And if the person keeping her company, taking care of her, could be Brady?

She chased that notion away, knowing it was dangerous to even entertain such a fantasy. Because in reality, if he knew and if he were there by her side for this, it wouldn't be because he wanted to be, the way Shane had, but because he felt he had to be, the way Buster had. And he would resent her the way Buster had. He'd resent her the way Buster resented Kelly. He would resent the baby the way Buster resented his twins. He'd resent being trapped....

Kate took a few deep breaths in an attempt to fight off another wave of nausea, feeling more convinced by the minute that thinking about Brady this morning was making her more ill than usual.

Or at least the tension of thinking about letting him know about the pregnancy certainly wasn't helping matters. Any more than actually telling him was likely to.

So, no, she was not going to tell him right away. Definitely not before the divorce was over and done with and he was a free man again.

Then, when he knew without a doubt that she wasn't angling for anything from him, when he had proof that she wasn't interested in trapping him into being married to her, then she'd tell him.

The deep breaths—or maybe having come to a decision and found a semblance of a plan—helped stave off another bout of sickness, and Kate was left standing at the sink, staring at herself in the mirror above it.

Not a pretty sight, she knew. Certainly not a sight for a man who didn't love her. Who probably wouldn't even like her if he felt forced to be with her.

So could she pull off keeping this a secret until the time was right? she asked herself.

Looking for an answer, her gaze dropped from her messed-up hair and almost-gray face to check for other signs of what was going on in her body, to be sure there was nothing overt enough to give her away before she was ready for Brady to know.

She pulled down on the T-shirt she'd worn to bed, making it flatten against her, and turned to look at her profile.

Her breasts were bigger, fuller. But that was only an improvement, since she was not normally busty. And there was only the tiniest pooch in her ordinarily flat stomach, which the doctor had told her wasn't really more than the hormones relaxing her muscles in preparation for stretching to accommodate the growth that would take place.

It was still a pooch, though.

She stood up straighter, pulled her shoulders back and let go of the T-shirt to see what happened if she practiced good posture and wasn't molding the shirt to her abdomen.

Invisible, she decided, reassuring herself that no one would notice anything.

Which was good. Because that way she could keep her secret as long as she needed to. Long enough for the divorce papers to be filed and for her to pick and choose when she'd let the world know she was going to be a single mother. A single mother who didn't need any man, let alone one who wasn't with her solely because he wanted to be.

And if, deep down, she recognized a little part of her that wished Brady *did* want to be with her through this?

That was probably just a remnant of Dwight's damage, she told herself. The damage that had left her self-esteem battered, that had left her craving a man like Brady, who found her attractive and desirable. The damage that had gotten her into this mess in the first place.

It didn't have anything to do with Brady himself.

Or his eyes that seemed to sear through her.

Or his big, callused hands she barely remembered the feel of.

Or the lips she'd wanted much too much to kiss last night....

But those weren't thoughts she would let herself have.

Because for one brief period of time she might have sacrificed her dignity to the passion that those eyes and hands and lips had evoked in her.

But that time had passed.

And she'd lost all the dignity she ever intended to lose.

Even if he did smell like heaven and have the power to melt her insides with a smile.

Luckily Kate's date with Brady wasn't until one o'clock that afternoon, because it took nearly until noon for the morning sickness to subside. When it finally did, she showered and dressed in an oversize camel-colored turtleneck sweater and a pair of black slacks.

She swept her curly hair up to her crown and held it there with a halo of tiny butterfly-shaped clips, applied just enough blush to hide the pallor of her skin and a little mascara to darken her eyelashes.

Then she gave herself a firm talking-to about keeping her perspective with Brady, and went out to the kitchen where everyone who was home today was gathered for lunch.

Lunch was a more casual affair than dinner. Brady, Buzz, Ry, Shane, Matt and little Andrew sat around the U-shaped breakfast nook. The men were talking horses, and Andrew was playing with a plastic replica of one while Junebug piled their plates with chili, thick hoagies, potato salad, pickles, olives and carrot sticks no one was touching. Maya, Tallie and Jenn sat on bar stools around the counter island at the opposite end of the kitchen, dining on lighter fare and discussing Buzz's upcoming eightieth birthday bash when Kate joined them.

She tried to be a part of the discussion but in truth she found it difficult to take her eyes off Brady even from that distance.

She wasn't watching him directly, of course. Only peripherally, except for the few occasions when a burst of male laughter or a comment tossed across the span of the kitchen gave her an excuse to look his way. But still, she was very much aware of every detail.

He'd already been seated in the nook when she'd arrived, but she could still see that he was wearing snakeskin cowboy boots and faded blue jeans under the table. Above the table he sported a navy-blue Western shirt beneath a leather vest that looked like an old friend.

He was clean shaven, and his hair was combed but not so neatly that it appeared as if he'd taken pains with it. Instead it seemed as if he might have tended to it after his own shower and since then had run a hand or two through it.

He looked much like her brothers did—cowboys all,

in for the midday meal after half a day's work. But for some reason to Kate, Brady stood out from the crowd.

Maybe it was his darker coloring, she thought as she gingerly ate half a turkey sandwich and tried to figure out why her gaze kept tracking to him like a heat-seeking missile.

Maybe it was the voice that was only slightly lower than her brothers' but seemed to draw her attention every time he spoke despite the fact that he wasn't talking to her.

Or maybe what made him seem so unique was his laugh. A full, booming, uninhibited laugh filled with gusto and a zest for life.

Or maybe it was just some primitive, elemental connection between the two of them because of the baby that secretly joined them.

Whatever the cause, to Kate he seemed head and shoulders above her brothers in every way. He seemed more striking looking. More animated. More appealing. More charming. More masculine. More of everything potent and powerful and irresistible.

More of everything that clouded her thinking and put all her senses into overdrive.

Which was why she shouldn't be spending the afternoon alone with him. But there was no backing out of it now and she knew it would only be a waste of energy to try.

He's just a guy, she told herself, trying to regain that perspective she'd promised herself on the way out of her rooms. Just a guy like a gazillion other guys her brothers had brought around over the years.

And maybe if she could actually convince herself of that, the next few hours would be okay.

Everyone finished eating shortly after one, and the men slid out of the breakfast nook, ready to get back to work.

Buzz shuffled Andrew out of the kitchen for a nap, Ry and Shane kissed their wives and headed for the barn, and that left Matt and Brady to join everyone else at the island counter.

"Why don't you guys take my truck," Matt said then, aiming the suggestion at both Kate and Brady, and obviously referring to their imminent departure to check out the properties.

"We can use my car," Kate countered in an attempt to maintain as much control as she could—in outward things, even if she wasn't having much success with the inward.

"Brady'll be as uncomfortable in that little go-cart of yours as we all are when we have to ride in it," Matt argued. "I don't need the truck today, so take it." Then, as if that settled it, he pulled a full key ring out of his pocket and held it up like a bone for a dog. "Who's driving?"

Kate snatched the keys before Brady had a chance. "Me. I'm the one who knows where we're going, remember?"

"Not until I tell you, you don't," Matt reminded. But then he went on to explain which ranches were up for sale and how best to get to them.

"You sure you don't mind her drivin'?" Matt asked Brady when he'd finished.

Brady looked at her as if he sensed her need for feeling in command and didn't mind conceding to it. "Nah. No big deal," he answered without taking his blue-gray gaze off Kate.

"You better get goin', then," her brother urged. "You have a lot of ground to cover for one afternoon."

And with that Kate had no choice but to slip off her bar stool and lead the way out to Matt's truck where it was parked in front of the house.

She made sure of one thing, though. She climbed in behind the steering wheel before Brady could open the door for her or give her a hand up or do anything that might put her in closer proximity to him than she needed to be.

He was there to close her door once she'd gotten in, but she only called a curt "Thanks" through the rolled-up window. Then she concentrated on starting the engine, trying not to watch him in the rearview mirror as he rounded the vehicle from behind.

Of course, nothing was aided by his joining her in the cab and bringing with him that spicy scent she liked so well, but what could she do about that? She just tried not to let herself think about it.

"You can drive a rig like this?" Brady asked without preamble, referring to the big pickup truck with dual rear wheels that Matt had bought himself only the month before.

"I grew up on a ranch, remember? I was driving trucks and tractors when I was twelve," she assured him.

He was sitting at an angle, facing her, with one thigh resting sideways on the seat so his ankle could be propped on his other knee. He also had a long arm slung across the top of the seat back, his hand near her nape—something else she didn't want to be so aware of.

As a matter of fact Kate wished he wasn't positioned

the way he was at all. It made his attention so directly focused on her that it seemed as if the heat of his eyes was a tangible thing.

But what could she do? She couldn't tell him to face front and stop studying her. At least, she couldn't say that without sounding ridiculous. So instead she just had to add one more thing to the list of what she was working to ignore.

"The Barton place is the closest," she said as she pulled away from the curb and headed for the main road. "Do you want to start there and work our way out, or start at the farthest and work our way back?"

"Let's hit the Bartons' first."

That would have been her choice, just so they wouldn't be in that truck for too long with him sitting the way he was. Maybe when they got in it again he'd sit straight in the seat and quit giving her the once-over.

"Beautiful day," she commented, hoping he might change position to look out at the countryside bathed in warm sunshine. March had definitely come in like a lamb with five consecutive sixty-degree days.

But Brady didn't budge. He just muttered, "Beautiful," without so much as glancing out the window.

Then he said, "Tell me about the Bartons."

Gladly, Kate thought, eager for something to distract her, even if she couldn't seem to distract him.

"Mr. and Mrs. Barton are both nearly seventy," she began. "Their land used to be part of our ranch, but about a year after Buzz bought it he decided he needed an influx of cash for livestock and to build the house, so he sold off several parcels to Ted Barton. My brothers have talked about buying it back if Mr. Barton ever decided to sell. Matt must want you around pretty badly to have talked everybody into letting you have first stab at the place."

"County needs a crop duster," Brady said as if it were the reason Matt had given him.

That was all the time it took to reach the Barton's small white farmhouse, and Kate pulled to a stop in front of it. But as she turned off the engine she continued to tell him about her neighbors. "They have one son who's a stockbroker on Wall Street. He isn't interested in taking over the place but they wish he was, so that's why it isn't formally up for sale. They can't run it anymore, it's more of a drain on them financially than anything else, and the son is urging them to sell. He even has a condominium all ready for them to move into if they'd just do it. But they haven't completely made up their minds. So don't be surprised if they seem a little reluctant."

"Good to know."

Brady got out of the truck and so did Kate, again in enough of a hurry to preclude him from coming around to open her door. But he didn't go up to the house until she had rounded the pickup and could go ahead of him.

As she did, Kate had the distinct sensation that he was taking a better look at her from behind than at the house he could be buying. She cast a glance back at him to see if she was just imagining things and caught him with his gaze on her rear end.

Knowing he'd been found out, he raised his eyes, but his expression didn't show any contrition. Instead he smiled a lopsided, mischievous smile.

"You're in pretty fine shape today," he said as if his open scrutiny of her had been her own fault for looking the way she did.

Mr. Barton came to the door, apparently having seen them coming. But before Brady acknowledged their host he shot Kate a wicked wink that caused her cheeks to heat. Only then did he turn his attention to the elderly gentleman as Mr. Barton invited them inside.

Kate spent the next hour and a half having tea with Mrs. Barton while Mr. Barton showed Brady around the house and then took him out to the barn. Mrs. Barton was a lovely older woman who kept up a lively chatter, but Kate had trouble following the conversation because her mind—and eyes—kept wandering to Brady whenever he came into sight through the plate glass window beside the kitchen table where the two women sat.

Kate couldn't help asking herself what things might be like if she and Brady hadn't eloped in Las Vegas. If they'd merely had a good time together on that trip but never taken things that last, disastrous step. She couldn't help asking herself what things might be like if she hadn't gotten pregnant. And if Brady were in Elk Creek merely for a visit and to look at some property now.

Would she have been giving free rein to the attraction she couldn't deny she felt? Would she have been relishing the time with him? Would she have been basking in the chemistry that seemed to be between them?

The answer, she decided, was yes, to everything.

Yes, she might have let the attraction have free rein, because although she didn't know much about him, what she did know led her to believe he was a good, decent, honorable man.

Yes, she probably would have been relishing this

time with him because no matter how much she wished it weren't true, she liked being with Brady. Even now, when it was against her will and when she was trying *not* to like being with him. The truth was, she still felt more alive, more energetic and more buoyant just being around him.

And, yes, she would likely have been basking in the chemistry that seemed to be between them, because in her experience that was something hard to find, something to be nurtured and explored when she did encounter it.

But New Year's Eve and ending up pregnant *had* happened, she reminded herself. And because they'd happened, nothing was the way it might have been. Because they'd happened, a simple attraction, a simple pleasure in his company, a not-so-simple chemistry, couldn't run their course, couldn't be indulged in.

And she had to remember that, she told herself sternly. She had to fight against the attraction running any kind of course at all. Because if she didn't fight, if she let things between them go the way they seemed inclined to, she could later be faced with Brady's whole different interpretation of what went on. The way Kelly had been. Like Buster—when Brady *did* learn she was pregnant—he could turn around and say it was all just a ploy she'd been using. A lure. He could say she'd just been pretending things were clicking between them so that when she dropped the bomb of the baby she'd have some emotional leverage.

Besides, to allow things between them to go the way they seemed inclined to was likely to get her in deeper herself. It was likely to get her hurt. The way she'd been hurt by Dwight.

Dwight.

Oh, no, she didn't want to go through that again.

She *wouldn't* go through that again.

And if there had been even the slightest inclination to give in to her attraction to Brady in any way, the memory of Dwight doused it completely and solidified her resolve.

Because no matter what her natural inclination might be, no matter how strong the chemistry between them, it was worth the fight to keep from ever feeling the way she'd felt over Dwight.

Chapter 5

Brady's tour of the other two properties took equally as long as the Barton place had. By the time he was finished for the day, darkness had fallen and he and Kate were on the southernmost outskirts of Elk Creek.

"Looks like we'll be late for supper," Kate observed as they got in the truck to go home. She'd been coming up with inane small talk like that all afternoon for no reason other than to fill time and space with inconsequential noise that helped block out her own thoughts about Brady.

"I was hoping we'd get through early enough for me to take a look at Elk Creek itself," he answered. "Think we could skip supper at the ranch and grab a bite in town so I could still do that?"

And here she'd thought this day was going to end.

Before she could answer, Brady leaned over so that

his mouth was nearly at her ear. "I'll make it worth your while and pick up the tab," he said in a seductive voice meant to be a joke.

It worked on both levels, though. It made her smile and proved too alluring for her to resist.

"You only have two choices of restaurants," she warned. "The Dairy King and Margie Wilson's Café—Maya's mother owns that one. The food is good and substantial but nothing fancy."

"Good and substantial will do. But how about we take that drive around town first and eat afterward?"

"Okay."

Since they came into town from the south end they drove past the train station and The Buckin' Bronco honky-tonk owned by Linc Heller, one of Elk Creek's more prominent citizens.

Kate didn't know a whole lot about the people or places that made up the small town, since she'd only been living there a little over two months herself, but what she did know she shared with Brady as they drove down Center Street, the main thoroughfare.

She pointed out the general store, owned by Linc's wife, Kansas, and a number of other shops and businesses all housed in quaint old buildings of one, two and three stories, some brick, some not, but all kept up with obvious care and pride. Then they drove up and down most of the residential streets, too, just so Brady could get the full feel of the place.

"Do you like it here?" he asked when they backtracked to the storefront café they'd decided on earlier, with its red-and-white-checkered half curtains in the twin picture windows that bracketed the entrance on to Center Street.

"I do," Kate admitted, even though she was tempted to bad-mouth the small town so he might think twice about moving there. She wasn't sure why the idea of that bothered her so much. She told herself she should be glad he'd be in closer proximity to his child. Close enough to be a part of that child's life.

But at that moment the only thing she could think was that it meant more time seeing him from a distance and fighting what that sight did to her.

It was that more selfish side that won a brief victory when she said, "But if you're not from a small town and don't know what it's like to live in one you might be careful. It isn't for everyone. People who are used to cities aren't always very happy in a place like Elk Creek."

"I'm not from a small town but I am from a rural community. I was raised on one of the biggest dairy farms in an area just outside of Oklahoma City. But I think I'll do fine here," he concluded, glancing around the café as if he were surveying his kingdom and finding it more than acceptable.

Margie Wilson wasn't working tonight, but a teenage girl seated them at a table not far from the soda counter. The restaurant was nearly filled with customers, some of whom Kate had met since coming to town. She exchanged pleasantries and introduced Brady before taking her seat facing him and the soda counter.

It was the first time she noticed a countdown board hanging on the wall behind it. In large black letters it said Weeks Until Margie's First Grandbaby Arrives, and a hook held a card with the number twenty-two.

The sight of it gave Kate a stab, and again she felt envious of her sister-in-law. Maya's coming baby was anticipated with such delight, while her own was surrounded by drastically different circumstances and had so far brought more fear, worry and turmoil than joy.

Her feelings must have been reflected in her face because Brady said, "You don't like the specials of the day?"

She hadn't even realized the teenager who'd seated them had brought water and recited the specials.

Kate forced herself to focus and said, "I'm sorry. I wasn't paying attention."

As the young girl repeated them, Brady craned around to look behind him at the countdown board that had caused her momentary preoccupation.

When the waitress left them to decide what they wanted, he said, "You did say this place belonged to Maya's mother, didn't you?"

"Margie. Yes."

"But the sign is a surprise to you?"

"No, I was just thinking how nice it is for Maya that her baby is so wanted."

"Why wouldn't it be?"

Kate shrugged. "Some aren't, you know."

"Sure. But Maya and Shane are happily married and a good age for it."

"What about you? Do you want kids?" Kate heard herself ask, when the urge to know became too great and the opening seemed to present itself.

"Someday," Brady answered without hesitation, but also in a way that said it was too far off for him to actually consider it seriously.

"Is that why you're moving to Elk Creek? To settle down?" Kate persisted.

"I suppose it's a beginning of that. It's not as if I

have a plan or a time limit or anything like that. I'm movin' to Elk Creek because the farm in Oklahoma really belongs to my brother. He's worked it since our folks passed away, while I've been off flyin' and doin' my own things. I still technically own half of it, but it just doesn't seem like mine anymore. I want a place of my own, even if I have to start small and build up. So I've been workin' my tail off the past few years, savin' everything I could since I paid off the plane, and here I am. But I want a decent house to bring a wife to and a few years alone with her, when I find her, before we bring kids into the mix."

He might not think he had a plan, but it certainly sounded to Kate as though he did. A plan that had nothing to do with her or a baby in seven months. And for some reason she didn't understand, that knocked the wind out of her.

"What about you?" he asked then. "You want kids?"

"Yes," was all she said, in a voice more quiet than she'd intended.

It wrinkled Brady's brow and made him laugh at the same time. "Don't sound so thrilled about it," he said facetiously. "Kids are fun. Look at your nephew. Andrew has more personality than a dozen adults. This morning he had to have coffee with Matt and me— in a coffee mug. We just put a splash in his milk, but he sat there and drank every drop, holdin' the cup the way we were, mimicking everything we were doin'. It was a riot."

Kate nodded. "I know. He loves to play little man," she said, trying to regain her equilibrium.

The waitress came back then, and they ordered. Pot

roast and potatoes for Brady, nothing but a bowl of soup for Kate, who had suddenly lost her appetite.

"So tell me about good old Elk Creek," Brady said when the waitress had left.

He was apparently finished with the remote notion of children, and Kate had to concede and change the subject. What else could she do? Especially when she didn't want to alert him prematurely about her pregnancy by showing undue interest in whether or not he wanted to be a father anytime soon. But she was still dispirited and had to put some effort into hiding it when she began to tell him about the small town they'd both chosen to move to.

"The people here are friendly and nice," she said, forcing enthusiasm into her tone. "And neighborly. Plus there are some fine workmen for hire—carpenters, a plumber and an electrician. I'm opening an accounting office just up the street, and my remodel crew seems to be on the ball and doing a great job. But like I said, it is still a small town. That means everybody knows everybody else's business and there aren't a lot of amenities like a wide variety of restaurants or a shopping mall or things like that."

She'd finished less upbeat than she'd begun. Not intentionally, but she really was going back and forth on the issue of Brady living in Elk Creek. She just couldn't seem to get ahold of her own roller-coaster emotions where he was concerned.

But he swung the pendulum back toward the positive on his own. "Elk Creek has some things a lot of other small towns don't have. There's a doctor, a dentist and a school. And Matt says the general store will order in about anything you want even if it isn't normal stock."

"That's true. And I guess you have the plane to fly in and out whenever you want, so the isolation won't bother you. You'll probably get some charter business, too."

"The place has a good feel to it," Brady said as their meals were served. "Warm. Welcoming. Laid-back. Some signs of prosperity but no urban sprawl."

"So you think you'll want to stay," Kate concluded.

"You don't sound like you want me to," he observed with a slight chuckle.

"No, it isn't that," she was quick to say. "What I meant was, did you like one of the properties you saw today?"

He didn't look as if she'd fooled him, but he didn't push it. "Matt was right—the Barton spread is the best of the lot."

"And Mr. Barton seemed pretty taken with you by the time we left. I think he wanted to adopt you."

Brady just smiled his acknowledgment of that fact. "It'd be a good spot for me, too. We could do some co-oping, you McDermots and me. But maybe you wouldn't want me so close by."

So he did know she was dragging her feet about that.

But she didn't admit it. Instead she said, "Why? Would you be a bad neighbor?"

"I don't think so. But you might not want to be lookin' at my face that often."

She looked at it now, studied it in a way she'd been trying to avoid doing all afternoon. His beard was beginning to shadow his cheeks and jaw but she liked the slightly scruffy look it gave him. And those eyes of his, so pale, so gorgeous, could melt her insides with a glance. Not to mention the sharply carved planes of his face, every feature, every angle as perfect as if it had been cut with a confident sculptor's hand.

He was nowhere near hard on the eyes. Which was why it would be so hard on every other part of her to have him within sight whenever she turned around.

"Kate?" he said as if calling to her from a distance.

She realized belatedly that she'd let too much time elapse since he'd wondered aloud if she might be against looking at his face as often as she would have to if he lived next door.

"I'm sure it would be okay," she blurted out, feeling like an idiot. Again.

Brady breathed a wry chuckle. "It took a while to think about, though."

"Well, you know, I don't like to make snap decisions," she joked to cover up.

"Couldn't prove that by me," he returned, teasing her with one raised eyebrow.

"New Year's Eve notwithstanding," she qualified.

"And it helps to ply you with a little champagne."

"A little? Buckets of the stuff is more like what I was plied with *that* night."

His smile was mischievous once more. And oh, so charming. "So if I promise to keep you in a constant supply of champagne, can I buy the Barton place?"

"Will you have it written into the deal as a ransom clause?"

"Maybe just a contingency clause."

"Okay, but I only want the good stuff. No cheap domestic swill for me."

Where was this coming from? she asked herself

even as she bantered—and, yes, flirted—with him. Lord, but the man could induce her to behave unlike herself.

Brady was staring at her again. Closely. Intently. As if he were seeing something he hadn't seen in her before. And liking it.

And she liked that he liked it. Heaven help her....

They'd finished eating by then, and Brady paid the check so they could leave. But before Kate even noticed, he'd grabbed Matt's keys off the table where she'd set them.

"My turn to drive," he announced, standing to pull her chair out—and she hadn't seen that coming, either.

"I don't know if you can handle the truck," she heard herself tease him, still not understanding what had gotten into her. "It's not some puny little airplane, you know," she added as they went out into the cool night air.

"'Puny little airplane'? Watch what you're sayin' about my pride and joy."

He opened the truck's passenger door for her, and while she knew just how dangerous it was, she couldn't help reveling in the feel of his big hand at her elbow, helping her up into the cab. Any more than she could help drinking in the sight of him walking around the front end on long legs that had just a hint of swagger to them.

Then he climbed behind the wheel and adjusted the seat and mirrors, fitting much better there than she had.

He started the engine, turning an ear to it as if to hear it more clearly and said, "She does purr, doesn't she?"

"I beg your pardon. I do not purr." Kate pretended

to be offended, knowing perfectly well that he was talking about the truck and not her.

"Careful, you're talkin' to a man who knows better," he said with a sly sideways glance at her as he pulled away from the curb.

"Oh, that was low-down and dirty," she said with a wicked laugh of her own that she didn't know she even had in her.

He grinned a broad, devilish grin. "But true," he boasted.

She hit him. A playful smack on the arm, the kind she'd have given any one of her brothers for teasing her.

But somehow it didn't feel the same. It sent a shock wave of awareness of hard, bulging biceps that reverberated all through her.

"It's good to see you loosen up," Brady said. "You've been wound tighter than a clock since I got here."

"Well, it isn't easy for a woman to face her defiler," she said, still joking and unsure where it was all coming from. Except that it *had* helped her loosen up and she felt so much better than she had lately that it wasn't something she wanted to let go of.

"Defiler?" he repeated, sounding shocked but laughing at the same time.

"Isn't that what you are? A defiler of young virgins?"

"Oh, geez, don't ever say that anywhere near any of your brothers or I'm a dead man."

"Behave yourself, then, and only do what I tell you to. Or else."

"Blackmail?"

"What can I say? There's an evil side to me."

She had him laughing hard now and she liked it.

Oh, who was she kidding? She liked *him*.

When his laughter had subsided to a chuckle, he glanced at her again. "How did I go without meeting you until Las Vegas?" he asked as if he felt deprived because of it.

"Just lucky, I guess."

"I don't think so," he said more to himself than to her. Then he said, "Seriously. I've been friends with Matt since we were freshmen roommates in college. I'd met all your brothers and your folks before. Where were they hiding you?"

"The cellar. That's where they hide all the virgins in my family."

"Seriously," he insisted on another laugh.

"I was in college, too. I skipped a grade in elementary school, so Matt and I were in the same graduating class. I went off to Denver University when he went to Texas A & M and met you. After that I stayed in Colorado—summers and all. I only went home for the occasional visit. I suppose we were just never visiting at the same time. I'd heard about you, though."

He looked at her from the corner of his eye. "Good things or bad?"

"All bad. What else is there?"

He chuckled again, shaking his head.

They'd arrived home by then, and as Brady turned off the engine he looked at her through eyes so approving she could feel the caress of his gaze. "Well, it was my loss," he said as if he meant it.

He held her mesmerized for a long moment, and Kate had a sudden vivid recollection of being with him in Las Vegas. Of having spent time with him the way they just had, having fun together, teasing, flirting.

And then, as if they were right back there, he reached out a long arm and cupped the back of her head in his hand, pulling her to meet him in the center of the seat so he could kiss her. Only briefly. Just a peck on the lips. But a kiss nevertheless. A kiss with enough impact on her to knock the wind out of her for a second time that night.

But just that quickly it was over, and Brady was out of the truck and coming around to open her door for her. Holding out a hand for her to take to help her out.

Still dazed by his kiss and not thinking clearly, she took his hand, slipping into it as perfectly as if her own had been cut from it, and for the moment he was holding it she savored the feeling of power restrained by gentleness.

But he didn't continue to hold her hand once she was out of the truck and instead let go so they could head for the house without any indication of what had just passed between them.

"I'd better...do some things in my room," she said as soon as they were inside, knowing she needed to distance herself from him before things went any further.

Brady just nodded his acceptance of that and said, "Thanks for today. And tonight. For everything."

"Sure. Thanks for dinner."

He smiled down at her with those thermal blue eyes once more and murmured, "Anytime."

"See you tomorrow."

"G'night," he answered, still studying her.

And oh, how she wanted him to kiss her again! Now, when she was prepared for it and could relish it, rather than be barely aware of anything but the shock and surprise she'd been aware of in the truck.

But he didn't kiss her again.

And she was afraid if she didn't do as she'd said she would and go to her room, she might take the initiative and kiss him herself.

So she muttered an answering good-night and forced herself to turn on her heels and leave him in the entryway.

But she took with her an inordinate urge not to go to her room at all. To go instead past it to his room, to be waiting when he got there.

Of course she didn't do that.

But even after she got to her own room and had closed the door securely behind her, she still imagined that she could taste his kiss on her lips.

And it only tormented her.

Because in spite of everything, she just wanted more.

Chapter 6

"Heads up!" Brady said by way of greeting, when he found Matt alone in the kitchen early the next morning.

Matt raised his head in response, and Brady tossed him the keys to his truck.

"You were behind closed doors when I got in last night," Brady explained. "I thought you would probably rather not be disturbed so I hung on to the keys. Hope you didn't need them before now."

"It's barely 7:00 a.m. Where would I have gone before now?" Matt countered, pouring a second cup of freshly brewed coffee to go with the one already steaming on the counter.

Then Matt picked up both cups and headed for the breakfast nook, nodding to Brady as he did.

Brady accepted the silent invitation and slid into one side of the nook about the same time Matt slipped into the opposite end.

"So how'd it go?" Matt asked after they'd both had a little coffee.

Matt could have been referring to how things had gone in terms of the properties Brady had looked at the day before, or he could have been referring to how things had gone between Brady and Kate, since Matt wasn't making any attempt to hide the fact that he was matchmaking.

Brady opted for assuming his best friend was asking about the properties.

"It went pretty well. You were right about the Barton place being the best of the three. The house needs some work. I don't think the Bartons have painted in fifty years or replaced the carpeting or fixed a shingle or a gutter."

"Yeah but compared to the shacks on the other two spreads, it's a palace."

"True. And there's a great barn plus a good water source. I'm going up to do a fly-by on all three today, get an idea of the terrain of each of them. But I think Bartons' is where I'll make my bid."

"Did he seem agreeable to selling?"

"He didn't sound too reluctant by the time I finished with him yesterday. He said his son had finally convinced him he'd never come back here, so there was no point in their hangin' on to the place. Seems like I should have a pretty fair shot."

"Good."

Matt was participating in the conversation, but Brady could tell he'd chosen the wrong interpretation of his friend's question.

Matt said, "When will you make an offer?"

"Today, maybe. Before the Bartons have too long to

think about putting the place formally up for sale and puttin' some competition into the bidding."

"Great. I hope they accept it. Now tell me how it went with Kate."

Brady had to smile at the impression he had of Matt champing at the bit as he waited for an opening to get back to what he'd really wanted to know in the first place.

And Brady just couldn't resist holding out any longer.

"She found the other two spreads without any problem and didn't put any dents in your new truck," he answered, being purposely obtuse.

"And you didn't make it home for supper," Matt persisted. "Which means you stretched yesterday afternoon into the evening."

There was a cue in that for Brady to expound upon. But he wasn't through giving his friend a hard time yet.

"Oh, yeah, I nearly forgot. We stopped off at a justice of the peace between the Bartons' and ranch number two, got married, had triplets between seein' the second place and the third, then got divorced after that because things weren't working out. Irreconcilable differences."

"Funny," Matt said. "How'd things really go with you guys?"

Brady took a deep breath and willed himself to have patience. "What am I gonna tell you, Matt? I think Kate is great. She's beautiful. She's sweet. She's funny. She's fun to be with. But maybe I've lost my touch with women since Claudia, because Kate just isn't interested." Why else would it have taken him so long to break through her defenses just to get her to laugh a

little, to joke a little, to lighten up? And between New
Year's morning and last night she'd made it damn clear
that she didn't want anything to do with him.

"You're wrong," Matt said point-blank.

"She tell you somethin' she's not lettin' me in on?"

"No. And I know she's actin' as if she's not interested. But she is."

"Ah, great Swami, and how do you know this? Tea
leaves? A crystal ball? Eerie voices that come to you
in the night?"

Matt pointed a finger at one of his own eyes. "I can
see it all right. She gets herself spruced up when she
knows she'll be crossin' paths with you. She watches
you when you're not lookin'. Kinda like you do with
her," he added slyly. "Only the two of you just keep
pussyfootin' around."

New Year's Eve had not been pussyfooting around.
And then there had been last night. Kissing her didn't
qualify as pussyfooting around, either. It did, however, count as something he couldn't believe he'd done.

Kissing Kate had been an impulse. A spur-of-the-
moment thing. He'd gotten carried away by some inclination, even when he'd been trying like hell *not* to get
carried away by his attraction to Kate, because he knew
it was a mistake. The same mistake he'd made with
Claudia—a mistake he wasn't going to make again. No
matter how nice a day he and Kate had had together or
how damn good it had felt to kiss her again.

"I think you ought to give this up, Matt," Brady said
then, thinking it was advice he needed to take himself.
"Kate isn't my biggest fan." Which explained why she'd
hardly responded to that kiss last night and then run

off the minute they hit the entryway, as if she'd had all she could take of being with him.

"You're wrong," Matt repeated. "She's just shy. Quiet. Inexperienced."

Not as inexperienced as she'd been before New Year's Eve.

But Brady sure as hell couldn't say that!

"You guys just need to get to know each other," Matt continued. "You couldn't have done any of that in Vegas. You were with the whole group of us almost every minute there."

"No, Las Vegas wasn't a good get-to-know-you place, and we hardly did any of that," Brady admitted because it was true. If you didn't count sleeping together. And maybe then what she'd gotten to know about him she hadn't liked. "But still—"

"'But still' nothing. She's watchin' you from under her lashes and you're watchin' her from under yours, and all you need is to stop bein' so wary of each other. Take some time to tell her your stories, to listen to her stories, to find out what you both like and don't like, and you'll see—we could end up more than friends and neighbors."

Yeah, we'll end up ex-brothers-in-law before you know we were ever brothers-in-law to begin with.

"You must've had a little start in that direction yesterday," Matt insisted. "You weren't out past supper time without talkin' to each other. Take your opportunities where you can. Like today, for instance. Kate's plannin' to drive into Cheyenne to do some shopping for Buzz's birthday on Saturday. You'll be taking your plane up, anyway. Why not fly her into the city?"

Brady sighed long and loud. "She's not interested,

Matt. And I'm tryin' to avoid what I did with Claudia when *she* wasn't interested."

"Kate is *not* Claudia. Kate is what you deserve. And you're what she deserves after that Dwight jerk."

"Dwight jerk?"

Matt grinned. "I'm not tellin' you about him. Ask her—it's one of her stories."

There just didn't seem to be any getting through to Matt.

"I told you, I've lost my touch with women," Brady said again.

"Well get it back."

Brady rolled his eyes. "Easier said than done."

"Claudia just shocked you. But just because you struck out with her doesn't mean you've lost your touch."

Brady would have liked to believe him. But Kate had disproved it. In a big way. On New Year's morning and again since he'd flown into Elk Creek.

"Take her to Cheyenne today," Matt urged. "Just get to know her. Let her get to know you. Then if it doesn't work out, well, hell, we can still at least be neighbors. I'll fix you up with Jenn's friend Greta when she comes into town for our wedding."

Brady just shook his head, hating that everything Matt said about getting to know Kate only encouraged what he was inclined to do himself. Hating that he *was* inclined that way.

"Come on," Matt coaxed. "You'll thank me in the end."

"Or want to shoot you," Brady said under his breath. But somehow that didn't sound like the hard line against pursuing Kate that he knew he should be following. Maybe he just never learned.

"I don't know, Matt. I just don't think it's a good idea."

And yet, good idea or bad idea, he knew deep down that he was probably going to do just what his friend was pushing him to do in spite of his show of unwillingness.

Because at the same time Matt was pushing, something else seemed to be pulling him.

And all in the direction of Kate.

Kate was not happy about ending up in Brady's plane. With Brady. Flying to Cheyenne that afternoon.

She'd actually been looking forward to the solitary drive into the city, to a leisurely day of shopping by herself. Especially after all the internal uproar she'd been in since Brady's arrival, topped off by a long, sleepless night of thinking about him and that kiss and what it had done to her. Her afternoon in Cheyenne had seemed like a much-needed reprieve.

But had she gotten that much-needed reprieve? No, she hadn't. Thanks once more to Matt and his machinations and her earlier agreement with Brady to pretend to play along with her brother's attempts at matchmaking.

"The Barton place still looks the best," Brady was saying as he carefully kept an eye on all the dials on the instrument panel as well as the wide blue expanse of a March sky so clear it looked as if milk had been poured into the darkness of night until it was just right.

He went on to talk about the lakes and ponds and sections of the river available to each property—water rights, the ranchman's mantra—but Kate couldn't concentrate on what he was saying. She was too busy reminding herself of all the reasons why she shouldn't be where she was at that moment. All the reasons she shouldn't be noticing how incredibly sexy he was in his black wire-rimmed sunglasses and the worn leather flight jacket that looked so soft it seemed to beg to be touched. All the reasons she shouldn't be so aware of his big hands on the control yoke, deftly keeping the flight steady and smooth.

All the reasons she shouldn't still be thinking about that nothing-of-a-kiss the night before.

But reasons or no reasons, she was noticing and thinking about it all. Along with how good he smelled again. And it was warring inside her with a confusingly heavy heart that made her wonder what was wrong with her.

She knew where the heavy heart was coming from, but knowing its origin and understanding it were two different things. The coup de grâce that had made her agree to this day in Cheyenne with Brady had been when—in the middle of Matt's maneuverings—Brady had leaned over and whispered in her ear that they could have the divorce papers notarized in Cheyenne without any worry of gossip.

From the moment he'd said it she'd known she had to concede to her brother's gambit, but from that very same moment she'd had this heavy heart feeling.

And she definitely couldn't figure out why.

It couldn't be some divorce-related reaction because there was nothing about her that felt married. But there it was—a reluctance, a sadness, a desire to drag her feet.

Which she certainly couldn't do.

Just because Brady made her blood run faster in her veins whenever he was around didn't mean she should—or could—refuse to finalize the divorce that had been her idea in the first place.

Besides, he really would feel trapped if she showed any hesitancy about signing the papers and then told him she was pregnant to boot.

So she'd said yes to this trip into Cheyenne with him, put the divorce papers in her purse to take along and now had to suffer through World War III going on inside her.

Of course, it also didn't help that Brady seemed so eager to get the divorce done. He apparently really did want out. And the faster the better.

It made her worry about what his response might be to learning she was pregnant.

And it also stung. Which was weird, too. Because it shouldn't have. She should have been able to take it in stride. After all, she didn't want them to stay married. Even above and beyond being determined that Brady not feel trapped, *she* didn't want to stay married to a man she hardly knew. Regardless of the fact that he was the father of her baby. That would be insane and archaic and would no doubt lead to more and more problems, until the inevitable divorce really was traumatic.

But maybe he should *want* to stay married to her, she thought, knowing even as she did that it was unreasonable and irrational.

And that was when she figured it out.

The idea of Brady not wanting to be married to her smacked of Dwight again and was pushing those buttons in her. So of course it made her feel bad. That was all there was to it. It didn't have anything to do with Brady or her attraction to him or even anything to do with the pregnancy or the baby. It was just pouring salt into her old wounds.

So everything was okay, she assured herself.

It wasn't as if any part of her actually wanted to stay married to Brady. It was just those old wounds she was struggling with.

What a relief.

"I figure we'll look for a notary as soon as we get to town," he was saying, the first thing to penetrate her preoccupation. "Might as well get that out of the way."

"Sure," she agreed as if she'd never had another thought on the matter.

But it still tweaked her.

And even believing she understood why now, it didn't feel great.

Maybe because no matter how she looked at it, there were two men in the world who'd made it clear they really *didn't* want to be married to her.

One, a man she'd believed she loved.

The other, the father of her baby—and the sole person who had ever made her feel like a real woman.

The notary was a tall, thin man with a very bad comb-over and a nose so hooked it looked like a beak. He didn't seem to care what Kate and Brady were signing, once he was satisfied they were aware of the contents of the document themselves and agreeable to it. Then he checked their identification, had them autograph the divorce papers and his record book—complete with the date—and he pressed his seal into the space provided, signed it himself and that was that.

"Well, happy divorce," Brady said on the way out of the notary's office.

"Happy divorce," Kate responded.

"Or at least it will be a divorce when I send the papers to the lawyer and he files them. Feel better?"

Not at all, was what Kate would have said if she were being honest. But she'd been the one to demand this so she could only say, "Yes. You?"

"Sure. Want to know why?"

Maybe not, she thought. But she played along, anyway, as they stepped out into the cool clear air. "Why do you feel better now that the divorce papers are signed? Because you were afraid you were really going to get stuck with me?"

He was looking down at her and he hadn't yet replaced his sunglasses, so she could see in his eyes that that wasn't what he'd been thinking and he was slightly offended that she might believe he had been.

"I feel better because you were so freaked out by this whole thing and I'm hoping now that it's taken care of—basically—maybe we can put it behind us and really start over the way we agreed to do the first night I got to Elk Creek."

"The clean slate," she said, referring to that same night.

"Right."

"Okay," Kate said, but for some reason it didn't seem to appease him, and she had the impression he had something else in mind.

"You know," he said. "We've said we'll be friends and that we'd pretend to go along with some of Matt's maneuverings to get him off our backs, but I'm just thinkin'—what if we really did put some effort into gettin' to know each other? For real. Would that be so bad? I mean, is that just totally what you don't want or could we give it a try?"

Could they? she asked herself. Could they make a genuine effort to really get to know each other?

It was tempting. It was something she realized she wanted to do. But should she? Wasn't it also dangerous, given her already strong attraction to him?

But then it occurred to her that if they were going to have a child—which they were, whether he realized it or not—they were going to need to have a relationship of some kind. Not a romance, because she was convinced that wasn't what she wanted. But at least a friendly, hopefully considerate, compassionate, adult relationship. A relationship in which they knew a little something about each other, if for no other reason than to be able to answer questions their child might pose down the road. And in the interest of that, what he was suggesting seemed like the smart thing to do.

As long as she could keep the whole attraction element out of it.

"Look, if you don't want to, it's okay," he said then, probably because she'd let too much silence pass as she'd pondered his proposal.

"No!" she said in a hurry. "I *do* want to!"

Okay, too eager now.

She toned down the sound of her voice and the feelings that had prompted it. The feelings she was supposed to be keeping at bay.

"I think that's a good idea," she finally assured him in as businesslike a manner as she could muster. "After all, you are Matt's best friend, and you'll probably end up being my next-door neighbor, and we'll both be living in the same small town. What could make more sense than to honestly get to know each other?"

"Maybe not a ringing endorsement of my own merits, but does that mean we have a deal?"

"Yes. Where should we start?"

Brady grinned at her. "Let's not attack it like it's a school assignment. How 'bout if we just relax a little and let it evolve on its own?"

"And in the meantime I can get my shopping done?"

"Absolutely."

"Great."

And with that they launched an afternoon that turned out to be better than Kate had anticipated.

Somehow she'd forgotten why she'd liked Brady so much in Las Vegas. But shopping in Cheyenne reminded her. The plain, undeniable truth was that when she did as he'd advised and relaxed a little, she and Brady clicked on so many levels. More levels than she had remembered from the New Year's trip.

Their senses of humor were similar. Their tastes were similar. Sometimes it even seemed as though they thought the same thoughts at the same time.

And it felt good to temporarily suspend all the weighty issues that she'd been carrying around with her. To revert to the way things had been between them before New Year's Eve. To rediscover not only the fun she had with him, but the fun he brought out in her.

The day was productive in other ways, too. Kate found the perfect leather-bound album for the gift she had planned for her grandfather, and Brady decided to get Buzz a birthday present of his own. He chose a silver belt buckle that Kate knew her grandfather would have picked out for himself if he'd had the chance.

While they were at the Western store buying the buckle, the display of Stetsons caught Brady's eye, and he decided to get himself a new hat. It meant trying on a variety of them—wide-brimmed, narrow-brimmed, felt, leather, even one that looked more like a straw sombrero than a cowboy hat.

But he finally found one that suited him—a buckskin beaver felt with a narrow black leather band—and then went to work with the hat creaser, discussing the subtle differences between a cattleman's crease, a quarter-horse crease and a cutter crease, to decide which would look best on him.

Kate observed that part of the proceedings from a distance, sitting in a barrel chair near the dressing rooms and fighting a laugh at what she was witness to. Because no woman had ever had so serious a deliberation about any form of clothing or hairstyle.

Not that she wasn't enjoying the sight, though, because she was. How could anyone *not* have liked looking at the tall, broad-shouldered cowboy standing with long, thick legs apart, running his fingertips lovingly along the hat brim and tipping it just so on his head?

And she had to admit, the hat did look good on him. Especially once it was finished and had just the right dip to the front brim, giving both man and Stetson a cocky, sexy accent.

But getting to know Brady was one thing. Noticing things like that was another. That was just what she shouldn't be doing, so Kate tried to sigh away the effects.

Just friends, she reminded herself. Just friends…

It was after seven by the time they'd done all they needed to do in Cheyenne and Brady suggested dinner at a steak house, where the food was incredible but the country-western music was so loud they could hardly talk to each other over the noise.

Then they went back to the airport.

"Buckle up, baby, and I'll fly you to the moon," Brady joked as they took their seats in his plane again and he did a preflight check.

Kate liked watching that, too. Watching his expertise and seeing the evidence of the fact that he was intelligent as well as gorgeous. Of course, it only mattered to her in terms of the genes he might have passed on to her unborn child, she told herself. It wasn't as if her appreciation had anything to do with him as a man or her as a woman.

Then they were in the air again, and the pitch-blackness of the night sky made her feel as if they were the only two people in the world. Not a feeling she minded, she realized, even though she knew she shouldn't really be indulging in it.

But where was she going to go to stop it?

"You know," Brady said then. "You're wrecking my pilot-and-the-beautiful-but-scared-passenger fantasy."

That made Kate laugh. "I beg your pardon?"

"Well, here I have you all alone, up in the air, and if you had some white-knuckled fear of flying I could be a hero."

"Wouldn't you have to be a *dashing* hero?" she teased him.

"It goes without saying," he said with mock humility. "Did you want to pretend? Say, tremble a little or something, so I could show you my stuff?"

"I don't think I want to see your *stuff*," she said, unintentionally putting some innuendo in that last word.

"But I don't get this chance too often, you know."

"I don't believe that. I'll bet you use this plane as your come-on. Instead of inviting women to your loft to see your etchings, you probably invite them to go flying with you."

He grinned in a way that let her know he'd done exactly that a time or two. "So is that a no? You won't even pretend to be afraid? What if I do this?"

He put the plane into a sharp dip and then yanked it up again.

But Kate took it in stride.

"You're forgetting I have four older brothers," she said, only laughing at his attempt to scare her. "I've been hung by my ankles off the barn roof, taken on every roller coaster they ever got me near, dragged off a cliff by a bicycle while I was wearing roller skates, had to hang on to the hood of a truck for dear life while Matt raced across an open field, been set backward in the saddle of a horse whose rump got slapped so it would run away with me and awakened from a sound sleep to find my nose pressed to the ceiling because they'd put my bed up on stilts. A little air turbulence just won't do it."

He half frowned, half grinned at her. "They did all that to you?"

"And more. Much, much more. I was their own private plaything when it came to practical jokes, pulling the wool over someone's eyes and just plain orneriness."

"That's bad."

"Tell me about it."

"Now I just feel guilty for wanting you even a little nervous."

"Good," she said with a laugh. "Then do something else."

"Like what?"

"Like… Tell me about your family."

"My family," he repeated as if he were trying to come up with something worthy of the telling. "Okay. Well, you know how people say they were childhood sweethearts? That was my folks. My mom's family moved across the street from my dad's family when they were both eight years old. My dad always said he fell in love with my mom the first time he laid eyes on her and it never changed from that minute on."

"What about your mom?"

"She said my dad had cowlicks and his hair stuck up so she thought he was funny looking. But he was tireless in his determination to win her over—"

"At eight?"

"Even at eight. And he didn't give up until he'd done it. But it took until she was nine."

"And they were married at ten?" Kate joked.

"Now that would be too far-out," he deadpanned. "No, they were sweethearts all the way through school and got married the week after they graduated. They were together—happily—until the day they died."

Because neither of them felt trapped, Kate thought, for no reason she understood. But it added strength to her own resolve, anyway.

"How did they die?" she asked more solemnly.

"Car accident. A drunk driver hit them head-on. It's been about three years now. But as bad as it was to lose them like that and so young, my brother and I agreed that it would have been worse to see them go one at a time, later in life. They really were two halves of a whole, and either of them would have been lost without the other."

"So that's what you're looking for, I'll bet—a love like that."

Brady seemed to think about it. Then he chuckled slightly. "I've never looked at it that way."

And maybe he didn't want to look too closely at it that way now, either, because rather than delving into it, he gave her a sideways glance again and said, "What about your folks? I've met them, and Matt's talked about them here and there, but how'd they get together? And wasn't there some problem with Buzz because of it?"

"*Big* problems with Buzz because of it. My parents met at the Stock Show in Denver the winter my mother was seventeen. My dad was twenty. They say it was love at first sight—sort of like your dad, only my dad didn't have cowlicks so my mom was head-over-heels in love with him from the get-go, too. But he lived in Texas and she was still in high school. There was no way Buzz was going to let his only daughter, his only child, drop out of school the way she wanted, to marry some guy who—to make matters worse—would take her off to Texas to live. So they eloped, and my mother didn't have any contact with her parents again until I was seventeen and she started to see things through her father's eyes. Then they reconciled and they've been on good terms ever since. My mother calls Buzz at least once a week now even though she and my father are traveling the country."

"But basically your parents did the Texas-Elk-Creek version of Romeo and Juliet, huh? Sounds like you have some pretty high standards to live up to in the romance department yourself."

"Maybe all that love-at-first-sight business is what got us both to the altar in Las Vegas," she said.

"Maybe. But we wiped that slate clean, remember? We're not talking about it."

"Mmm."

"You're right, though," Brady went on. "When you grow up seeing two people as crazy about each other as my folks were, it's a hard act to follow. You want it for yourself, but sometimes you get to thinking that it just isn't out there for you."

"Are you getting melancholy on me?" she asked, teasing him to ward off feeling exactly that way herself. And for the same reason. She'd always looked at what her parents shared and wished for the same thing. And worried that she wouldn't ever find it.

"Melancholy? Me? Nah. How could I be melancholy with a new hat back there in its own seat?"

Kate laughed, recalling that he'd actually buckled the hat into a seat belt as if it were precious cargo.

Brady concentrated more closely on his flying then, because they'd passed over Elk Creek and were about to land in the pasture his plane had been in since his arrival. He smoothly eased the aircraft to the ground not far from where Matt had left his truck for them to drive back in. Then, when the plane came to a standstill, he cut the engines, and quiet wrapped around them, heralding the end of their trip and their day together.

And Kate felt an awful pang of regret that it was coming to a conclusion.

She fought it, though. Telling herself just how inappropriate the sentiment was under the circumstances she was determined to impose upon them.

They transferred all their packages from the plane to the truck and exchanged small talk on the short drive from the north pasture to the house. No one was in sight when they let themselves in through the kitchen's French doors and they both headed for the hallway that led to their bedroom suites.

From that direction they passed Brady's door first, and he set his hat can down in front of it before taking the remainder of the packages he was carrying for Kate to her room.

"I can take those," she told him when she'd opened her own door, thinking that if she had him bring the bags and boxes into her room, she wouldn't want to let him back out again.

Brady didn't protest, he just handed everything over.

And then there they were, Brady in the hall facing her as Kate stood in the doorway looking up at dark-molasses hair that was a little mussed from all the hat trials, and blue-gray eyes peering down at her from a face that was handsome enough to make her heart skip a beat.

"Thanks. I had a nice day," she said then in a voice that was softer, breathier than she'd wanted it to be.

"First Las Vegas and now Cheyenne—we do know how to do a town up right, you and I, don't we?" he said with a slow smile.

"Cheyenne will never be the same after today," she agreed as if they'd done something wild and woolly rather than merely shop.

But it made his smile grow even wider, and suddenly Kate was all too aware of every inch of the man.

Of broad shoulders and solid chest and the whole long length of him standing there in all his masculine glory and that pure sexuality that she could feel in the air around them as sure as if it were a living thing.

He reached a hand to her arm in a gesture that began as no more than any friend touching another friend as he was about to say good-night. But in that instant, when his touch seared through the sleeve of the light sweater she wore, what was ignited inside Kate was something so much more than feelings of friendship. Something warm and full and alive. Something rich with needs and desires and cravings for more.

His smile was gone, replaced by an expression that said he could well be feeling the same things and that he was as taken aback by them, by the speed with which they'd hit, as she was.

But his resistance must not have been any greater, because he raised his other hand to her other arm, and there was most certainly not mere friendship in his drawing her nearer, in adding a little pressure from strong fingers that massaged and caressed and sent glittering shards of light all through her.

Then he bent over just far enough to press his lips to hers, and if his touch alone had awakened things inside her, it was nothing compared to what his mouth against hers inspired.

And this time the kiss wasn't only the brief peck of the previous evening. This time his lips parted over hers. This time he even let them linger long enough for her to savor the soft feel of his mouth, to taste the warm sweetness of his breath, to let her head fall back in surrender to something she knew she should stop but couldn't muster any inclination to—

The sound of voices going into the kitchen from the recreation room drifted to them, and Kate broke away in a hurry.

It appeared as if the sounds from the kitchen penetrated Brady's consciousness only after she'd ended the kiss, and for a moment he seemed slightly crestfallen.

But Kate whispered, "Someone's coming," to let him know that was the reason she'd so abruptly ended what she had really wanted to have go on and on.

Brady nodded with merely the tilt of his chin and took a big step backward himself, putting distance between them.

But whoever had gone into the kitchen stayed there, never venturing into the portion of the house where Kate and Brady waited to be discovered.

The intimate moment between them had passed, though. And as much as Kate yearned for him to take her in his arms, to kiss her again—and again and again—he didn't do it.

Instead he said a quiet good-night and disappeared with his new hat into his own room.

Kate followed suit, closing her door behind her and then leaning against it, still hanging on to her forgotten packages and reliving that kiss in her mind.

And as surely as she knew she shouldn't have let Brady kiss her again tonight, she also knew that she wished he were right there with her still, kissing her until her lips were numb. Touching her until she tingled all over. Holding her in those enormously strong, powerful arms. Undressing her with deft fingers. Taking her to bed to do those things she only had a blurry memory of from New Year's Eve....

"Friends," she muttered to herself. "We're just going to be friends."

The trouble was, no friend she'd ever had before had made her feel what Brady made her feel. And she wondered how a person took those feelings he brought to life in her and turned them platonic.

Because she was failing miserably....

Chapter 7

It snowed the next day. One of those heavy, wet snows that pile up on the grassy areas but turn instantly to slush on the pavement and sidewalks. Spring snow.

But it made for the perfect afternoon for Kate to stay inside with Tallie, Maya and Jenn to begin their preparations for Buzz's eightieth birthday party by doing some early decorating of the living room—something they could do since the party wasn't a surprise.

They had the house to themselves. Buzz had gone into town to play cards with his cronies, and the rest of the men in residence—including Brady and little Andrew—were out in the barn.

That meant that Kate and Brady hadn't crossed paths at all today because he'd already had lunch and gone outside with her brothers and nephew by the time the morning sickness had passed and she'd emerged from her rooms.

She counted avoiding Brady as the one advantage to the illness she was waking up with every day now.

By late in the afternoon the women moved into the kitchen to inventory the ingredients for the food they'd be preparing in the next two days, and to make sure they had enough paper plates and plastic silverware.

As everyone else dealt with the food, Kate took the job of paper plate counter at the center island, facing the French doors that looked out onto the back patio and the barn beyond it. So she was the first to see the men emerge from the barn and go to work on what appeared to be a snow fort for Andrew. Although, it looked as if the little boy was only the outward excuse for the big boys to play in the snow.

But regardless of the reason, Kate found it difficult to tear her eyes off the scene framed by the French doors.

Well, she found it difficult to tear her eyes off one member of the scene framed by the French doors, anyway.

Brady joined in the construction with vigor, and wherever he was at any given moment, Kate's gaze seemed to follow with a will of its own.

He cut quite a figure, there was no denying it. He had on cowboy boots and faded blue jeans that fitted his thick thighs and incredible derriere as if they'd been made by a London tailor. On top he wore layers for warmth—a red Henley T-shirt next to skin she fought not to think about, a chambray shirt over that and a short denim jacket over the shirt.

But even all the clothes couldn't disguise the breadth of straight shoulders or the bulk of biceps or the pure power of his chest. And not even distance diminished Kate's appreciation of it all.

Not that she wasn't looking for a flaw in him, because she was. Anything that might turn the tide for her.

But could she find even one? A repulsive bump in his nose? An unattractive angle to his jaw? That he threw like a girl when the snow fort was built and a snowball fight erupted?

No, she couldn't.

His nose was great. His jaw was sharp and chiseled. And when he threw the snowballs he so expertly packed, he looked like an Olympic athlete.

No matter how hard she tried, there just wasn't anything about him that she could come up with to counteract the undeniable attraction she had to him.

And she was trying. Why else would she have had to count the paper plates three times now?

As she started on the fourth attempt, her sisters-in-law and soon-to-be-sister-in-law caught sight of the antics outside. They all moved to the French doors to watch and joke about the boyishness of their respective men, but Kate stayed where she was, pretending to have no interest in the snowball fight.

But the truth was it wasn't boyishness that kept her gaze surreptitiously riveted to Brady, that had her subtly altering her stance so she could see him between Maya and Jenn. It was the grace of his movements, the simmering sexuality that seemed to present itself even in his bending over to scoop up snow in big gloved hands. It was the striking curve of his back when he launched his snowy missiles with true aim and the accompaning joyfully wicked smile she'd seen a time or two.

And every return hit he took was evidence of the solid wall of powerful male body that Kate yearned to snuggle up against.

Things would definitely have been easier if he were a gargoyle of a man. Or even if he were just on Dwight's level—okay looking but nothing to turn heads. Plain, really.

But, no, Brady was spectacularly handsome. Spectacularly sexy. Spectacularly man. Way, way more man than Dwight had been.

And she hadn't been woman enough even for Dwight....

That thought made Kate finally able to take her eyes off Brady.

It was good to remember her limitations, she told herself. If she couldn't find a flaw in him, at least she could keep things in perspective by remembering that she was a woman who had a long history of being utterly resistible to the opposite sex. Even to lesser men than Brady.

Yes, perspective, that was important. Keep things in perspective, she reaffirmed. Because pregnant or not, Brady was out of her league. Far out of her league. It was something she had a lifetime of evidence to fall back on.

Brady might have had a little bit of an attraction to her—that was something she'd inspired along the way in several guys. But when it came to more than that? There just *wasn't* more than that. Not enough to maneuver through the obstacle course her brothers had put up all through school. Not enough to hang on to

Dwight. Certainly not enough to have a future with a man like Brady.

And not to remember that was to risk having unrealistic expectations. Unrealistic expectations that could get her hurt. Really hurt. The way she'd been hurt by Dwight. The way she never wanted to be hurt again.

The way she wouldn't *let* herself be hurt again. No matter what she had to do to keep it from happening.

"I'm going to get them in here before they're all sopping wet," Tallie said then, her voice invading Kate's thoughts.

Kate's sister-in-law opened the French doors and shouted for the snow warriors to come in and have hot cocoa.

Kate took that as her cue to escape back to her rooms before she ended up any nearer to Brady and the potency of his effect on her. Better to avoid the potency of that effect when she knew she didn't have that same potent effect on him.

So as men and boy brushed the snow off before heading for the house, she announced that she had to make a phone call to her contractor and slipped out of the kitchen.

And with her she took her lowered expectations, the recognition of her limitations and that newfound perspective, wrapping it all around her like a suit of armor.

Dinner that night—like every other meal when so many of the McDermots were in attendance—was a noisy affair. Kate didn't mind. It was fun, and being among so many other people made it somewhat easier for her to keep some control over the onslaught of things Brady stirred up in her.

When everyone had finished eating and the kitchen was cleaned, she excused herself and holed up in the den with a box of old photographs and a second box that contained mementos, both of which she wanted to go through.

She was congratulating herself on making it for a whole day without being alone with Brady when he knocked on the door and poked his head in.

"Hey, stranger. I was wonderin' where you'd gone off to. You avoidin' me today?"

"Didn't we just have dinner together?" she countered, playing innocent.

"We had dinner in the same room, but I don't think you could say we had it *together*." He poked his chin in her direction. "What're you up to?"

"Is Buzz within earshot?"

Brady reared back enough to look around then slipped into the den and closed the door behind him. "All clear. Is this top secret?"

It didn't take more than his entrance to make the air in the room seem charged. And as much as Kate knew she should do her best to get rid of him and continue her reprieve from what he did to her insides every time he got near her, the excitement he brought in with him was intoxicating and left her knowing she wouldn't do any such thing.

Instead she said, "I'm putting my gift to Buzz together."

"Is that so?" Brady strolled to the leather sofa where she sat with a few pictures already on the coffee table in front of her and a roaring fire in the fireplace nearby. "And what exactly is your present going to be?" he asked.

"You know I bought the album in Cheyenne yesterday. I thought I'd turn it into a sort of scrapbook for him. Since he wasn't a part of our lives until we were all basically grown-up, he missed our childhoods. So I'm going to use pictures of Shane and Ry and Bax and Matt and me when we were kids and a few keepsakes—ribbons we won, things like that."

"Nice," Brady said, infusing the single word with sincerity. "Can I help?"

"I don't know how. I just need to go through all the old pictures and things and decide what I want to use."

"Then can I just look at the old pictures while you do? I'm a sucker for stuff like that."

She couldn't come up with a reason why he shouldn't see the photographs, so she said, "Sure. Okay. If you want."

If he heard the lack of enthusiasm in her voice he ignored it. Instead he sat beside her on the couch. So close beside her that his thigh brushed hers and suddenly made the jeans she had on feel as warm as a heating pad.

Great. Now he's giving me hot pants, she thought, wishing his nearness didn't feel good enough to want to lean in even closer to him.

As usual he smelled wonderful. Apparently he'd shaved before supper, and that clean scent only added to the headiness she'd been feeling ever since he'd come in.

How was she supposed to fight the emotional effects of the man, she wondered, when there were so many physical effects to go along with them? It was a double whammy.

"I thought I'd start with pictures of us as babies,

maybe put them around a snapshot of the ranch we grew up on in Texas since Buzz never got down there to see the place," Kate said as they began to sort through the photographs that were merely thrown haphazardly into a toaster-size box. "Then I'll try to work my way up through the years to high school and college graduations, and finish with a picture I had everyone sit for two weeks ago, all of us together."

"Sounds like a good plan," Brady said, studying each photo closely before trading Kate for the ones she took from the box first.

"Here's one of you as a baby," he announced when he happened across a shot of Kate at about four months old, sitting on her mother's lap.

"Are you sure?" she asked as she glanced back and forth between two others to decide which she wanted to use.

"Positive. You're the only McDermot with curly hair and that particular shade of green eyes. Besides, I don't think any of your brothers would have let a picture of them in a pink-flowered dress survive."

Kate took the photograph, verifying that it was indeed her. "That's a good one of me to start out with."

"You were a cute baby."

"All babies are cute."

"Not true. My brother was a homely little cuss. Actually, he was a homely big cuss. Nearly twelve pounds at birth. He looked like a Sumo wrestler."

"Twelve pounds?" Kate repeated in awe tinged with trepidation, hoping her own baby didn't take after its uncle. "What about you?"

"Now I was a beauty," Brady said without skipping a beat.

He made that sound as if he were exaggerating wildly but she couldn't imagine that he'd been anything less than a beautiful baby.

"How big were you?" she asked.

"'Bout nine pounds."

"Wow," Kate breathed. "Your poor mom."

"Mmm," he agreed, obviously not having a clue as to why she was so interested in the subject.

"Here's Ry and Shane," she said then, pulling out a shot of her dad juggling both twins at once.

"Geez, I thought they looked a lot alike now but your folks must have had to mark an A and a B on their bellies when they were born to know which was which."

"Don't worry, they got plenty of mileage out of switching places and fooling people."

Brady laughed out of the blue then but clearly not at what Kate had said. He was staring intently at yet another picture. "What happened to your hair here?"

Kate leaned in slightly to peer at the photograph and felt more of the warmth of Brady's body as she did. She wasn't having much luck not being ultraaware of every nuance, every tiny effect, almost of every breath he took.

"Oh, that one," she said. "Bax gave me a haircut. Daddy had taken all the boys into the barbershop to have haircuts for Easter, and I was mad because I'd been left out. So Bax did the honors."

"Good thing he didn't become a surgeon," Brady said with another chuckle at the misshapen, lopsided, bald-in-some-spots abomination of a haircut her brother had given her when she was four.

"Better add this to the album. It's too funny to leave out," Brady suggested.

Kate took the picture from him and also lost the excuse to lean against him. Something she regretted more than she'd expected to, when she straightened up.

Maybe he regretted it, too, because he leaned her way then, renewing the contact, to poke a finger at a picture still in the box rather than pick it up himself.

"Early *Sports Illustrated* swimsuit modeling?" he asked.

Kate lifted the photo out of the box and held it so they could both see it. In the picture she stood on a beach, the ocean behind her, dressed in a two-piece suit. She was all of five or six.

"I was getting some practice," she confirmed in a deadpan.

Brady took the picture from her and looked at it more closely. But only when he ran his thumb over the spot that showed the heart-shaped birthmark she had just above her left hipbone did it occur to her what he was thinking. He'd done that same thing New Year's Eve only on the genuine article when he'd discovered it.

"Your broken heart," he murmured, referring to the fact that although it was an almost perfect heart shape, it was separated directly through the center for about half its length. "I'd forgotten about that."

Among a lot of other things about her and that night that he'd no doubt forgotten about, Kate thought, slightly dejected by the reminder of just how unmemorable she was. Even if there was a whole lot about Brady and that night that *she* didn't recall.

"You said your mother had always told you it was the only broken heart you'd ever know," Brady added then, as if just remembering that now, too.

"How wrong she was," Kate heard herself say before she'd even realized she was going to.

But she didn't want to think about the heartbreak that hadn't been confined to her birthmark. Or talk about it, either.

She also didn't want to go on feeling the way she was feeling, watching Brady caress that spot on the photograph much the way he'd caressed the birthmark itself that other night. She didn't want to go on feeling so warm that the fire suddenly seemed to have been a mistake. Feeling an immense craving to have Brady run that blunt thumb across the birthmark itself again right that minute....

"Here's one of Matt," she blurted out then, nearly shoving another photograph at her brother's friend to distract him from the beach shot. "I think I'll save the swimsuit picture for *Sports Illustrated* when they come calling," she added to let him know it was time to dispose of it.

Brady didn't give up the beach shot easily, but he did finally hand it over to Kate, accepting the picture of his friend instead.

He had a good laugh at Matt in his superhero Halloween costume and that helped to diffuse some of what had been going through Kate, it helped her relax and get back to business.

They spent the rest of the evening that way—looking through the box of photographs and sorting small plastic trophies, award ribbons, report cards and various other keepsakes in the other one.

Somewhere along the way Kate slipped down to sit on the floor with her back against the front of the sofa.

Somewhere along the way Brady did, too, only he

sat on one hip, almost facing her profile, with an arm resting on the couch cushion behind her.

Somewhere along the way they stopped studying pictures and mementos separately and passing them off to each other and instead just checked them out together, usually with Kate holding the item in question and Brady looking on, near enough for her to feel the heat of his breath, to indulge in the scent of his aftershave, to be almost cocooned by his big body.

And somewhere along the way Kate forgot she was supposed to be keeping things in perspective. She forgot her limitations. Forgot everything and started to just have a good time.

She reveled in walking down memory lane with him. In sharing childhood memories and anecdotes with him. In letting him see her family history.

Before either of them realized it, it was midnight and they'd reached the bottom of both boxes. There weren't any other sounds coming from anywhere outside the den, and it seemed apparent that they were the only two still up and about.

Kate had a tall pile of what she'd chosen for the scrapbook, and the remainder they repacked. Then Brady gave a great stretch, raising his long arms into the air and arching his back, and Kate heard his spine crack.

"Ouch. Was that as painful as it sounded?" she asked.

"Nah, felt good."

Well, it *looked* good, too. But she tried not to notice.

When he was through stretching he got to his feet and reached a hand down to help her to hers.

She knew it was a mistake to take it, to allow herself the physical contact that the whole evening had been just short of. But she had to do it. Not only so she wouldn't seem standoffish, but also because she just *had* to do it, because she had to indulge.

So she did, slipping her hand into the undeniable strength of his workman's hand and letting him pull her to stand before him.

For a moment after she got there he looked down into her eyes, and she expected something more to follow. Another kiss maybe?

But rather than that he gave her a mischievous smile and said, "How bad would it be if we got into some of the ice cream for the party?"

"Ooh, bad. Very bad," she said with a voice full of wicked delight just the same.

"Unforgivable?"

"Maybe not *that* bad."

"How 'bout if we figure we'll eat our share tonight and skip it at the party?"

"That seems fair," she finally agreed.

They made their way to the deserted kitchen where they took two gallons of ice cream out of the freezer—one Black Forest and the other plain chocolate.

"I suppose we have to use bowls?" Brady said.

"I think we'd better," Kate confirmed. While she got out the ice cream scoop, he took two bowls from the cupboard and brought them to the island where they each perched on a tall stool and helped themselves to both flavors.

"This is heaven," Brady said rapturously when they dug in.

"Maya's mom made it just for the party."

"Well I'm a connoisseur of ice cream and I can tell you this is fantastic."

"A connoisseur of ice cream, huh? Is that just a nice way of saying you're a glutton?" she teased with a glance at his full bowl.

"I beg your pardon. I spent three summers in high school dishing it out in a little parlor near where I lived."

Kate couldn't suppress a smile. "You were a soda jerk? Did you wear the little hat and a little bow tie and everything?"

"Just a plain white shirt. But I'll have you know that folks came from miles around for my banana splits."

He put a lascivious spin on that and made Kate laugh.

Then he added, as if confiding in her alone, "It was a great way to get girls."

"As if you had problems in that department," she countered just before eating another spoonful of the icy confection.

"Has Matt been talkin' out of school?"

"As if I couldn't guess," she said, feasting as much on the sight of him as on the ice cream. "I'll bet you collected way more than your fair share of female hearts," she persisted, suddenly wanting very much to know.

"I was pretty lucky with the ladies," he conceded. "'Course it took me until just recently to find out it really had been luck and that that luck could run out."

"When you met me," she said, jumping to the conclusion.

It made him frown slightly. "You make that sound like you're some kind of bad penny. My luck ran out be-

fore I met you. Just before, as a matter of fact. Hooking
up with you in Vegas… Well, that was the first bright
spot I'd had in two months."

Until New Year's morning when I went ballistic,
Kate thought. But she didn't say it. Besides not wanting
to ruin the mood between them she was more curious
about exactly how his luck with the ladies had run out.

"What happened two months before Las Vegas?"
she asked.

His eyebrows lofted as he swallowed a mouthful of
ice cream. When he had, he said, "Claudia Wence."

He gave the name a dire tone.

"The evil princess?" Kate queried as if they were
narrating a cartoon.

Brady chuckled lightly, but somehow she could tell
there was nothing light about this subject for him.

"She probably couldn't be called evil, no," he said.
"But she was the first woman I'd ever wanted who
didn't want me back."

Now it was Kate's turn to raise her eyebrows. "You
actually made it to two months before your thirtieth
birthday without ever being rejected by a woman?"

He had the good grace to look sheepish. "I know.
It's hard to believe. But it's true."

"It's not only hard to believe, it must be some kind
of record."

"For the *Guinness* book? I don't think so."

"So what happened?"

"We met in an elevator. Hit it off. She actually asked
me out. Very suggestively, in fact. Things went pretty
quick—again under her initiative. After about six
weeks of seeing each other she moved into my place,
started talkin' about our future together. Long-term."

"And that didn't set off any alarms in you? I thought you weren't ready to settle down yet."

"I admit it set off a few alarms, and I was a little worried that she might be rushin' the relationship. But I really cared about her, and it wasn't as if she was talkin' about eloping on the spot or anything. And actually thinkin' about us bein' together down the road felt good."

"So what happened?" Kate repeated.

"Three days before her birthday, at the end of October, she came home and announced as she was packing, that she'd fallen out of love with me—that's what she said. Just like that. With a shrug. As if it were no big deal. She'd met another guy she wanted to date, and she was moving out. So long. It's been fun."

"And you had a rude awakening in the form of your first rejection ever."

"Not only in the form of my first rejection ever, but also in the form of how hard it was to take."

"It's never easy."

"Well it nearly wiped me out. I didn't even know myself for a while."

"And then you met me when you were on the rebound."

He flinched. "That sounds so bad. And not like anything that was goin' on in my head at the time."

"Oh? What *was* going on in your head at the time?"

He grinned that devil's grin that delighted her for no reason she could name. "At first I was thinkin' damn Matt and his matchmakin', and that I'd just like to run the other way because getting involved with my best friend's little sister seemed like the fastest route to ruinin' that friendship."

Kate nodded her understanding. She had a lot of experience with men shying away from her because of her brothers.

"But then when I laid eyes on you," Brady continued, "I was thinkin' that you have hair like winter wheat on a sunny day and eyes the green of the ocean far out to sea and a body that wasn't half-bad, either."

"A body that wasn't *half-bad?* Now there's faint praise."

He grinned the devil's grin again, letting her know he was teasing her with understatement. Then he nudged the air with his chin. "What'd you think of me?"

Oh, good, turn-about. But Kate knew she had that coming.

"I thought you were tall," she said, dealing out some teasing of her own as she took their bowls to the sink and rinsed them.

Brady came to stand beside her at the sink, leaning his hips against the counter's edge. "Talk about faint praise."

Kate put the bowls in the dishwasher and headed for the light switch and the hall that led to their rooms. As she did she said, "I thought you looked like you had a nice personality, too."

Brady laughed quietly as they headed down the hall so as not to disturb anyone behind the other doors they passed. "Try to keep the compliments to a minimum so I don't get a big head," he said facetiously.

They had reached her door by then, and Kate turned to smile at him, unable to resist the opening to tease him yet again by purposely misinterpreting his words.

"No, I didn't think your head was too big. Your feet though, those are a different story."

"You're just being mean now."

She decided to cut him some slack. "I thought you had great hair," she said, looking up at the dark, dark fullness of it. "And great eyes," she added before she realized she was going to, as those blue-gray depths caught and held hers.

Then he smiled and stretched the smile into baring his very white, straight teeth. "And how 'bout my choppers? Did you think they were okay?"

"Pretty okay," she confirmed in a voice that had somehow grown breathy when she meant for it to still be teasing him.

He moved his jaw back and forth. "And how 'bout my strong chin? Did you notice that?"

Kate laughed lightly. "Now you're just fishing for flattery."

"True. But remember, I've recently had my ego damaged. It could use some boosting."

"I think it's had all the boosting it needs."

He smiled down at her again, but this time it was sweet and warm and it seemed to wrap her in a golden glow.

"Well, maybe not *all* it needs," he said in an oh-so-quiet, sexy voice.

He went on looking into her eyes, his own alight with mischief and that special brand of life that seemed to shine there. And then his hands were at her shoulders and he'd leaned forward just a bit, enough to let her know he was going to kiss her.

He didn't make any sudden moves, though, so she

had the time and opportunity to say no if she didn't want him to.

But she *did* want him to, she realized, and so she didn't move away. In fact, she tilted her own chin in invitation and let her eyelids drift closed just as his mouth met hers.

Only this time—unlike the kisses he'd given her the last two times—it was a kiss to knock her socks off. A kiss with his arms around her. With his fingers kneading her back. With his lips parted and urging hers to part, too. With his tongue coming to call, tentatively at first, the tip barely tracing the sensitive inner rims of her lips, then trailing along the very edges of her teeth, then finding its way inside, finding the tip of her tongue to say hello. To invite it to play. Teaching her the warm, slippery feel. Instigating games that courted and seduced and began to erupt sparkling things inside her.

Her arms were around him, too. Although she wasn't quite sure how or when they'd gotten there. But still her hands filled themselves with the hardness of his back, and one even rose to the nape of his neck where soft bristles of his hair seemed incredibly intimate.

Her breasts were pressed to his chest and she felt her nipples harden, yearning to be noticed, to be paid some attention as her mouth opened wide in response to his and their kiss went to a new, deeper, more passionate level.

And suddenly Kate could only think of pulling him into her room. Of the fact that her bed was waiting just a short distance away. Of making love with him the night through and replacing the foggy images and unclear memories she had of losing her virginity with him in Las Vegas with the bright, vivid images and memories they could create tonight....

But that was when she recalled they'd already created something. And that at the end of this night—no matter how she spent it—she'd wake up obviously ill as a result of that creation, and Brady would have to know what was going on.

Not to mention that pulling him to her bed, only to have him find out at the end of their night together that she was pregnant, would seem too much like luring him to the trap she didn't want him to ultimately see this baby as.

So she forced herself not to pull him into her room the way she was picturing in her mind, the way she was itching to do. But to push him away instead. To stop the kiss. To step back as if it wasn't what she wanted. To hide the fact that she really wanted so much more.

"Maybe we should say good-night," she told him in a raspy voice that seemed to give her away.

Brady looked down at her from beneath a frown, with an expression on his handsome face that she couldn't read.

But there was too much chaos in Kate to delve into it. She just needed to escape to the safe confines of her room before her tenuous resolve disappeared and she yanked him in with her after all.

"Okay," he agreed in a husky, reluctant voice.

"Good night, then," she said firmly, stepping into her doorway.

"'Night," he answered softly. So softly she couldn't help thinking that it was probably the way he would have said it at the end of hours of lovemaking when they were both exhausted and falling asleep in each other's arms....

But thoughts like that didn't do her any good, and she pushed them aside, grasping the edge of the door as if it were a lifeline and beginning to ease it shut.

"See you tomorrow," she said, so he knew it was coming and it wasn't as if she were closing the door in his face, even though he was still standing there, studying her.

"Yeah," he responded, sounding maybe a little crestfallen. Or did he sound angry maybe? Or disappointed?

She wanted to tell him not to be any of those things, but she couldn't do that any more than she could drag him into her room, to her bed.

So instead she whispered another "Good night" and really did close the door between them.

But not even that solid oak panel could take away what she was feeling.

And what she was feeling was that every inch of her body was alive with wanting the man who was her baby's father.

The very man she couldn't have.

Chapter 8

Apparently, once the Bartons made up their minds to sell their ranch they didn't want to waste any time. Because Brady got word the next morning that his offer had been accepted.

He arranged to meet the local lawyer who was handling the sale at the Barton place after breakfast to sign some papers, and once he'd had a hearty meal of waffles, eggs and sausages with the McDermot men, he decided to walk across the fields to keep the appointment.

It was a hike of a little over two miles from one door to the other, and he could have driven Matt's truck. Matt had offered it. But after the previous day's snow, the sun was bright in a crystal-clear blue sky, and Brady opted to walk because it seemed like a good chance to clear his head.

And he desperately needed to clear his head. But

not of thoughts of buying the Barton ranch. That whole deal had gone through with surprisingly little thought. Instead his mind was filled with something completely different.

It was filled with Kate McDermot. And since talking about Claudia the night before, it was also filled with the reminder that had been.

A reminder that had stayed with him all through the night. A reminder that was still with him this morning.

A reminder about what had gone on with him after Claudia had bailed on him.

He'd gone into some kind of conquest mode that had come out of an obsession to get her back. He wasn't proud of it, but that was how it was.

He'd kept calling her, sending her emails, sending her flowers, gifts, messages through friends. He'd put all his energy into wooing her in any way he could come up with.

Just recalling it all now made his hackles rise.

At the time it had seemed like he was meeting a challenge. As if that was all it would take to win her back. But that hadn't been how things were, and he'd had to finally face the fact that her feelings for him weren't the same as his feelings for her. Regardless of what she'd said or how she'd acted before the breakup. And in retrospect it felt degrading to have gone to such lengths for a woman who hadn't wanted him.

Sure, he'd finally come to the point where he was over her, but what he'd gone through before that was something he never wanted to do again. What he needed to think through as he walked across the open fields that separated the McDermot ranch house from the house that would be his, was whether or not that might be happening again, with Kate, even though he didn't want it to.

He wasn't in the midst of the same kind of full-court press, he knew that. But in a more subtle way he was sort of wooing her. And not without what seemed to be some reluctance on her part.

Okay, so there wasn't *total* reluctance on her part the way there had been on Claudia's once she'd moved out. But still, Kate was sending mixed messages. Running hot one minute and cold the next. Which to Brady meant that she had more reluctance to have anything to do with him than he had about having anything to do with her.

Who was he kidding? he asked himself. He didn't feel reluctant at all. Much as he wished he did. Much as he knew it would be better if he did. But instead he actually wanted to be with her. Despite trying to fight it.

And he was trying to fight it. Not successfully, but...

Well, hell, how was he supposed to fight it when he was in the throes of a potent, powerful, red-hot attraction?

A potent, powerful, red-hot attraction that kept her on his mind almost every waking hour? That made him want to spend his every waking moment with her, that had made him go searching for her after supper the night before when he'd known he should just accept that she'd gone on about her business without him? A potent, powerful, red-hot attraction that made being with her for hours seem like mere minutes, that made him want it never to end.

So, no, fighting the drive to be with her, to get to know her, to woo her, wasn't doing much good.

But at the same time he also couldn't help worrying that he could very well be pursuing another woman who didn't want him. Because when Kate was running cold, that was the impression he had. And that was how every meeting with her began.

Sure, she seemed to have a good time when they were together. But at the start it always seemed as if she didn't really want to be with him. As if she was actually avoiding him. Hell, she was as skittish as a colt.

Granted it wasn't as bad as New Year's morning. Or as bad as Claudia's rejection. But it was still there—that feeling that she'd rather not be with him. That he made her uncomfortable for some reason he couldn't figure out. That he was thwarting some plan to keep away from him.

So why didn't he just keep away from her? he asked himself. The way he should have kept away from Claudia.

But that was where things got dicey for him. Because besides the potent, powerful, red-hot attraction that was driving him, she always warmed up once he got past that first hurdle. More than warmed up if you counted last night's kiss. Because that kiss in particular had sure as hell not been cold.

No siree. She'd been as involved in that kiss last night as he'd been. She'd been kissing him back. She'd had her arms around him. Her hands in his hair. There was no mistaking that and he'd thought, It's okay, this is nothing like Claudia....

Until Kate had put a stop to it and acted as if kissing him wasn't what she'd wanted at all.

Hot and cold.

And he'd thought, What the hell am I doing feeling

the things I'm feeling, doing the things I'm doing, if she doesn't want it just as much as I do?

Brady shook his head and kicked a fair-size rock with some vengeance.

If she were someone else, he might have thought she was playing games with him. But he didn't have that sense about her. Instead it was as if she were torn, now that he thought about it.

But why would she be? Either she liked him or she didn't.

Unless she really didn't but good manners were behind her being outwardly friendly and polite once she was with him. Good manners that forced her to be pleasant when she really would prefer he keep his distance from her.

But if that was the case, those were some kind of amazingly good manners that had her kissing him the way she had. And he didn't believe anybody had manners *that* good.

Nah, something was definitely going on with her. He just didn't know what it was. And he might never know. So if he had any brains he'd just let her be, he told himself. Better that than risk looking back on this the way he looked back on Claudia, disgusted with himself for putting effort into something he should have walked away from.

"So do it," he said out loud, his words crisp and clear in the silence of the open countryside. "Just cool it with her. Better safe than sorry. Red-hot attraction or no red-hot attraction."

The only problem was that he wasn't sure he could just let her be. Because here it was, ten o'clock in the morning, and he was already champing at the bit to see her again, wondering if she'd be at lunch, thinking about how to get her alone later on.

"Just let'r be!" he shouted at the sky.

But a quiet little voice in the back of his head told him that wasn't going to happen. Not as long as every time he looked at her something in his chest ached. Not as long as every time he heard her voice it made his heart smile. Not as long as every time she laughed he felt like a kid on Christmas morning.

He guessed he just had to hope that what was causing these feelings in him was causing something similar in her and that he wasn't chasing after the unattainable, because Kate was triggering that conquest mode in him again.

And in the meantime, he also had damn sure better not forget about or discount her reaction to him the morning after they'd made love in Las Vegas. Along with keeping his eyes and ears open so he didn't get in too deep and end up finding himself in the same kind of pain he'd felt with Claudia.

Kate needed to make a trip into Elk Creek that afternoon to check the progress of the remodel of her office. Junebug needed a few last-minute items for Buzz's birthday party the next night, so Kate drove them both into town.

Their first stop was the general store and then they went two doors down to the small corner building Kate had rented, where the contractor worked with two of his men on her bathroom, and Junebug's son Jace was building Kate bookcases that filled a whole wall, floor to ceiling and end to end.

Carpentry wasn't Jace's main employment. He

and four of his five brothers ran the family ranch—a smaller spread than many in Elk Creek, so most of the Brimley men also did odd jobs for extra money. When Kate had seen Jace's handiwork on the bookcases in the den, she'd asked Junebug if he would consider doing some for her office, too.

Jace, like all of Junebug's boys—as Junebug still referred to her grown sons—was a mountain of a man and as handsome as they came. It was something Kate hadn't overlooked since moving to Elk Creek and meeting them.

But today it struck another chord in her when she realized that in spite of how bowl-her-over handsome Jace was, the only thing that came to mind when she first looked at him was that it didn't cause her heart to flip-flop the way every glance at Brady did.

It was disconcerting. Especially because just today she'd ordered herself all over again to get some control over her attraction to Brady so she could deal sensibly with what she needed to deal with. But how successful was she being at that when the sight of another gorgeous hunk of man only made her pine for Brady?

"What do you think?" Jace Brimley asked after he'd greeted his mother and Kate.

Of course he meant what did Kate think about the bookcase, but what went through her mind was, What I think is that I'm in trouble with Brady Brown in more ways than one.

She could hardly say that, though, so instead she said, "They're beautiful."

They were, too. Jace had used solid oak and turned all the edges to give them a fancy finishing touch.

"I have a little more sanding to do, then I'll stain and seal the wood and you'll be all set."

"I can't tell you how much I appreciate this."

"My pleasure," he answered with a warm smile that would have made any woman's knees melt.

But Kate smiled back, feeling absolutely nothing except a desire to hurry home to see Brady.

Oh, yeah, she was definitely in double trouble.

"Will you be home for supper tonight?" Junebug asked her son then.

"Sure. I don't have any other plans," he answered.

"Don't be late," she ordered, and then Junebug marched out the door, ending the visit without another word.

Kate just shrugged as if to say, *I guess that means we're leaving,* said goodbye to Jace and followed the large woman out onto the brick-paved sidewalk where Junebug was surveying the office.

"Glass's broken," the imposing three-hundred-pound Amazon of a woman informed Kate when she joined her.

Kate's glance followed Junebug's pointing finger until she finally spotted what couldn't have been more than a hairline crack of about two inches in the uppermost corner of the picture window.

"Good grief, how'd you ever find that? You must have eagle eyes," Kate said as they both got in her car parked nose-first at the curb.

"I got eyes all right," Junebug assured her, buckling her seat belt. "Speakin' of which, how long you been in the family way?"

Kate felt the color drain from her face. "Excuse me?" she said, glancing at Junebug.

Junebug arched a brow at her. "Got me six sons. Six times I was in the family way. I know it when I see it."

Kate put her eyes on the road and headed out of town, debating about what to do now. But there wasn't an ounce of doubt in the other woman's tone, and in the end Kate simply said, "No one else knows, do they?"

"Not likely. Not that I've heard anybody say. Just you and me. Or does the daddy know, too?"

"No!" Too quickly. Too panicky. Kate took a breath and tried to calm herself down. "I didn't think anyone but me knew. And I just found out a little while ago."

"How far along are you?"

"Slightly over two months."

"And sicker'n a dog every morning. That's why you never come out of your room till noon."

"Is it that obvious?"

"Only to me. Everybody else thinks you're just sleepin' in."

"I wish that was all I was doing," Kate groaned.

"Not a lot of help for it. Tried crackers on your night table?"

"That's usually the first thing to come up."

"My Jace did that to me. Hard on ya."

"Mmm," Kate agreed.

"Helped havin' a husband there by my side."

Kate had been enjoying having someone to talk to about the pregnancy. But it ended with that.

"Where's the daddy?" Junebug asked bluntly.

Kate just shook her head, keeping her eyes on the road.

But Junebug took that the wrong way. "You don't know who the daddy is?"

"No! I mean, I know who he is. But *he* doesn't know."

Junebug nodded, pondering something before she said, "Two months gone—back to February, back to January… Ahh, that explains a lot."

"Excuse me?" Kate repeated.

"That trip to Las Vegas you all had such a good time on. Matt's friend Brady was there, too, if I'm not mistaken. Seems I recall hearin' how the two of you hit it off then."

"Junebug—"

"That's why you're actin' so funny around 'im now, isn't it? He's the daddy."

"Junebug—"

"When're you gonna tell 'im?"

Again, denying anything seemed futile, so Kate didn't try. Instead she said, "Soon."

But that must not have satisfied Junebug because she said, "You are gonna tell 'im, though. Man has a right to know."

Spoken like the mother and champion of six sons.

"Yes, I'm going to tell him. I'm just waiting for the opportune moment." She didn't think she needed to compound things by telling Junebug about the Elvis-impersonator wedding she was waiting to have dissolved first. But she did add, "I don't want him to get the wrong impression."

Junebug laughed out loud at that. "What wrong impression would that be?"

Kate sighed. "I don't want him to think I want anything from him."

"Like marriage."

"Like marriage."

"In my day a man did right by a woman he got in the family way or he wasn't no kind of man at all."

"What if the man were one of your sons now, though?" Kate challenged.

"He'd do right," Junebug answered without skipping a beat.

"And if doing right meant a loveless marriage that made him feel trapped?"

"I'd remind 'im that he liked 'er well enough to diddle with 'er in the first place and tell 'im to go from there lookin' for love. It could come. I've seen it happen."

"And you'd want that for your son? Even if love never did happen and he just always felt trapped and resentful?"

"Babies need a momma and a daddy," Junebug decreed.

"But not necessarily married to each other or living together."

Kate could feel the weight of Junebug's disapproval. But she ventured a question, anyway. "They would feel trapped, wouldn't they? I know my brothers would. I've heard them say it about other men who've been in this situation."

"Is that what you set out to do? Trap 'im?" Junebug asked, rather than answer Kate's question.

"I didn't *set out* to do anything. It just happened."

"And he did his fair share of willingly participatin'? Of chasin' and persuadin' and seducin'?"

"Yes. It wasn't as if I lured him into my bed."

"Then maybe he's more willin' than you think. Seems to me he likes you well enough."

"Liking me well enough and getting all the way to

the altar are not the same things. Believe me, I know from experience."

"Could be different with this man," Junebug offered.

"How could it be different with this man when *I'm* not different?" Kate said quietly as she pulled up in front of Junebug's house. "There's already been one man who didn't want me, and that was before, when things were a whole lot less complicated and he'd put in a whole lot more time on a relationship with me. Now, with Brady, who I barely know—"

"Now you're carryin' this man's baby, though."

"That only makes me less appealing."

"Maybe you should let him be the judge of that."

And when Brady himself judged her even less appealing—the way Dwight had? How much would that hurt?

"You didn't answer my question before," Kate reminded Junebug then, for some reason feeling driven to hear what the other woman had to say on the subject. "Don't you think your sons would feel trapped?"

The stern older woman still didn't answer right away. In fact, she waited so long, Kate started to think she couldn't bring herself to.

Then Junebug finally said, "Maybe. Some."

And even though it confirmed exactly what Kate thought, it didn't make her feel any better to hear it.

"But they'd deal with it," Junebug added with conviction. "They'd still have to be told what was goin' on."

"I'm going to tell him. Eventually. But I wouldn't marry him even if he asked. He'd only be asking out of some sense of duty. And it would be a mistake."

Junebug scowled at her, full-bore.

Kate pretended not to notice.

"And please, this is just between you and me," she added.

"No it ain't. This is just between you and the daddy," Junebug amended. "But nobody'll hear it from me, if that's what you're sayin'."

"That's what I'm saying."

But still Junebug sat there, staring at Kate. Then she said, "One of my boys was the daddy, I'd trust 'im to do right *and* to handle any kind of feelin's that came along with it."

Kate just nodded in response to the advice that statement seemed to hold, even if she didn't agree with it.

Apparently Junebug didn't have anything more to say on the subject, so she got out of the car and headed up the walk to her house, again not bothering with a goodbye.

Kate drove off, wishing the older woman had said something to convince her that things might work out for her.

But she'd only helped convince her that what Kate had thought before was true and that there was no way Brady wouldn't feel trapped when he found out she was pregnant.

No matter how toe-curling that kiss they'd shared the night before had been.

But it was good to have her theory reaffirmed, she told herself. Especially now.

Because after that kiss she'd had a hard time not entertaining fantasies about happy families. About happy futures. About things she wasn't going to have with Brady. And talking to Junebug reminded her that they really were only fantasies and that she'd better not lose sight of what the reality was.

Unfortunately that was easier said than done.

Particularly when she found herself in a lonely bed wishing Brady were there with her....

Chapter 9

It was a little after five o'clock when Kate got home from dropping off Junebug. She parked her car in the garage out back and crossed the patio to go in through the kitchen doors. But as she approached them she had second thoughts.

She could see through the glass, and what she saw was Brady alone in the expansive, well-appointed room, doing something at the island counter.

He looked as terrific as always, dressed in boots, tight jeans that hugged his narrow hips and thick thighs, and a gray Henley T-shirt that cupped every muscle of his torso and biceps and exposed his forearms where the sleeves were pushed up to his elbows.

She was curious about what he was doing, but just seeing him from that distance was enough to make her pulse race and her knees go weak. So she decided it was better to walk around to the outside door of her own sitting room and go in that way. At least then she could avoid running into him until supper time.

But just as she was going to alter her direction and head for the side of the house, he looked up as if his radar had been alerted and spotted her.

She knew she'd look foolish if she merely waved and still went around to the other door, so she had to finish her original course and go in through the kitchen.

"Hi," Brady greeted as she came in.

"Hi," she responded, catching his quick head-to-toe once-over that took in her tan slacks and the red cardigan sweater she wore buttoned up the front.

"What are you doing?" she asked with a nod in the direction of the butcher's-block top of the island counter where his massive hands adeptly wielded a knife to slice water chestnuts.

"I'm making rumaki. Maya put a roast in the oven for dinner, but it won't be ready for a couple of hours yet. Everybody's hungry so I thought I'd do a few hors d'oeuvres to tide us over."

"Rumaki?" Kate repeated. "What is that?"

"Classically it's water chestnuts and chicken livers wrapped in bacon, but I'm not big on the chicken livers so I just use the water chestnuts. I marinate them in port wine, then wrap them in the bacon and broil them until the bacon is crisp."

"Ah," Kate said, trying to keep her surprise at this heretofore unseen side of him out of her tone. But she could only accomplish so much. "You cook?"

"Yes, ma'am. I have a pan comin' out of the top oven over there before too long. Sit and visit a few minutes and you can see for yourself."

Kate sat all right. She perched on one of the bar stools across from him even though she knew she should make up some excuse and retreat before that potent charm of his seeped in and left her even more susceptible to him. But he'd really roused her curiosity now. Not to mention that there was a fascination in watching his big hands so adeptly and expertly fashioning the small appetizers.

"None of my brothers cook much," Kate said then. "They can heat up whatever Junebug tells them to and make coffee and cereal, but that's about it."

"Guess you either like to or you don't. I started likin' it in college."

There was a mischievous half grin and a double entendre to that, but Kate pretended not to catch either one. "When you were on your own for the first time and had to cook or starve?" she guessed.

"No, when I went away to a college that cost more than my folks could afford. I needed to work to help with my tuition. My uncle owned a restaurant not far from school so he hired me. I was a busboy to start out. Planned to be a waiter once I learned the ropes, but for some reason the cookin' part of things got me interested and I ended up doin' that instead. Maybe it harked back to my soda jerk days, fixin' malts and banana splits."

"What kind of restaurant did your uncle own?"

"Semifancy. Not four-star but not a burger grill or a diner, either. Appetizers, steaks, chops, lobster, a few pasta dishes. My specialty was a blackened pork tenderloin that I came up with. It was a big seller. It'd melt in your mouth. And then of course there were some fancy desserts."

"You bake, too?" More surprise echoed in her voice.

"No, that's the one thing I didn't get into. The pastry chef was a little toad who was afraid somebody would steal his secrets. I steered clear of him. But I did everything else at one time or another before I finished college."

"A rancher, a pilot, a soda jerk, a chef—what haven't you done?"

"Brain surgery," he joked, crossing to the oven to open the door so he could peer in at his rumaki.

The smell of bacon cooking hadn't been too strong in the big kitchen until he opened the oven door. But it hit Kate full force then.

Ordinarily it was a smell she liked. But this time it made her stomach lurch. The way her stomach lurched every morning now even without provocation.

She swallowed hard and fought it. This hadn't happened anytime after noon before. Why now?

She got up and poured herself a glass of water from a pitcher in the fridge, breathing deeply of the cold, clearer air that came out with it until she managed some control over the sickness. Then she went back to the bar stool at the island counter about the same time Brady returned there, too.

"You don't look so good all of a sudden," he observed with a concerned frown creasing his brow.

"No. No, I'm fine," she said too quickly, realizing after the fact that she could have lied and said she might be getting the flu. But her immediate thought had been that to admit she was ill at all was to give herself away.

Brady's frown deepened with doubt. "Are you sure my cookin' isn't botherin' you?"

"No, why would it? I like bacon." Although at

that moment just the thought of it threatened to make her gag.

She took a sip of her water and turned the subject back to him. "And here I thought you just flew planes."

"Well that is my first love."

"How did you get hooked on that?"

"My dad. He was a plane fanatic from way back. He got my brother and I nutty for them by the time we were knee high. The three of us would build model airplanes together and fly the remote-control kind. Dad'd take us to every air show to come around. But that was where it stopped for Dad and Jack—a hobby. They didn't have the bug I did to actually pilot one myself. So after college I joined the air force and got myself into flight school. Flew jets eventually."

Kate was getting an image of Brady that she hadn't had before. "So you're not the kind of person who could be content sitting on the sidelines or working on the peripheries, are you? You're a doer."

He inclined his head and chuckled a little. "I guess you could say I'm always in the thick of things, yeah."

"A man of action. Better off without ties that bind." Like unplanned parenthood. "You must like having a lot of options."

He laughed at that. "*Everybody* likes having a lot of options."

Another wave of nausea took Kate by surprise just then, strong enough to bring her fingertips to her lips as if that would stop the inevitable.

She swallowed hard and fought the rise of her gorge once more, this time under Brady's watchful eye, his handsome face again pulled into the deeply etched lines of an alarmed frown.

"Are you sure you're okay?"

She nodded, wondering why she was torturing herself by staying in the fumes of that bacon.

But she just couldn't seem to make herself leave.

When she had things settled some, she seized her earlier thought about a way of explaining the sickness and said, "Maybe I'm getting a touch of the flu."

"Maybe you should go lie down."

It was the perfect opportunity to end their conversation and seek the solace of her room. But she was enjoying his company too much—*again*—to do the smart thing.

So instead she took another sip of her water and said, "I'm fine." Then she went back to their former subject. "Have you ever flown commercial jets?"

It took a moment of his scowling scrutiny before he accepted that she didn't want to talk about the way she was feeling and answered her question.

"I flew for a small airline for about a year, just long enough to save up the down payment on my own plane. Then I did charters and crop dusting. I like being my own boss."

"Footloose and fancy-free," she supplied.

"On the work front, anyway," he agreed. "That's why I figured investing in a ranch was a good way for me to go. I can run my own place and hire out for dustin', too."

Kate nodded, still trying to will this new bout of sickness to pass.

Why now? she asked herself again. Wasn't it bad enough to wake up this way every morning? Did it have to assault her in the middle of the day, too? In front of someone else? In front of Brady, of all people?

The oven timer went off then, and Brady retraced his steps to open the door again.

And once more the bacon smell intensified. In fact, it seemed overwhelming.

Kate took another sip of her water, marveling at how something as simple as a common scent could do this to her. Maybe she was just imagining it, she told herself. Maybe if she practiced a little mind over matter she could conquer it.

"All done," Brady said, using a dish towel to protect his hands as he pulled out the cookie sheet full of rumaki and brought it with him to set down on the island counter. Directly in front of Kate.

Mind over matter was not succeeding as she looked down at the small hors d'oeuvres, the bacon still sizzling in little puddles of its own grease.

And never had she seen anything more stomach churningly unappealing.

The smell was all around her now. Inescapable. Awful. Overpowering.

Overpowering enough that she knew she wasn't just imagining the sickness that was gaining a rapid stronghold as surely as it did every morning, mind over matter or no mind over matter.

And this time when her hand went to her mouth it wasn't merely a reflex in response to a wave of simple nausea.

It was a necessity as she ran like mad for the nearest bathroom.

Kate woke up an hour later. She'd been sick so many times she'd lost count before succumbing to the accompanying exhaustion and falling asleep on the bed.

She felt better, though. In fact she felt just fine. Fine enough to even be hungry, although she was leery of leaving her rooms and rediscovering the bacon smell and the sickness all over again.

She got up and went to the sink in the bathroom, grimacing at the first sight of herself in the mirror above it.

Her mascara had melted into black crescents beneath both eyes, her skin was pale and her hair was a total mess. If she decided to venture out of her rooms for something to eat she couldn't do it looking like that, she decided. So she brushed her teeth thoroughly, washed her face and brushed her hair into a curly top-knot held at her crown with an elastic scrunchee.

Vanity took hold from there and she reapplied mascara and blush because she couldn't stand the thought of encountering Brady without it—crazy as she knew that was.

Her clothes still bore a faint trace of the bacon smell, so she stripped them off and went to the closet for something fresh. Opting for comfort over fashion, she chose a black fleece jumpsuit and slipped into it, appreciating the downy-softness of its inside against her bare skin since she'd even shed her bra, figuring the two large pockets over each of her breasts allowed for enough camouflage to allow that.

There was a knock on the sitting-room door as she pulled the zipper up the front, stopping a few inches below the hollow of her throat.

Brady was waiting in the hallway when she opened the door, bearing a tray and a surprised expression as his gaze took her in.

"Wow. Now there's an improvement," he said in greeting.

Kate smiled, glad she'd gone to the trouble of cleaning up.

"You seem to have made a miraculous recovery," he added.

"I have. I fell asleep and when I woke up a few minutes ago I felt perfectly fine again," she explained. "Must have been a fast-moving flu."

"I knew you were asleep. I came to check on you and when there was no answer to my knock I sent Maya in to see if you were okay. She said you were asleep and we all decided it was probably better to leave you alone. I've been listening for sounds of life since then, and when I heard them I fixed you tea and toast in case you felt up to it." He raised the tray slightly to indicate that was what was on it.

Kate appreciated the gesture. And the care and nurturing that came with it. "Tea and toast, huh?" she said, craning forward to peer at the contents of the tray.

"I can get you something else if you're hungry. Just not rumaki."

Kate wrinkled her nose at the mere mention of the word. "Definitely not rumaki. I am hungry, though. And tea and toast are probably about as brave as I should get for now. Is there jam, too?"

"No, but if you take the tray I'll go get you some."

"You don't have to."

"It's the least I can do since I made you sick with my cooking."

He'd made her sick all right, but not with his cooking alone. Of course, she couldn't say that, so instead she said, "That would be nice," even as she told herself she should have declined the offer, taken the tray and avoided spending any more time with him today.

But now that she felt good again she couldn't resist the opportunity to have more of what they'd been sharing in the kitchen when she'd gotten sick. Wise or not.

"I'll be back," Brady said, handing over the tray and turning on his heels to return to the kitchen.

Kate didn't mean to look at his derriere as he did, that just seemed to be where her gaze landed at that instant before she yanked her eyes off him and took the tray to the coffee table.

She set it down and then sat on the sofa, pouring the tea from a small silver pot into the china cup he'd brought, while still keeping an eye on the door. Not only was she eager to see him again but the moment he reappeared she said, "Would you close the door? I'm afraid of the bacon smell coming in here."

He did as she asked, then joined her on the couch. "You're making me feel guilty," he told her, referring to her most recent mention of the bacon.

"Good," she teased, not meaning it.

Brady leaned forward and put the strawberry jam on the toast for her.

"I think I can do that myself," she said with a laugh.

"Take advantage while you can," he advised.

She accepted the slice when he was finished with it and took a bite. "How did your rumaki go over with everyone else?" she asked then.

"Nobody but you ran out of the room with their hand over their mouth, so I guess it was a hit," he joked.

Kate held up the slice of bread to take another bite. "I can attest to your culinary skills with toast if that helps make up for my earlier insult to your talents."

"Makes me feel much better," he assured as they both settled back on the sofa, Kate with her tea and Brady sitting at enough of an angle to her to study her as if she were a sight for sore eyes.

Then, out of nowhere, he said, "You know I've been thinkin' that you never did tell me the details of that 'saving yourself for marriage' thing. How did you manage that? I mean, you're great looking. I would have thought there would have been a lot of hot pursuit of you that would have worn you down long before New Year's Eve."

"Hot pursuit of me?" she repeated with a laugh. "Hardly. I was a geek. Believe me, no one was in any kind of pursuit, hot or otherwise."

"I don't believe it."

"It's true. It took plastic surgery to have my ears pinned back to stop me from looking like Dumbo the Elephant Girl, and four years of braces on my teeth to correct nature's dastardly dentistry in my mouth."

"No," he said dubiously, looking more closely at her ears and then her teeth.

"I wouldn't lie about it. Didn't you notice what a sight I was in those old photographs we put in the scrapbook the other night? I was a horrible geek until I was seventeen."

"Okay, so you were a geek until you were seventeen. That still left a lot of years between then and New Year's Eve."

"You're forgetting I also have four older brothers."

"What did they do? Go out on your dates with you?"

"Dates? I didn't date. Nothing ever got that far. Even the few nerdy guys who showed the slightest bit of interest in me got chased off by my brothers before they so much as asked me out."

"You didn't have a single date all through high school?" Brady recapped with disbelief.

"Not a single one. My brothers thought it was hilarious to scare off anybody who came within ten feet of me."

"Big dumb jerks," he said affectionately.

"I called them a lot worse than that," Kate assured him. "But it never did any good."

She'd finished her tea and toast so she set the cup on the coffee table and curled her feet up underneath her, pivoting slightly toward Brady to look at him while they talked.

There was a sense of closeness to sitting there like that with him and she was aware of just how nice it was. Not to mention that she was relishing the look in his eyes as he kept his gaze focused on her. A look of warmth. Of fondness. Of something more. Something that seemed very sensual.

And very dangerous because of the way it made her feel.

But she didn't want to analyze it. She didn't want to fight it. She just wanted to indulge in that sense she had that he found her so desirable he couldn't imagine that she'd ever been anything less to any other man.

"What about college?" he asked then. "You went away for that. There must have been guys who were after you on campus."

Kate held up two fingers. "It wasn't as if I'd developed great skills of flirtation," she admitted. "Or knew what to do with guys when they actually stuck around awhile and asked me out. I was awkward and, well, geeky, and after a couple of dates I never heard from either one of them again."

"And that was it? All through college you only went out a few times with two different guys?" Brady said, again as if he couldn't believe what he was hearing.

"That was it."

"What about after you graduated?"

That question took them to the present and to memories too painful for Kate to talk about as glibly as she'd told everything else.

Brady must have seen the change in her expression because he said, "Oh-oh. Here's where the inexperience hurts." He stretched an arm along the top of the sofa back behind her and squeezed her shoulder with one of those big hands.

It was a simple gesture of support, but just his touch was powerful enough to make Kate feel more than comforted. It also set off little sparks from that spot to rain all through her. Sparks that had absolutely nothing to do with comfort or compassion, and everything to do with bringing to life the kind of feelings he'd brought to life in Las Vegas. The kind of feelings that had made her throw caution to the wind.

Kate tried to ignore those feelings and said, "It wasn't the inexperience that hurt me. It was Dwight Mooney."

"He preyed on your innocence?" Brady guessed.

"No, in fact it was exactly what he was looking for, because he was just as inexperienced. By choice, though. His family was very old-fashioned and very religious. His father was a minister, in fact. They believed in not having sex out of marriage. Our both being virgins was a big deal to him."

Brady's eyebrows rose. "How long were you together?"

"Five years. After college I was busy concentrating on my career and still didn't date more than a couple of one-time deals. Then I met Dwight."

"You were together for five years and he never touched you?"

Kate had to smile at the complete shock in Brady's tone. "He kissed me," she offered.

"But that's all?"

"That's all."

"Wow."

"I know, it sounds pretty extreme. But that's what he was committed to, and I thought the ability to make such a strong commitment to something—especially something as tough as that—was a good sign. A sign of character. And since we got engaged a year into the relationship, I honestly thought that anytime we'd be getting married and the wait would be over."

"And even once you were engaged? Nothing?"

"Kissing. Only kissing. Anything else was against his religion."

"Were you okay with that?"

Kate thought about it. "Well, I don't know. I didn't expect the engagement to go on for so long, that's for sure. He kept putting off setting a date and I didn't like that. But I thought Dwight was a good man. He treated me well. He was attentive. Caring. He said we were building a foundation to base our life together on, and I hoped that was true. I hoped his passion for his religion and his commitments would translate into passion for me once we were married and he felt free to…consummate it."

"Okay, I guess I can see that," Brady conceded.

"Plus, I loved him and I felt as comfortable with Dwight as I did with my brothers. I thought that meant I had found my other half, the man I was meant to be with. And the fact that he was someone who wouldn't expect me to…know what I was doing in the bedroom made the whole thing seem like he was the guy for me."

Brady's face creased into a pained kind of smile, and he dropped his head to the top of hers. "Oh, Kate," he said, sighing her name into her hair. Then he raised his head again and said, "I'd like to take all four of those brothers of yours, hog-tie 'em and hang 'em by their heels in the hot sun."

Kate laughed. "Why?"

"Because their foolin' around made you think you had to settle for a guy who could keep his hands off you for five years."

She hadn't thought of it like that.

"Tell me you finally saw there was somethin' wrong with good ol' Dwight and gave him the heave-ho."

"I'd like to tell you that, but it wouldn't be the truth," she said softly, because in spite of Brady's more flattering perspective, Dwight had hurt her deeply.

"What happened?" Brady asked kindly.

Kate took a deep breath to shore up for telling what she hadn't admitted to many people since it had happened. "I thought we were on the verge of finally setting a date for the wedding. I'd even told my friend Kelly to keep April—next month—open so we could have a spring wedding. I was all ready to start picking out bridesmaids' dresses and flowers and a caterer—" An unexpected catch in Kate's voice stalled her a moment while she tamped down the pain, rejection and humiliation she'd thought she'd put behind her.

"The idiot broke it off with you?" Brady asked with another full measure of disbelief that helped bolster her.

"Worse," she said. "Dwight eloped with a woman who lived in the apartment across the hall from me. She was a stripper who ran so many men in and out of her place that Dwight and I had wondered if she was—"

"Playing for pay?" Brady supplied.

"Yes." She took another deep breath and consciously attempted to sigh away the bad feelings the subject had raised.

"How did Dwight get from saint to sinner so fast?"

"He moved her couch one night."

Brady laughed, picking up on the levity she was trying to inject into this subject that was so difficult for her.

"He moved her couch," he repeated. "That'll do it every time."

"They had come up on the elevator together one night, and when she recognized him from seeing him going in and out of my place she asked if he'd help her out. He told me afterward that he'd only agreed because it was the Christian thing to do."

"Right," Brady said facetiously.

"Anyway, I didn't think anything about it. After all, he was so good at resisting me, it didn't occur to me that he'd have any problem resisting anyone else. Especially someone he'd talked about with such scorn before that."

"What was he doing, just covering up the hots for her all along?"

"According to his explanation on the phone from

Reno, the couch moving had only been the beginning of something between them that he *couldn't* resist. They'd been seeing each other on the sly since then, and he'd discovered a drive in himself that he hadn't known he'd had when he was with me. He said it was just something he couldn't do anything about, and since he still didn't want to act on it outside of marriage—"

"He eloped with her."

"He eloped with her."

Brady closed his eyes in a tight grimace and shook his head. "Incredible."

Then he opened his eyes again to look at her with that penetrating blue gaze. "And that was why you were more than ready to shed your virginity a little over a month later in Las Vegas," he concluded.

"Sort of," she agreed.

"But not really?"

"There was just a lot more to what happened in Las Vegas than that."

"Shall I guess? Dwight's elopement was all it took to make you feel the way you had before meeting him— undesirable, unappealing, not pretty enough. And a little fling was a good ego booster."

"Yes," she admitted tentatively, amazed that he understood her so well. "But that wasn't all there was to it, either," she added then, not wanting him to think what she was afraid he thought. Especially when it wasn't true. "I wasn't using you."

He laughed lightly at that. "Ah, Kate. There's nobody quite like you. I never thought you were using me."

"I mean, you were so much fun to be with and I was having such a good time—" She'd almost said she'd also been so attracted to him that she just hadn't been able to help herself, but stopped short of that. Instead she said, "I just got carried away by it all. Losing my virginity... Well, yes, I was ready to do that, but it wasn't as if I'd planned to do it. It was actually the last thing on my mind until... Until things started happening between us."

Brady put a knuckle to her chin to make her look directly at him. "I *was* fun to be with and you *were* having a good time? All past tense?" he said, his tone teasing but edged with a note of seriousness, too, as if he were concerned she might be telling him things had changed now and she wasn't enjoying his company.

"We were talking about the past, weren't we?" she reminded him, rather than expose just how much she did like being with him.

"Okay, then what about now?" he persisted with a half grin that was pure devil, the kind Dwight would never have known how to give.

And Kate basked in it.

"Now you're making me sick," she teased, referring to the bacon incident.

But Brady missed the reference and went on the alert. "Right this minute? Again?"

Kate laughed. "I was talking about this afternoon. I feel great now." More than great. She felt warm and comfortable and relaxed and alive all at once. And very aware of those sparks that he'd ignited in her, still dancing through her veins as if they were electrical wires.

Brady's expression eased and he smiled again. Slowly this time, with those eyes so bright they made her heart ache.

"You *look* great," he said with so much of what

sounded like genuine appreciation that Kate believed him in a way she'd never believed it before. "But tell me that you're still having fun with me," he ordered, not letting her off the hook that easily.

"Okay, okay, I'm still having fun with you," she finally admitted.

It pleased him because his smile turned into a grin. A grin she got lost in.

"Now tell me you don't hate it that I'm hanging around so much."

"I don't hate it that you're hanging around so much."

"And I'm not forcin' myself on you?"

She laughed. "Forcing yourself on me?"

"When you'd rather be readin' a book or somethin'."

"I haven't felt forced upon, no."

Her responses—even though they were prompted—seemed to please him because his grin reappeared moments before he kissed her.

His knuckle at her chin somehow became his hand caressing her jaw and the side of her face to guide her as his mouth came over hers in a soft kiss. But soft or not, after having talked about Dwight, Kate couldn't help comparing even that fledgling kiss to kisses her ex-fiancé had given. No wonder they had the power to do so much to her, she thought, because even that tender, beginning buss was so much better, so much more intriguing, so much more potent than anything Dwight had ever bestowed.

And when Brady deepened the kiss, when his lips parted and urged hers to part, too, when his tongue came to say hello, he left Dwight in the dust. In fact, he wiped Dwight right out of her mind as his arms came around her and pulled her up against him, his hands massaging her back through the velvety fleece of her jumpsuit.

Between his kiss and his touch those sparks dancing along her veins turned into little flames that made her answer his teasing tongue thrust for thrust, taunt for taunt. They brought her arms around him, too, and inspired her hands to fill themselves with the hard expanse of his back, with the roll of honed muscles and the breadth of shoulders strong enough to bear the weight of the world.

Her breasts were pressed to his chest, yearning, striving for attention. For the kind of attention that Kate barely remembered from Las Vegas and yet craved with a sudden intensity that nearly drove her wild. Wild enough to arch her back, to press them more insistently into the wall of a man that was Brady.

Oh, how she wanted him to touch her!

Just then one wonderful hand began a slow slide from her back to her side, slower still to the straining globe of her breast until he cupped it in his big palm.

A small moan of pleasure escaped her throat with that initial contact, and she instantly wished the jumpsuit would disappear so she could feel the full impact of his skin against hers.

Their mouths were open wide by then in a seeking, hungering kiss that gave Kate the courage to slip her own hands under the knit of his Henley shirt to his bare back. Hot satin over steel—that was what it felt like—and she couldn't get enough of it, digging her fingertips into taut sinew in a way that unconsciously mimicked the kneading her breasts were crying out for. So much so that her spine had arched even more, insinuating that single globe firmly into his adept hand.

He seemed to be perfectly in tune with her, with her needs, because just when she thought she couldn't endure a moment more of the barrier of cloth, he deserted her breast altogether so he could pull the zipper of her jumpsuit down. Inch by snail's-crawl inch until it was finally low enough for him to give her what she wanted, what she needed, so desperately—her bare breast engulfed in his bare hand.

Another groan echoed in her throat as bliss washed through her with such force she nearly felt faint. She'd realized that pregnancy had made her breasts more sensitive, but she hadn't known there would be so much more pleasure in that sensitivity until that moment when nothing came between his kneading, teasing, seeking hand and her oh-so-aroused flesh.

In fact, the pleasure was so great, so intense, it tore her mouth from his kiss as she nearly writhed beneath the exquisite things he was doing to her. Her nipple kerneled into a tight knot in his palm. A knot he rolled gently between his fingers, traced round and round, and tormented so deliciously she almost couldn't contain herself as everything inside her came awake with a jolt of need, of wanting, of desire for even more of what he was doing to her. For his mouth to be where his hand was. For his hand to be lower still. For more than his hand to find that place between her legs that was thrumming to life....

But that was when he stopped. Suddenly. As if something had just occurred to him.

Just when she wanted so much more, his glorious hand slipped completely out of her jumpsuit, zipping it up to her throat.

"Brady?" she said in a husky whisper that sounded more vulnerable than she wished it had.

He kissed her again, but only softly, quickly, before he laid his cheek to hers for a moment and then sat back.

"I don't think we better push this after your being so sick this afternoon," he said in a voice as raspy as hers had been.

"I'm fine. Really," she heard herself say before thinking better of it, before realizing how much of her own need it revealed.

But even that didn't matter.

"Fine is how I want you to stay feeling, too," he said with a conviction that sounded as if it were warring with a hunger as strong in him as the hunger that was still coursing through her.

And yet, despite that hunger, there was something else in his expression that kept her from saying more. Something in his eyes. A look she couldn't read.

But what popped into her mind after a split second was the thought that somewhere in the middle of things he'd figured he wasn't going to make the same mistake he'd made in Las Vegas no matter what raw desire might be urging him to.

And that stabbed her as surely as any knife might have, even as a part of her was still wishing he would pick up where he'd left off.

But he didn't take her into his arms the way she wanted him to. He didn't kiss her again or touch her. He certainly didn't carry her off to bed to make love to her.

Instead he stood and said, "Get some rest."

It was on the tip of her tongue to say she'd just had a nap. But she didn't. If he didn't want her, he didn't want her, and nothing she said could change that—she knew it only too well after her experience with Dwight.

"If you get sick during the night and need me—need anything at all—just holler," he said then.

"I'll be fine," she told him stiffly but very, very quietly as old feelings of rejection set in.

He stood there staring at her, frowning, searching for something she couldn't fathom. But he wasn't about to let her in on it because he just said, "Sleep tight then," and turned on his heels to go out of the room on long strides that seemed to pound thorns into her heart with every step he took away from her.

Then he was out the door, closing it behind him, and Kate was left even more confused than she'd been before.

Confused and hurt and wanting him so much it was an empty ache inside her.

Chapter 10

Kate was just getting over the next day's morning sickness when she had a phone call. She took it in her bedroom with the door closed, because she had a good idea who her caller was even before she picked up. She also had a good idea what they'd be talking about.

Kate's best friend, Kelly McGill, had been scheduled to return from her vacation in Mexico late the previous night, and Kate was expecting to hear from her.

Sure enough, the voice on the other end of the line that answered Kate's hello belonged to Kelly.

"Well?" was all Kelly said.

Kate didn't need any more explanation than that. She knew Kelly wanted to know if the doctor in Cheyenne had confirmed that Kate was pregnant.

"Yes," Kate answered in a quiet voice.

"You're pregnant," Kelly said with a sigh.

"Yes."

"Shall I say congratulations or I'm sorry?"

Kate laughed a little at that. "Congratulations. I think."

"Okay. Congratulations. And whatever you do, don't marry the father."

Kate laughed again, understanding perfectly her friend's comment. "Speaking of Buster…" she said. "How did he do with the boys while you were gone?"

"About the usual. Not well. They were happy to see me and glad to leave him, and he made it clear he was just as glad to have them go."

It was Kate's turn to sigh. "I keep hoping he'll finally step up to the plate, but he just doesn't, does he?"

"No. And if he hasn't by now, he never will. He's out of work again, too, by the way."

"Not again."

"And, as always, according to him it's my fault."

"Same old song and dance?"

"Yes. If I hadn't gotten pregnant and he hadn't had to marry me he'd have finished college the way he'd planned and now he wouldn't be getting passed over for promotions in favor of people with degrees."

"I suppose it's also your fault that he mouths off or storms out of his jobs on a whim."

"Of course. I'm responsible for ruining his life and that's why he has a bad attitude—that's what he tells me every time. As if I was alone in that backseat that night or planned to get pregnant. Like I said, don't marry the father, whatever you do. It's better for you and the baby to avoid this kind of resentment. Before and after the inevitable divorce that comes out of some guy marrying you because he thinks he has to."

Kelly said that matter-of-factly and with a minimum of bitterness because Buster's resentment was a plain fact she'd been living with for so long now. A plain fact Kate didn't want to experience for herself.

"Believe me, I don't have any intention of marrying anybody," Kate told her friend, feeling a renewed conviction that came with the reminder of how even what had begun as a loving relationship could deteriorate so disastrously.

"Is the dad there at the ranch?" Kelly asked then.

Kate had told her originally that Brady was due for a visit within days of her doctor's appointment.

"Right in the room beside mine. And he's buying the place next door, too."

"You'll be neighbors. Is that good or bad?" Kelly asked in the same tone she'd used to inquire if she should offer congratulations or sympathies on the pregnancy.

"I don't know yet," Kate said honestly.

"You haven't let him know you're pregnant?"

"I haven't let anybody but you know I'm pregnant— well, you and Junebug. But she guessed. I haven't told my family or Brady, either."

"I know you'll tell your family eventually. But are you going to tell Brady?"

"I don't think there's any way around it, do you?"

"And depending on his reaction, it could be good that he'll be close by to actually be a father to the baby or bad if he acts like Buster does."

"That's about it," Kate confirmed, not adding that it could also be bad to have Brady so nearby, where she would have to watch him go on with his life—his life with other women—and how painful that might be for her.

But Kelly knew her too well. "What about your feelings for him?" she said as if she were privy to Kate's thoughts. "You really liked the guy in Las Vegas. He's been almost all you've talked about ever since."

"I haven't been that bad. Have I?"

"Pretty much. We haven't had a single conversation that you haven't brought him up one way or another."

Kate knew Brady had been on her mind almost non-stop since January, but she hadn't realized she'd talked about him that much. She wasn't heartened to be made aware of it now. "He's a nice enough guy," she hedged.

"You're liking him more and more, aren't you?" Kelly said, again reading Kate like a book.

"I'm trying not to," Kate confessed.

"Oh, Kate," Kelly said as if she'd just heard something that scared her.

"I won't do anything dumb," Kate said firmly. "But it would be better for everybody if we had a civil relationship."

"Civil, yes. But don't forget you have happy hormones at work. Nature designed them to make you look at the father of your baby and think he's a prince whether he is or not. Keep that in mind."

"You weren't thinking Buster was a prince when he didn't show up in the delivery room because he was playing softball and wouldn't leave."

"I'm just saying—"

"I know. It's easy to want to believe in the happily ever after fairy tale."

Kelly didn't say anything for a moment. Then she switched gears. "Of course, just because things didn't work out for me, doesn't mean they won't work out for you. Maybe this Brady guy *is* a prince. Maybe he's always wanted a family and he fell in love with you at first sight in Las Vegas and he'll be thrilled to his toes to find out he can have the whole package all at once."

"He is a nice guy. But he's already said he isn't ready for a family yet."

"You were fishing?"

"Maybe a little. Just to get a feel for how he might react when I tell him. And believe me, I'm the last person on earth with any illusions about my being such an irresistible force that he'll change his mind on the spot."

"Just because you weren't an irresistible force to Dwight doesn't mean you won't be to someone else."

Kate laughed. "How many pregnant irresistible forces do you know?"

"Don't get down on yourself, Kate. You're great, pregnant or not pregnant. Dwight was just an idiot."

"That's me all right…great," Kate said with false bravado.

"So when are you going to tell him?"

Kate explained her decision to wait until the divorce papers were filed so it would be clear she didn't want to stay married to him.

But even as she was saying the words, she was thinking that, when she did finally tell him about the baby, everything would change. That what had begun to happen between them in these last few days and nights would end. And so would the way he made her feel—attractive, desirable, sexy, irresistible….

Maybe what was going through her mind echoed in her tone because when she was finished Kelly said, "Are you going to be okay?"

"Sure," Kate said with more confidence than she felt.

"Why don't you duck out and come here to stay with the boys and me for a while? To get away."

"Thanks but I'd kind of like to wait things out here so as soon as I know the divorce is final I can tell him and get it over with."

But that was a lie. The truth was that being presented with an option to put some real distance between herself and Brady only pushed Kate to realize she didn't want to be too far from him. From all those things he was making her feel.

"Well, if you won't come to stay you can at least call and talk through what you're going to say to him beforehand. Practice on me," Kelly offered.

Kate laughed again. "I might do that. Dress rehearsal."

"But if you don't you'll let me know when you do tell him?"

"You know I will."

"And you also know I'm here for you, don't you?"

"You always have been." Sounds of angry voices had been coming from the background on Kelly's end of the line for several minutes, and they seemed to have gained heat and volume suddenly. "Are the boys fighting?"

"I think they're trying to kill each other."

"You better go break it up before they do."

"I know. I'm just worried about you."

"I'll be fine," Kate assured. "Go take care of your kids."

"We'll talk soon."

"Soon," Kate confirmed before they said their goodbyes and hung up.

* * *

"Oh, man, is it beautiful up here! I don't know why you got the bug to take me flyin' today, but what a day for it—not a cloud in the sky, the trees just beginnin' to bud, fresh snow in the high country—incredible! And worth all those peeved looks we got when we said we were duckin' out for an hour while everybody else gets things ready for Buzz's party tonight."

Brady smiled at Matt's enthusiasm, barely noticing the splendor his friend was talking about as Brady piloted his plane to the farthest reaches of the McDermot property and beyond.

The view wasn't the reason Brady wanted to get Matt up there. His real purpose was to get away from Kate. Only this time, he wanted to get away from Kate not because of the hot, simmering attraction he had for her. This time he just wanted to make absolutely sure she didn't overhear what he needed to ask her brother. He wanted to make sure no one overheard it.

"You don't look like you're enjoyin' this as much as I am, though," Matt said then. "In fact, you look like you've been up all night and could use some sleep."

"A touch of insomnia last night," Brady said as if it were nothing, when in fact he hadn't been able to sleep for good reason. He'd been up pacing the floor, thinking things he was determined to have confirmed or refuted this morning.

But not in any forthright way. So, as if he were merely changing the subject because his sleeplessness was too negligible to discuss, he said, "How's Kate been since Las Vegas?"

"What're you doin'? Lookin' to find out if she missed you?"

"No, it's just that she finally told me about that Dwight guy and how she was comin' off his eloping with someone else when we met. I wondered if Las Vegas helped and she was back to her old self afterward."

Matt gave him a sly smile. "Or maybe what you're really wonderin' is if she might be ready to move on to a new relationship now," he said, gloating over what he was apparently choosing to believe was his successful matchmaking.

"Has she been seein' anybody?"

Again Matt interpreted that to suit himself and his own goals. "No, you've got a clear field there. She's about been hibernating. Has hardly left the ranch except to get things goin' for her office. Been doin' a lot of sleepin'."

"She hasn't dated anyone at all?"

"Not a soul. At least not anybody around Elk Creek."

"But how about outside of Elk Creek? Any trips anywhere else? Somewhere she might have hooked up with somebody?" Brady asked.

Matt turned his head to look straight at Brady. "I can't believe how off your game you are since Claudia left you. What are you? Scared of competition? That isn't like you."

"I'm just thinkin' that Kate could have something goin' on with somebody outside of Elk Creek."

"She hasn't taken any trips anywhere. I told you, she hasn't left the ranch except to go into town, now and then. The truth is, we've been figurin' she's still mendin' a broken heart over Dwight. She's seemed kind of under the weather. She's pale. Not a lot of energy. Not eatin' much. And like I said, sleepin' way more than any of us have ever known her to sleep. She was perky enough in Vegas, but it didn't carry over once we got her back here." Matt grinned slyly as he added, "Maybe it's just you who makes her feel better."

Brady ignored the comment. "So she was the same before Vegas—sleepin' a lot, not eatin', under the weather? Vegas was a change of pace for her and then she went right back to it?"

Matt thought about that. Then he said, "Now that you mention it, no, she wasn't doin' that stuff before. She was unhappy. Real down in the dumps. But she was eatin' fine. And *not* bein' able to sleep was more her problem then. She was stayin' up later than anybody every night and out in the kitchen in the mornings before us all. It's only been lately…"

Matt did a mock glare in response to his own words sinking in. "Hey, did you do somethin' to my sister in Las Vegas that made her worse off?" he joked.

Unfortunately there was nothing funny to Brady in that possibility. Still, he didn't want to raise his friend's curiosity or suspicions so he said, "Nah. We had a good time in Vegas. You just said yourself she was in a better mood when we were there. Maybe she just got away from her troubles for that time and then got the blues all over again when she got back."

"Yeah, that makes sense," Matt agreed.

"I'm not sure what you're talkin' about when you say she looks pale, though," Brady said to segue into the other questions he had. "In fact, I was wonderin' if she might've done something to herself."

"Done something to herself?" Matt repeated. "What do you mean? Like new makeup or hair or something?"

"Yeah. Or even like plastic surgery."

Matt cast him a glance that said he thought Brady was crazy. "Plastic surgery? As in a nose job or somethin'?"

Actually what Brady was thinking about was south of her nose. Pretty far south.

"It's not her nose, no. I just thought there was something a little different about her," Brady persisted.

"Nah, she didn't have plastic surgery," Matt continued. "I told you, she's been at the ranch the whole time since Vegas." Then Matt laughed. "Oh, I get it. She's lookin' even better to you now than she did New Year's and you're tryin' to figure out why."

It wasn't so much the way she looked as the way she felt. But Brady couldn't say that to her brother.

Matt chuckled again with obvious pleasure. "Things startin' up with you two, are they? No wonder you've spent more time with her than with me since you got here."

Brady forced a smile that seemed to confirm that, all the while thinking that he was afraid something might have started up with Kate but not what Matt was figuring on.

"Hey, who is it who's been busy with a woman?" Brady countered.

Matt grinned. "Yeah, I know. I spend every minute I can with Jenn. I wasn't complainin' about you bein' with Kate. My findin' Jenn was the best thing that ever happened to me. I can't tell you how I feel about her. One look at her face and I just fill up inside. Makes me want that for everybody. Especially for my best friend and my sister."

"How about working out?" Brady said when another possibility occurred to him in the middle of what Matt had been saying. "Has Kate been exercising or lifting weights to…you know…build herself up or something?"

"Working out? No, she hasn't been working out. Like I said, she's been sleepin' till nearly noon every day. Says she's takin' advantage of her time off while she has it." Matt poked him in the ribs with an elbow. "She's *really* lookin' good to you, huh?"

"Yeah," Brady admitted truthfully. "She's really looking good to me."

"And how's she actin'?"

"How's she acting?" Brady repeated.

"Did you take my advice and get her to open up to you? Get things rollin' so she'd develop an interest in you?"

An interest in him? Brady supposed it could be called that. But he had to hope there was more to it than simple interest. Especially after the previous night when she'd just about driven him wild with wanting her. So wild that he'd been headed for making love to her again until it struck him that something was different about her. About her body. And even though he'd tried to write it off to his memories of New Year's Eve being too foggy to be reliable, the more he'd touched her, the more he'd begun to believe that his memories might be more reliable than he thought.…

"I can't be sure what's going on with her," Brady said, belatedly answering Matt's question about whether or not Kate was interested in him.

"Is she still keepin' you at arm's length?"

Brady could hardly tell his friend that Kate had let him get a whole lot closer than that, so instead he said, "We've both just learned to be cautious."

"I think you both just worry too much."

"Maybe," Brady agreed, all the while thinking that he just might have more to worry about than Matt realized.

Maybe a whole lot more....

Chapter 11

Kate chose her favorite dress for her grandfather's birthday party that evening. She'd tried it on a few days earlier, and although it still fit, she knew it was likely to be the last time she could wear it until after the baby was born. It was an ankle-length cashmere tube the soft-brown color of milk chocolate. And while it wasn't formfitting, it didn't have much room to spare.

She showered late in the day and washed her hair, leaving it to air dry with a few finger-scrunchings along the way to ensure that it curled enough to wear loose, and with the hour the guests were to arrive fast approaching, she slipped the dress on over her string-bikini panties and bandeau bra.

The bandeau bra was a necessity because the dress had a wide boat neck that would expose straps. But she loved the three-inch V-split the neckline took in the center at the base of her throat so it was worth the slight sense of insecurity to go without straps.

The sleeves were three-quarter length, freeing her wrists for the dozen small beaded bracelets she and Maya had each bought on a whim in town the week before.

A little blush and mascara were the only dabs of makeup she applied. Then she combed her hair into a wild array of curls that ended in a blunt-cut at her jaw. She slipped her feet into a pair of thin-heeled strappy pumps and took a close look at the finished product in the full-length mirror, turning to the side for the most important view.

The increase in her bust size caused the cashmere to fall far enough away from the slight bulge of her belly so that her pregnancy was hardly noticeable at all. She could rest assured that no one was likely to guess at her condition.

"But even if they do, it's okay," she reminded herself.

It was okay because she'd already made up her mind that she was going to tell Brady about the baby very soon, whether the divorce papers were filed or not. She'd decided that signing them was message enough of her intentions and that she would reinforce that when she told him by insisting the divorce still be finalized. But in the meantime, she'd be taking some action. Before it was too late.

Her talk with Kelly had brought her to the conclusion that it was best not to keep the secret any longer. What had happened with Brady the night before had been on her mind, and realizing she was dragging her feet about getting away from him when she'd spoken to Kelly had set off warning bells inside her. The conversation had left her knowing more than ever that she was playing with fire to let things go on the way they had been.

It wasn't a matter of just forming a friendship or a civil relationship on which to base their co-parenting, the way she'd tried to convince herself it was. Friends didn't keep ending up in each other's arms. They didn't keep ending up kissing each other. Touching each other. Very nearly making love to each other. And she had to stop fooling herself that friendship or mere civility was all there was to it.

At least for her.

She couldn't be sure what was happening on Brady's side. But she had to face the fact that she was getting in over her head.

"As if having his baby doesn't already count as getting in over my head," she muttered in response to her own thoughts as she applied a light lip gloss.

But still, she knew that the feelings that were coming to life inside her just as surely as the baby itself was, were only compounding her problems. The plain truth was that no matter what she'd told herself along the way, and no matter how dangerous she knew it was, she was coming to care for Brady.

Maybe Kelly was right and it was those happy hormones her friend had talked about, but she just couldn't let what had gone on so far keep going on. Keep progressing. And since her willpower was nearly nonexistent when it came to Brady, she'd decided that the best thing to do was to drop the bomb she believed would change everything for her whether she liked it or not. And put an end to what needed to be ended.

Before it was too late and her feelings for him got any stronger.

Before it was too late and Brady looked back on everything that had happened between them since he'd arrived at the ranch and wondered if it had all been devised to trap him.

So she was going to tell him. At the first possible moment.

And maybe then things would be put on the straight and narrow where they should have been all along.

And hopefully it wouldn't hurt too much.

Since Buzz had been born, raised and had lived his whole life in Elk Creek, the party to celebrate his eightieth birthday was a big one. His only daughter— Kate, Ry, Shane, Bax and Matt's mother—had intended to be there but had been kept away by a case of bronchitis that had prohibited her from flying in. She was hardly missed, though. With so many of the townsfolk there it seemed as if the entire citizenry had come to pay homage to the elderly man who held court in the living room.

Kate and the rest of the McDermot women, along with Junebug, were kept busy seeing to the needs and comfort of their guests, so it should have been easy for Kate to have been completely oblivious of Brady. To not even notice him.

But that wasn't the case.

All of her brothers put effort into introducing him around, making sure every person there met him and learned he'd just bought the Barton place and would be a member of the community. But somehow those introductions never took place far from where Kate was. And even as Brady engaged in conversation that she could tell was already making him well liked, each time Kate glanced up she found his gaze crossing to her as if he were still more aware of her than of anyone else in the house.

Of course, despite the crowd and her own chats with everyone, Kate was still more aware of Brady than of anyone else in the house, too. It was just impossible for her not to be.

This realization really didn't make sense to her, but like the previous day in her office—when it had occurred to her that the sight of Jace Brimley didn't have the same effect on her that the sight of Brady did, even standing in the midst of five of Junebug's six strikingly handsome sons—it was still Brady who caught Kate's eye.

He wasn't any taller than the Brimley men. Or broader of shoulder or narrower of hip. His dark, longish hair wasn't any more remarkable, and while there was no disputing his drop-dead good looks, Junebug's sons were like a gallery of gorgeous men all standing around in a circle. And yet not one of them riveted Kate's attention the way Brady did.

Happy hormones, she told herself. That's all it was.

But whether or not that was true, nothing changed the fact that she was attuned to his every movement. That she devoured the sight of his thick thighs and tight derriere in the black jeans he wore. That she feasted on the sight of him in the dove-gray Western shirt that hugged his waist, while his mile-wide shoulders were saddle-bagged in a black design that came to points over pectorals she wanted stripped bare before her so she could run her hands over the honed chest muscles.

And try as she might she just couldn't seem to stay distracted from him even at a distance. As far as she was concerned they might as well have been alone in the house, even though they rarely got near enough to speak.

At the first sign that the guests were beginning to leave, Junebug started a surreptitious cleanup so that by midnight, when the last of them were gone and Buzz had taken himself off to bed, there wasn't anything left to do that couldn't wait for the morning.

"Just let the rest be, until tomorrow," the imposing housekeeper instructed as she put on her coat and headed for home with her family in tow.

No one seemed inclined to go against the housekeeper's wishes and instead good-nights were in the process of being said as Kate bent over to remove her shoes, because she didn't think she could stand them long enough to walk to her room.

But when she straightened up it was to find herself alone in the kitchen with Brady as everyone else wandered off to their rooms.

He was watching her with the same quiet study that had been in his blue-gray eyes all evening, and it was beginning to make her wonder what he was thinking about to put it there.

But he didn't give her any clue when he said, "Nice party."

"I hope everyone thought so," she responded, as the deep rye whisky of his voice seemed to wash her in warmth for no reason she could put her finger on.

"You know what I didn't get, though?"

She knew what she hadn't gotten—time with him to appease the unwanted craving for it.

But all she said was, "What?"

"Birthday cake. How about it? Are you up for a birthday cake nightcap?"

There it was—the perfect opportunity to sit down with him and tell him she was pregnant.

But now that the moment had presented itself, Kate hesitated.

It was very late. She was tired. Wouldn't it be better to wait until tomorrow, when she was rested and so was he? When it didn't come as some sort of afterthought?

Okay, so maybe she was only hedging. But what harm would a few more hours' postponement do?

"Birthday cake sounds good," she heard herself say, even as a voice in the back of her mind was warning her she was playing with fire yet again.

"I'll tell you what, you've worked all day, so you go to your room where you can be comfortable, and I'll serve you for a change."

Kate figured her fatigue was showing, and in truth she really was too tired to fight a suggestion that was so appealing. So she said, "Just a little piece of cake for me," and did as she'd been told.

She'd hardly had a chance to drop her shoes, sit on the sofa in her sitting room and put her feet up when Brady followed, carrying two plates.

He handed her one and then pointed a finger of his free hand at his boots. "Do you mind?"

Kate shook her head, and off came his cowboy boots before he joined her on the couch and propped his feet beside hers.

A flood of emotion welled up in her at the intimacy of his two big feet so casually next to her much smaller ones, and she tried to fight her reaction. But there was something about him being in his stocking feet that just made her feel that way.

I must really be tired if something that inconsequential can move me, she thought.

"Good cake," Brady observed then, after his second bite.

Kate forced herself to concentrate on that, rather than on their feet, and tasted it herself.

"But no ice cream," she countered once she had.

"We already ate our share of that, remember? That was the deal—we had ours so we couldn't eat any tonight." Then he gave her a half grin. "Besides, I looked and it was all gone."

Kate didn't want to like him as much as she did at that moment, but she couldn't help that, either. Although, in an attempt to keep her perspective she did force herself to say, "Have you sent the divorce papers to the lawyer yet?"

That sobered Brady somewhat. "Not yet," he said. Then he added, "I'm sorry, but I think there's a law against talkin' about stuff like that while eatin' cake this good. And I'll have to enforce it."

"Ah," she said with a slight laugh.

They ate in silence for a little while. Brady seemed somewhat lost in thought, and Kate had the oddest sense that he might be trying to tell *her* something.

Or maybe she was just projecting her own thoughts on to him. But somehow, coupled with the abrupt ending of what had been happening between them the previous night, she was slightly unnerved by the possibility that he might actually be looking for the right moment to say his piece. Maybe to say that he really had stopped short because he felt it would have been

a mistake to go any further. That he was uncomfortable with the directions things had taken with them
again....

But just as Kate's fears mounted Brady said, "No
sickness tonight?"

There wasn't anything in his tone to lead her to
think he had anything else on his mind, and she relaxed a little. "You mean like last night?" she asked
for the sake of clarification.

"Mmm," he confirmed as he took another bite of
cake.

"No flu tonight," she said honestly, setting her plate
on the coffee table because she'd had enough.

Brady finished his slice and then hers, too, without
any indication that what she'd been worried might be
going through his head was a reality.

Then he proved he wasn't thinking about telling her
he was uncomfortable with the direction things had
taken with them because once he'd leaned forward to
pile the dishes together on the coffee table he hooked
his arm around her legs and brought them with him as
he sat back, swiveling her so that she was sideways on
the sofa with her legs across his lap. And the intimacy
of their feet together on the coffee table was nothing
compared to that.

"I didn't get a chance to tell you how great you look
tonight," he said as he angled himself to get a more
direct view of her, settling in to massage her calves
and ankles with a familiarity that only increased the
sense of intimacy.

"Thank you," she said in a breathier voice than she'd
intended as his hands set glittering things to light inside her.

"I kept trying to get close enough to tell you that earlier, but every time I headed in your direction you seemed to go the other way."

"Not on purpose," she said. "I was just busy playing hostess."

The man should have been a masseur, Kate thought as he continued working on her legs, chasing away the weariness in them.

"I thought maybe you were steerin' clear of me because of last night."

"You were the one who seemed to want space last night," she reminded.

"Space? Was that what I wanted last night?" he said with a sly smile.

"That's how it seemed. I thought it was the logical conclusion when you left in such a hurry."

He gave her a devil's grin. "Logical? There wasn't anything logical about last night."

"What was it then?" she challenged, as his hands around her ankles did wicked things to those glitters, sending them into a wild dance.

"Last night was crazy and overpowering and... great. It was great."

"So great you had to stop as if you'd been burned and were running for your life."

"Oh, are you wrong," he said with a chuckle and a shake of his head.

"Explain it then."

"Let's just say it had to do with how good you felt to me and with things that were goin' through my head."

He raised one of her legs enough to press a light kiss where her ankle curved into her foot.

Tell him now and get it over with, a little voice in

the back of her mind recommended. *Tell him now and stop this before it goes any further....*

But already those glittery things he'd set to life were burning brighter, turning to sparks, and she knew she wasn't going to do any such thing. Not right then. Not when it *would* end things....

"Why do we keep circlin' around each other, Kate?" he asked then, running his thumbs up her shinbones in a stroke that made her pulse pick up speed. "We keep goin' round and round, like two scared foals, comin' together in the center to bump noses but always backin' up again to circle each other some more."

"I don't know about you but I'm just sitting here," she joked in a voice more breathy still.

He took hold of her legs and pulled her nearer, so that she was sitting with her rear end against one of his thighs. Then, at that closer range, he looked into her eyes with a piercing intensity.

"I don't want you to be scared of me, Kate."

"I'm not scared of you."

"Yes, you are. But you don't need to be. I won't hurt you. I won't hurt you," he repeated with emphasis on each word as if to make what he was saying sink in.

But she knew better. She knew he'd already made her want things that would never be and not having them would hurt.

"Trust me," he commanded in a near whisper of a voice that beckoned, too.

Then, while one hand stayed resting on her knee, the other came to the back of her head to bring her to the kiss he pressed to her lips. Softly. Sweetly. A kiss that added to the enticement of his words, his voice.

And somehow Kate knew that tonight he would

go through with what he'd so prematurely ended the evening before. That if she didn't stop him now, he wouldn't stop himself. He'd make love to her.

But should she let him? Should she go through with it knowing what she knew?

Then it occurred to her that maybe she should go through with it *because* she knew what she knew. *Because* she knew that once he found out she was pregnant things would take a different turn. And that when they did she wouldn't have this chance again. The chance to have his hands on her the way they had been in Las Vegas. To have him wrapped around her, every part of their bodies entwined and touching. The chance to have him make love to her just one more time before she put everything else in motion.

Still, she probably shouldn't let anything happen, she told herself.

But her thoughts didn't have much impact. Because no matter what lay ahead, no matter what happened or what he might end up thinking, she wanted this single night, she wanted him too much to deny herself.

So she would trust him. She would trust him not to hold it against her when he found out she'd known she was pregnant and kept it a secret while indulging in this time with him. She would trust him not to think it had been any kind of trap. To believe that it was what it was—a deep desire, a deep need, just to connect with him on a much more intimate level than their bare feet sharing the same coffee table or her legs crossed over his. On the most intimate of all levels. To have him want her so much that he couldn't resist her any more than she could resist him.

And that was when she gave herself fully over to his

kiss. To him. That was when she pushed aside all other thoughts and allowed herself this moment, this night, without worry. This night to indulge in mindless, primal passion the likes of which she'd feared after Las Vegas she would never experience again. The likes of which she might not ever be allowed to experience again after tonight.

But tonight, unlike New Year's Eve, she was clear-headed. There was no liquor in her system to dull her senses, to dim her awareness, to fog her memory, to numb any sensation. Tonight she could truly savor every nuance, every spark Brady lit in her blood.

And savor it she did as he deepened their kiss, as his mouth opened over hers and invited her to do the same so their tongues could meet again in playful abandon.

As if he could read her mind and knew she was his for the taking, he slid one arm under her knees and the other around her back and stood, carrying her with him as his mouth still plundered hers.

He didn't set her down until they'd reached the side of her bed where he let her feet fall to the floor without releasing her from his hold.

By then Kate's arms were around his neck, her hands in his hair, and she was lost in the minuet of his mouth over hers, in the game of hide-and-seek with his tongue, in the feel of his body against her.

His hands went to her back in a massage much like the one he'd done on her legs, arousing, enlivening, easing away all tension, all turmoil, all tiredness.

Those same strong hands rose to her shoulders, slipped over to her collarbone and then came forward, taking both breasts into their magical grip and sending a whole new maelstrom of that glitter all through her.

Her body responded with a will of its own—her back arched, thrusting those ultrasensitive, much-fuller orbs into his palms, her nipples taut and straining and feeling as if they might burst right through her clothes. Clothes she wished would disappear.

With that thought uppermost in her mind, she tore Brady's shirttails from his jeans, not caring that some of the snaps that held it closed popped in the process. In fact, she opted for finishing the job herself to leave his shirtfront open, the ends dangling around his hips.

She plunged her hands inside, pressing her flattened palms up his chest to his shoulders and smoothing the shirt off until it fell to the floor at his feet.

He'd had to leave her breasts to free his arms and, rather than return, he reached around again to lower the zipper of her dress.

Good! Good! Get rid of it! was all she could think as she rolled her shoulders a little to aid him as he pushed dress, bra and panties down at once.

But he didn't leave her the only one nude for long. Instead his hands went to the button and zipper of his own jeans, making quick work of shedding everything else he had on.

Then he raised his hands to hold her face cradled in them as he kissed her even more deeply, even more soundly, before he abandoned her lips to look down at her body, bare before him, as if it were some rare work of art he were viewing for the first time, something awe inspiring and incredible to behold.

And that was how she felt—genuinely beautiful and not at all bashful or ashamed or embarrassed by her own nudity. How could she be bashful or ashamed or embarrassed by anything that had the ability to affect him so profoundly?

And it did affect him. Kate knew not only from the expression on his handsome face and the deepening of his breathing at just the sight of her, but also because she let her eyes do some roaming of their own—down massive shoulders and carved pectorals to his flat stomach and farther still to the long, thick hardness of his obvious desire for her.

His hands guided her face upward so he could recapture her mouth with his, hungrily, urgently, his lips apart and his tongue thrusting into her mouth to conquer hers, to incite her pulse to race, her blood to run hot in her veins.

Then all at once he stopped again, lying on the bed and pulling her with him to rest beside him even as he rose above her to kiss her, to cup her face with his palm for a moment before sliding it to the side of her neck where he flipped it so that the back of his hand ran down the center of her, between her breasts.

Breasts that were engorged and yearning, with nipples knotted into diamonds of need.

But down, still, went that hand. The backs of his fingers grazing her stomach, veering to her thigh before switching course to retrace the path, this time whispering across one of those kerneled nipples in such torment her spine arched, bringing her inches off the mattress.

That was when he took hold. That warm, strong hand closed around the full globe of her breast, gently at first, then firmly, filling itself with her, letting the crest tense in his palm as he lifted and kneaded and worked wonders so great it made her moan somewhere deep in her soul.

He kissed a similar path down the side of her neck to the hollow of her throat and then farther still, kisses that were like a necklace of glimmering pearls that fell between her breasts before he chose just one breast to take into the warm black velvet of his mouth, drawing it into that moist cavern of delight. His tongue found her nipple, circling it, toying with it, flicking it tip to tip, rolling that incredibly aroused peak between tender teeth until she thought she might pass out from the pure pleasure of it.

But he had so many more gifts to give as his hand began another descent. A slower, ever more tantalizing glide that paused at her middle, exploring the new, resilient curve of her stomach before he continued on, ending between her legs with gentle, seeking fingers that slipped inside her and took her breath away with the wonder of his touch.

Memories of New Year's Eve were fuzzier than she'd realized because never in any mental reliving of that night had anything he'd done felt so incomprehensibly spectacular. Every nerve ending seemed to rise to the surface of her skin, alive and as sparkling as shards of glass.

She needed this man. She wanted him so much it had a life force of its own and she couldn't have fought it if she'd tried.

He came over her then, above her, finessing his way between her thighs, fitting himself into that spot that seemed fashioned for him alone.

Carefully—oh, so carefully—he entered her, giving

her her heart's desire in that moment when his body filled her. When his body completed her.

And as he began to move it was a swell she rode, a rise and fall that she answered with her breasts thrust upward, with her arms around him, with her body in harmony and rhythm with his.

Faster and faster he went and she kept pace, striving, straining, yearning for every moment, for every movement that brought them both closer to that pinnacle she'd known only once before.

And when she reached that point, it was nothing like she remembered. It was so much more glorious, as they clung together and climaxed at once. Her fingers dug into Brady's back, her legs wrapped around his, her hips thrust up into him to take him so totally within her that she thought he might actually reach the baby he'd made in her that single time before. White light seemed to erupt within her, white hot light that blinded her to everything but the exquisite rapture and exultation of their united bodies and spirits combined into an immeasurable bliss.

And then the feeling began to ebb. The light. The exquisite pleasure. The ecstasy. Bringing them both back to earth slowly, slowly, leaving Kate feeling sated and languorous and more wonderful than she could ever recall feeling in her life.

Brady's breathing was heavy against her ear as he settled atop her, and she felt his every muscle relax. But he only allowed himself a moment of that before he took his own weight onto himself again by raising up onto his elbows even as his brow came to rest against hers.

"Are you okay? I got carried away."

Kate couldn't help laughing at that because he hadn't been any more carried away than she had. "I'm fine," she assured him. "A whole lot better than fine."

"I didn't hurt…anything?"

"Did you hear me cry out in pain?" she joked.

She felt rather than saw him smile. "I heard you cry out, but it didn't sound like pain."

"Because it wasn't."

He slipped out of her then and rolled to his side, taking her with him to lie in the lee of his arm, her head on his chest.

"Can I stay the night?" he asked in a passion-raspy voice that was about as sexy as anything she'd ever heard.

"Oh, yes," she breathed against the satin over steel of his pectoral, thinking only that she wouldn't have been able to bear his leaving right then and not taking into consideration the illness she was prone to each morning.

"And we'll worry about tomorrow when it comes?"

She wasn't sure what that meant, but she was too tired to ask. In fact she was so exhausted she couldn't keep her eyes open.

"Tomorrow," she barely managed to murmur before a long sigh escaped her in response to the unadulterated joy of lying there in Brady's arms, cocooned by his big body and bathed in the warmth of his breath as she and his baby fell asleep.

Chapter 12

When Brady woke up just before dawn the following morning, he felt as if everything was right with the world. He had a lot on his mind. A whole lot. But Kate was asleep on her side in the curve his body made around hers, and the crystal-clear memory of making love to her was enough to temporarily put a rosy glow on even the deepest of his concerns.

It felt amazing to be in her bed, to be lying the way they were, with her head beneath his chin, her back snuggled against his chest, her small rear end in his lap, and his arm tracing the length of hers so their fingers could be entwined on the pillow in front of her face. It felt so amazing that he didn't want to disturb anything. And he certainly didn't want to leave her.

But he could see the sun beginning to come up through the window, and he knew her brothers would be stirring any minute. He didn't want to meet one of them, coming out of Kate's room. And he also didn't want to risk Kate feeling as panicked as she had New Year's morning at that same thought.

So he kissed the top of her head and eased himself away from her, making sure she was well covered by the sheets and blankets so she would stay warm.

Once he'd pulled on his jeans, he scribbled a quick note on a piece of paper to let her know why he'd left and propped it behind the faucet in the bathroom where she'd be sure to see it.

He gathered up the remainder of his clothes and then debated about whether to leave through the door to the hallway or through the outside door from the sitting room.

He ended up opting for the French doors that led out onto the porch, rather than risk meeting her family, and slipped into the sitting room of his suite next door just as stealthily.

But once he was safely inside again, Kate was still uppermost on his mind.

Not that that was unusual for him lately. She'd held a prominent place there from the moment they'd met. But these last several days with her had left him unable to think about much else. Only now he knew he needed to consider some things he *hadn't* been thinking about. And fast. Things like what his feelings for her were, what was happening between them, where they were headed. Where he wanted them to be headed. Because now that he thought he had an idea what was going on with her, he couldn't just play around.

Play around? Was that what he'd been doing with

her before now? It wasn't, he told himself as he went through his bedroom into his own bathroom to shower.

Okay, maybe in Las Vegas, before New Year's Eve, he'd only been playing. Having a good time. No strings attached. Falling into some old patterns with women. Old patterns he'd followed before Claudia. Before Claudia had pulled the rug out from under him.

But getting to know Kate even just a little in Las Vegas, spending that night with her, had changed things for him. He just hadn't recognized it before, because of the way they'd parted that next morning.

But the truth was, the way he'd felt about Kate then and the way he felt about her now were different from the way he'd ever felt about anyone else. Different from the way he'd felt about Claudia, even.

With Claudia he'd felt as if he were infected with something. Something that hadn't always been good, but that he'd been consumed by nevertheless.

With Kate... Well, he was powerless to control the feelings she brought alive in him, but none of them were bad. They were all great. Great enough to have pushed him to look past her reticence about being with him. To work to override her hesitations. But not in a crazed, obsessed mind-set, the way he'd been after Claudia had rejected him. And not because Kate had seemed like some kind of challenge he had to conquer.

No, with Kate he hadn't felt the frantic need to please, to win her over, even in view of her reaction New Year's morning. He hadn't felt the kind of desperation he'd felt with Claudia—the things Matt thought had come out of shock at being rejected for the first time in his life.

With Kate he'd felt relaxed and able to be himself. He'd felt calm and content and comfortable.

That sounded very big brotherish, he thought as he soaped himself up.

But big brotherish was definitely not how he'd intended it. Because along with that calmness and contentment and comfort, he'd also been totally churned up over her. He'd wanted her again so much it had nearly hurt.

And that seemed like a pretty terrific combination to him. Certainly it wasn't at all like the desperate determination he'd felt to win Claudia, coupled with the underlying self-disgust that had made him wonder at himself and at what the hell he was doing.

No, his feelings for Kate weren't what he'd felt for Claudia. They weren't what he'd felt in pursuit of Claudia. They weren't tinged with that insanity he believed his feelings for Claudia had been.

In fact, they seemed altogether pretty healthy. Robustly healthy.

But what about Kate's feelings for him?

That thought gave him pause as he rinsed off under the spray of the shower.

As time had passed since his arrival in Elk Creek, and he and Kate had grown closer, he hadn't been worrying as much that she couldn't stand the sight of him, the way he'd been afraid might be the case after New Year's morning. But how much deeper did her feelings go?

He couldn't be sure, and since that rejection still had the power to sting he knew he had to factor it in.

But when he really thought about it, objectively, he decided there were grounds for writing it off to circumstances that didn't reflect on him personally. Because in retrospect Kate's reaction seemed like a fairly natural response to the impromptu wedding and losing her virginity under the influence. He didn't know any woman who wouldn't have been upset, now that he thought about it.

But that still didn't tell him what she *did* feel about him.

What if she was just playing around with *him?*

The very idea of that made him chuckle as he turned off the water and dragged his hands through his hair.

Kate just playing around with him? No, not Kate. She wasn't that kind of woman, and he knew it. She had too much substance, too much character. She wouldn't just play around with anyone on a lark, not with anyone she didn't have feelings for, regardless of what had happened in Las Vegas.

And if she wouldn't play around with anyone she didn't have feelings for, that must mean that she *did* have feelings for him. Maybe even serious feelings.

Brady stepped out of the shower stall and grabbed a towel to dry off, satisfied with the conclusions he'd come to.

He cared about Kate and thought there was a strong possibility that she cared about him. And that was a good thing.

Because he was also reasonably certain that they were in a pretty delicate position. A delicate position that they were going to have to deal with together.

And the sooner the better, as far as he was concerned.

"You're taking my sister breakfast in bed?"

Kate heard Matt's muted voice coming from the

hallway outside her room, and she willed what she was afraid was about to happen, not to.

"I want to talk to her about something. Thought I'd ply her with food, yeah," Brady responded, confirming her worst fears.

She'd only been awake a little over an hour. An hour in which she'd found Brady's note in the bathroom because she'd been in there being sick. And while she would rather have been able to wake up in his arms this morning, she was glad he hadn't been there to watch her make her daily mad dash to the john. She certainly wasn't ready for company yet, though, since the morning sickness was still in its ebb-and-flow cycle, and despite the lull she was in at that moment she knew it could strike again at any time. The last thing she wanted was to have Brady there when it did.

But after that brief exchange in the hall, the knock on her door let her know she was out of luck.

She wanted to call, "Go away," but that would have been rude, so she refrained. Instead she took a brief inventory of her appearance, glad she'd washed her face, brushed her hair up into a curly knot at her crown and put on her dark-blue velvet bathrobe. At least she didn't look as awful as she felt.

When the second knock came she had her hand on the knob and, taking a deep breath, she opened the door. But only a few inches.

"Mornin'," Brady said from the other side, smiling a smile that almost looked sympathetic. Although she didn't know why that should be.

He looked as great as always. Standing tall and straight and strong. Dressed in blue jeans and a crisp white Western shirt. His hair was combed rakishly back and his breathtakingly handsome face was freshly shaven.

But the scent of his aftershave—which she ordinarily liked—didn't help the nausea she knew by then was unstoppable and so rather than return his greeting, she said, "I woke up with another touch of that flu. I'm not up to company."

His expression was unreadable, but his response to her flu excuse was to shake his head in denial. "Let me in, Kate. I brought you tea and toast." He raised the tray he was carrying to prove it. "You can eat or not, but we need to talk."

His tone was part cajoling, part commanding. But it didn't change how she was feeling.

"Honestly, I'm not up to—"

"I know what you're up to," he said, the commanding tone overpowering the cajoling one. "Open the door and let me in."

He knew what she was up to? What did that mean?

A cold clamminess washed over her, even as she told herself he couldn't possibly know *what she was up to*. Maybe he thought she was just spurning him the way she had New Year's morning. Maybe that was what he believed she was "up to."

"I'm really sick, Brady," she said as if that would disabuse him of the notion that what she was doing bore any resemblance to that other morning.

"I know you are. Let me in, anyway."

How did he know she was?

That cold, clammy feeling got worse, and Kate knew what was going to happen as a wave of nausea reared its ugly head.

"Just go away!" she said in a hushed, curt whisper,

more worried about fighting down her sick feeling than about imparting the message that this wasn't like New Year's morning.

"No, I won't go away," Brady insisted stubbornly.

But Kate couldn't argue anymore because at that moment she had to turn and run for the bathroom.

Fifteen minutes later, after being ill, brushing her teeth and rinsing her mouth with mouthwash, she walked out of the bathroom to find Brady in her bedroom.

He'd left the tray of tea and toast on the nightstand beside her bed, pulled her desk chair so it was facing the room rather than the corner desk and sat there, one ankle atop the opposite knee, his arms crossed over his chest. Waiting.

"Please go away," she said, calmly now, sounding almost as weak as she felt.

This time Brady didn't even shake his head to address her request. He just stared at her. "How much longer were you going to wait to tell me you're pregnant?" he asked then, in a quiet voice.

For a moment she thought about denying the truth. But what was the point, when she'd been going to break the news to him anytime now, anyway? Besides, she didn't have the strength at that moment to play games, so she just let herself wilt onto the edge of the mattress and, out of curiosity, said, "What makes you think I am?"

He shrugged one of those broad shoulders. "A couple of things," he said matter-of-factly, giving her no clue as to how he felt. "I had a neighbor in Oklahoma who came over to my place on Sunday mornings to fry the sausage he liked for his breakfast because his wife was pregnant and would lose her cookies at just the smell of it—like you did the other night over the rumaki. And then the sickness would pass and she'd be right as rain—just the way you were. Plus there are the changes in your body. Your face and arms and legs are thinner than they were two months ago, but when I touched you… There's more up top, and instead of that flat stomach you had before, there's a little rise."

"I didn't think you remembered that much about the night in Las Vegas."

"There are a lot of things that are fuzzy, but I've been dreamin' about that body of yours in vivid, living color ever since—there wasn't anything about you that I didn't remember."

He didn't seem angry or upset, so it was difficult for Kate to tell what was going on with him. Until it occurred to her that he might not have realized the baby was his.

But just about the time she thought that, he said, "I did some checkin' with Matt—not so he'd be suspicious, he thought I was just showin' an interest in you—but I know you haven't so much as had a date since we were together. And with my being your first… I know it's mine."

It…

Somehow that sounded so cold. So removed. So impersonal. So different from how she felt about the baby.

But it was good in a way. It seemed to confirm her every thought about how he'd react—how any man would react to an accidental pregnancy—and it gave Kate a renewed strength in her convictions.

"It doesn't matter," she said then.

"It doesn't matter? It sure as hell does matter," he said, obviously not appreciating the remark.

"I meant, you don't have to worry that I'll expect or need anything from you. I've already decided that I want the baby and I'm perfectly capable of raising and supporting it myself, so you can do as you like."

"What does that mean—I can do as I like?"

"You can be a part of the baby's life—the way any divorced dad is—or you can go on about your business as if the baby isn't even yours. You can even resell the Barton place and leave town if that's what you want to do. I won't hold it against you, and I won't come after you for anything."

He looked at her as if she were out of her mind. "What kind of man do you think I am?" he demanded, his tone full of offense.

She actually did think about what kind of man he was for a moment. Realistically. And in the process she realized why even the suggestion that he would turn his back on the baby would aggravate him.

"You're the kind of man who probably thinks he should do right by me—that's Junebug's turn of phrase. But what I'm telling you is that what that involves can be flexible."

"I don't know how. I'm the father of this baby and I'm going to *be* the father of this baby. There's no question about it. I've done plenty of playin' in my time, and I always knew that if I got caught at it this way I'd step up and do what needed to be done."

If he got caught?

If ever Kate had had a doubt about her assumption that he would feel trapped, that statement and the way he'd said it took that doubt away. Caught in the trap of an unplanned baby was what he meant, and she knew it as surely as she was sitting there.

"Understand this—you are not 'caught,'" she said firmly, a little righteous anger of her own sounding in her voice. "You have the option to go on as if this had never happened. I'm not asking anything of you. You can be around or you can not be around. It won't make any difference."

"I can be around or not be around—those are my only choices. Look on from the sidelines or high-tail it out of here?"

"I didn't say anything about only looking on from the sidelines. There can be visitation."

"Visitation."

Why was it that every word she said seemed to strike him wrong? Was he disappointed that she wasn't begging him to make an honest woman of her?

"You can be as much or as little a part of the baby's life as you want. Plain and simple," she reiterated.

"And what about being a part of your life?"

"Well, we'll be coparents, I guess, if you want to be included in things."

"Coparents. And is that what we've been doin' since I got here? Practicin' to be coparents? Is that what we were doin' in that bed last night?"

She felt as if another of her fears had come to pass. "There wasn't any ulterior motive, if that's what you're thinking. It wasn't a plot to lure you in so I could trap you. I want to be clear about that. Maybe I got carried away, again, but my friend Kelly says it's because of happy hormones. Something left over from primitive days when women needed the father of their baby to appeal to them so they'd want them around to provide for them. But that's all there was to it, and now that you know about the baby—"

Brady stood up so abruptly, so fiercely, he nearly knocked the chair over. "You expect me to believe that this was some hormonal thing?"

Okay, so no, it didn't feel like simply some hormonal thing. It felt like a whole lot more. But she wasn't going to admit that. Not in the same conversation in which he'd referred to himself as "caught."

"It was a lapse," she amended, hoping to make it sound better. "Like in Las Vegas. There's just some kind of chemistry between us that seems to make us end up in bed. But it didn't have anything to do with anything else. And now that you know about the baby, well, we'll just have to have more restraint. We'll have to be more responsible."

"How 'bout responsible enough to stay married?"

"*Stay* married?" Kate repeated. "You say that as if it was a viable marriage in the first place, when all it really was was a technicality. Besides, the divorce papers are signed and notarized—we're more divorced than married."

"Not until the papers are filed, we're not."

"Well I *want* them filed," she said forcefully. "This doesn't change a thing. I don't have any illusions about what a disaster in the making it is for us not to go through with the divorce. Staying married is just asking for a simmering pot of regret and resentment that will boil over and burn everyone in its path. Baby or no baby, papers filed or not filed, you're still free as the breeze as far as I'm concerned."

Even though it made something ache inside her to think about that.

"You said yourself that you're not ready to settle down," she continued. "And I'm telling you that you don't have to. You can go on just the way you planned. You can see the baby, be a part of the baby's life, but you won't have me or the baby as a burden of any kind. I won't be a noose around your neck."

And she wouldn't rely on him the way she'd come to rely on Dwight, either. She wouldn't count on Brady being there for her or for the baby, so if she turned around one day and found him gone, it wouldn't hurt the way it had when Dwight had left her.

"And if I told you I might be falling in love with you?" Brady said then, very, very quietly.

To Kate it sounded like testing the waters, as if he thought if he said that it might convince her to do what some sense of duty or obligation was urging him to do.

"You're only suggesting that because you think you have to, and I'm telling you that you don't. It's just better if we both keep our heads about all this."

"That's very clinical of you. Obviously those happy hormones aren't clouding your thinking with anything like emotions or feelings for me."

Kate was suddenly too sick again to argue with him. To tell him she couldn't *let* emotions cloud her thinking.

"Please just go," she said desperately, pressing her fingertips to her mouth as she fought another swell of nausea and some unexpected tears that pooled in her eyes.

"Tell me you don't feel anything for me, Kate," he challenged, rather than leaving the way she wanted him to.

"My feelings aren't the feelings that count. Yours

are. The ones that make you feel caught in some trap I never set. And I won't have anything to do with that. Now go!" she nearly shouted, not wanting him to be there through another bout of her illness and especially not wanting him to see her cry, since she was feeling less and less able to stop it.

"So this really is just a replay of New Year's morning," he said more to himself than to her.

Maybe she did sound as shrill as she had then. But she couldn't help it. She knew better than to foster her feelings for Brady, let alone admit to them. Feelings that could cause her to make the wrong decisions. Decisions that would lead her to what they'd led Kelly to. That could lead Brady to hate her. To hate the baby. And she didn't want that.

"Just go!" she said as heartsickness and morning sickness seemed to join forces, and she had to run for the bathroom again.

Chapter 13

Kate didn't leave her rooms that day, and by early evening Matt came looking for her. He knocked on the sitting room door but didn't wait for an invitation to poke his head in.

"Somebody have you tied up in here?" he joked.

Kate was still in her bathrobe. She'd gotten over the morning sickness, as usual, but hadn't had the impetus to get herself dressed. Not after she'd come out of the bathroom and found that Brady had finally taken her at her word and left her room. Because even though it had been what she'd told him to do, she'd still somehow felt as if the world had come crashing down on her.

So she was sitting with her legs curled underneath her on the overstuffed chair, watching the sunset through her window.

"Are you sick again?" Matt asked before she'd had the chance to answer his first quip.

"This morning, but not anymore," she said because through the whole day of moping and thinking, she had finally come to the conclusion that it was time to tell everyone what was going on.

"Come in," she urged her brother. "I wanted to talk to you, anyway."

"Good, because I want to talk to you, too. What the hell went on in here this morning? I saw Brady bringing you a breakfast tray—of all things—and the next thing I knew, he was moving out."

"He moved out?" Kate responded dimly. She'd heard some sounds from his rooms, but she hadn't thought for a moment that he was packing his bags. In fact, she'd assumed he was still here, and that's why she hadn't left her rooms all day—she'd known she couldn't see him and keep up the facade that she didn't have feelings for him. Not today. Not when she felt as miserable as she ever had in her life, including when Dwight had eloped with someone else.

"What do you mean Brady moved out?" she asked, trying not to let any of her emotions sound in her voice.

"I mean just what I said—he moved out. The Bartons' son sent movers to clear the place out yesterday and the plan was for Brady to stay here while we did some painting and repairs. Then he was going to send for his furniture and move in. No hurry. But one minute I see him headed in here with breakfast, happy as a lark, and two hours later he announces that he's movin' over to the new place now. Today. Without anything done to it and without a stick of furniture in it. He said he has a bedroll he keeps in the plane, he'll sleep in that. And boom! He's gone. I couldn't talk him out of it. He even bit my head off for tryin'. So what the hell happened in here this morning?"

Matt had crossed the room by then and was sitting on the arm of the couch, a frown on his face to go with the accusatory tone in his voice.

Obviously, Brady hadn't told him any of what had happened between the two of them, and Matt was taking his friend's side by default. So the time had come for an explanation.

But Kate didn't find it easy to give, despite her decision to do just that. Especially when she was working so hard not to break down in tears at the thought that Brady had high-tailed it out of here—away from her— as fast as he could. Even though it was something she'd told him to do if he wanted to. She guessed that deep down she just hadn't wanted him to want to.

"I have a lot to tell you, Matt. I just don't know where to start," she finally said.

"At the beginning."

"The beginning was in Las Vegas. Brady and I got a little closer than we let anybody know."

Kate went on to tell her brother what had begun over the New Year's holiday, how she and Brady had indulged in the inebriated impromptu wedding, the resulting pregnancy she'd so recently found out about, along with what had transpired since Brady's arrival in Elk Creek, up to and including this morning's argument.

It took Matt some time for everything to sink in, and his shock was evident in his expression. But once he'd grasped the whole picture, he said, "So when Brady found out you were pregnant he ran out of here?"

Matt's allegiance had suddenly switched to Kate.

But Kate couldn't leave her brother with the wrong impression of his best friend. "No, it wasn't like that. Apparently, he'd figured out I was pregnant before, on his own. He came in here this morning to ask when I intended to tell him. And as for his leaving, well, I didn't order him to pack his bags and get out, but I urged him to go on as if nothing had changed. And when he suggested we not file the divorce papers and stay married, I made it clear I wasn't going along with that no matter what."

"Why would you do that?"

"Why *wouldn't* I do that?" she countered with enough incredulity to match his.

"For crying out loud, Kate, you're *pregnant!*"

"That doesn't make any difference."

"It makes every difference. What were you thinkin'? You're already married to the guy, even if it was through a joke wedding. Why would you send your husband and the father of your baby packin' when you need him most?"

"I don't *need* him," Kate bristled, even as it occurred to her that while it might be true that she didn't *need* Brady, it didn't take away any of the wanting that was still there to torture her.

"Brady doesn't *want* to be married to me," she insisted. "He only offered to stay that way to do the right thing."

"And you said no, leave?" Matt asked with raging disbelief.

"Of course I said no. But I only said for him to leave if he wanted to. That he didn't have to stick around. That even if he did I still wanted the divorce to go through."

Matt shook his head. "You've made such a huge mistake I can't believe it. No wonder he got out of here. He must have felt like he was relivin' Claudia."

"The woman who dumped him."

"Yes the woman who dumped him and left him burned to a crisp. That's why he was tiptoein' around you at first. But it seemed like he'd gotten past it there at the end and was lettin' himself get close to you. And then what do you do? You push him away. Pregnant and all."

Matt was making her angry.

"He would feel trapped, Matt," she said as if he should see that for himself. "You know that. He'd feel trapped just like Buster did. Just like I've heard you and Ry and Shane and Bax say more than once about guys who end up having to marry someone because they've gotten them pregnant. Do you think I grew up with four brothers and don't know how you all think about these things?"

Matt had the good grace to look shamefaced. "Ah, Kate, that's just guys talkin'."

"It is not. Buster wasn't just talk. He hates Kelly, and he's not too much more fond of his own kids. He blames Kelly for every bad thing that happens to him even now. He tells her outright that she ruined his life. Do you think for one minute that's what I want?"

"Brady is not Buster."

"No, Buster was madly in love with Kelly before she got pregnant. Brady and I were just— Well, I don't know what we were. But I know he isn't madly in love with me, that's for sure. The most he'd say was that he might be falling in love with me—"

"He said that?" Matt cut in. "He admitted even in

the face of you tellin' him to take a hike that he loved you?"

"It was marginal, believe me."

"Probably because you were pullin' a Claudia on him at the time. But to even admit that much, then, is a big deal, Kate."

"It's not a big deal. It's just something he felt he had to say."

"Brady doesn't say anything because he thinks he has to. And why would he have had to? You were giving him his walking papers—all he *had* to do was take them and leave. It sounds to me like what he was really doin' was trying to get it across to you that he cares about you and wants to stay married to you and be a father to his baby without going too far out on the limb you were already sawing off."

"So everything's my fault?" Kate said, her temper flaring more and more.

"A lot of this is, yeah. You said yourself that he knew you were pregnant before this morning. What did he do with that information? Did he run while he still could have without you or anybody else knowing why? No, he stuck around."

He stuck around and made love to her....

But Kate didn't say that, she just let her brother rant on.

"Then he brings you breakfast in bed to talk about the situation, puttin' himself in my sights when I caught him at it and not carin'. He tells you he loves you—"

"Marginally," Kate reminded, feeling as if they'd both reverted back to bickering kids.

"Marginally or not, he let you know he has feelings

for you. He tells you he wants to stay married to you, and you still kick him to the curb."

"Thanks for understanding, Matt," Kate said face-tiously.

Matt ignored her tone. "Why the hell would he have felt trapped when you made it clear he could turn his back if he wanted to and he let you know he didn't want to? That's not being trapped, that's makin' a choice. The same choice I'd make if it was Jenn and me in your situation. Happily."

"You're already engaged to Jenn and you're crazy about her. The sun rises and sets in her where you're concerned. But Brady was only thinking to do what was right, not what he wanted to do, and certainly not *happily*. He'd be settling, and eventually he'd regret that. He'd resent it. He'd resent me and the baby. He'd look at me and he'd realize he'd been trapped by the world's most resistible woman!"

That last part had come out on its own as part of the full head of steam she'd worked up by the end of what she'd been saying. She regretted it because it revealed too much of what she'd been feeling since Dwight's elopement. Too much of a portion of her that was so vulnerable she was afraid to let it out into the light.

But Matt caught it and wouldn't let go. "So you still have some baggage of your own that's playing a role in this?"

"Why don't you just go away, Matt. You're not helping anything," she blurted out in a fit of temper.

But again her brother ignored her. "Oh, Kate," he said on a sigh, apparently not caring that she hadn't confirmed his opinion. "Brady was tryin' to put his baggage behind him, but you let yours ruin things."

"That's not true," she defended feebly.

"Bull. You're so busy protecting yourself from the kind of hurt you had when Dwight left you in the dust that you aren't seeing what's right in front of your face."

"I see what's right in front of my face perfectly clearly every time I picture Kelly."

"But Brady isn't Buster," Matt repeated. "And how could Brady feel trapped if he's getting what he wants?"

"It isn't what he wants."

"I think you are."

"Well you'd be wrong."

"That's good, dig in your heels. Don't give him a chance. Take not only your past but Kelly's past and present, too, and pull it all around you like a coat of armor. See what it gets you. It won't be what you want. It won't be what I'm betting Brady wants. It won't be what's best for your baby. But, hey, what difference does that make?"

"Sometimes I wish I were an only child."

"Sure, push everybody away. It's safer like that, isn't it?"

"Matt…" she said in the same warning tone she'd used when they were kids and he was going too far in his teasing of her.

"Don't blow it, Kate," he said anyway, not heeding the warning. "Brady's a good man. I've watched the way he's been with you since he got here. I've seen the way he looks at you. Things could work out with him. If you let them." Matt stood then, his hands on his hips, frowning down at her. "Get your rear end over to the Bartons' place and talk to him. *Listen* to him. And quit puttin' the past and other people's problems between you. Just look at him for what he is."

Matt left without waiting for a reply, and Kate sank farther into her chair, as if willing it to swallow her alive so she didn't have to deal with any of what her brother had said. With any of what she was feeling.

But the chair didn't swallow her alive.

And like it or not, she couldn't disregard what Matt had said, even if she did go on trying to disregard what she was feeling.

She'd never been more confused.

What if her brother was right? she kept asking herself.

A lot of what he'd said seemed to have some validity. After all, he'd known Brady much longer than she had. So was she seeing her past and Kelly's problems when she looked at Brady and her own situation rather than seeing Brady as Brady?

It was just so hard to say for sure.

She knew she was afraid of reliving that past, afraid of ending up in the same kind of mess Kelly had ended up in—that was a given. She certainly knew she was afraid that Brady would feel trapped by a woman he came to see the way Dwight had seen her—as a woman so resistible Dwight had had no problem maintaining years of celibacy with her and then had turned around and been propelled by such a burning desire for someone else that he'd eloped with her.

And, yes, she guessed that qualified as baggage.

But it was also what had happened, so she believed she had cause to worry. To more than worry. She had cause to be paralyzed with self-doubt.

She knew what Kelly would say to that, though.

And what Matt would say to it, too. That obviously Brady hadn't found her resistible or she wouldn't be pregnant. That if he'd found her resistible he wouldn't have been rooting around the way he had been since getting to Elk Creek. He wouldn't have made love to her again just last night.

And Kate wanted to believe that. She honestly did. It just wasn't easy. Besides, even if it were true now and had been true in Las Vegas, what if it wasn't true for the long haul? Buster had found Kelly irresistible before he'd had to marry her, but afterward he'd hardly touched her—something that had been a huge blow to her friend's self-esteem, too.

Brady isn't Buster....

Kate heard Matt's words in her head as clearly as if he were there to repeat them himself.

But Brady was a man. A man like her brothers, who had all talked that "trapped" talk. A man who had referred to himself as "caught."

Forgetting about that was as difficult as trying to let go of her own sense that she was ultimately resistible.

And how could she discount such thoughts when he'd told her himself that having a wife and a baby right now were not part of his plans? How could she even entertain the notion that he wouldn't look at a forced change in those plans without regret and resentment?

Although, truthfully, Matt was right. She wasn't forcing Brady. She'd opened the door for him. And, yes, she'd probably urged him out of it with enough vigor to remind him of that other woman's rejection. But, still, he might well have suggested they stay married out of a sense of duty. And if that was the case it would result in the same things, wouldn't it—regret and resentment?

She thought it would.

On the other hand she could be wrong about everything. Wrong about Brady. And Matt could be right when he said that Brady might feel the way Matt would if he and Jenn were in the same situation—that he'd be only too happy about it.

Okay, so a part of her wanted to believe that. Who wouldn't?

But what if it were true? What if that's what Brady would have said if she'd given him half a chance?

Temptation washed through her. Temptation to go to Brady the way Matt had told her to, to give him more of an opportunity to talk than she had this morning. To listen to him without letting her own baggage get in the way.

But should she do that? Was she only looking for an excuse to see him again? An excuse to hang on to hopes she shouldn't hang on to?

That was a hard question to answer. Because after a day of misery she knew she *wanted* an excuse to believe things could work out. She wanted it more than she'd ever wanted anything in her life.

So maybe you should take your brother's advice and go to Brady, hear him out, a little voice in the back of her mind suggested. *Would that be such a mistake?*

Possibly not. Because if she listened very closely, very carefully, then one way or another she'd know what was really on his mind. Even if it was what she was most afraid of, what she'd already assumed he was thinking. And if what he had to say wasn't enough to convince her he genuinely did want to try to make their marriage work, if it wasn't enough to make her believe his feelings for her—and only for her—were behind it, then she could still make sure the divorce went through....

Kate finally got up from the easy chair and headed to her bedroom to get dressed.

"I hope you're right, Matt," she muttered to herself.

Because if Brady was only thinking in terms of duty or obligation she would still have to turn her back on him.

Only, she wasn't too sure how she could bear to do that again....

There was no welcoming porch light when Kate got to the Bartons' place. Brady's place now. But the front door was open, and a dim glow came through the screen from a fire she could see burning in the fireplace in the living room.

Wondering why Brady would have left the front door open when it was so cool outside, Kate got out of her car and started for the house. She was craning for sight of him through the screen when his deep whisky voice came from the shadows at the far side of the porch.

"What are you doin' here?"

She jumped with fright and stopped dead in her tracks rather than climb the stairs, refocusing her eyes to find him. "You scared me to death," she said, holding a flattened hand to her heart, which was beating faster even than it had been with the tension that had kept her company on the drive over.

Brady didn't apologize. He didn't say anything at all, apparently letting his initial question stand.

Kate took a bolstering breath and climbed the steps to the porch, finding him sitting with one hip atop the railing, his back against a support pillar. He had a bare foot riding the railing, too, so his bent knee could prop a single arm. His other foot was on the porch floor and his left hand was jammed into the pocket of his jeans.

He wore a chambray shirt, but it was open down the front, the tails flying like flags at half-mast around his hips, and he looked as sexy as she'd ever seen him.

Which, for no reason she could name, inspired an image in her mind of him pulling on his clothes after a romp with some female company he might have escorted out only moments before her arrival.

Kate's stomach lurched at the thought, and before she could get control of her own responses she said, "Did I just miss someone?"

"Who would you have just missed?" he asked in a not particularly friendly tone.

"I don't know. You just look...I don't know," she stammered.

"I was workin' on this place all day. I took a shower to clean myself up and came out here to cool off."

Relief was a living thing inside her, even though Kate felt like a fool for what she'd been thinking. Of course, his explanation made more sense.

"Is that why you came over here? To check up on me?" he asked then, almost as if he'd known what she'd been imagining.

"No," she said quickly, quietly.

"Then why are you here?"

Kate mentally called upon some badly needed courage and said, "I had a chat with Matt a little bit ago. A pretty heated chat. I told him everything."

"And you came to warn me to head for the hills before all four of your brothers come to string me up?"

"I'm who Matt's disgusted with," she said into the shadows as a shiver shook her voice in an involuntary reaction to the cold that was seeping in through the denim jacket, crew-neck T-shirt and jeans she had on.

Brady seemed to notice the shiver because he came off the railing and said, "Let's go inside."

There was only a hint of concern in his tone, but Kate held on to it hopefully. Maybe if he cared that she was cold he cared about her.

He went ahead of her to the door, opening the screen and waiting for her to go in.

Kate didn't hesitate to step into the warmth of the living room. She made a beeline for the fireplace and the heat it was giving off, stopping only a few feet from the hearth as Brady followed, closing the door behind them to shut out the chill.

He ended up at the fireplace, too, standing with an arm braced on the mantel so he could see her face. His weight was slung onto his right hip in a way that made the side of his shirt fall away from his body, so that his expansive chest was gilded by the golden illumination of the dancing flames below.

"What's Matt disgusted with you about? Sleepin' with me?" Brady asked then.

Kate dragged her gaze off the delectable sight of his naked torso so she could concentrate on the conversation.

"No. My brother gave me what-for for doing more talking than listening this morning. He said it sounded like I didn't give you a chance."

"You didn't."

"He said I let my own baggage get in the way and probably reminded you of yours in the process."

"Smart guy, your brother."

"So I came for a do-over."

Brady watched her intently, his blue-gray eyes boring into her so fiercely she was afraid he was going to just tell her it was too late, that he'd given her her only opportunity this morning.

But instead he said, "I didn't handle things too well myself. I expected you to jump at the idea of stayin' married. And when you didn't—"

"Matt said I 'pulled a Claudia.'"

"I had some flashbacks, yeah."

"I'm sorry."

"I just want to know how much like Claudia this morning was," he said in a gruff voice that let her know she really had scratched old wounds.

"How much like her I was?" she repeated, unsure what he was asking.

"I thought she had feelings for me and she didn't."

Ahh...

"I'm not like her at all in that area," Kate admitted, her voice quiet once again, because she knew she was venturing out onto a limb of her own.

But that didn't seem to be enough for him, because he just stood there, watching her as if he were waiting for her to say more.

"This isn't easy for me, Brady," she blurted out. "I have this friend—my best friend—and she got pregnant just out of high school. The father was the love of her life. They were planning to get married after college, but when she got pregnant and they couldn't wait, everything changed. It's been horrible for both of them and for the twins they had, ever since. The marriage ended in divorce. He says she ruined his life. He hates her. I didn't want to end up like that. I didn't want *us* to end up like that. And when I factored in that I'm a person who my ex-fiancé didn't find attractive enough to be in any hurry to get into bed, along with a lot of guy talk I've heard over the years from my brothers about men getting trapped, and then you saying yourself that you were caught... Well, I just thought it was better for everybody to cut you loose, no matter how I felt about you."

He didn't say anything for the longest time, and it was very unnerving for her. Especially in light of the fact that she'd just opened herself up so completely to him. And all Kate could think was that maybe she'd poured her heart out to a man who didn't care. Who maybe didn't even like her. A man who maybe she *should* turn and run from before she embarrassed herself any more.

Then he said, "You really do have baggage," as if it were all inconsequential now that it had been aired.

"I just wanted you to see that I wasn't 'pulling a Claudia' this morning and rejecting you. I thought I was giving you what you—or any other man—would want by not asking or expecting anything from you. By making sure you knew that you were still free in spite of the baby." Kate stopped herself from going on, realizing that once again she was doing all the talking. "I'm not saying anything else. I came to listen."

Brady nodded and went on watching her awhile longer before he finally said, "The first thing I better tell you is that I burned the divorce papers in this fire when I started it tonight."

"You did?"

"I decided today that I wasn't lettin' you go. I just hoped to hell I wasn't doin' what I did with Claudia. I've been hopin' to hell all along that that wasn't what I was doin'."

"What did you do with her?"

"I made a fool of myself chasin' after her. I didn't want to make the same mistake with you—chasin' after you after Las Vegas when you let me know in no uncertain terms that I was your biggest nightmare."

Kate flinched. "You were a long way from my biggest nightmare. I just couldn't believe what I'd done."

"Yeah, I came to that conclusion myself. That's why I thought we had a shot at makin' this work out. Till you made yourself clear this mornin'."

"I just—"

"I know what you *just*. But you're wrong. I was crazy about you from the start, Kate. Do you really think that if you hadn't acted as if you wanted to shoot me New Year's morning I wouldn't have gladly let all your brothers know I was interested in you? I hadn't been hidin' anything before that. I agreed to keep everything secret because that was how you wanted it and because no, I wasn't wild about the idea of lettin' them know we'd had what you were determined was only going to be a one-night stand and that after that one-night stand you wanted nothin' to do with me. Keepin' that from your brothers was purely an act of survival. But if you hadn't insisted on things bein' hushed up, or gettin' away from me that morning, it would have only been the beginning for us."

"It would have?"

"You remember when I told you about my father

never giving up until he'd won over my mother? And you asked me if that was the kind of love I was lookin' for? Well, I'd never thought about it before, but you were right. And the thing is, you're it. Pregnant or not pregnant—you're it. You were it from the minute I set eyes on you in Las Vegas. I just didn't realize it until I sorted through everything in my head today.

"Yeah, maybe a little of this morning was me doin' the right thing. But after a day of scrubbin' this place from stem to stern and spendin' all that time thinkin' about nothin' but you, I can stand here now and tell you without a doubt that I'm in love with you, Kate McDermot. That even if there was no baby, I'd still be in love with you. I'd still want you to stay my wife. That's why I burned the divorce papers—because no matter what you said New Year's morning, no matter what you said this morning, I figured I was goin' by your actions instead, and you didn't act like somebody who didn't want me."

Okay, so maybe she owed Matt a big kiss.

"I don't act like somebody who doesn't want you because I'm *not* somebody who doesn't want you."

"Meanin' you *do* want me?"

Kate nodded because her throat was suddenly constricted with too many tears to answer him.

"I'm in love with you, Kate," he repeated, just in case she hadn't caught it the first time.

"I'm in love with you, too, Brady," she whispered, because it was the most she could manage.

"And I'm not givin' you a divorce. Not now. Not ever. You're my wife and you're stayin' my wife. If that makes *you* feel trapped then that's just too damn bad."

She could only laugh at that as the tears flooded her eyes and ran down her face.

Seeing them made Brady push away from the mantel and close the space between them.

"What're these for?" he asked, wiping the moisture with a gentle thumb at each cheek.

"I love you," was her only response.

"I more than love you," he said. "I want you so much it's like a thirst I can't quench."

He took her into his arms then, kissing both damp cheeks before his lips pressed to hers in that way that was familiar now but that she still knew she would never get enough of.

And that was all it took for sparks to fly between them. For hunger to be awakened and passion to ignite. Passion greater than either of the other times they'd made love.

Kate wasn't sure if it was because this was the first time they'd come together with love stated and out in the open, knowing they had an unbreakable bond, a commitment to each other, but something made her feel more free, more uninhibited, more able to savor every kiss, every caress, every movement of his hands on her.

Clothes were shed in a hurry and they lay down on the floor in front of the fire, too much in need of bare flesh pressed to bare flesh to even seek out Brady's bedroll.

His mouth was everywhere. His hands were everywhere. And the driving desire he orchestrated in her body was like nothing she'd ever felt before—hot and wild and demanding.

When he slipped inside her, she was more than

ready. Her back arched and a groan of the purest pleasure rolled from her throat. Deeply, deeply inside her
was the staff of life, driving them both in a relent-
less climb up a mountain of delight to a pinnacle that
flamed into an inferno, leaving Kate clinging to Brady
as she called his name in that moment of sublime ecstasy that made her spirit soar with his, that truly joined
them.

And when it was over and he eased them both back
to earth, Kate had a second surprise in the sense of
joy that filled her—body and soul—with the knowledge that this man loved her. That they would have a
whole lifetime of what she felt they'd just discovered
in each other.

After a few minutes of calming his breathing, Brady
took one more full breath and then exhaled in a replete
sigh and rolled to his side. He left one arm under her
head and his body half covering her, his thigh a wonderful weight across her lap.

"We have to do this more than three times in almost
as many months," he said as he relaxed.

Kate laughed. "The way I look at it we've done it
twice in less than twenty-four hours."

"That's more like it. We'll just have to keep *that* up."

"I'm game if you are," she said with a little nudge
into the juncture of his legs at her hip.

"Just give me a few minutes," he said wryly, bestow-
ing a sweet kiss full of promise before he abandoned
her lips again.

"So Matt knows we're married," Brady said then,
resting his head beside hers on his arm.

"And he's probably told everyone else by now."

"Good, then they won't think anything about you not comin' home tonight."

"And after tonight?" she asked, testing the waters.

"After tonight you can choose—we can stay here and live like Bohemians, or we can stay at your ranch until we get this place in order and furnished and can move in properly."

Kate thought about how comfortable she was, just lying on the floor with nothing but Brady's arm as her pillow, his body as her blanket, and she knew she didn't really need anything more than that.

"Let's stay here," she said, eager to dive right into their life together.

"Good choice," he said, kissing her temple this time. "I do love you, Kate," he added then. "Forget about that Dwight guy not wanting you. I want you enough for both of us. And I want this baby, too. Enough to surprise the hell out of me."

"You're sure?"

"More sure than I've ever been about anything except how much I love you."

"Good thing," she said with a laugh as his hand played at her stomach, exploring the slight changes the baby had made there already.

Kate smiled up into the face she loved so much it was almost an ache inside her, pressing a palm to his cheek as if only touching him could convince her that he was real. That his love for her was real. That the life they would have together was real.

That was when he rose above her again, recapturing her mouth with his, caressing her with those wonderful hands, nudging a knee between her thighs.

And as Kate felt arousal spring back to life once more, she knew she was right where she belonged. Right where she and their baby belonged.

With Brady.

Forever with Brady.

* * * * *

We hope you enjoyed reading this
special collection from Harlequin®.

If you liked reading these stories,
then you will love
Harlequin® Special Edition books!

You know that romance is for life.
Harlequin Special Edition stories show
that every chapter in a relationship has its
challenges and delights and that love can be
renewed with each turn of the page.

Enjoy six new stories from
Harlequin Special Edition every month!

Available wherever books and
ebooks are sold.

❖ HARLEQUIN®

SPECIAL EDITION

Life, Love and Family.

STEPHSE

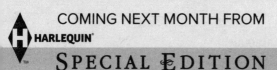
#2401 NOT QUITE MARRIED
The Bravos of Justice Creek • by Christine Rimmer
After a fling with Dalton Ames on an idyllic island, Clara Bravo wound up pregnant. She never told Dalton the truth, since the recently divorced hunk insisted he wasn't interested in a relationship. But when Dalton discovers Clara's secret, he's determined to create a forever-after with the Bravo beauty and their baby...no matter how much she protests!

#2402 MY FAIR FORTUNE
The Fortunes of Texas: Cowboy Country
by Nancy Robards Thompson
On the outside, PR guru Brodie Fortune Hayes is the perfect British gentleman. But on the inside, he's not as polished as he seems. When Brodie is hired to fix up the image of Horseback Hollow's Cowboy Country theme park, one lovely Texan—his former fling Caitlyn Moore—might just be the woman who can open his heart after all!

#2403 A FOREVER KIND OF FAMILY
Those Engaging Garretts! • by Brenda Harlen
Daddy. That's one role Ryan Garrett never thought he'd occupy...until his friend's death left him with custody of a fourteen-month-old. He definitely didn't count on gorgeous Harper Ross stepping in to help with little Oliver. As they butt heads and sparks fly, another Garrett bachelor finds the love of a lifetime!

#2404 FOLLOWING DOCTOR'S ORDERS
Texas Rescue • by Caro Carson
Dr. Brooke Brown has devoted her entire life to her career—but that doesn't mean she isn't susceptible to playboy firefighter Zach Bishop's smoldering good looks. A fling soon turns into so much more, but Brooke's tragic past and Zach's newly discovered future might stand in the way of the family they've always wanted.

#2405 FROM BEST FRIEND TO BRIDE
The St. Johns of Stonerock • by Jules Bennett
Police chief Cameron St. John has always loved his best friend, Megan Richards—and not just in a platonic way. But there's too much baggage for friendship to turn into romance, so Cameron sets his feelings aside...until Megan's life is threatened by her dangerous brother. Then Cameron will stop at nothing to protect her—and ensure their future together.

#2406 HIS PREGNANT TEXAS SWEETHEART
Peach Leaf, Texas • by Amy Woods
Katie Bloom has fallen on hard times. She's pregnant and alone, and the museum where she works is going out of business. Now Ryan Ford, the one who got away, walks into a local eatery, tempting her with his soulful good looks. Ryan's got secrets, but can he put Katie and her child above everything else to create a lifelong love?

When Harper had gone back to work a few days after
the funeral, Ryan had offered to be the one to get up in
the night with Oliver so that she could sleep through. It
wasn't his fault that she heard every sound that emanated
from Oliver's room, across the hall from her own.

Thankfully, she worked behind the scenes at *Coffee
Time with Caroline*, Charisma's most popular morning
news show, so the dark circles under her eyes weren't as
much a problem as the fog that seemed to have enveloped
her brain. And that fog was definitely a problem.

"Do you want me to get him a drink?" she asked as
Ryan zipped up Oliver's sleeper.

"I can manage," he assured her. "Go get some sleep."

Just as she decided that she would, Oliver—now clean
and dry—stretched his arms out toward her. "Up."

Ryan deftly scooped him up in one arm. "I've got you,
buddy."

The little boy shook his head, reaching for Harper.

"Up."

"Harper has to go night-night, just like you," Ryan said.

"Up," Oliver insisted.

Ryan looked at her questioningly.

She shrugged. "I've got breasts."

She'd spoken automatically, her brain apparently stuck somewhere between asleep and awake, without regard to whom she was addressing or how he might respond.

Of course, his response was predictably male—his gaze dropped to her chest and his lips curved in a slow and sexy smile. "Yeah—I'm aware of that."

Her cheeks burned as her traitorous nipples tightened beneath the thin cotton of her ribbed tank top in response to his perusal, practically begging for his attention. She lifted her arms to reach for the baby, and to cover up her breasts. "I only meant that he prefers a softer chest to snuggle against."

"Can't blame him for that," Ryan agreed, transferring the little boy to her.

Oliver immediately dropped his head onto her shoulder and dipped a hand down the front of her top to rest on the slope of her breast.

"The kid's got some slick moves," Ryan noted.

Harper felt her cheeks burning again as she moved over to the chair and settled in to rock the baby.

Fall in love with A FOREVER KIND OF FAMILY by Brenda Harlen, available May 2015 wherever Harlequin® Special Edition books and ebooks are sold.

www.Harlequin.com

Love the Harlequin book you just read?

Your opinion matters.

Review this book on your favorite
book site, review site, blog or your own
social media properties and share
your opinion with other readers!

JUST CAN'T GET ENOUGH?

Join our social communities
and talk to us online.

You will have access to the latest
news on upcoming titles and special
promotions, but most importantly,
you can talk to other fans about your
favorite Harlequin reads.

Harlequin.com/Community

Facebook.com/HarlequinBooks

Twitter.com/HarlequinBooks

Pinterest.com/HarlequinBooks

HARLEQUIN®

A *Romance* FOR EVERY MOOD™

**Stay up-to-date on all your
romance-reading news with the
Harlequin Shopping Guide,
featuring bestselling authors, exciting new
miniseries, books to watch and more!**

The newest issue will be delivered right to you
with our compliments! There are 4 each year.

Signing up is easy.

EMAIL

ShoppingGuide@Harlequin.ca

WRITE TO US

HARLEQUIN BOOKS
Attention: Customer Service Department
P.O. Box 9057, Buffalo, NY 14269-9057

OR PHONE

1-800-873-8635 in the United States
1-888-343-9777 in Canada

Please allow 4-6 weeks for delivery of the first issue by mail.